Nun Too Soon

Bad Habit Book Club Book #1

Lissa Sharpe

www.smartypantsromance.com

Copyright

Chapter 1
Helen

This is not a romance.

...at least, not a very good one, not yet. I furrow my brow in a way that I hope looks as though I'm encountering a complex issue with the microfiche database, instead of struggling to find the right verb choice for my work in progress.

Moaned? Groaned? Whimpered? What should Rosamund do when Axel laps at her nipple through her lacy bra with his rough tongue? My go-to is usually a whimper, but I'm worried I'm beginning to overuse the word. Not that most of my writing group is probably paying that much attention to my synonyms or lack thereof, but I live in almost constant fear of betraying myself —making the one mistake that will out me for what I truly am.

"Kimberly. Hello, Kimberly?"

It takes me a belated moment to realize my coworker Erica is trying to get my attention. It's an easy enough mistake to make on my part, considering the fact that my name isn't Kimberly—it's Helen. Yet in all our time working together, Erica has never called me by the right name. It's been Kimberly since my first week, and that was almost two years ago now.

When Erica first called me the wrong name, I tried to correct her, but she always insists the misnaming is intentional: "Because you look like that girl, Kimberly? From *The Magic School Bus*, you know, that educational cartoon from when we were kids."

I tried my best to see the nickname as a sort of endearment, only when I

"

pulled up an old episode of the show to see what Kimberly looked like, I discovered there is no character named Kimberly.

It's impossible to know whether Erica's a little deranged or a mastermind manipulator, having cornered me into years of responding to the wrong name.

I quickly minimize my Word document, even though Erica is still across the room. "Yes, Erica?" Notice that *I* have managed to use her correct name. Just saying.

"Can you take over checkout?" Erica nods toward the clock, then clasps her hands together in the motion of a prayer, her lacquered pink nails gleaming under the fluorescent light. "I'll be late to my appointment if I don't go now."

I stifle a sigh. This is another point in favor of either Erica's delusion, or her genius. She has a standing weekly appointment with a "chiropractor" due to a "chronic back illness," though more than once my coworkers and I have spotted Erica at places that are definitely not the chiropractor's office during this time period: the movies, the nail salon, and perhaps the most depressing of all, just sitting in the back of a McDonald's by herself, eating a McFlurry and scrolling through her phone.

But Erica remains adamant that she has to get to her appointment every Monday at three, and so every Monday at two forty-five, out she goes.

"Sure." I log out of my computer, moving to the checkout counter. I can't blame Erica exactly, since I myself am using a little downtime at the library to fix the latest chapter of my WIP, but at least I wouldn't lie about it if anyone asked me. Or at least, not so egregiously.

As I approach the counter though, Erica suddenly straightens, pivoting back toward the computer. "Um, actually, I can stay a few more minutes." She tosses her hair a bit, sticking out her breasts.

This is all the warning I get as the Red Unicorn approaches the counter, carrying his usual haul of books in a way that nicely showcases the muscles of his forearms.

The Red Unicorn has become a frequent patron of the library, and he's earned his nickname (of which he is completely unaware) because he has a trifecta of qualities unusual in a man: the first is a sexy, if spotty, Southern accent; the second, a love of reading across multiple genres, including genre fiction and poetry, often scorned by men of his age/demographic; and the last is that he is an attractive ginger, which I don't personally think is all that unusual, but my friend Matilda assures me is a true rarity, especially combined with the other two aforementioned qualities.

It would be easy enough to find out what his real name is; I have it on file, after all, available every time he uses his library card. But I prefer to think of him as the Red Unicorn, a perfect fantasy man who may or may not exist as I imagine him, but who happens to stop in at my library at least twice a week.

In his presence, all thoughts of Erica's chiropractor appointment seem to have disappeared, and she is suddenly all attention—and all breasts, as she practically puffs out her chest on display, easy to do in her low-cut blouse that is unbuttoned just one button too low. I say this not out of judgment, but a little envy. I get nervous if even my clavicle is on display. Turtlenecks are usually my go-to, a few sizes too big.

"Hi there." Erica's voice is almost as low as her blouse, and unusually breathy, too, like she has asthma, but the sexy kind. "See anything you like?"

I can't blame her, honestly. The Red Unicorn is attractive enough to justify an over-the-top cleavage display and ASMR sexy voice. I might have tried the same myself, but it's hard to pull off a good boob display in a men's extra-extra-large turtleneck, and my sexy voice sounds unnervingly like Minnie Mouse.

Instead, I awkwardly linger, watching as Erica continues her aggressive chest-thrusting, and waiting to see how the Red Unicorn will respond.

"Just these, thanks." He seems distracted—not unusual, since he normally seems distracted and a little distant, but I thought Erica's breast showcase might have been enough to catch his attention. Clearly Erica did, too. With his lack of response, she looks a little crestfallen and loses some of her swagger.

Her dejection doesn't last long though, and she rebounds quickly with a lingering hand graze as she takes the last book from the Red Unicorn—brazenly enough that I can't help my eyes from widening, both astonished and a little impressed by Erica's moxie. This is one of my curses, I've been told; people can always read my every thought on my face. I like to imagine I would be extremely GIFable, were I to venture into reality television.

"Is there anything else I can do for you today?" Erica purrs.

"No." The Red Unicorn gathers the books, adding a curt "Thanks" before leaving without bothering to give either of us a backward glance.

An awkward moment follows, before Erica checks her watch again and groans in frustration. "Ugh, Kimberly, I'm going to be so late!" And with that, she snatches her purse and is gone so fast she leaves nothing but the faintest whiff of Juicy Couture behind her.

Silence descends. The room is virtually empty now, except for the few patrons using the public computers and Tom, a middle-school-aged child, doing his homework at one of the tables. He's here often enough that I know him by name. His mother will pick him up in about an hour and a half, looking frazzled and asking him which meal in a sack he prefers for dinner tonight.

Not for the first time, I remind myself that there are worse things than being perpetually, eternally single. My time is my own. I only have to worry about taking care of—and feeding—myself. I can only imagine how stressful it must be to be a single parent, working full-time, at the mercy of the public library system for free babysitting when necessity demands it.

Buoyed by the reminder, I grab my satchel, slip out from behind the counter, and stop at the table where Tom is studying. I wish I could say that I am some kind of child whisperer and that Tom and I have formed a magical bond during his hours spent at the library, but we mostly maintain a friendly distance from each other. For most of my life, children weren't something I considered a possibility, so I didn't put much time into practicing for future motherhood, and I can't say it's something that's come naturally to me now that it's (sort of) on the table. Still, I'm trying.

Tom looks up at me expectantly. There's really only one thing I've found to bridge the gap between our ages. I know nothing about video games, manga, or sports, so those are off the table, but we've found one common language that we share.

"Lemon bars," I tell him, pulling out my Tupperware. "They turned out okay. Tell me if you think there's too much lemon zest."

He's wolfed down one of the bars before I can even finish talking. "It's good," he says, mouth still mostly full.

That's pretty high praise, coming from Tom. I linger awkwardly for a moment, then give a half wave-salute. "Okay. Well. See you next Monday." Sunday nights are my baking night. I can't—or rather, *shouldn't*—eat the entire yield of the recipes myself, so I always share with Tom when he's here on Monday afternoons. "Enjoy!"

Tom grunts in response. Yes! Another gold star interaction with a youth.

"Hey, Helen of Troy!" A voice catches me as I make my way behind the counter again.

I turn to see one of the library regulars, Shane, standing at checkout. He is a mid-twentysomething, way too young to be considered a true romantic possibility, but I nonetheless enjoy his sweet puppy dog energy. Tall, lanky, and with an impressive mane of corkscrew curls that stand out in every direction, Shane radiates energy, cheerfulness, and a contagious enthusiasm for learning.

In true form, he has a small stack of books under his arm. I inspect them as I take them for checkout. "Quantum mechanics?" I raise an eyebrow, impressed. "Very ambitious."

At least once a week, Shane chooses a new topic to do a deep dive into, but usually it's more along the lines of jellyfish, or black holes, or clocks. Quantum mechanics is raising the bar substantially.

Shane nods eagerly. "Well, yeah, I gotta do something to impress the pretty librarian."

How pathetic is it that it actually takes me a moment to realize he means me? I know by now not to take Shane seriously—he is a chronic flirt, with anything and everything that has a pulse—but I still blush, more from being out of practice with compliments than being genuinely flustered. "I'll let Erica know," I joke back at him.

He grimaces. "Please, no. The last time I smiled at Scarica, I got an alarming number of 'accidental' texts from the library system, reminding me about Singles Saturday." He leans in toward me, waggling his eyebrows. "Definitely not interested in that, by the way, unless the Face That Launched a Thousand Ships will be there?"

I smile back at him, though not for the first time, I feel a little ping of uncertainty. Is he really just being friendly, or is the truth about me so transparently obvious that he pities me and is just trying to make me feel better about my sad, pathetic life?

"I'm not much of a Singles Saturday kind of girl," I hedge carefully.

"Darn." Shane's face seems guileless, his smile cheerful as he takes his stack of books back from me. "Wish me luck! I failed biology in high school."

"It's not biology," I try to call after him, but he's already halfway out the door, whistling to himself as his spiral curls bounce in time with his footsteps.

With Shane gone, a stillness settles over the library once again as I return to my desk. Glancing surreptitiously around, I pull up my document. I don't normally try to sneak in so much writing when I'm on the clock, but I'm supposed to do a reading for my writing group in a few days, which means my pages need to be sent out by tonight.

The cursor blinks at me tauntingly, reminding me I still haven't come up with the right verb. Something about my interaction with Shane has deflated some of my romantic energy, making it seem even more daunting than before to finish the paragraph. Which is stupid, because it's the moment when the hero and the heroine finally let down their inhibitions and give in to their passions. The entire novel is building to this literal (and figurative) climax, and yet I suddenly find that I have zero inspiration to finish it.

So I push aside the little squiggly moral inhibitions that tell me it's wrong and allow Axel's fictional face to be filled in by one decidedly more substantial and familiar. The Red Unicorn's features come to mind—his blue-gray eyes, his cleft chin, his strong, stubbled jaw. His tousled auburn hair, always looking slightly windblown, as if he is forever just finishing running his fingers through it.

Imagining someone I actually know as one of my characters always feels strange and a little sordid, especially when I'm writing love scenes. I know—it's skeevy! But I justify it to myself in a few ways, namely because the Red Unicorn is more a character to me than a living, breathing person. Despite seeing him around the library for weeks now, we've barely exchanged more than a handful of words and a few fleeting moments of eye contact. Further, the heroine of my story, Rosamund, is nothing like me. She is beautiful, daring, forthright—all qualities that could never be said to describe yours truly. So it isn't like I'm imagining the Red Unicorn doing a series of naughty things to *me*—and somehow, I hope, that makes it less creepy.

Suddenly, Axel comes to life in my mind—the subtle woodsy, masculine smell of him, the flash of his blue-gray eyes. Rosamund is helpless against him, overwhelmed by him—and yes, indeed, it is a keening *whimper* that escapes her throat as his tongue lavishes her breasts.

That ought to be enough to please the ladies of my writing group, I think as I finish the paragraph. They're always encouraging me to be a little bit racier with my love scenes, to go into more detail, and I'm really trying my best here, letting my imagination fully run away with me.

I just hope it will be enough to keep them off the scent, and that no one will realize they have a thirty-one-year-old virgin—and former nun—in their midst.

Chapter 2
Helen

It isn't that I think there's anything inherently wrong with virginity. Objectively, I know that what people do with their own bodies is their own choice, and that society shouldn't have any say in when or if a person decides to have sex. I also know that age shouldn't really be a factor—some people might be emotionally ready at seventeen, others might take significantly more time. Circumstances, sexual orientation, health, religious beliefs—all of these things can factor into a person's choice to remain celibate, and it doesn't make anyone more or less worthy of romantic love.

I can logically reason about all of these things, but every time I think about a romantic prospect finding out I'm still a virgin, I shrivel with mortification.

Being a former sister is a logical excuse as to why I was still a virgin at twenty-seven, when I made the choice to no longer renew my vows so I could try to live a normal life with a job, marriage, babies, and the like. Obviously, it made sense that someone who pledged to live a celibate life should remain celibate. This part of my story I think would be fairly easy for a romantic prospect to understand.

Four years after leaving the order, however, I'm still as much a virgin as when I first left. I've had a small smattering of blind dates and a brief dabbling into online dating (though I closed all accounts before I actually went on a date with anyone, because I am a coward).

But the truth is, I'm not just a virgin in the sense that I've never had sexual intercourse with another human being. I'm a virgin in every sense of the word when it comes to romantic encounters. I've never been kissed. I've never had a man hold my hand. I went on a couple dates before taking my vows, but I've never had a boyfriend. And, persuaded at a young age that I would go to hell for doing so, I've never even attempted to masturbate. My body as a sexual object is a completely foreign concept to me, and I'm certain that any man who gets close enough to sniff this out will go running for the hills screaming.

So I gradually closed my online dating accounts, stopped accepting blind date offers, and embraced the shapeless sweaters that keep me nice and toasty in the overenergetic library air-conditioning. I started baking Sunday nights. I've taken up knitting, badly. And on Tuesdays, I get Pizookies with the girls at Lou Malnati's Pizzeria.

For those sad, ignorant folk unaware of the beauty of the Pizookie, it is a pizza cookie: a half-baked, chocolatey dessert—crispy on the outside, gooey on the inside, and topped with cold, crisp vanilla bean ice cream.

I may have never had an orgasm before, but I'm pretty sure this is probably as close as it gets.

"Watch it, you're breaching into my territory," Matilda snaps as the three of us hover over the dessert in question, spoons engaged in a swift battle to ensure that no one gets shirked their full amount. This is a precarious situation, especially at a high-top table with a slightly wonky chair.

One of the things that I love most about my friends is that they love to eat. I've never known how to bond with someone who doesn't truly enjoy food.

"We didn't divvy out sections," I remind her, "and even if we did, this is clearly *my* third."

Our bickering might have continued, but we suddenly realize that quiet Antonina is stealthily infringing on our territory with her own spoon. Silence descends once more as we each hurry to eat as much as we can before it's gone.

Aside from our love of Pizookies, the three of us might not seem to have much in common. I'm the oldest at thirty-one, blonde, blue-eyed, round-faced, and completely swamped in my oversized sweater. What I like about the bulky sweater is that my actual shape underneath is impossible to tell, and I like the general, almost-androgynous roundness that my outfit gives me. ("Like a habit," Matilda pointed out to me once, and I guess that's true. Even though not all orders still wear the habit, and in mine it wasn't required, I always felt safely invisible in mine.)

Matilda, by contrast, is tall and sleek, with formfitting, chic clothes that show off her athletic frame. She is twenty-seven, dark blonde, with a chin-length, no-nonsense haircut, cool blue eyes, and a direct stare that matches everything else about her hard-edged appearance.

Then there is Nina, who is twenty-four and uncommonly, ethereally pretty. She has long wavy brown hair that reaches almost down to her waist, a petite but shapely figure that a Disney princess would envy, and big brown eyes that always look a little dreamy and distracted. I've noticed she can go several meals totally forgetting to eat (a completely foreign concept to me). The only time she really seems to come to life is when she is eating dessert.

Yet despite our numerous differences, readily visible to anyone looking from the outside, I'm connected to these women in a way that no one else will ever truly understand, closer to them than I am to my own brother.

It all began a few months after I left my community house, when my then-therapist recommended a support group for former sisters, like myself. As expected, most of the women in the group were significantly older than me, and their individual relationships with the Church and their former lives as nuns were in some ways far more complex than my own. Still, it was nice to be around other people who understood, to some extent, what I was going through, and it was encouraging to learn that most all had gone on to live normal, unextraordinary lives with marriages, kids, and careers.

But it wasn't until Matilda showed up that I truly felt as though I'd found a kindred spirit. Even though, as she likes to point out, she was a "real" nun, a cloistered sister who lived in a convent, and I was "just" a sister, a person who takes the vows of chastity, poverty, and obedience but still interacts with laypeople in the world. (I say I was a nun as a shorthand, since that's the term most laypeople recognize, but Matilda is technically right.) And a year after that, sweet Nina arrived. (For the record, she didn't even make it as far as taking her vows to become a sister, since she left when she was a novitiate. So, I'm more of a "real" nun than her. Not that there's a competition. Well, not that there's a competition to anyone but Matilda.)

The three of us are mainly tied by this one thing in our lives, but oh, what a thing it is. Though we've drifted away from attending the monthly support group meetings, our friendship provides a far more frequent (and delicious) form of moral support.

"I finished my chapter," I inform the other women once we all finish our share of the Pizookie and can therefore relax and actually speak to one another, since we are no longer in competition to scrape up the last morsel.

"The sex one?" Matilda asks with her usual bluntness, rubbing at her little food baby, prominent on her otherwise flat tummy.

"Yep. It's pretty steamy, considering it was based on pure imagination."

Matilda and Nina are some of the only people in the world who know the full truth about my situation, and as always, it's a relief to be able to speak candidly. They know where I'm coming from, even if their own situations aren't exactly the same.

"Believe me, imagination is always better anyway." Matilda lost her virginity as soon as she could manage it after receiving her dispensation to leave from the Pope, and she continues to keep a "booty call friend" on hand for whenever she "feels the itch." She has no inclination for dating or romance, claiming she doesn't want to finally reclaim her autonomy just to lose it again. And Antonina…

Well, actually, I don't really know Nina's status for certain. Nina doesn't talk much about herself, just listens with those kind, sympathetic dark eyes that make it seem like she's divulged her soul when in fact, she hasn't contributed anything. Still, I can't really imagine her setting up a "special friend" like Matilda has, and she's never mentioned any dates or crushes, so I'm guessing she's probably in the same boat as I am. Only Nina is twenty-four, not thirty-one, and ethereally beautiful, so it's only a matter of time before she gets snatched up by somebody.

As if on cue, a compact, mildly attractive man in a suit approaches the table, his gaze fixed on Nina as if he is Galahad approaching the Holy Grail. "I'm sorry to bother you ladies"—he says this as if addressing the entire table, though his eyes never leave Nina—"but I was wondering if any of you would be interested in attending the symphony this weekend. I'd love to bring you all as my guests."

It isn't his fault, really; he seems nice enough, but it's the third time our evening has been interrupted by some guy who can't stop gawking at Nina, and Matilda has clearly had enough. "We're all deaf. Go away." Uttered in her pragmatic, faintly Russian accent, it somehow sounds even more cutting.

The man's brow furrows. "But—"

"No one here wants to talk to you. Take the hint." Matilda shoos him, and befuddled, the man obeys, casting one last longing glance back at Nina.

For her part, Nina stares down at the table, never even so much as looking at him. I squeeze her hand encouragingly, changing the subject to distract from her embarrassment. "I'm going to read my chapter at my writing group on Friday, if either of you want to come."

I know it might seem weird to invite your friends along to a public reading of your first sex scene, but it will be reassuring to see my two besties in the crowd. Or mortifying. I've never done this before, so it's a real roll of the dice.

Seeing Matilda's already-forming protest, I add, "I'll bring those muffins you like."

"The red velvet ones?" At my nod of confirmation, Matilda purses her lips, considering it. "We'll see."

Beside me, Nina suddenly stiffens and sits up straighter. "Isn't that…?"

Matilda and I follow the little jerk of her chin in the direction of a far corner table, so shrouded in shadow that it takes me a moment to recognize the Red Unicorn. I straighten instinctively, then immediately slouch back, afraid he might look up and recognize me. Or not recognize me. It's hard to decide which outcome would be worse.

Though Matilda and Nina only infrequently visit me at work, both are well familiar with the legend of the Red Unicorn. I'd talked about him so often that it became necessary to procure a picture and prove, contrary to Matilda's doubts, that he was real; and since I've purposefully avoided learning his name and therefore can't stalk him on social media and find out something unsettling about him—like that he has a supermodel girlfriend, or boyfriend, or that he is an amateur DJ—I had to resort to other means to prove his existence. Namely, I once sneakily took out my phone and pretended to be texting a friend while I actually took a series of pictures of him to show my friends over Pizookies.

It's not a proud moment of mine, but when a man is that attractive, his face needs to be shared!

"Is he here with somebody?" Matilda voices aloud the very question I've been wondering, as I scan for any sign of who his dinner partner might be.

But there is only one set of cutlery on the table, one glass of water, one glass of wine. "He's eating alone," I realize out loud, not sure why I should feel this little twist of pleasure. It means nothing. He could still be dating someone. And even if he is completely single, it changes nothing for *me*. I won't approach him at the table, or slide him my number at the library. I just like looking from a distance, knowing that he is at least *in theory* still attainable, even if in practice he is very much out of my league.

"Eating alone and reading," Matilda adds, and for the first time I notice the book in his hands—an Agatha Christie he checked out earlier that day—and the reading glasses that somehow manage to make him look even hotter.

You are a ridiculous weirdo, I remind myself, even as I make a mental note to give Axel some glasses before I send my chapter off tonight to my writing group.

If this were one of my stories, the Red Unicorn might look up and notice me across the room. A spark of recognition might light his eyes before he crossed the room to me. "The librarian," he might say, teasing me in that faint, sporadic Southern accent of his. "I've been meaning to check *you* out." (Or something less cheesy. I'll have to brainstorm that one some more.)

But the Red Unicorn doesn't look up from his book, and eventually I manage to drag my eyes away from him and pretend to be interested in the conversation for the rest of the night, until finally I glance back and see that he's gone.

Chapter 3
Helen

Stepping into my compact, one-bedroom apartment, eager to devest myself of the sheer torture that is an underwire bra, I let out a groan of frustration when I see my cell phone screen light up with *Mom*. A rebellious little part of me wants to send it straight to voicemail, but I quickly remember the last time I did so: The Boston Catholic network went into action, and my mom's church friends' sons, who also happen to live in Chicago, showed up at my door. And because Quinn Sullivan and Dan O'Malley run Cipher Security, they had a whole team of security officers with them. It was a whole thing, and it's taken me almost a full year to convince my landlady that I'm not a war criminal. (Offerings of surplus baking goods have come in handy with this task.)

"You're just so new to the world," my father explained at the time. "We worried about you so much less when you were still a nun."

I could have reminded all of them that I've been living on my own now for about two years, after earning my MS in library science and saving up enough money to move to Chicago, even if it was into a shoebox (and a kids' small, at that). By pretty much all measurable determinants of what makes somebody a responsible adult, I tick all the boxes. I pay my bills, I have a steady job, I watch HGTV. Sure, I've never had sex or been in a relationship, but that's true for a lot of adults. Okay, maybe not a LOT, but some. I'm not the only one.

(Right?)

But to my family, I will always be the miracle baby, the chosen one, whose life was promised to God—all without consulting me, of course.

"Hi, Mom," I answer on the fifth ring, knowing I can't let it go much longer without fear of repercussions.

"Helen!" My mother, Pamela Flanagan, shouts my name way too loud, then adds, "Ken, it's Helen!"

I hear my father in the background, also shouting for no apparent reason. "Hang up and do the FaceTime. Helen, we'll call you right back on the FaceTime!"

"I don't really—" I start, but it's too late, because my mother has already hung up the phone, only to call back a moment later via FaceTime.

I answer, forcing a smile. "Hi."

"Sweetheart, did you get my text about Dean's birthday?"

The worst thing about FaceTime—even worse than not being able to pretend to listen attentively as someone talks while you actually play Tetris —is not being able to eye roll with abandon. "Yeah. I already texted you back."

"Oh. I haven't checked my texts yet."

Then why are you calling me, Mother? I want to demand, but keep my smile plastered on. I love my parents, I really do. They are good people, and they try their best.

But—and I think this with all the love and kindness in my heart—they need a hobby. Maybe several. I visited them over the Martin Luther King Jr. Day weekend, just a few weeks ago. We have a virtual Sunday dinner together every week. My mother texts me frequently throughout the day, usually about nonsensical, pointless things that she could have just as easily Googled. Mom is planning my brother's birthday a month in advance, seemingly because she has nothing better to do. My dad at least has his sports teams he follows, but I once heard him get into a long debate with a telemarketer, I think just because he was bored.

I know they worry about me, and Dean (well, maybe rightfully so with Dean), but they might worry a little less if they took up gardening or traveling, or maybe got a dog.

These suggestions seem to always fall on deaf ears, though, so I listen as they tell me about a great new show they discovered that they think I'll love. After listening to their back-and-forth explanation for a few minutes, I inter-rupt: "Are you talking about *The Office*?"

"Yes, that's what it's called!"

Lord, give me strength. Only one of the most popular sitcoms of all time, and my parents think they've discovered a hidden gem. "I'll have to give it a try."

"What's that on your face, sweetheart? Are you bleeding?"

Frowning, I examine my image on the screen, seeing the smudge in question near the corner of my mouth. "Um, no." I reach up, guiltily wiping it with my index finger. "It's chocolate."

Silence. "That's right," Dad says after a moment, too cheerfully. "You met up with your friends tonight, right? How was it?"

"Great." There was once a time when my parents were thrilled at my weekly meetings with Matilda and Nina—probably believing that being in such close contact with two other former sisters might remind me of what I'm missing and persuade me to renew my vows. When they slowly began to realize the opposite might be true, their enthusiasm about our weekly meetings dimmed considerably.

My mother changes the topic quickly, not wanting to dredge up the old fight. Actually, *fight* makes it sound more like a confrontation. Conversations with my mother are never direct—they are passive-aggressive boxing matches where we dance around each other and mutually agree to pretend we don't notice she is taking jabs. "Don't forget we'll be in town next week for Aunt Linda's birthday. I'm looking forward to attending mass with you at St. Michael's."

Again, I must suppress an eye roll, knowing that my mother can see my face, though it almost feels worth it to chance it. Every time my mother visits me in Chicago, she insists on doing a self-made tour of all the most beautiful Catholic cathedrals in the city, as if this will trick me back into sisterhood.

I still go to church, I do. But I'm happily a once-a-week worshiper these days, and no cathedral, no matter how stunning, is going to convince me to give up my free will. Or my Pizookies.

"Maybe," I say noncommittally, mostly to avoid an argument, then fake a yawn. "Early shift tomorrow. Better get to bed."

They let me go, telling me to sleep well and that they love me, and I bid them good night. As I get ready for bed, I wonder how it's possible for two people to make me feel both smothered by their love and also like I'm a constant disappointment, in practically the same breath. They act like my choice to stop being a sister was the worst thing that's ever happened to them, as if it's so outrageous that I should get any say in my own life.

I wonder sometimes if that's part of why I have such a hard time letting go of some parts of my life from back when I still had a vocation. The baggy clothes, for example. I know in theory that it wouldn't be a big deal for me to wear normal clothes in which my figure is not just an amorphous blob of fabric. Even Nina, with her shirts always buttoned to the top of her neck and long skirts down to her ankles, at least has a silhouette. I suppose I have a silhouette, too, in my big bulky sweaters—only it resembles the Kool-Aid Man more than a human woman, which is what I should be going for, probably.

Freed from my bra, wearing my sleep shorts and T-shirt, I take stock of myself in the full-length mirror. It isn't a dislike of my body that keeps me from dressing in a more flattering way. I know I'm not a supermodel or anything, but I don't think I'm hideous. I'm tall—not Matilda tall, but taller than average—with blonde hair that brightens and darkens with the seasons, depending on how much sun I get. My eyes are bright blue, my nose just slightly crooked, but in a way that gives my face character, I think. Underneath the baggy clothes I wear, I'm not fat or thin, but somewhere in the middle. I like my hourglass figure, my surprisingly small waist, my toned calves and shapely ankles. I don't like the little pooch just below my belly button, or the cellulite on my thick thighs. I'm coming to terms with my voluminous breasts, which always feel a little bit overpowering and are therefore more comfortably hidden under baggy T-shirts and bulky sweaters.

I think my body is fine, all things considered. Maybe even attractive, on days when I'm in a good mood and I'm not on my period, or about to start my period, or just after my period—so, that one good week out of the entire month. It's more like I can't really reconcile putting myself in a position to be seen as an attractive, sexual being. I like being amorphous. It's safe, and comforting.

It's also likely why I'm still a thirty-one-year-old virgin.

Deflated by this assessment, I turn out the lights and go to bed. In the dark, I run my hands over my body, not for the sake of arousal, but assessment. If I ever do manage to have sex with a real human man, what will he feel when he touches me? Will he like my softness, my contours? Will he pity me for my lack of experience? Will it be obvious, off-putting?

It's a pointless hypothetical, since even getting a man this far is unlikely at best.

Chapter 4
Helen

It's with this same sense of gloom that I go to my appointment with Dr. Sandra the next morning. Her name is actually Dr. Fielding, but she's not technically my psychologist, although she is *a* psychiatrist, who lets me talk about my problems problems in exchange for scones.

Let me explain.

Remember that Boston Catholic network I mentioned? One of the only reasons my parents agreed to let me move to Chicago was because of their contacts in the city. And yes, I'm aware that it's absurd that an adult woman should need permission from her parents. My parents are friends through church with the Sullivans and the O'Malleys, and their sons—Quinn Sullivan and Dan O'Malley—live in Chicago with their respective wives and children. As also previously mentioned, they run a pretty impressive security operation, so my parents were convinced I'd be safe as long as Dan and Quinn kept an eye on me.

I knew Dan and Quinn growing up in Boston, but not well. They were family friends I knew mainly through my parents, too old to be in my group of friends but close enough that I idolized them from afar as part of the cool, handsome, older crowd. They knew me as a kid, an awkward teenager, a sister, and now as a laywoman. We are on the exchanging-Christmas-cards level of friendship but not the hang-out-at-a-weekend-BBQ tier.

So I was surprised how much Quinn—and to a lesser extent Dan, since he had moved back to Boston—took me under their wing when I moved to

Chicago. Anything I've needed has been provided without question. When I showed up at my apartment for the first time, expecting to spend all morning moving in my boxes, I was met by professional movers who assured me they had everything covered and that I could go relax at a local nail salon, courtesy of Quinn. When I casually mentioned to my mother that my air conditioner was acting up one summer, I had a repairman show up to my house within the hour, his fee already paid.

And when my health insurance wouldn't cover a therapist, I got a call from Dr. Sandra.

Dr. Sandra is red haired and beautiful, and has a friendly but no-nonsense demeanor that feels somehow softened by her spunky Texas drawl. She has a way of making you feel like you're talking to a friend, but a friend who will absolutely not let you get away with any horse manure.

Dr. Sandra insists that I can't pay her since she isn't my psychologist or psychiatrist, just someone who happens to have a medical degree in psychiatry who meets with me regularly for homemade scones. At first I assumed Dan or Quinn must be subsidizing her fee, but now I'm not so sure. Along with genuinely acting like my friend, Dr. Sandra also seems completely fascinated with my transition out of the order, or my "no-sex cult" as she jokingly likes to call it.

After some gentle prodding in our first "nonsession," I told her the specifics of my own predicament, surprised at how quickly it all came spilling out. Leaving my community, the path I'd always believed was my life's calling, reentering the world and not quite knowing how to fit into it anymore. Oh, and the whole issue of being a virgin and trying to date for essentially the first time in my life. (I originally left out the details of having never had a boyfriend or been kissed, not wanting to seem like too much of a loser to Dr. Sandra, though that came out over time. She's sneaky that way.)

Dr. Sandra listened quietly on that first visit—which I assumed would be our only meeting, a onetime pro bono advice session from a friend of a friend—then recommended that we continue to meet bi-monthly until I "found my footing." I guessed this was essentially psychotherapy speak for "We're gonna need a bigger boat." A one-off discussion was not going to cut it for this weirdo.

And now, after almost two years, I'm continuing to see Dr. Sandra, though now only once a month. It's helpful to have someone to check in with and talk to about my progress. I have Matilda and Nina, and to a lesser extent, my parents, but it's nice to have someone who doesn't have a horse in the race, so to speak. Dr. Sandra doesn't care if I become a sister again or never go back to church or start calling myself Madonna. (Well, that last one might raise at least one well-manicured eyebrow of concern.) She's simply here to listen.

I spot Dr. Sandra now, waiting on the park bench that's our spot, unless it's too cold outside—even by hardy Chicagoan standards. It's bitterly cold today, as a matter of fact, but we're both bundled up in hats and gloves and huge puffy coats that make my usual baggy sweaters seem practically skintight in comparison. Plus, I've brought along thermoses of my favorite Mexican hot chocolate, along with a flask of whisky in case Dr. Sandra wants to make them a little Irish, too.

Meeting outside is easier unless it's snowing or gusting with ice-cold wind, since we don't have to worry about anyone listening in too closely. When we used to regularly meet in a coffee shop, there was one guy who I'm pretty sure was following us so he could write a screenplay about me, until Dr. Sandra got him talking about himself and made him cry in under half an hour. It was impressive, honestly, and a little frightening.

"Helen," she says today by way of greeting, standing to give me a hug. "Cute shoes. Any sex yet?"

I realize this might sound like a totally inappropriate way for even a pretend-therapist to talk to their pretend-patient, but we've been meeting long enough by now that it just makes me laugh. I throw up my hands. "Yep. I'm all cured. Have a good life."

"Honey, just you wait. There's a whole bucket of therapy waiting for you *after* you have sex the first time. It's not a magic cure-all, I'm afraid." She's smiling, but her eyes are shrewd, studying me carefully, as we settle ourselves under an afghan—one of hers, not mine. I'm still working on my first hat; a blanket would be like my Everest. "What's going on? You seem…unsettled."

If Dr. Sandra hadn't become a counselor, she could have had a career as a psychic, she's so attuned to reading people's moods. I sigh. "I spoke to my parents last night."

"I see."

That's therapist-speak for "continue," so I do. "My mother just made one of her comments, and it kind of sent me into a spiral."

"What kind of comment?"

"About my life choices. How much of a disappointment I am, etcetera."

Dr. Sandra studies me. "Did she actually say that, or is that what you inferred?"

"Inferred," I admit, a little sulkily. "But in my defense, my mother is not one to speak her mind. Not if she can speak in circles around it, anyway. Which really isn't fair, since I'm the *good* one."

"The good one?" Dr. Sandra echoes.

I take in a bracing breath. I've mentioned Dean to her before, but never gone into depth on it. "You know my brother, Dean? Well, we're the classic sibling opposites. I'm the good, rule-following oldest child, he's the wild, rule-breaking baby of the family."

That's maybe underselling it a bit. Dean has been in and out of jail, in and out of rehab. All things considered, leaving my order pales in comparison.

"It's interesting that you call yourself the *good* one. That's kind of a loaded word, isn't it? And it comes with a lot of pressure, too."

I shrug, though her words land hard. "I guess I always felt like I had to be good. That expectation was made very clear for me, but Dean's never been held up to the same standard."

"Why do you think that is?"

"I'm not really sure." Actually, I have a bit of an idea, but it's something I'm too scared to say out loud, even to Dr. Sandra. Instead, I deflect. "Maybe because boys will be boys, and girls will be nuns?"

Dr. Sandra obviously isn't buying it, but she doesn't push either. "You know, the word 'good' can have a lot of meanings. It can be a reflection on people's morality, or their worth. But like any value judgment, it doesn't have one fixed meaning. It's subjective. Maybe instead of feeling trapped by your parents' expectations of what 'good' means, you should ask yourself what it would mean to *you*—to be a 'good' person."

I blink at her as I take in the words, really process them. What would it mean to me, really, to decide for myself what "good" means? How freeing might that be, to separate that from what anyone else expects from me? Groaning at the weight of it, I put my face into my gloved hands. "Why do you have to be so wise and insightful?"

The corner of Dr. Sandra's mouth twitches, just a little. She winks at me. "So that you'll keep bringing me scones."

I take a deep breath, considering Dr. Sandra's point more seriously. "You're saying there isn't just one way to be good? And I get to decide for myself what being a good person means?"

Dr. Sandra grins, popping a bite of blueberry scone into her mouth. "Wow, it sounds even better coming from you. I *am* good at this."

I take a bite of my own chocolate chip confection, pondering. "It's not like I'm even doing anything *bad*. I'm boring, by most people's standards. I go to work, I come home. I knit." It was Dr. Sandra, actually, who'd gotten me into knitting. I'm nowhere near as good as her, but I'm improving, I think. Not enough for my creations to be seen in public, but improving nonetheless.

"When I really want to let my hair down, I have a glass of wine. It's like my mom thinks I'm out carousing with random dudes all the time." Realizing how judgmental that sounds, I correct, "Which *she* would disapprove of. Not me."

"Are you ever out 'carousing with random dudes'?"

A sigh. "No."

"What about nonrandom dudes?"

I level her with a glare. "Do you think I'd be here talking about my parents if I'd finally gotten some action?"

"What's the problem? Do you believe your mother's version of you—is that what's preventing you from making a connection?"

"Maybe." I shake my head, realizing it's not right, not fully. "No, that's not it. It's more like—there's this disconnect. Like, I look in the mirror and I see someone who looks fine. I mean, not to be rude, but I know much uglier people than me who've had sex, so that can't be the only issue, right?"

"Of course not. You're a snack." Another ghost of a smile from Dr. Sandra. "What's the issue, then?" More gently she asks, "Are you afraid of sex?"

"I don't think so." Realizing how tentative this sounds, I laugh nervously. "I like the idea of it. I like imagining it. I can write fiction about other people doing it."

A moment passes as Dr. Sandra considers this. "Have you ever looked into the asexuality spectrum?"

I nod. "Yeah. I thought about that. But I don't think that's me. I want to have sex." That is maybe the understatement of the century. "And I know I could just get sex, in theory, but it's more than that. I want a romantic connection. It's like…it's like I started out on the same spot as everyone else, but with every life experience they took another step further and further away from me, until suddenly I looked up and everyone around me was miles away. And I know I should catch up, but how?"

Silence. Then Dr. Sandra sighs. "Well. I guess you start by taking it one step at a time. No one's expecting you to run a marathon on your first time out the door. But you aren't going to get anywhere by standing still."

Chapter 5
Helen

I'm doing my very best to stand as still as possible.

Arriving at work after my appointment with Dr. Sandra, I was dismayed to learn that the heater had gone haywire. The usual toasty wintertime warmth of the library has become a hot, sweltering stuffiness not nearly so agreeable to my wardrobe—my usual black leggings with one of my oversized knit sweaters that's more of a dress than a top.

The easy solution would be to just remove the sweater, but there are a number of barriers to this plan. Namely, that I am only wearing a tank top underneath said sweater. For most people, wearing a tank top in public wouldn't be anything all that remarkable, but I like the ambiguous bulkiness of my turtlenecks. In one of my sweaters, with no makeup, big glasses, and my hair tied up in a topknot, I can be invisible.

A tank top allows no such luxury. A tank top shows off arms and shoulders and a generous scoop of neckline when you have natural double Ds. A tank top fits to one's form, suggesting the shape of the body underneath.

Paired with my leggings, a tank top practically begs the world to look at me and say, *This is my body. These are its contours, ambiguity be damned. Behold, and be amazed!* (Or something along those lines.)

So my alternative solution is to push up my sleeves, put up my hair into a stereotypical librarian bun, and try to stay very, very still in the hopes of preventing my body temperature from rising. I'm still sweating like a sinner in church, but right now it's a sort of tolerably gross, damp state of being, and I don't want to tip the scales into the territory of *intolerably* disgusting.

"Kimberly." Erica—blithely wandering around in her own tank top, her skirt rolled up to the point where I half wonder why she even bothers wearing the thing anymore—drops down into her swivel chair with a dramatic flourish. "Take over restacking. I've been doing it for hours and it's soooo hot."

It's been twenty minutes. I hesitate, not wanting to be a jerk and not contribute my share, but also realizing that taking over restacking will sabotage my genius plan of not moving. "Umm. Maybe we can wait until the heater's fixed, or at least until tomorrow?"

Erica purses her lips, giving me a none-too-subtle once-over. "Look, I don't want to be *that person*, but you *did* come in late today because of your 'therapy'"—this said with skeptical air quotes—"and you know how those books add up if we don't get them back on the shelves in a timely manner."

Funny how Erica doesn't seem to care so much about the books piling up when it's *her* turn to restack the shelves but she has to leave early for a date, or a concert, or "drinks with the girls," or one of her mystery chiropractor appointments.

I motion down to my outfit, trying to appeal to her sense of pity. "It's so hot."

"I know. Maybe next time you should bring a change of clothes," she says, as though I'm being completely unreasonable for not having anticipated that the heater was going to break out of the blue.

Come to think of it, Erica could have given me a warning, since she'd been at work for an hour and a half before I arrived. It would have been an easy detour to stop off at my apartment on the way over and grab an appropriate change of clothes. Gritting my teeth against this new realization, I do my best to shove my sleeves up even higher, then push the cart into the stacks.

I only make it two and a half aisles before I admit defeat. It's just too hot to be wearing a woolly-mammoth sweater. Besides, the library is virtually dead due to the overenthusiastic heating, so only Erica and a few of the die-hard public computer users will see me—and most of the latter are so consumed in whatever it is they're using their computers to do that they probably won't even give me a second glance.

That settled, I remove my sweater, giving an audible gasp of pleasure as the offensively hot piece of clothing is discarded. The toasty air hits the bare, damp skin of my arms, my collarbone, my shoulders, and it is glorious.

Sure enough, I encounter no one in the stacks as I finish unloading the cart. I wheel back toward the front desk, anticipating my bottle of water and upcoming break, when I'll be able to stand outside in the freezing air for fifteen spectacular minutes.

"Kimberlyyyyyy!"

The irritation and urgency in Erica's voice makes me stop in my tracks, teeth clamping down in instinctive aggravation. *Lord, give me strength.* For one moment, I allow myself the luxury of hiding behind one of the stacks before—taking in a deep breath—I peek my head around the corner. "I'm here!"

No sooner do the words leave my mouth than I freeze, stunned to see the Red Unicorn standing at the counter, a flustered Erica standing opposite him. It's unusual to have a second sighting so close in the same week, so I hadn't even considered the possibility of running into him in my current tank-topped state.

The Red Unicorn's own concession to the heat is that he's unbuttoned the top few buttons of his shirt and rolled up his sleeves, revealing tantalizing glimpses of muscled, tattooed forearms and a broad chest faintly visible through the top of his white undershirt. The edges of a tattoo creep up over the rim of his collar.

Somehow, it feels even hotter all of a sudden.

Erica raises her voice, managing to sound both relieved and irritated at the same time. "There she is. I'm sure an error's been made." Her tone leaves very little room for interpretation as to who might have made this error. She gestures for me to come over.

You're not my boss, I think irritably, not liking how Erica is trying to show off for the Red Unicorn and make it seem like I'm her underling. But I also can't refuse to help a patron, no matter how annoying Erica is being.

I'm so flustered by Erica's behavior that it takes me a moment to remember the tank top of it all. Right now I'm partially concealed behind one of the stacks, but I'll have to walk across the room, right in front of the Red Unicorn, on full display.

You are ridiculous, I tell myself sternly. *It's just a tank top.* But as I force myself to take one step forward, then another, I feel as though I might as well be completely nude, being sweater-less under the Red Unicorn's gaze. I avoid his eyes, but it suddenly feels extremely difficult to do something as ordinary as walking across a room. What do I normally do with my hands when I walk? Why are they just pointlessly hanging there like that…?

I swallow down a relieved sigh as I reach the counter, feeling at least a little more concealed now that my bottom half is hidden behind something. As this is my considerably larger half, it's probably the better part to have obscured. "What seems to be the problem?"

"This gentleman has a book on reserve, but I can't seem to find it. *Someone* must have shelved it wrong."

Gee, Erica, could you be *a little more obvious?* I think in my best snide Chandler Bing voice. To the Red Unicorn, I offer a polite smile. "Okay, let's see if we can figure out what happened to it." I hesitate. The easiest option would be to look up his name, but I've been avoiding knowing it for all this time. I don't actually want to know *who* he is. I want him to remain the nameless Red Unicorn, an anonymous, safe, almost-fictional man who can never disappoint me. "What was the name of the book?" I ask instead.

"*Death on the Nile.*"

Smiling to myself, I remember seeing him reading a Poirot mystery the night before. He must have finished it already and ordered the next. I'm the same way with mysteries, exercising as little restraint with them as I manage with Pizookies. "Of course—another Agatha Christie."

Too late, I realize my mistake. I've just unwittingly betrayed that I've been keeping track of his books. The Red Unicorn looks perplexed, furrowing his brow a little. "What?"

I paste on my blandest smile, even as my heart races, knowing my only hope is to play it completely and totally dumb. "Agatha Christie wrote *Death on the Nile*, another one of her many mysteries!"

The pucker in the Red Unicorn's brow increases, but he doesn't comment, and I hope that I've convinced him, or at the very least confused him enough that he won't know what to think.

"Hmm." Grateful for the distraction, I focus on the computer screen in front of me. "I'm not seeing any order for *Death on the Nile*. When did you make it?"

"Last night."

"And you received confirmation that it was here?"

Erica lets out an irritated groan. "I already asked him that." She smiles, sickly sweet, at the Red Unicorn. "I'll check in the back. See if it got misplaced." She offers one last accusatory glare at me before disappearing into the back room.

The Red Unicorn clears his throat. "It's not important. I can come back for it later."

I hate the thought of him—of any patron, really—wanting a book and not having it available. If he ordered the book last night, it must have been after he finished the one he'd been reading in the restaurant. He might be playing it cool now, but I know from experience it's such a disappointment to think your book is waiting at the library only to have it not be there after all.

I offer him a sympathetic smile. "I don't mind looking through the reserves again, just one more time, if you want to wait."

He shrugs, so I turn my back to him and begin looking through the spines of the books. It's tedious work but it takes my full attention for a few minutes, distracting me from his presence.

Well, mostly. He's so silent that I glance over my shoulder a moment later, just to make sure he hasn't disappeared. What I see makes me do a double take in surprise.

The Red Unicorn is doing a slow, leisurely perusal of my body, starting from my feet and winding up over my calves, my thighs, my backside, lingering there for a long moment before continuing up past the small of my waist, my back, and finally meeting my gaze over my shoulder.

For a brief but intense moment we just look at one another. Then the Red Unicorn slides his gaze away.

I resist my first instinctive urge, which is to awkwardly cover my body, and I force myself to turn around to face him. I will use my most normal, everyday voice because what happened isn't a big deal. He just looked at me, that's all. People look at each other all the time. This is not an event! "I'm sorry." My stupid, traitorous voice sounds suspiciously winded, like I've just come running up a flight of stairs. "I'm not seeing it."

"I'll come back." I see a muscle in his jaw pulsing, and then—as if he can't help himself—his eyes dart down to my breasts, and just as quickly away again. He stands there for a moment, not speaking, then abruptly leaves.

I stare after him, baffled. The Red Unicorn, who has not so much as looked at me once the entire time he's been coming to the library, has by all appearances just…checked me out. As absurd as it sounds, I don't know any other way to describe what just took place.

Holy. Cow.

Chapter 6
Helen

As anticipated, Nina is supportive—in her calm, reserved way—of this new development, as indicated by her single heart emoji in response to my text. Matilda, as usual, has stronger opinions, on every subject.

So what? she texts back. Heterosexual men like boobs. You have larger than normal breasts. Ergo, he looked.

I know Matilda is right, at least in theory. Most women on any given day can probably expect to be ogled at least a handful of times, just going about their normal business: grocery shopping, drinking coffee, walking to their car. That doesn't make it right, of course, but it happens—to other people. I, unlike most women, do not get ogled on a regular basis. The way I present myself was designed to result in this very outcome, and it has worked very well for me. I can walk by a construction site completely unnoticed; it's one of my superpowers. Because…I don't want to be noticed. I don't want to be catcalled. I spent so much of my life not allowing myself to think of my body as being in any way sexual that the thought of some stranger thinking of me in that way makes me feel physically ill.

The point isn't that *some guy* looked at my boobs, though. The point is that *the Red Unicorn* did. And in that moment, all the anxiety, the unease, the fear that I've associated with my body being noticed was missing. I felt…excited that he was seeing me. A little unnerved, yes, but also…anticipatory. I liked knowing he was looking at me. I like imagining him thinking about me the way...

The way I've been thinking about him.

———

The feeling is nice enough that for the first time in a very long time, I find myself at a loss as to what to wear to my Friday night writing group. Normally what to wear anywhere is a no-brainer—I have enough leggings, sweaters, and baggy T-shirts to last me through every day of the week, including laundry day.

But tonight, I decide—wildly, recklessly!—I'm going to take that first baby step, like Dr. Sandra suggested, and see if I can grow more accustomed to having a little bit more of my shape on display. My writing group is a safe place to test the waters, after all. Aside from occasional visits from Matilda and Nina, the group consists of mostly middle-aged and elderly women, with the exception of Frank, who is gay. The group is always advertised on the library's events board, but the last time we had an outside visitor was 2015, and the man—a serious, horn-rimmed-glasses type, who talked a lot about his typewriter and seemed like he was really into Hemingway—never resurfaced again.

So the writing group is not likely to notice much if I shake things up a little. Actually, that isn't true—they will most certainly notice, and offer their opinions; this group is not shy about offering their opinions. But aside from a very slight stir, no one will very much care.

Despite the earlier events of today, I don't think I'm quite ready for tank top-and-leggings level of exposure, but maybe, hidden behind all the turtle-necks in my closet, there is some kind of compromise between the two extremes. I search into the dark, rarely visited crevices of my closet, finding a pair of jeans, so long neglected that I have to shake them out to ensure there are no spiders nesting in them, and a cream-colored sweater that will hint at a body underneath without hugging my figure too closely.

It's the type of outfit that most people would not think twice about wearing, but I have to stop myself from going back into my apartment to change.

Baby steps, I remind myself. *Baby steps...*

As expected, there is a mild commotion when I enter the small event room at the back of the library where the writing group meeting will be held. Florence wolf-whistles; Kathleen takes me by the hips and forces me to turn full circle so they can all take a look at my backside.

All totally normal, nonintrusive behavior.

Frank sits in the corner, disinterested. In his usual T-shirt and Walmart-brand jeans, Frank is not what most of the women in the group hoped he would be when they found out a gay man would be joining our ranks. From conversation, I gathered that a few of them had been half expecting Jonathan Van Ness—which, on the one hand, great for them for joining in on the inclusivity love fest! On the other hand, there's some room still to grow in thinking every gay man will automatically be like one of the guys on *Queer Eye*. Frank is about as fashion savvy as my aunt Linda, which is to say, socks with sandals are considered to be a valid lifestyle choice. He could not care less about my outfit change.

But Barb and Deb more than make up for his lack of enthusiasm. "Whoo! Look at that tiny little waist," Barb enthuses.

"And that ass like one of those famous sisters," says Deb.

I wave them down. "Okay, okay. Let's save the booty talk for my pages, please."

The ladies obligingly simmer down, just as Matilda and Nina arrive. Matilda doesn't notice my outfit at all, her eyes honing in on the red velvet muffins, and she marches past with a brisk "Hi," before going over to claim her territory.

Nina and I exchange an amused glance. "You look nice," Nina says with her fairy princess smile.

Her muffin already one-fourth gone after an impressively sized bite, Matilda looks up. "Who looks nice?" She does a double take at the sight of me, processing my outfit before shrugging her approval. "It's an improvement."

Matilda is the friend I know with one hundred percent certainty would help me bury a dead body—but she is also the friend who would critique me on bungling up the murder and buying the wrong kind of shovel.

I grimace-smile. "All right. If we're done commenting on my clothes, can everyone take their seats so we can get started…?"

The room obliges, with Nina scuttling to be closer to Matilda and everyone else taking their usual spaces. Florence glances at Matilda, sitting to her left. "How do you stay so skinny when you eat like that?"

Some people might demure—*Oh, no, I'm really not that skinny*—but not Matilda: "I have a very high metabolism due to some genetic factors, but also because I try to practice a nonsedentary lifestyle." She shoves another piece of muffin into her mouth. "Also, I generally eat a low-carb, high-vegetable diet, except for on special occasions, or when the food is free."

"Oh," says Florence. Because what else can you say to that?

Once everyone is finally settled, I take my place at the podium at the head of the room, pulling out my printed pages. Everyone, with the exception of Matilda and Nina, has already read my excerpt in advance and prepared notes to give me, but it's part of the tradition of the group for the author to do an oral reading of the piece first. The selections are kept short, since everyone knows if they read for longer than their allotted fifteen minutes, they will be roundly booed by Deb. (A retired schoolteacher, Deb is a real stickler for following the rules.)

"Esteemed ladies and gentleman," I say, taking a bracing gulp of my wine. I've had to read so many times for the group that I'm usually no longer nervous, but tonight is the first night I'll be reading a love scene, and I'm a little paranoid. I haven't written anything egregiously different from the other romance novels I've read, but what if I made some error, some telltale sign that I have no actual experience in the subject matter I'm writing?

"This is an excerpt from my work in progress, *The Knight Librarian*," I inform the group, keeping my voice as level as possible. "As you recall, last time we left them, Axel and Rosamund were forced to hide in the back room of the library so the mob wouldn't realize they'd overheard their plot to launder money through the reserve system—"

Matilda makes a bored, move-it-along motion with her hand.

I swallow, realizing that I am, in fact, dragging out the moment when I'll have to read, aloud, all of the steamy things I've written. I take another swig of my wine, reminding myself that I trust these people. They are my friends.

The door at the back of the room opens, and I squint against the light, trying to make out the features of the new arrival. Everyone from the group is already here.

"Sorry I'm late," comes a deep, masculine voice, and I feel the color drain from my face as I recognize him only milliseconds before he takes a seat in the corner, his face coming into view.

The Red Unicorn.

Chapter 7
Helen

I stare in dry-mouthed, sweaty-palmed horror as the Red Unicorn settles into his chair, fixing his blue-gray eyes on me. Words come out of my mouth, that much I know. They must even be somewhat coherent, because no one interrupts to ask me why I'm babbling, or tells me to get to the point already (and the "no one" in this scenario is clearly Matilda).

But even for a million dollars, or one of the Hemsworth brothers' phone numbers, I could not repeat back anything said in that first minute or so after the Red Unicorn entered the room. My mind is racing, trying to figure out how and why the Red Unicorn is sitting in on my writing group.

Logically I can piece together that he must have seen the flier on the library's community board. But why now? Why *this* meeting, when I'll be reading aloud my first full-on smut scene, in which the hero is only a thinly veiled replica of him?

This feels like it must be a punishment, for becoming a layperson maybe, or eating too much refined sugar. My mother warned me against both, and here I am, making my atonement.

Finally I realize I can stall no longer: "So, without further ado...*The Knight Librarian.*"

There's nothing to do but to read from the pages. I can't change anything last-minute; my writing group has already read the excerpt and will notice anything but the minutest of details being altered. I briefly consider trying to read Axel's hair as blond instead of strawberry blond (thank God I didn't make it full-on auburn, at the very least), but realize that will probably draw even more attention to the detail.

So, sick to my stomach, I read.

"With their bodies pressed together, Rosamund found she had a hard time focusing on her fear. Something new was building inside of her, as she stared into his...blue-gray eyes." What an idiot. Why couldn't I have just made them blue? "Something she had never felt before, not like this. Certainly not at the hands of the bumbling Wilfred."

This line earns a laugh from the regulars of the writing group. Their early notes were that poor Wilfred was too unbelievably inept to be an effective rival to Axel, though Kathleen has weirdly developed a crush on the underdog character and insists she's rooting for him to win Rosamund's heart in the end.

"Axel's throat bobbed as he swallowed heavily, making Rosamund wonder if maybe, just maybe, he felt something, too." Why did nobody tell me how terrible this book is? I will just have to leave the room as soon as it's over, move to Guam, and never return. "As she shifted, and felt the growing proof of his attraction pressing against her thigh, Rosamund no longer had to wonder."

The group gives a supportive burst of noise, some clapping, others whistling. Matilda, through a mouthful of muffin, calls out, "Finally!"

Buoyed by this response, I continued reading through Rosamund's and Axel's nervous but heartfelt declaration of feelings, leading up to the frenzied kissing that results in clothing being meticulously removed. More whistling, some foot stomping.

This is actually sort of fun, I realize as I lose myself in the pages. I would be enormously enjoying myself if it weren't for...

The Red Unicorn. I've been studiously avoiding his gaze, trying my best to pretend he isn't there, but my rebellious eyes dart to him on their own, at precisely the wrong moment: "...building toward a frenzied climax," I stammer, then swallow.

His face remains impassive, his watchful eyes trained on me. I grip on to the podium, swallowing again as I stare down at my pages. "At last, Axel clapped a hand over Rosamund's mouth to keep her gasps of pleasure from reaching the ears of the mobsters on the other side of the door. A moment later, he followed after her, tumbling into ecstasy. Satiated, spent, Axel half collapsed on top of Rosamund, pressing his chest against her bare breasts, their two hearts synchronizing and slowing together."

Enthusiastic applause follows, and I gather my pages back together, grateful to have something to occupy my hands. I exercise all of my willpower to keep my gaze from returning to the Red Unicorn, hoping this will keep me feeling professional, confident. This is *my* writing group; these are my friends. I shared a story from my imagination, and any resemblances to persons living or dead is entirely coincidental. If he assumes otherwise, that just proves he's arrogant—even if he happens to be right.

First comes the round of compliments, in which the group members tell me what they like about my writing. Then comes constructive criticism. I pull out my pen, ready to take notes.

Deb thinks the pacing is a little too quick, and they can take more time removing their clothing. Frank thinks the voice is too passive in some areas, and I ought to use a thesaurus since I repeat words too frequently. (Darn you, whimper!) Barb wants there to be more tension, with the mobsters lurking on the other side of the door, and Florence wants a little more buildup. Kathleen doesn't have any major issues, just wishes there was more Wilfred.

No one points out that Axel seems to have a striking resemblance to the mystery man who let himself into the room moments before I started reading. Just when I think things are wrapping up and that I've somehow, miraculously managed to escape from Dante's second circle of hell unscathed, the Red Unicorn shifts.

He clears his throat.

A silent, reflexive prayer escapes my thoughts. *Yea, though I walk through the valley of the shadow of death...*

Florence shushes everyone. "I think the handsome, mysterious newcomer wants to say something."

The Red Unicorn glances at her before fixing his gaze back on me. I resist the urge to press my eyes shut in the hopes that this will render me invisible. This is the moment, I'm certain, that he's seen straight through me, and I will be outed as a perma-virgin.

"Where did his gun go?"

Of all the things I feared the Red Unicorn would ask me, this is not one of them. For a very brief moment, I wonder if he's using a euphemism for Axel's penis, but that doesn't seem likely. "Sorry?"

"You mention Axel is wearing his service weapon at the beginning. Then about midway through when they're"—the Red Unicorn shifts slightly—"tearing each other's clothes off, you don't mention him removing it and setting it down. So when she's ripping off his pants with her teeth—"

"The gun would go clattering to the floor and let the mobsters know they're hiding in the back." Deb nods her agreement. "Well spotted."

Surely this can't be all. Surely I cannot get off this easily. (No double entendre intended.) "Okay. Great. I will make sure Axel sets it on the shelf before"—I feel my cheeks pinkening—"Rosamund removes his pants. Thank you."

It is maybe the longest exchange the two of us have ever had in the several weeks that the Red Unicorn has been coming to the library. My gaze catches on his for a moment and holds. I wonder what he thinks of my pages, beyond the detail of the gun. He was paying attention, that much is clear from his comment. But what does he think? Did it…stir him in any way?

I don't have too long to dwell on the thought, because Barb starts going over the details for the next meeting, coordinating everyone's schedules and arranging for Frank to send out his pages. All the while, I do my best to pretend to be engaged, though I half worry, half hope the Red Unicorn will leave just as silently and mysteriously as he arrived, before I have a chance to…what? Talk to him? Ask him if he thinks Rosamund should moan or whimper when Axel's tongue laps her nipple through her lace bra?

Finally, the meeting adjourns, and the Red Unicorn makes no sign of moving. Florence rounds on him immediately. "So, who are you and what are you doing here and what do you write and are you single, in that order, please?"

I am also very curious to hear the answer to all of those questions, but Kathleen has the audacity to interrupt my eavesdropping with more notes about my writing: "…can see why Axel's the hero. He sounds so hunky. But I think, with age, you'll find that Wilfred is really the type of guy your heroine should go for…"

It's impossible to focus on her *and* listen to the Red Unicorn's answers. Darn Kathleen and her fixation on Wilfred—normally I find it charming, but at the moment it's all I can do to keep from screaming that for Pete's sake, Kathleen, nobody cares about Wilfred!

By the time I manage to successfully end the conversation, the Red Unicorn has not only ceased revealing tidbits of information about himself, but he's also left the room.

My heart sinks in my chest. As disconcerting as it was to have him here, as much as I know I'll go back to seeing him semi-regularly at the library and that this is the extent of the relationship I want with him to avoid being disillusioned by his human imperfections—I can't help but feel disappointed. It surprises me, this feeling. I thought that maybe…

What? He'd be so turned on by my prose that he'll see me, really see me, for the first time, and it'll turn out he really is the perfect guy, and we'll live happily ever after?

This is not a romance, I remind myself again, for the millionth time.

I planned to get drinks afterward with Nina and Matilda, but Matilda has roped Nina into helping her wrap up the leftover muffins, so I go into the hallway to wait for them. Despite everything, I have a last, fleeting hope that maybe the Red Unicorn will be waiting for me there, but the corridor is empty.

I move to the drinking fountain, filling up my reusable water bottle and reminding myself, once again, that I am an idiot.

The door to the men's bathroom opens and I jump at the unexpected movement, heart racing. The Red Unicorn holds up a hand in what looks to be an instinctive gesture, my startled reaction startling him. He smiles, just a little, as I stare at him, dazed. It's the first time I've ever seen him smile.

"Sorry," he says. "Didn't mean to spook ya."

I wave him off. "No, you're fine. I startle easily."

The conversation has a surreal quality to it. I'm experiencing two simultaneous and contradictory emotions. The first is disbelief at the fact that I'm standing here, having a conversation with the Red Unicorn outside of normal library hours. And the second is surprise that this feels completely natural, because this man has played a central role in so many of my daydreams and fantasies that it feels like I actually know him.

I hold my breath, waiting to see if he'll try to continue the conversation. Which he'll need to do, because frankly I have no idea what's supposed to happen next, and I don't want to come across as a gibbering idiot.

He raises a hand, running it along the back of his neck. "I liked your story."

"Oh, thanks." I feel myself flushing, and in my self-consciousness, my mouth takes off without my permission. "There was a lot of sex in it."

The faint flicker of a smile appears on his face. "I noticed that, yeah."

"I don't usually write that much sex, but my writing group has been telling me to go a little deeper." I wince. "Stretch myself." A flinch. "Wow, there really isn't any way to say that that doesn't sound like an innuendo, is there?"

He gives a short, coughing laugh, rubbing the back of his neck again. Is that a self-conscious gesture? If so, it's strangely endearing. "Well, you should listen to your writing group more often."

"It's a great writing group. Was tonight your first time?" I, of course, know the answer to this, but he doesn't *know* I know the answer to this, and it's a perfectly natural segue to find out why he's here tonight.

He nods, glancing back toward the room. "Yeah. I saw the fliers in the library."

I nod, too, in what I hope is a polite and not overenthusiastic way. "Do you write?"

"Well," he replies, with another short, staccato laugh, "not really. I read, though."

We are both half smiling, just looking at each other, and the moment feels strangely charged—charged enough that even I can't miss it, and I can be oblivious to a lot of things like this.

Taking in a deep, bracing breath through my nose, I decide to be bold. "Detective novels, right? I recognize you from the library. I have a good memory for books."

"Ah, yeah. I recognized you, too." He extends his hand. "Thaddeus Hughes. I go by Thad."

A name! The Red Unicorn has a name. I've held off on this moment for so long that I have to fight a wince at hearing it, but I suppose it was inevitable that at some point he would have to move beyond a fictionalized character in my mind. Still. It feels, somehow, terribly intimate, to know this very public piece of information.

Thad Hughes. I test it out, trying to wrap my head around it. I hesitate only briefly before taking his hand. This is the most physical contact I've had with a nonrelated male in a very long time, and I don't want to do anything too weird.

His palm is warm, his fingers firm but not too tight as they close around my hand. I am so worried about making the situation awkward that I feel like I've turned to stone at his touch, afraid to move or breathe too quickly or grip too tightly. But he doesn't seem to feel any such compunction. His thumb brushes over the back of my hand, then again, like he's touching an especially soft blanket and can't quite help himself. Goose bumps break out on my arms, and my skin suddenly feels incredibly sensitive, responsive. "Helen Flanagan," I manage to say, though my voice sounds a little too breathy for just a simple introduction.

We're still holding hands, just kind of *looking* at each other, and for a moment I panic, worried that he might think I'm strange for not pulling away, until it occurs to me that he hasn't pulled away yet either, and what is happening?!

The door behind me opens and I jump, turning to see Matilda and Nina coming into the hall. They stop in their tracks at the sight of me with Thad, and only then do I realize we're still holding hands. I pull back, embarrassed.

Matilda and Nina stare. Nina's eyes are even bigger than usual, and Matilda is actually gaping, open-mouthed, for a full three seconds (which might not sound all that long, but *feels* LONG).

Nina is the first to recover, smiling brightly at us. "Well, have a good night, Helen. We'll see you later."

Matilda blinks in confusion. "I thought we were supposed to get drinks."

For such a smart woman, she can be so incredibly oblivious sometimes. I feel Thad's eyes on me as a blush rises up the back of my neck, and I wonder what I can possibly say to make it not completely obvious that I was supposed to leave with my friends but now they're trying to leave me behind so I can talk to Thad longer—only one of the friends clearly hasn't gotten the memo and is making everything super awkward.

"That's tomorrow night," Nina says quickly, her quiet voice brooking no argument. She links her arm through Matilda's, half dragging her toward the door, which is impressive both because Matilda is not one to be dragged *anywhere* and also because Nina is basically half her size.

"But tomorrow's puzzle night!" Matilda's loud voice rings out through the empty hallway before Nina pulls the door shut behind them.

Awkward silence hangs in the air. I dare a glance at Thad, whose face I can only half make out in the shadows of the corridor. "I don't suppose there's any chance you didn't hear that?" I ask him.

He laughs.

Somehow, and I'm still not entirely sure how, I'm walking out to my car, and Thad—nee the Red Unicorn—is at my side. The two of us are doing that sort of dawdling, deliberately slow walk that people do when they want to linger and spend more time together. At least, that's what I think we're doing? It's possible Thad just thinks I'm a slow walker and is trying to be polite.

But for once, I actually don't think so. The air between us is charged with an intense electric current, making everything sharper and brighter. It's the sort of thing I've read about hundreds of times in my favorite novels but have never experienced for myself until now. I feel hyper-aware of everything around me, every detail that might otherwise fade into the background standing out in sharp relief. The crinkles around his eyes when he smiles, the faint red stubble on his cheeks, the freckle just below his chin. The purple-black of the night sky and the cold, biting air, and the city lights reflecting on the building windows. The way my body moves and the sound of my breath and the weight of my hands and the overwhelming awareness of my lips, heightened by the little leap my heart gives every time his eyes dart down to them.

Is he going to kiss me? The thought seems entirely possible, when only a few hours before it wouldn't have even been plausible. I mentally run over everything I've eaten today, wonder when I last put on Chapstick, worry over what I should do with my hands.

And while all of this is racing through my mind, somehow I'm managing to keep up a conversation. I couldn't for the life of me recall what I said in those few minutes, not even under oath, not even if my life depended on it. Maybe something about writing, probably something about the library, possibly something about quiche, although I can't imagine why but it seems to ring familiar.

When we reach my car, I turn to face him with an attempt at a smile. "This is me."

"Ah." He puts his hands into his back pockets, rocking back a bit. Nervous, maybe? The thought is endearing, even if it feels implausible. "I'm just over there."

He doesn't move, though, and neither do I. We just look at each other, caught in that strange, invisible current. "It was nice to finally get to meet you, properly, I mean. I know all the other regulars by name but you've been holding out on me."

"Huh," he says.

I wait a moment for something more, but Thad stays silent, and now he's looking vaguely embarrassed. Oh, shoot. I *did* read the situation wrong, and he's trying to figure out a way to leave, and I'm making things weird.

I back up a step. "Well, I should—"

His voice catches me before I can retreat. "Do you like working at the library?"

I blink at him in surprise, then feel a surge of nervous pleasure as I realize *he's* now the one trying to extend the conversation, keep me here. "Um. Yeah. I do. I mean, I love books and I like helping people find the right books for them."

"You're the best one there. Sometimes I just turn around and leave if I see you aren't working."

It is, I realize, the most I've heard him say. He isn't a particularly verbose man—it doesn't come across right away, because his eyes are so expressive, and his face can change so much with just the slightest shift. But he's a mostly one- or two-word-answer kind of guy, until he goes and says something so unexpectedly sweet it floors me.

I blush. "That's really nice of you to say." Loyally, I can't help but add, "We all have our own strengths—"

Thad scoffs. "Carlos always wants to chat and Marsha is way too slow and Nadia hides in the stacks with her phone. And don't get me started on Erica."

I almost laugh at the very accurate picture he's painted of all my coworkers, until it registers just how clear of a picture it is. "Wow, you've really been paying attention."

Something shifts in Thad's eyes—hard to identify, but almost like a little light has been snuffed out. He sobers visibly, his lips thinning out. "It's my job, noticing the details."

"Your job?" I echo. Something else is shifting, too, although I can't entirely figure out what, and a part of me doesn't want to. I just want to hold on to this exciting pre-kiss moment where anything seems possible.

"I should've mentioned." He sounds almost regretful, like he doesn't want to say it. "I'm a bounty hunter."

"Wow, I've never met a bounty hunter before." I smile, still a little worried by that sudden shift in his tone but trying to tell myself I've imagined it. "So. A bounty hunter who reads crime novels—isn't that a little on the nose?"

Thad is smiling, too, though now I see it no longer reaches his eyes, which are noticeably crinkle-free. "I'm not much of a reader, actually. But I had to find some reason to be in the library so much."

I feel almost as though I'm being steered into a script, but I don't know how to escape it. "Why did you need a reason to be in the library?" I ask dutifully, dreading the answer.

"To watch you." Thad holds my gaze, his blue-gray eyes no longer bright but dimmed, blank. "I've been looking for your brother, Helen. He's in a lot of trouble, and I need you to help me find him."

And whatever sliver of shiny little hope I had snuffs out for good as the dread of those words sinks in.

Chapter 8
Thad

If this were a noir, Helen would play it coy—bite her lip, give me big, sultry bedroom eyes across the cafe table as she hems and haws about her brother's whereabouts, playing whatever games she can to throw me off the scent.

I know this isn't a noir, know that I need to stay focused and present if I'm going to find Dean Flanagan in time, but it's difficult not to let my mind wander when I'm standing so close to Helen. Difficult not to imagine her biting her lip and peering up at me with those big baby blues. Difficult to not be distracted by the formfitting outfit she's wearing that suggests I wasn't inaccurate all those times I watched her moving around the library and guessed what her shape was like underneath those loose, baggy sweaters. I got a tantalizing glimpse here and there—her sweater slipping down over one shoulder as she rearranged a ground display, or her sweater riding up as she stacked books on a high shelf, so I could see the full roundness of her ass underneath.

It always made me feel a bit skeevy, truth be told, especially because it's so obvious she doesn't want anyone noticing her body. I tried to respect that, not pay her more attention than she's due as the sister of the man I'm trying to locate, but she makes it damn difficult—the sexy librarian, the femme fatale goddess with a true hourglass shape and a tendency toward biting her full lower lip whenever she's really focusing on something.

And then tonight…God help me, tonight. I thought it was time to finally make contact with her, and the semipublic setting of the writing group seemed ideal. I didn't know she'd be reading though, and I certainly didn't know *what* she'd be reading. Listening as Helen took Axel and Rosamund through foreplay into full-on intercourse required a self-discipline I didn't know I possessed. It was hard not to let my mind cast her in the role of her heroine as she read out loud some truly filthy, lurid stuff. I'm not a prude or anything, but I had no idea romance novels are so *detailed.* It puts a whole new spin on those bodice rippers I always saw on my meemaw's nightstand.

Repressing a shudder at the thought, I reach for my beer. I don't normally drink when I'm actively on a case, but after the night's entertainment, I needed something to dull the edges. Something to stop me from imagining the way Helen's mouth looked when she read the part about Rosamund getting railed against the library bookshelves again and again by Axel's throbbing cock. The self-conscious little way she tucked her hair behind her ear, that embarrassed-but-pleased glint in her eye as she glanced around the room, like she could hardly believe what she was reading even though she'd been the one to write it, which must mean she'd imagined it, which must mean…

Another sip of the beer. I clear my throat. "When was the last time you saw Dean?" I sound formal and businesslike, which is good, because this is an important case and I can't afford to screw this up.

Helen holds her hands around her cup of hot cocoa, though I notice she hasn't actually drunk any of it yet. "Um. Last Christmas, probably?"

"Your family's not close?" I keep the judgment carefully out of my tone. It's been longer since I've seen my family, so I'm really not casting any stones. It just would be a lot more helpful if the Flanagans were a family who kept tabs on each other.

Helen's voice is apologetic, like she's embarrassed to be called out. "I see my parents more often. But Dean's always…done his own thing." She gives me her big blues, the worry in them palpable. "What is he into this time?"

I might've questioned the "this time," only I'm too familiar with Dean's arrest record to mistake the meaning. Dean Flanagan started committing minor felonies when he was fifteen, even spending three months in juvie for vandalism, and his record has been a hodgepodge since then of drug charges, petty larceny, and the like. Then, the last few years his record went silent. In my experience, there are four possible reasons for this: the person is dead, incarcerated, came to Jesus…or they just got much, much better at covering their tracks.

From the tone of Helen's voice, I'd guess it's the last option. The family knows he isn't squeaky-clean, even if they don't know all the details of what he's up to.

Still, I don't want to tip my hand too much. In all likelihood, Helen really doesn't know what Dean's mixed up in, but it wouldn't be the first time a family member's played dumb with me to feed information back to their loved one. I keep my response intentionally vague: "Illegal gambling."

Helen reaches up to rub the bridge of her nose, taking in a sharp breath. "Okay. Okay. That's bad, right? But it's not like he killed anyone."

She says it almost hopefully, like she's waiting for me to confirm it. I'm almost glad I didn't tell her the rest of it, if only so she won't know just how much trouble her brother is in. Still, I'll have to make clear how serious this is. "Let's just say I'm not the only one looking for him." At Helen's blanched face, I add as gently as I can, "Let's just say other, much-less-friendly people who aren't just worried about him skipping bail."

Helen does a quick little cross over herself.

"If there's anything you know that can help me find him, you need to tell me." I prompt, "Do you know places he might go? Friends he might stay with?"

Helen shakes her head, looking overwhelmed. "He really doesn't talk about anything like that around me. Probably because I was a—" Her eyes dart up to mine, something sharp and nervous in them. "—really religious person."

I pretend to buy that obvious slipup, just to keep her talking. I don't know if whatever she's covering up has to do with Dean or not, but there's definitely something Helen doesn't want me to know.

"When's the next time he'll visit your parents in Boston?"

She flinches a little when I say Boston—probably processing that I really have done my research about her family—but answers anyway: "His birthday, I guess."

That's only about a month away, but I don't know if Dean Flanagan has that long. "You have his phone number, yeah? Could you try texting him?"

Helen's hands return to the cocoa mug. "I can try. But he'll think it's weird. We don't normally just *catch up*. We're on a family group chat, but that's mostly just used to coordinate holiday stuff and birthdays."

"Can you try?" I don't add on *for me*, but I might as well have. The two of us are staring at each other again, that weird, charged thing between us that I don't quite know how to name. Attraction, sure, but there are plenty of nice-looking girls that don't make me act like a complete dickwad. Like I'm fifteen again and have never touched a girl's boobs before and it's all a beautiful, scary mystery.

Almost as if she's read the thought, Helen's eyes dart down to my lips. She bites her own.

Shit. I keep my face carefully neutral. That kind of thing isn't an accident. She knows the effect she has on me, and she's using it to some end. I don't buy the innocent, big-eyed thing. No one with tits like *that* is as Bambi as she's pretending to be.

And anyway, two can play at that game.

Helen holds my gaze another beat before nodding, then once again says, "I can try."

I watch as she sends off the text. I'm an old hand at this, and I know I'll have to keep an eye on her if she's going to stay true to her word. I look over her shoulder as she types out the message—a generic: Hey, what's new?—to make sure she isn't going to pull a fast one on me and warn Dean someone is looking for him. I was once a more trusting soul, and I might have fallen for the shy, sweet librarian with the big electric-blue eyes at one point in my life, but not anymore. In fact, the sweeter Helen Flanagan comes across, the more I nurse my suspicion of her. She's Lana Turner in *The Postman Always Rings Twice*. Rita Hayworth in *Gilda*.

She's trouble.

As the two of us wait for some response from Dean, I drum my fingers on the tabletop, trying to keep my eyes from darting down to her breasts. Truly, the woman is making me feel like a teenager again, and it's irritating as hell. It's taking everything in me not to scowl at her, let her know I'm onto her game. I have to try to play nice for now, keep her on my side. Let her think her act is working.

"So how does one become a bounty hunter?" Helen asks, jarring me from my thoughts.

Now I do glare at her, before catching myself. "Family business." I know what she's playing at, trying to get me talking so I'll get distracted. I have no doubt she already knows about my dad.

But those big, guileless eyes say otherwise. "Oh, really?"

At first I'm not going to answer her, but then I change my mind, wanting to call her out. "My dad is Darius Hughes." At her continued, questioning gaze, I tag on, "*Bama Bounty*? It was a pretty big show about five years ago."

Something shifts in her eyes, and inexplicably, she starts to blush. "I, um, wasn't watching too much TV then. I must have missed it."

Okay, sure. She's never heard of my dad. I'll pretend I believe that. "Anyway, Alabama started to feel a little crowded, so here I am."

I watch her face to see if she'll react to that. If she really does know who my father is, then she'll know exactly why I left to relocate to Chicago. Well, technically, my office is in Indiana, since the state of Illinois doesn't allow bounty hunting. I keep a place in the city, though, specifically for cases like this.

But there's no flash of recognition, nothing. Either she's very good at pretending, or she really has no idea what I'm talking about. "So that's why sometimes you have a bit of an accent, I guess? Although sometimes it sounds Southern and sometimes a bit Midwestern."

I stare at her. What's she getting at? "I grew up in both places. My mom lives here, my dad's in Mobile."

"Oh, wow. I hear Mobile is beautiful."

She is so fresh-faced and sunny, her voice so bright, clearly trying to make *me* feel comfortable, that I falter for a minute. Maybe I really have misjudged her. Maybe she really is just the human equivalent of cotton candy—all sweetness and lightness.

Then she lowers her lids, biting her lip again as she glances down at her phone. "I honestly don't know if we're going to hear from him. With Dean it's usually either five seconds or five hours."

I stifle a laugh. She almost had me. I raise an eyebrow, deciding I'll call her bluff. "If we're going to settle in to wait, we might as well do it someplace more comfortable. Your place or mine?"

Helen's eyes widen, as if she can't quite believe what I just said. Then a little flush starts in her cheeks, and despite myself, I feel something stir at the sight. She might be taking me for a ride, but she *is* just as attracted to me as I am to her. At least that much isn't forced.

"Um…" She seems to be choosing her words carefully. "We can wait at my place. It's just down the street."

"Perfect." I rise to my feet and wait for her to lead the way, getting an eyeful of her voluptuous backside. I might not be an easy mark, but I'm no saint, and that ass in those jeans is something else.

And now I'm on my way to be alone with her, in her apartment, where I'm somehow supposed to keep a clear head and not be taken in by her sexy mind games.

Jesus, take the wheel.

Chapter 9
Helen

P raise baby Jesus, but for once I tidied up my apartment before I left for work in the morning. I have a few loose shoes hanging around the entryway and a mug out on the coffee table, but there are no stacks of dishes in the sink or bras hanging over the shower rod, so I will take that as a win.

"I have some wine," I say over my shoulder to Thad, trying my best to sound casual, as if this is something I do all the time—entertain gentlemen callers with alcohol, alone in my apartment. The thought is so absurd that I almost break down into giddy, nervous giggles, though I manage to bite them back. "Do you like red?"

When I glance back at Thad, he's giving me a wary expression that stops me short. "Sure," he says at last, "I guess this is what we're doing."

I blink at him, perplexed. No one's ever looked at me like that before, like I'm...untrustworthy? It's disconcerting. I've always been good little Helen, the school treasurer and the girl everyone knew was going to someday become a nun. "I can run out and get some white if you prefer...?"

"No, no. Red's just fine."

Thankfully my kitchen is out of view of the small living room, so I manage to pour myself a small glass to settle my nerves before I regroup to join him. "Do you live nearby?" I call out ahead of myself.

The sight of the Red Unicorn on my couch draws me up short, nearly taking my breath away. He's picked up one of my books and is studying the back cover, his brow knitted together as if in deep concentration. He has a wonderfully lined face—which might sound out of place for someone roughly my age, but with his defined jawline and full lips and stubbled cheeks, it just kind of works. It makes him look lived-in, in the best possible way.

He looks up finally, reaching out to take the glass from me. Our fingers brush, just lightly, but enough to send a shiver through me. Our gazes lock, holding. There was some weirdness at the cafe and I thought maybe I imagined all of it—this current between us—but now it is snap, crackle, popping all over again. I swallow.

So does he. "Sorry, what?"

It takes me a moment to remember I asked him a question. "Do you live nearby?" I force myself to sit and take a sip of my wine, willing myself to treat this situation like it is normal, to *be normal*, darn it!

"Not too far." It's an evasive answer, but he's been kind of evasive all evening. I still don't fully understand why he's looking for Dean, or how he thinks I'm going to help him, or why he was so cagey about his dad, and all of these things should be more concerning to me, but in truth I'm so horny it's difficult to focus on anything but Thad's lips and his hands and how much I want to interact with them. There's probably a prettier, more romantic way to try to spin it, but we are about fifteen years past subtleties. I have never wanted anyone so badly, have never fully let myself understand what it is to want like this.

I'm so discombobulated that when I try to take a sip of my wine, aiming for sexy and sultry, I drink too much, too fast, and end up spilling it onto my shirt.

Hot.

"Oh, shoot." I dart an embarrassed glance at Thad, but to my surprise he looks sort of—resigned? Like he's been expecting this to happen. Although that obviously doesn't make any sense. "Sorry. Let me just go change."

"Sure, sure. Get nice and comfortable."

He looks so guarded. But maybe he's just nervous, too? I start out of the room, when his voice catches me: "Leave your phone behind." At my perplexed look, Thad continues, "In case Dean texts back while you're chang-ing. We wouldn't want to miss him."

It feels strange to surrender my phone. I'm not glued to technology or anything, but it sort of feels like leaving my journal behind. My password-protected journal with nothing even remotely interesting in it, but still. Thad's gaze almost looks like a challenge, though, like he is waiting for me to put up a fight, so I shrug. "Sure. Just call out if he does. I'll only be a minute."

In my room, I quickly realize that might not be true. I have no idea what I should change into. My top is completely soaked and my jeans are spattered, so I'll have to get entirely re-dressed. It feels like putting on a whole new outfit would be trying too hard, but it also feels like putting on pajamas would be a little too intimate. I desperately want to text Matilda and Nina to ask them their opinions, but of course, I've left my phone in the other room with Thad.

It's ridiculous to spend this long debating over something that doesn't matter at all. "Everything okay in there?" Thad calls after a moment.

I force my response to be bright: "Yeah, just going to the bathroom!" I cringe as soon as the words leave my mouth. Why did I say that? Now he probably thinks I'm back here pooping since it's taking so long.

That settles it—I put on the first thing I have on hand, which happens to be a pair of yoga pants and a slouchy T-shirt. It isn't quite pajamas, but it is comfortable, and it doesn't look like I'm trying too hard. This should be fine.

I immediately second-guess myself, though, when I reenter the room and see the slow appraisal Thad does of my outfit as I approach. It's the same look he gave me in the library earlier today when the heater was broken. I suppose the pants are a little on the tight side, but the T-shirt is long and loose enough to counteract that. Or so I thought. Then again, it's also loose enough that the sleeve keeps slipping down my shoulder, revealing my bra, which is nothing all that special but is still technically underwear, so. There is that.

I think about turning right around to go change again, but then Thad meets my gaze and sighs—not a depressed sigh, but more like an *I'm going to give in and eat a piece of cake even though I'm supposed to be dieting* sigh.

"Come here," he says, motioning to the couch cushion next to him.

Swallowing, I obey, wondering why it's so oddly sexy to have him issue a command like that. All manly and gravelly voiced. I can't quite meet his gaze as I sit down, pretending to be absorbed with my phone. "Any word from Dean?"

Thad shakes his head. "Doesn't seem likely we'll hear from him tonight."

The words send a jolt of panic through me. Does that mean he's going to leave? I look up to find him much closer than I expected, his eyes on my lips. He reaches out and touches a strand of my hair, tucking it behind my ear, and I think my ovaries might explode from the contact.

"We shouldn't be doing this," Thad says quietly.

I manage a breathless "Shouldn't be doing what?" before Thad leans in, and I realize what *this* is with a little jolt of surprise, before I find myself, bizarrely, leaning forward and kissing him, as easy as that, like I do this sort of thing every day.

His lips are nice, and so soft, and his hands are warm as they touch my face, my neck, my shoulders, drawing me closer. For a moment, instinct takes over, and I just genuinely enjoy myself: the sensation of his tongue against mine and our bodies pressing together.

And then…my mind starts going, and I start to panic, wondering if I'm doing everything right. If it's obvious that I don't have much experience with this—and certainly no experience with this level of *this*. And now, I begin to second-guess myself, wondering if Thad can tell that I'm a complete novice. Thad doesn't know that I'm a former sister, after all—or does he? If he's been trying to find Dean, maybe he looked into *my* background, too, and knows all about my history. Of course, I left my order years ago, so maybe he assumed that, like a normal person, I've already gotten back on the saddle, so to speak. Like Dr. Sandra is always saying, I can't hide behind my vows forever because it wasn't my time as a nun that keeps me from pursuing romantic relationships, not entirely; it's my own hang-ups that I have to overcome. I desperately want to ask Thad if I'm doing okay at kissing but I sense that this will be worse than just *being* a bad kisser, so I'm kind of stuck.

I can't be too bad, though, since Thad runs his knuckles along the neckline of my shirt with one hand, the other sliding down to my waist to pull me closer. I instinctively suck in, wishing I didn't eat that second red velvet muffin, and then I remember that my mom used to always call red velvet "Satan's cake," and the thought is so absurd that I find myself giggling.

Only this is no quick, passing giggle. It's a hysterical, burbling thing that begins to run rampant as soon as it escapes from my throat. Thad pauses, stiffening a little before pulling back. "Are you…okay?"

"I'm fine," I say—or at least I try to through uncontrollable laughter. "I'm sorry, my mind was just wandering and I thought of something that happened the other day that was really funny." Afraid of follow-up questions, I add, "You would have had to have been there!" I take in a deep breath, attempting to steady myself. "Sorry."

"No problem." But whatever was happening between us is clearly over. Thad doesn't look upset or disgusted or anything, but he certainly doesn't look overcome with passion. He looks kind of confused, truth be told, and I can't really blame him.

Wanting to make things up to him, and to distract from my weird outburst, I spontaneously rise to my feet. "Oh, I have something for you." I cross to my bookshelf, beaming as I pull out the book I have in mind for him.

He takes it, still looking perplexed. "*Death on the Nile?*"

"It was the book you came in for today, but we didn't have it." I fold my arms over my chest, realizing too late that it might seem kind of stalkerish that I remember this. "I'm also an Agatha Christie fan, so I thought you might not want to wait to dive in."

"Oh. Thanks." Thad holds the book like he doesn't quite know what to do with it. Catching my gaze, it's his turn to look uncomfortable, even a little sheepish. "This is nice of you. I just don't actually read that much."

I stare at him, gobsmacked. "But you're in the library all the time. You go through so many books." It's one of the things I like most about him—beyond the obvious physical attraction.

Thad runs a hand over the back of his neck. "Right. I was keeping an eye on you in case Dean made contact, so I'd just pick up something to make it look like I had a reason to be there." He motions again to the book. "This is really nice, though. I hear she's good."

It feels like a punch to the gut. That's dramatic, I know, but it's true. All the times I imagined the conversations we'd have about how much we both love reading, and it was all a lie. He's *heard Agatha Christie is good*, for goodness' sake! The bestselling novelist of all time, creator of two of the all-time greatest literary detectives, and he's never even picked up one of her books. Well, no, he picked them up, all right, he just never actually read them.

And that's just really the tip of the iceberg, I guess, which is that I have no idea who this person is. I thought after seeing him at the library, knowing what kind of books he read, I could paint a picture of who he was. But it was only just a fantasy, wasn't it? It's more than just the fact he doesn't like to read. He's been pretending everything about himself from the moment we met, trying to use me—making himself into what he thought I'd want him to be. The books, the long, lingering glances, the chemistry *I've* been feeling—it was all just an act.

I search for something to say—and am luckily interrupted by the chime of my phone. It takes me a moment to process the sound, to remember what we've been waiting for, and then Thad and I make quick eye contact before I pick up the phone, breath catching when I see the name flashing on the screen.

"It's Dean," I confirm. "He wants to call me."

Chapter 10
Thad

I watch as Helen bites her lip, remembering its soft plushness. Along with being incredibly unprofessional, kissing her was everything I've been imagining since I first saw her in one of her ridiculously oversized sweaters, smiling brightly at me over the counter as I handed over an Agatha Christie novel. It was just something that didn't look too girly or literary I picked at random off the shelf, but she seemed so enthusiastic about it that I thought it might come in handy as a conversation piece down the line. So I waited the appropriate number of days—how long did it take to read a book, anyway, two or three days?—and went back for another Christie novel, then another, then another.

Except for a few cursory pages when I needed to pretend to be engrossed in my reading, like when I followed her to dinner with her two friends, I've never actually read any of the books. Believe me, I do enough reading in my line of work—public records, paper trails, social media pages of whoever I'm following—that reading for fun doesn't sound particularly appealing to do more of when I'm trying to unwind. I like the classic movie channel with the old film noirs, which you can watch in basically any run-down motel—a real perk in my line of work. Guys in trench coats and fedoras, knockout dames who don't take shit from anyone, cool one-liners, and bad guys who aren't all bad and good guys who aren't all good.

But Helen looked so crestfallen when I admitted the truth that I almost wish I had read at least one of the books. Which is stupid, because I know she's just playing a game to distract me from finding Dean—only, what the hell kind of game is it? I assumed with the whole wine-spilling trick that she was going to seduce me. It isn't normally the type of thing I let myself fall for —not anymore—but apparently I have an untapped thing for the whole sexy-librarian schtick. The combo of the shy smiles and blushes with those sultry lips and that knockout body that's all boobs and ass is potent stuff. I wasn't going to let myself actually sleep with her, but I didn't see any harm in fooling around. I figured she was the one calling the shots, so it wasn't taking advantage.

But for someone who's trying to play the femme fatale and seduce me into a stupor, the giggling was a weird move. Maybe it was meant to confuse me? If that's the case, it worked like a charm. Still, as a method to make me succumb to her womanly wiles, it was an odd choice. The giggling didn't seem forced, either—if anything, it read like she couldn't quite get control of herself. Maybe she hasn't really done this kind of thing before. I find that hard to believe with all the hip swaying and lip biting and the whole sleeve-slipping-down-the-shoulder thing, but it's possible she's new at this kind of game.

The thought makes me feel unexpectedly tender toward her, like I want to give her completely unsolicited and nosy advice to stay away from this whole scene. Find some nice, boring accountant to marry and let Dean fend for himself.

Then came the actual text from Dean, and any thoughts of warning Helen to stay out of it fled. Actual contact from Dean, the guy who has proven so unexpectedly elusive he is nicknamed "The Ghost" among me and my contacts. And he wants to call Helen.

The phone starts ringing a few moments after the text chimed, and for a moment, both Helen and I just stare at it. She starts to answer but I catch her arm. "Okay. Here's what you're gonna do. Answer it, try to sound like you just want to have a normal catch-up conversation, try to work in something about where he is now. Don't let him know I'm here with you."

Helen stares at me wide-eyed, deer-in-the-headlights terror on her face. "I'm not good at lying."

Sure. I do my best to refrain from giving her a skeptical look. "You'll be fine."

Taking in a bracing breath, Helen answers the phone. "Dean, hey." She listens for a moment, brow furrowing. "Yeah, okay." She covers the receiver, doing an exaggerated stage whisper. "He wants me to put him on speaker."

That's...odd. Something uneasy prickles in my gut. "Okay..."

She does so, setting the phone down on the counter. "You're on speaker, Dean."

Dean's voice comes over the speaker, a little crackly, like maybe he has bad reception or is calling from a pay phone. "Whoever's there with my sister, I wanna talk to you."

I shoot Helen a sharp, accusing look. I can't believe I fell for her act for even a second. "You warned him."

Helen looks genuinely flabbergasted, though I no longer give my perception of her that much weight. She's a better actress than I anticipated. "How could I have? All I said to him was 'Dean, hey.'"

Fair point. And I had the phone while she changed, and the rest of the time we were together, so I don't quite know how she managed it, but I'm sure she did somehow. I don't know how I keep falling for this bullshit, but I clearly need to stop being so trusting.

"Helen didn't tip me off, asshole. I'm just not an idiot. When my sister who never texts me wants to get in contact, I can put two and two together."

Helen looks a little guilty at being called out like this. "I text you, sometimes. We coordinated Mom's Christmas gift a few months ago."

"Come on, sis. Any text from you after nine p.m. is a huge red flag. Aren't you usually in bed by now?"

The blush climbing up Helen's cheeks confirms this to be true. She darts a quick glance at me, then looks away. "I stay out after that sometimes."

This whole thing is confusing. Have they coordinated some kind of brother-sister game to make me think Helen is some spinster who sits at home on Friday nights knitting? Either she really doesn't know anything about where Dean is, or they're trying just a little too hard to throw me off the scent.

But the blush. A person can't fake that, can they?

"So who are you?" Now Dean is speaking to me. "FBI? Or one of Cadorna's guys?"

It's my turn to feel a little embarrassed. I resist the urge to look at Helen. "Um. Bounty hunter."

"Jesus Christ. Whoops—uh, sorry, Helen." Why is Dean apologizing to Helen for saying that? Before I can ponder it too much, the younger man continues, "Look, you're in way over your head, man. Leave this to the big dogs. And leave my sister out of it."

I'm going to lose him if I don't act quick. "That's pretty rich advice coming from you, Dean. I'm not the one who's in over my head. Jumping bond is the least of your worries, from what I've heard."

Helen gasps, her face paling. "What?" She looks at the phone, aghast. "Dean, what have you gotten into?"

Dean goes on as if he hasn't heard either of us: "Look, asshole, my sister's a nice girl. She doesn't need to get mixed up in this."

Helen goes from horrified to affronted. "I'm older than you. Don't act like I'm some innocent who can't understand that you're in serious trouble."

Dean's voice turns petulant, the way only a sibling's can. "You might technically be older, but you're younger in the ways of the world—"

Helen rolls her eyes. "That is such bullarky—"

Bullarky? What is she, thirteen? As if realizing her blunder, Helen corrects herself: "Bullshit." But it sounds weird coming out of her mouth, like someone trying to pronounce a word in a foreign language who hasn't quite gotten the accent right.

Dean laughs, not nicely. "It's not a bad thing, Hel, but some of us were living out in the real world while you were hiding behind Jesus in that convent."

What…?

I blink at Helen, whose face has gone tomato red. If I needed any confirmation that Dean is speaking literally, not metaphorically, I guess I have it. Helen was in a convent? "Like a nun or something?" I hear myself asking out loud, furrowing my brow at her quizzically.

Was I just making out with a nun?

It doesn't fit with the whole sexy-librarian vibe. But it does put her giggling fit into new perspective. Oh, God. The realization falls down on me like a cold deluge. She was nervous because she's not used to kissing people. Maybe has *never* kissed anyone. Same with the wine spilling. Everything I took as a seduction tactic was actually just ineptitude.

I stare at her, perplexed. I've been so focused on finding Dean that I figured Helen was just a means to getting to her brother. Turns out, she's maybe even more of a mystery. Just who is this woman, anyway?

Whatever is on my face makes Helen look away, unable to make eye contact. Over the speaker, Dean continues, "Yeah, like a nun. She's a good girl, not mixed up in any of this, so let's keep it that way."

"Fine," I agree. "Tell me where you are, and we can meet up, make a plan—"

But Dean's already hung up.

For a moment, silence stretches out between us. Helen stares at the ground, refusing to look up, so I take the opportunity to study her. I made so many assumptions about her, most of them not very good. On the one hand, I wouldn't have minded playing hardboiled detective to her femme fatale; on the other, I'm honestly relieved she isn't some kind of master manipulator, and that the sunny, sweet thing isn't an act. There are no mind games. She's a *good* person—and an inexperienced one who doesn't know what the hell she's doing. This isn't some film noir, I'm just a douchebag who tried to cop a feel on a nun (ex-nun?) because I thought she was leading me on a merry chase.

Dean is right. She really shouldn't be involved in any of this.

I clear my throat. "Guess that's a dead end. Sorry I wasted your time."

Helen reacts like the words were a hit, turning her face away from me, but not before I see her electric-blue eyes flooding with tears. Shit. I take an instinctive step toward her, surprising myself, before holding myself back. What would be the point? She probably should think I'm an asshole, for her sake. I wasn't exaggerating before when I said Dean was in a lot of trouble, and there's no need to drag her into it, especially now that it's obvious she doesn't know anything.

Still feeling like a piece of shit, I back toward the door. "Thanks," I say. Then realizing how stupid that sounds, I figure it's better to just leave. So I do.

Chapter 11
Helen

It's stupid to feel heartbroken over Thad. We only shared one measly conversation, one stupid kiss. I know hardly anything about him, actually, since it turned out he made up part of his personality, and his only real interest in me was trying to find my brother. Thad made that incredibly clear when he all but ran out of my apartment after Dean hung up the phone.

There was nothing between us, except for my fantasies of who I thought Thad *might* be.

I know all of this, on a logical level. But on an emotional level? On an emotional level, I feel deflated, crushed. The look he gave me when he tried to kiss me and I couldn't stop laughing…it springs back into my mind at the most unexpected, inopportune moments, like an incredibly sadistic jack-in-the-box, and no matter where I am or what I'm doing, I have to cover my face in mortification.

Luckily I already had plans to get coffee with Matilda the next morning. We meet up at Philo's, the coffee shop down the street, an hour before I'm scheduled to open the library for the day. Matilda might not be the most caring audience, but her matter-of-fact briskness can be weirdly comforting sometimes.

"He was never going to be a long-term relationship anyway. He has *tattoos*." Matilda shakes her head as she scrolls through her emails. As a paralegal, Matilda is always working, even when she's not technically working, and she's incredibly good at multitasking, so I don't take it too personally that she's on her phone during my meltdown. "You do not belong with a tattoo guy."

I feel like I ought to be offended, but I know what Matilda means. Thad looks like he should have a glamorous girlfriend who used to be a supermodel. And I…well, I look like I should be with someone who wears a cardigan and house slippers. So, basically Mr. Rogers.

"You got to make out with the guy you've had the hots for. That's as far as it was ever going to go anyway. I see this as a win."

Matilda can be so wise, sometimes. I shake my head, sighing. "You're right. You're so right." There's no way that someone like Thad would fit into my world. I can't imagine him at puzzle night, or baking with me on the weekends, or wanting to be in bed by nine p.m. with a good book. That's probably when he starts his nights, with his glamorous supermodel girlfriend who loves to go clubbing. This woman is entirely hypothetical, of course, but I imagine she's the clubbing type, and I myself am most definitely not the clubbing type. Thus, Thad could have only ever have been a fling.

"What you should be worried about," Matilda continues, "is the laughing-during-kissing thing. No one's going to like that, whether he's a fling or not."

There it is. Matilda's unflinching honesty always adds a little sting to her advice, no matter how good it is. "It wasn't like I meant to giggle," I defend myself.

"Exactly. That's the problem. You need more practice making out with people. Random people, maybe, so it won't matter if you make an idiot out of yourself."

"Gee. Thanks."

Matilda either doesn't hear the sarcasm in my words, or she chooses to ignore it. "There's a guy at my firm I could set you up with. He seems kind of desperate, so he won't care if you're bad at it…"

I know from most people, that would be a passive-aggressive dig at me, but Matilda isn't being mean, just pragmatic. In her mind, it makes sense that I should want to practice with someone who isn't picky or judgmental. She's helping, or trying to, and I honestly don't know if that makes it better or worse.

Luckily, Matilda has to leave to get to an appointment on time, so I don't have to hear any more on *that* subject. *Or is it unlucky*, I reflect later, after I've started logging in all the books returned through the outside drop box, *if Matilda is heading to meet up with the so-called desperate man she wants to set me up with…?*

I hastily pull out my phone, reiterating via text what I told Matilda in person: Do not set me up with your coworker. I mean it!

Someone clears his throat, pulling my attention from my phone. For a brief, pulse-pounding moment I think it might be the Red Unicorn—*Thad*—but of course, that doesn't make any sense. He already got what he wanted from me—and anyway, the Red Unicorn isn't really a beautiful ginger who loves to read. The Red Unicorn is dead.

With that melodramatic thought in mind, I meet Shane's sunny smile with an attempted smile of my own. "Hey, Shane. How's quantum mechanics going?"

Shane shakes his wildly curly hair. "Not so great, I'm afraid. I have no idea what this book is talking about." He hands over the book he checked out a few days ago, then produces a new one he's pulled from the shelves.

I scan the cover. "Oak trees. That should be interesting."

"Right?" Shane nods enthusiastically. "Have you ever just looked at trees and thought, *whoa*?"

I can't help but be pulled into his enthusiasm. Smiling, I nod. "Trees *are* whoa, you're right."

I go through the motions of checking him out on autopilot, my mind wandering, unbidden, back to my encounter with Thad. There it is again—that *look* on his face when I wasn't able to stop laughing. I'm convinced it's burned into my retinas now, an image I'll be able to conjure no matter how many years pass. It will most likely be the last image I see before I die, that's how scarred it is into my memory.

"What are you doing tonight?" I ask Shane before I can check myself. It's a stupid, impulsive thing to do, but didn't Matilda just tell me I should get some practice with someone else—ideally, someone nicer and less interested in using me to track down my brother?

Shane blinks at me in obvious surprise. "Uh—nothing?"

This is really not in character for me, but I have to do something to purge that memory of Thad from my mind. And Shane is nice, sunny, cheerful. I could see him wearing a cardigan—probably not slippers, though, since he's always talking about being connected to the earth through being barefoot and whatnot, but one out of two isn't bad.

I do my best to look confident, maybe even a little flirty. "You know, you're always joking about me turning you down, but you've never actually asked me out?"

Shane's face stretches into a grin. "Really? You wanna have dinner with me tonight?"

"Yes." I nod decisively. "That would be nice."

We decide on a place and time, and Shane copies my number into his phone. When he's finished, he beams at me. "Whoa. My day just got so good. I always love it at the library!"

I laugh at his enthusiasm. "Well, I'm not promising to be as interesting as oak trees, but I'll try my best..."

Matilda is busy tonight on a case, but her texts are mildly encouraging. *He's tolerable,* she writes, which is pretty effusive, coming from her. *Much more your speed.*

Since Matilda is otherwise occupied, I enlist Nina for the time-honored tradition of helping me choose an outfit for my date. Honestly, it's a little weird being on my own with Nina; Matilda and I spend time one-on-one together because we've known each other longer, but I never really do anything with just Nina. I think she's a sweetheart, but truthfully, we have little in common outside of the very big thing we have in common, which is the whole nun thing. And even then, I was a sister for five years, whereas Nina left when she was still a novitiate, so there's also that divide between us. Plus, as nice as she is, Nina always feels a little removed, like she doesn't want to let anyone in too close. In a group of three, this isn't that big of a deal, especially since Matilda often takes over the conversation anyway; but one on one...

#Awkward

"Do you want anything to eat or drink?" I ask, only realizing as the words come out of my mouth that I already made this offer when Nina first arrived. The answer was no, since Nina is planning to eat with her family when she gets home and since she always carries around a water bottle (how practical!). Not wanting to seem as if I just forgot (which I definitely did), I decide to add something new to the table: "I made brownies the other day...?"

Nina looks up from the clothes she's perusing, giving me a small smile and a firm shake of her head. "No, thanks. I had that muffin yesterday."

For a moment I just stare at her, not sure how to compute what I just heard. Is Nina suggesting that because she ate something sweet yesterday, she's somehow filled her quota—for what, a few days? The whole week? That sounds like crazy talk. Then again, Nina is delicate and perfectly proportioned, so maybe she's onto something. Something that I don't particularly care to emulate, but *something*.

As I struggle for something else to say, Nina clears her throat quietly. "What were you planning on wearing?"

I truly haven't given it much thought beyond the instinctive stress I feel at the decision. "Clothes…?"

Another small smile from Nina. "You should wear something you feel good in. Comfortable."

"So, a muumuu?"

"Not that comfortable." There is an unexpectedly sassy edge to Nina's tone —a very quiet, muted sass, but sass nonetheless. She bites her lip, concentrating deeply as she pulls out a few items from my closet: a sweater dress, some boots, and a belt.

I stare at the ensemble. It's the kind of thing I would think is cute on anyone else, but that would make me feel incredibly exposed. The dress is fairly conservative, as far as dresses go, but with the belt…that's a lot of waist action happening there. Not to mention the exaggerated emphasis on boobs and booty.

"I usually wear my cardigan with that," I tell her, reaching for an oversized, mustard-yellow cardigan, with an extra button at the top so I can feel all nice and snuggly and covered.

Nina reaches out a hand, stopping me. "Not tonight."

Her voice is quiet and firm—so firm, in fact, that I can only gape back at her. "Not tonight?" I echo.

Nina shakes her head. "No."

Nervously, I eye the outfit again. "I think the belt might be too much." Without the belt, the dress will be looser and I might not feel so conspicuous if my shape isn't showing.

"It won't be." Again, the firm voice. This is a side to Nina that I've never experienced before, and I would probably like it, if it weren't directed at me.

Before I fully know what's happening, Nina ushers me into the bathroom with the outfit in hand. It only takes me a few minutes to change, but I linger behind the locked door, half hoping Nina might just get bored and leave.

"Helen?" Nina's muffled voice snuffs out that hope. "How does it look?"

I wordlessly open the door so Nina can see for herself. Nina takes me in quietly, critically, before meeting my gaze and giving me one of her little nods. "That's a date outfit."

"Are you sure it's not too…?" I almost say the word "slutty" but stop myself. I don't like that word, and it isn't something I would use about anyone else, truthfully. At the library I see all kinds of people—people who wear way less than this dress covers—and I never think of them as being slutty. But for some reason I've always been more critical with myself. "Is it trying too hard?" I ask instead.

"It's perfect," Nina reassures me. And it's so unlike my young friend to express an opinion of any kind so intentionally, that I find I have no choice but to go along with it.

Chapter 12
Helen

I immediately regret the decision to wear the outfit Nina picked as soon as I'm out of the house, on my way to meet Shane at the taqueria we agreed upon. As if the clothes weren't enough of a step outside my comfort zone, Nina also persuaded me into a bold eye shadow and a jaunty little half pony that I never would have attempted on my own. It turns out Nina is sort of pushy, but in a sneaky, quiet way that ambushes a person out of the blue. Like some kind of fashion ninja…?

As I wait for Shane inside La Chaparrita, I'm half tempted to leave on my big puffy coat so no one can see my outfit. If it weren't for how crowded the front room is, and therefore how warm it is with so many bodies filling the space, I might do it, too. But the thought of sweating through my dress finally forces me into taking off my coat. Surprisingly, there is no spontaneous sex riot at the sight of me in a formfitting outfit. I relax a little, reasoning to myself that the dress is a bigger deal to me than it is to anyone else. Shane probably won't even notice.

Then again, he's one minute late. Two, now. Maybe he won't show up at all! The thought is strangely relieving.

But then the door opens and he enters, wearing a nice shirt and actual shoes instead of barefoot-toe shoes, along with cologne I can smell from even a few feet away. It looks like he's attempted to control his wild hair, too, with little success, but still, the effort is endearing.

A flutter of anticipation courses through me, and I paste a smile on my face as he approaches…

And then walks past me. Confused, I look after him, observing as he scans the crowd that always congregates around the front counter. It appears that he's looking for me, which is weird, since he just walked straight past me.

"Shane!" I offer a little wave.

He stares at me blankly before blinking and taking me in. Jaw all but falling open, Shane does a full body scan, his eyes lingering longer than necessary on my breasts, before traveling again up to my face. "Helen?"

Embarrassed, I avert my gaze, tucking a strand of hair behind my ear. "It's me. My friend got a little carried away with my outfit, I know."

When I glance back at Shane, he's staring at my breasts again, but he snaps his gaze up to mine. "Your friend deserves, like, a trophy or something. A big one."

I laugh, mostly because I don't really know what to say, and I resist the urge to cover myself. "Should we get tacos?"

"Hell yeah." Shane unexpectedly leans in to kiss my cheek, then slides his hand over my shoulder, resting it there as he guides me to the back of the line. To my surprise, he keeps his arm around me, leaning in close to tell me, "This place is really great. Best tacos in Chicago."

I make a polite noise of interest, refraining from pointing out that he already told me this when we decided to meet up here earlier this afternoon. It isn't a big deal. Maybe Shane's nervous, or he just forgot about the conversation. Or maybe he brings a lot of girls here and it all kind of blurs together for him. This is only one date. He doesn't owe me anything.

I'm surprised, frankly, by his reaction to me. We've always mildly flirted in the library, but I never took him seriously; I thought tonight would be more practice than anything else. But even though I'm naive, I've read enough romance novels to know what it means when a guy takes every opportunity he can to touch you. Maybe he really is attracted to me.

But am I attracted to *him*? It's not something I've had to think about before in a real, concrete way. I try to peek over at him surreptitiously to assess him. He's not my usual type, but he's a good-looking guy, a little on the young side. But there's something kind of safe about someone younger. I don't feel so overpowered, so caught up in my hormones, like I was with—

No. I'm not going to think about Thaddeus Hughes tonight. I'm not going to spend my evening comparing him to Shane, or picking apart what went catastrophically wrong after he kissed me. I'm not going to notice that the guy standing a few feet ahead of us right now has hair just the same shade of red, or the same build. Thad even has a shirt like that, which always comes a little untucked in the back, something which I always found kind of endearing. Like, here is this absurdly beautiful man who looks like something off the cover of a romance novel but he doesn't know how to properly tuck in his shirts—

No, no, no. *That's not just a guy who looks like Thad,* I realize as the man turns his profile toward me. *That* is *Thad, the Red Unicorn in the flesh.*

As if drawn by my gaze, Thad glances behind him, then does a double take at the sight of me. Like Shane, it takes him a moment to fully recognize me, and when he does, he stares.

A week ago, I might have bought this whole act, when I hadn't yet heard firsthand just how long he's been tracing me, pretending to be an avid reader. Accidentally showing up at the same restaurant where I was meeting my friends. Popping up at my writing group. And now, surprise, surprise, here he is at the same taco place I chose for my date with Shane. What. A. Coincidence.

Thad holds my gaze for a long moment, seeming to debate internally before bracing himself and coming over. I fold my arms, determined not to fall for any of his bullcrap.

He opens his mouth as he approaches, but I'm done with the lies and the tricks. "What are you doing here? Did you follow me?"

Thad stops, glancing self-consciously at the cluster of people standing in front of us in line who are now obviously invested in whatever drama is unfolding. "I'm just here for tacos."

"Sure you are—"

I might have continued on with something more cutting, hopefully something a little clever, if it wasn't for Shane guffawing next to me. Thad glances over at him, and—just as he did with me—does a double take.

Shane reaches forward, clapping him on the shoulder. "Hughes—no way. Let me guess: you're looking for Dean Flanagan, too?"

Chapter 13
Thad

This is a new, and very bad, development. I didn't know Shane was after Dean Flanagan, too, but if that's the case, then Dean is in much deeper trouble than I previously realized. Finding him is even more of a priority now than it's already been; I can't allow anything to distract me, can't afford to take my eyes off the prize.

And yet, as it so happens, my eyes can't stop darting down to where Shane is touching Helen. Just standing there and *touching* her, like he's calling dibs on her for everyone to see. I didn't even realize they knew each other, and yet they seem to be on some kind of date. I've never seen her dressed up like this before and it's…nice. I like her with her messy bun and big sweaters, too, but this dress is a good dress. Not just because it highlights her hourglass figure—which, holy Jesus, I'm a fan—but also because she looks confident and happy.

Before seeing me, of course. I've managed to squelch that look right away. Good for me.

The thing that irks me about her pretty dress and the glowy thing her skin is doing is that Shane doesn't even deserve it. He's just using her to get to Dean Flanagan. And, okay, yes, I've basically been doing the same thing, but I don't have a reputation like Shane does. I keep things professional. Shane seems to exclusively find his pleasure mixed with business, which has always frankly baffled me. Between the Sideshow Bob hair and the stupid footwear, I do not understand what his appeal is.

"Long time no see, Thaddeus." Is Shane's expression actually smug, or does his face just look like that? "Looks like we're after the same booty." He lets that hang in the air a moment before clarifying, "I mean, bounty. I assume that's how you know Helen, too, right?"

Helen is literally open-mouthed, looking back and forth between us in what is at first astonishment, but which slowly becomes anger. I've never actually seen her look angry before. It's…cute. She has every right to be outraged, but with those big blue eyes she looks about as intimidating as Shirley Temple. "You have got to be kidding me." She rounds on Shane, turning some of her ire on him. That's a bonus. "You're a bounty hunter, too?"

"Private detective, sweetheart," Shane corrects quickly, shuddering as if being a bounty hunter is a fate worse than death. "Licensed in *Illinois*."

I ignore the dig—knowing it's in reference to me *technically* not being a licensed bounty hunter in this state—instead watching the chain of emotional reactions playing out across Helen's face; she has one of those transparent faces, where every feeling is broadcast in cinemascope. Irritation, first, at being called sweetheart. Then shock as she processes that Shane is a private detective. (She, like most normal law-abiding citizens, has probably never come across a private detective; I, unfortunately, can't say the same. Let's just say that the nickname "Private Dick" didn't come from nowhere.) Finally, worry as she registers just how much trouble Dean must be in for multiple people to be searching for him.

"You've…" Helen gulps, shying away now from Shane's touch. "You've been coming to the library all this time, undercover, trying to find Dean?"

Shane, as per usual, does not take the hint, retaining his hold on her lower back. "Not totally undercover. I mean, I kept my name. It's just easier that way. But I do have a persona I've been working on for cases. You know, happy-go-lucky, aren't-trees-awesome, shroom guy. What'd you think—did I nail it?"

He sounds like he genuinely wants feedback on his performance, from the person he's been conning for the last month or so, just like I've been doing. Once again, I feel a twinge of guilt for what I've put her through. She'll be second-guessing everyone she meets now, some of that open sunniness dimmed. Maybe forever.

Helen takes a step away from both of us, looking back and forth between us two idiots. *I'm not like this guy,* I want to protest, but realize it isn't entirely true. So I keep my mouth shut.

"Let me say this loud enough for any other undercover agents to hear," Helen says, with enough volume to draw attention from the long line, tacos temporarily forgotten in the face of this unexpected drama. "I have no idea where my brother, Dean Flanagan, is. We are not in contact. So please, please, leave me alone." She starts to go, then turns back, angrily pointing a finger in Shane's face. "You can use the outside drop box to return your book. It's due in two weeks."

She glances at me, and for a moment I think she might say something. But she just jerks her head a little, like she's having some conversation with herself that ultimately ends with *not worth it*, and walks away.

———

Shane waits until she's out of earshot before turning to me with a commiserating grimace. "Well, that was a real waste of a month." He claps an arm around my shoulders. "Come on, man. Let's get some tacos. My treat—I know how fickle bounty hunting can be, even for the sons of D-list celebrities…"

I grit my teeth, working through some of my anger management breathing exercises to help me keep my temper in check as I listen to Shane prattle on: "…did you know all of that was going on under those huge sweaters? Because I sure as hell didn't. I would have been playing a different angle than chummy library patron if I'd known she had tits like that."

Breathe in, breathe out. Think of a tree, with roots embedded deep into the earth, and branches reaching up high into the sky…

Shane turns to me with renewed interest. "She was pretty pissed at you, though, huh? Sounds like maybe you got in a bit ahead of me?" He elbows me in the ribs, harder than is necessary. "First time for everything, I guess."

I debate internally whether to correct Shane on his assertion that I "got in ahead of him." Presumably, he's insinuating that I've already slept with Helen? That hasn't happened, of course, though there was that weird kiss—less weird in hindsight, once I learned Helen's last serious relationship was with God. I wonder if Shane knows that, but decide not to bring it up; it definitely isn't my place to share that. I also don't especially want to hear the comments Shane might make about Helen having been a nun. Shane strikes me as the kind of guy who might take it as a challenge to devirginize a former nun—assuming that Helen's still a virgin. She's been out of the convent for a few years (I now know after some research), so things might have happened in the meantime. Probably. It's none of my business. Still, Shane will find a way to make it into some dumbass game, complete with puerile bragging rights.

God, I hate private detectives. I catch myself running a hand over the back of my neck, a nervous tic ever since I was a kid. I used to have these cowlicks at the back of my head—still would, if I grew my hair out longer—but I was scolded enough by my meemaw that I tried to make myself stop doing it. The result is that the impulse remains, but now I've schooled myself to just rub my neck, which is, for whatever reason, more socially acceptable.

Someone who doesn't seem to care about being socially acceptable, at all, is Shane, who holds out his hands in front of his chest, intimating the size of Helen's breasts. "Seriously, I'm not usually into full-figured chicks, but those were impressive knockers. Maybe I *am* into full-figured chicks?" Shane considers this, as though facing some great existential crisis to his perception of himself. "Kate Winslet, yes. Usually. Not when she's, like, grunged up for Oscar bait. I'm saying *Titanic*, not *Mare of Easttown,* you know?"

What the hell is he talking about? I search desperately for some way to change the subject—then realize, abruptly, there's no need whatsoever to stay in the conversation. Shane and I aren't friends. The tacos here are good, but not *that* good. There is literally no reason to put myself through the torture that is talking to Shane Feldstone.

"I'm gonna go," I say abruptly, cutting Shane off midsentence as he debates his feelings about Kate Winslet in *The Holiday*. Probably, I should have come up with some excuse for why I'm leaving, but I just don't feel like Shane deserves it.

"What? I thought we were getting tacos, man." Shane looks belligerent as he watches me duck out of line. "Don't be like that, Thad—just 'cause she asked *me* out on a date."

I pause at that, but only briefly, and continue on to my car.

As I drive around, trying to come up with a plan B for dinner—the problem is, now I have tacos in mind, but the tacos just aren't as good anywhere else—I can't get that last parting shot from Shane out of my mind. Helen asked *Shane* out on a date? By some miracle, Shane and I hadn't run into each other as we were both staking out Helen at the library, but during my time watching Helen, I'd flattered myself that there was a connection between us. Not that people can't be connected to more than one person; I don't have any rights over Helen's romantic interests. She can like who she likes. But… *Shane*?

Granted, Shane mentioned he was playing some kind of character during his interactions with Helen. That's another thing Shane has a reputation for, in law-enforcement-adjacent circles: he likes to play "characters" when he's undercover. Rumor has it that he's a Second City reject and his backup plan was becoming a PI. The point being, the "Shane" he showed to Helen was likely very different from the Shane I (unfortunately) know all too well.

Still, the thought of Helen having romantic feelings for Shane Feldstone does not sit right. A sudden thought draws me up in the driver's seat, making me sit a little straighter and grip the wheel a little tighter. The night I went to Helen's reading at her writing group, and she read that sexy story, the hero—Ansel or Ajax or whatever—had wavy hair. For whatever reason, that detail stuck out to me, amongst all the other more interesting details about bras being ripped open and members being grasped and whatnot. Maybe I just latched on to some pointless tidbit to keep from getting a hard-on as I listened to Helen read those shockingly filthy words out loud (she can't still be a virgin, right?), but I remember thinking it was weird how many times Helen mentioned his hair was wavy. Wavy, wavy, wavy.

Isn't that another word for curly? Like Shane's wildly curly hair?

The thought has me gritting my teeth and abruptly pulling into a Taco Bell drive-thru. Quality be damned, I'm gonna get some tacos.

As I wait my turn in this much shorter line, something else niggles at the back of my brain, some small detail that I've managed to overlook. I groan to myself. If there are other clues that indicate Helen's spending her evenings fantasizing about riding astride Shane's muscular thighs, and then writing it all down, I do not want to know about it. I'm going to get my tacos, and drive home, and put on *The Killers*. Let Ava Gardner forever and always be the ultimate reminder: women, especially beautiful women, cannot be trusted.

Although…Helen is beautiful. And trustworthy. She's just a good person who's been pulled into a bad situation.

No sooner has the thought crossed my mind than the irritating, nagging thing that's been bothering me suddenly appears as a fully formed thought in my head: Helen mentioned the last time she had significant contact with Dean was to help plan their mother's Christmas present. Dean Flanagan might be caught up with some bad people doing some bad things, but he's still a mama's boy at heart.

The mom. She's the key to finding Dean. And Helen just might be *my* key to getting to Mrs. Flanagan.

But it would be wrong to pull Helen back into my search for Dean. I don't want to draw the wrong kind of attention to her, be the reason a bullseye is painted on her back.

Then again, if Shane's already been sniffing around her, who knows who else has been? Someone even worse than Shane. Someone even worse than me.

I can't just leave her to the wolves, can I?

Chapter 14
Helen

It probably isn't a good sign, having one's sort-of therapist gape in open-mouthed surprise. Considering all the things psychologists likely hear on a daily basis, it has to be something pretty shocking to get a reaction like that. Dr. Sandra recovers quickly, but still, the gape has happened.

"So both men you tried to practice dating turned out to be undercover agents looking for your brother," Dr. Sandra summarizes, her voice calm and professional, though I notice she is blinking more than usual. "How did that make you feel?"

Because of the snow flurries forecasted for today, we opted to meet in a cafe rather than at the park. Today would have been a nice time to have the anonymity of the outdoors, but the weather had other ideas, I guess.

"Not great." I slink down in my oversized sweater, hoping no one around us is paying too close attention. I'm back to billowy clothes and messy buns. No more makeup. No more formfitting dresses. No more hope. "I think I might try getting a cat. Maybe a Chia Pet."

"Is that what you really want?"

I raise a finger at her. "I know that might *sound* like giving up, but hear me out. What would a romantic relationship bring to my life, anyway? Companionship? That's what the cat is for. Someone I have to take care of who doesn't clean up after itself? Chia Pet. For the rest, I have GIFs of Sam Heughan."

Dr. Sandra presses her lips in a way that means she's trying not to show that she's amused. "There is nothing wrong with choosing to live one's life alone. Many people have very fulfilling lives as single individuals. *However*" —she gives me a look—"there is a difference between embracing what makes you truly happy, and giving up because of setbacks or fear. So I will ask you again, is that what you really want?"

I consider it. The life I'm imagining isn't an unfulfilling life. It's the life I've pretty much been living since leaving my order, minus the cat and the Chia Pet. If this is all I ultimately get out of life, it wouldn't be such a bad thing. I'm content.

But, at the risk of plagiarizing Foreigner, I want to know what love is. It's a concept I've only ever experienced secondhand, vicariously. Not everyone who looks for love in life finds it, and I've always known this was a possible outcome for me. If that ends up being the case, it wouldn't be the end of the world. Life will go on. But to miss out on the opportunity because I'm too afraid to try? *That* would be what I regret.

"I'm encouraged by the steps you've been taking. Approaching a handsome stranger, asking out an acquaintance to get to know him better, trying new outfits that let you show off, instead of giving you something to hide behind." Dr. Sandra pointedly does not look at the even-larger-than-usual turtleneck I reverted to today, though I get the message all the same. "This is all movement forward. Can you imagine the woman who first came to me being brave enough to do any of those things?"

I smile ruefully to myself, remembering the straight-out-of-the-community-house Helen and how terrified she was of everything. "No. I can't."

"The outcome may not have been what you were hoping for, but the *progress* is something worth celebrating." Dr. Sandra smiles at me. "Can I ask, how did you feel wearing the makeup and the dress?"

I scrunch my face, wishing I had a pillow to hide behind, I'm so embarrassed to admit it. "Pretty."

"That's a good thing, isn't it?"

"I've spent so long trying not to be noticed, it's hard to purposefully do things that make me stand out. I feel like I'm trying too hard. Like I'm betraying some past version of myself."

Dr. Sandra nods, pondering this for a moment. "Maybe that's a good place to start, then. We can't control what romantic interests might come into your life, or who may or may not be an undercover bounty hunter." She allows the rare wisp of a smile. "But what you can take charge of is your relationship with your own sense of self. The way you dress, the way you present yourself. Your sense of attractiveness, and how you do or don't want to share that to the world. I don't mean you have to throw away all your sweaters, though you certainly may if you choose. And I would help you. But what's something that you could do, independent of anyone else's response, that would help you get in touch with yourself as an attractive, sexual being?"

That…is a very good question. I stare at her for a moment. "I have a feeling you won't take 'Chia Pet' for an answer."

"No." Another press of her lips. "But you can take your time. Really think about it. Remember, this isn't about proving something to me, Helen. It's about proving something to yourself."

I sigh, nodding in deference to her superior wisdom. "Okay. I think I can try that…"

We hug in parting, quibble over whether Dr. Sandra will take the leftover scones—we always do, and she always eventually does—and make plans for our next meeting. We usually don't meet so frequently, but recent events demanded we bump up our regularly scheduled programming.

As Dr. Sandra and I start out the door, we run into Dan and Quinn coming in. It shouldn't be too unexpected, since I chose the cafe baed on its proximity to Dr. Sandra's building on East Randolph, and Quinn lives there, too—it's a whole thing, where a bunch of their friends all live in separate apartments in the same complex, and Dan still visits regularly.. I think Quinn owns the building or something, since I was also offered an apartment when I first moved here at an unbelievably low rent; but despite the price point, I declined. I thought, considering the source of the offer, this might make me a little too easy to access by my mother.

"Hey, fellas, what's shaking?" Dr. Sandra quips in a sassy screwball comedy voice.

Before I can echo her greeting (well, not *her* greeting specifically, because coming from me it would sound unhinged), Dan and Quinn both stop abruptly at the sight of me, freezing in place like they've just seen a ghost. For a moment, they just stare. Then both avert their gazes, like looking at me too directly might turn them to stone or something. Dan swipes off the beanie he was wearing, twisting it in his hands.

"Hi, Sister." They don't quite say it in unison, but close enough.

Dr. Sandra looks at me and rolls her eyes. "So as you can see, Helen, your fears about transitioning back into society are completely unfounded," she deadpans.

As embarrassing and awkward as the whole exchange is, I know it doesn't come from a bad place. Dan and Quinn, like myself, were both raised super Catholic, and it's hard to unsee someone as a member of a religious order when you've known them that way for a long time. I try my best to smile unaffectedly. "Hi, Dan and Quinn. It's just Helen now."

"Sorry, Sis—" Dan shakes his head, correcting himself, and grits his teeth to say, "Helen."

My name sounds so unnatural coming out of his mouth that for a moment, we can all only stare at each other. Then Dr. Sandra blows out a breath. "Oh, brother."

Quinn claps Dan on the shoulder. "We'll work on it." Though I notice, he doesn't even attempt to say my first name. Piercing me with that intense blue gaze of his, he asks, "Do you need anything?"

When I first met Quinn, his severity intimidated the Hootie and the Blowfish out of me. Now…it still kind of does, but I know it comes from a place of caring. Extremely intense caring. "I'm fine. Thanks."

I give Dr. Sandra a look that I hope conveys, *Don't you dare mention the private detective or the bounty hunter*, and Dr. Sandra gives me a look back that seems to say, *Girl, please, I would never reveal a confidence!* Or maybe, *Next time can you bake a raspberry scone?* It's hard to convey a whole lot with just your eyes.

As wonderful as all these people are, I'm eager to escape back into the anonymity of people who have no idea I used to be a sister. "Well, enjoy your coffee. I'll see you next month, Sandra."

"Remember what I told you!" she calls after me. "Prove something to yourself this week!"

Her words stick with me as I head back into the Chicago winter chill. There is one thing I've been meaning to try, something that I don't need Shane or Thad or anyone else to accomplish.

Something that—after having one devastating kiss and one humiliating attempt at a date—I just might be brave enough to finally do. After all, what's left of my dignity to lose?

Chapter 15
Thad

Femme fatale–nun is up to something. I watch her from my car, parked a few rows behind her in the parking garage of the Water Tower Place mall. She is acting…shady. That's really the only word for it, honestly, and that's not me being biased. She keeps looking around, like she's afraid someone might see her. She's wearing a trench-style winter coat, and even though she's inside and underground, she puts on a pair of huge sunglasses. Surely it's too on the nose for someone who looks like a film noir goddess from a '40s movie to be on a secret mission wearing a trench coat and sunglasses, but she's also acting way too shifty for it to just be a coincidence.

And there she goes, popping her collar. Oh, yeah. She's definitely up to no good.

I trail behind her through the mall, never getting close enough that she could actually clock me, but close enough that I can keep an eye on where she goes and who, if anyone, joins her. I'm not really sure what my game plan is. I'd intended to ask her today for advice about approaching her mother for help with finding Dean, but with the way she's acting…something isn't adding up.

Is it possible Dean has been in contact? That he might even be here today?

Yesterday I would have said no way. But with the way she's moving today, like she doesn't want anyone to see her, all furtive and sneaky… Maybe.

Hanging back, I keep an eye on the back of her blonde head, picking up my pace to keep from losing her as she turns this way and that, making her way purposefully toward her destination.

I don't pay too much attention to what store she goes into. I'm fairly confident in my ability to blend into my surroundings, even with my distinctive hair (a baseball cap helps) and my big frame. If it's a clothing store she's going into, I can duck behind some racks, or if I'm lucky, a display, and wait to see if Dean joins her.

But as soon as I enter *this* store, I stop short, immediately realizing my mistake. This is no run-of-the-mill clothing store. If the lavender walls and chandeliers didn't give it away, I'd have figured it out from the nearly nude mannequins in lacy negligees and barely there wisps of cloth.

Lingerie store. It's a lingerie store.

And not only am I the only man in the room—but in my baseball cap and flannel shirt, I look about as out of place as a bull in a ballroom. Realizing my error, I try to retreat as fast as possible, but not before I spot Helen a few feet away.

She's pushed up the oversized sunglasses to the top of her head, her profile turned toward me. Though she's still hiding behind her coat collar, she looks more relaxed now that she's actually in the store, a little smile playing on the corner of her mouth as she looks through a display of—

Oh, God. I swallow. Lacy panties.

Lacy *red* panties. I don't know why that makes it worse, but it does. Images, unbidden, spring to my mind, despite my best efforts to keep them at bay. That round, juicy ass barely contained in those very thin, very sheer panties…

I need to go. I start to back out of the room, trying not to draw attention to myself, and promptly bump into a mannequin wearing a sheer turquoise panty set. Swearing under my breath, I try to pull away, but somehow the damn thing's creepy plastic fingers have gotten stuck in my coat collar. Reacting more on instinct than on common sense, I twist this way and that, trying to loosen myself. Damn mannequins with their weird blank faces and bendy body parts!

Instead of freeing me, the whole mannequin falls off the display, on top of me. I hold it up with one arm, trying to reach with the other behind my back to detach its thumb, which seems to have gotten caught in that hanging loop just under my collar. I'm so caught up in the task that it only belatedly hits me that I'm causing quite a scene. I realize, too late, that I'm holding the mannequin up by one of its unnaturally firm butt cheeks, and that in all the scuffle, the mannequin's head has dipped down, perilously close to my crotch.

Freezing, I look up, to find Helen looking back at me. Our gazes lock. We stare at each other.

Helen's mouth drops open.
Oh, shit.

Chapter 16
Helen

For a moment, I can't quite believe what I'm seeing—for more than one reason. First and foremost, I have no idea why Thad is feeling up that mannequin, but somehow even more absurd than this sight is the reality of him being here, in this lingerie shop, right now. After literal years, I finally work up the nerve to sneak into a lingerie store and there he is, standing three feet away from me. Probably here to buy lingerie for his sexy, super-model-esque girlfriend, of whom there is no proof of existence, but who must exist nonetheless because she always does.

We stare at each other for a short eternity, as I run through all of the plausible scenarios to explain why I'm here that don't include my own stunted, burgeoning sexuality: I'm here to buy a gift. A sexy gift for a friend—no, that's too weird. I've wandered into the wrong store, maybe? Or I've been hired as a secret shopper.

Or maybe, just maybe, there's nothing that strange about an adult woman buying herself underpants. I know this logically, but somehow it still feels tremendously embarrassing to be caught. Especially since I'm currently looking at *red* panties, which everyone knows is the horniest color.

It's not as embarrassing as feeling up a mannequin, though, so at least I still have the moral high ground.

Thad tries to step toward me, but seems to remember all at once about the mannequin and does his best to drop it. It seems to be hanging on to him by his coat, though, which might have been funny under any other circumstance. Instead, I watch stone-faced as he grows increasingly flustered trying to shake the mannequin off before he abruptly pulls off its arm with a loud pop and lets the rest of the mannequin drop to the ground with a heavy thud.

If I didn't know better, I might think Thad was blushing. Actually, maybe I don't know better, because I'm almost positive that's a blush climbing up his neck. "I—" he starts to say, but I cut him off, stepping forward and reaching over his shoulder to detach the mannequin arm still dangling from the back of his coat. There's no way I'm going to be able to have a conversation with him swinging that thing around like a tail.

In a matter of seconds, he's free. I set the arm down carefully on a display stand before looking back at him—and I promptly swallow. Absorbed in the task, I hadn't realized just how close I've moved to him. I'm gripping his forearm, my breasts pressed up against his bicep. Our faces are *close,* so close that I feel the air sucked out of my lungs as his blue-gray eyes lock on to mine.

Thad clears his throat, brows knitted together gruffly under his baseball cap. "Is Dean in the back?"

I frown, matching his expression as I take a step back. "Is Dean in the back of what?"

He gives an irritated grunt. "Of the store."

It takes a moment to process. "You think I'm meeting my brother in a lingerie store?" I ask him slowly, not quite believing I even have to answer such an accusation.

A look of dismay flashes through Thad's eyes, but his jaw remains clenched tightly. It's like he's messed up, and he knows he messed up, but rather than admitting it, he has to double down. "No one would suspect it."

"Because no one would have that sort of relationship with their brother, outside of *Game of Thrones.*" The thought of having a discussion of any kind with Dean around sexy lingerie gives me the heebie-jeebies. I shudder and take another step back, not wanting any closeness between us to muddle my brain. "Dean is not here. Like I told you before, I have no idea where he is." I fold my arms as a new idea strikes me. "But I guess this proves you're still following me. I hope it's been worth your time, stalking me while I watch Netflix and read in bed. Pretty wild stuff."

His eyes flicker down to the red lacy panties still gripped in my hand, then back up to me. He clears his throat, looking discomfited. "I haven't been watching you in bed. Only in public."

"Oh. Well. As long as it's only in public." I give a dramatic flourish to my eye roll, suddenly no longer caring that I've been caught holding panties. I am not the ridiculous person in this situation, *he* is. I'm pretty sure whatever vestiges of a crush were left have been finally, firmly snuffed out.

Thad clenches his jaw, a muscle in his cheek flexing. He looks around the store, like he's afraid someone might overhear him, then leans in closer to me. "I have a theory."

I truly don't know who Thad thinks might be listening in on this conversation—the sales girl texting furiously on the phone she thinks we can't tell she's hiding behind the counter, or the mom pushing a stroller with her sleeping baby while she examines a pair of crotchless panties. (Interesting.) Either way, he's a little too close for comfort now, close enough that I can smell his soap and see the unexpected flecks of green in his eyes.

Okay, so maybe not entirely, one hundred percent over the crush.

"Oh, yeah?" I challenge, irritated at how breathy my voice sounds. "What's that?"

"You may not know where Dean is, but you do know how to find out."

I command my face not to betray anything, but I know my face. It is not a poker face, and I am no Lady Gaga. My expressions are as transparent as these panties.

Thad sees my hesitation and grins at me, triumphant and cocky, and something about it makes me feel squirmy in my bathing-suit areas. "There it is again. You know something."

I do my best to channel my inner sister, the one who taught middle school English for a year at an inner-city Catholic high school. Think *Sister Act 2*, but without the singing, or the fun, or Whoopi Goldberg. I'm not a natural disciplinarian, but one has a steep learning curve with prepubescents, and I can be tough. When forced to be. And no other alternatives present themselves. "Maybe. But even if, hypothetically, that's true, why should I tell you? Frankly, you haven't done anything to show me I should trust you."

"You don't have to trust me," Thad returns easily, folding his arms in such a way that (distractingly) shows off the tight muscles in his forearms. "But you should trust this: Dean is in a lot of trouble. On the scale of people looking for him, I'm a hermit crab. But there are barracudas, stingrays, even great whites who are on the hunt, too, just waiting for a chance to get a bite out of him."

That sounds…ominous. I frown at him, not wanting to relent too easily. "Killer whales are actually the apex predators of the sea. But I get your point. Who are these people and what do they want with Dean, anyway?"

"Not entirely sure. But rumor has it that Dean has majorly pissed off the Chicago mafia."

For a moment, I can only stare at him. "Like, the *mafia* mafia? Like Tony

Soprano, Marlon Brando, *I'm gonna make you an offer you can't refuse* mafia?" I shake my head. "That doesn't make any sense. Dean's an idiot but he's only been arrested for petty crimes. Drunk and disorderly conduct, peeing in alleys, that kind of stuff. What does the mafia want with him?"

Thad scoff-laughs. "Someone's been feeding you a spoonful of bullshit if you think that's true. Dean's been dabbling in the big stuff for a while now." He slides open his phone, switching through a few screens before handing it to me. "Here. Take a look for yourself."

I stare in surprise at the different charges on Dean's record: racketeering, sports gambling, extortion, loan sharking. Most recently he was arrested for health-care fraud.

And every single time, someone bailed him out. The only person who would do that is Pam Flanagan, which means that Mom has to know about all the different charges on Dean's criminal record. Knowing my mother, she refuses to believe most of them, but she at least knows of their existence.

Despite my worry for Dean's well-being, I can't help but be irritated by the entire situation. Dean is literally in and out of jail and seriously jeopardizing my parents' finances by skipping bail, and yet somehow *I'm* the problem child because I only go to church once a week now and I maybe/someday/hopefully will have sex. Explain that one to me, slowly.

Thad must read the warring emotions on my face as something more benevolent than they really are. "I can tell you care about your brother. Let me help him."

I snort. "By putting him back in jail?"

"In custody, away from the mob? Yeah, I'd say that's much safer than whatever game he's playing right now."

I debate this idea internally, weighing out the pros and cons. More to buy myself time than anything, I fold my arms back at him and ask, "How do I know you're really who you say you are? According to Google, bounty hunting is illegal in the state of Illinois." Yep. I did some research. I put my MS in library science to good use. "Maybe you're part of the mob and trying to trick me into leading you to Dean."

I don't actually think this is true, but it feels like something I should clarify, just to show I'm not as naive as everyone seems to think I am.

Sighing, Thad changes screens on his phone and pulls up…YouTube?

"Is this your swearing-in ceremony, or something?" I ask as the video loads. "Do bounty hunters have swearing-in ceremonies?"

"Shush," he orders me. "Just watch."

What follows is the most amazing five minutes of my life thus far. A brief, thirty-second introduction clip for a show called *Bama Bounty* plays, with overlays of a city I don't recognize, juxtaposed with swamps and alligators, cheesy graphics, an older man with a faint resemblance to Thad—but with a blue mohawk!—and Thad standing back-to-back with two other twentysomething guys who also faintly resemble him. And all of them, every last one, has matching mohawks: Thad's is his natural shade of red, while one guy has dyed his green and the other purple.

Thad clears his throat. "My brothers. And the first guy is—"

"Your dad," I finish for him, watching eagerly as the clip continues.

The scene is a brief one from what appears to be a reality television series following Thad and his bounty hunter family as they arrest people who break their bail. All of them have very thick Southern accents, much more defined than the occasional hint I get from him every now and then.

"Is this in Mobile?" I ask, remembering what he told me about splitting his time between here and there.

Thad clears his throat. "Yep."

In the clip I'm watching, Thad's father—Darius, according to the chyron on the screen—breaks down the information about the perpetrator and his criminal record for Thad and Thad's brothers (Orpheus and Amadeus—I'm not making this stuff up, I swear). The three sons make a lot of colorful interjections about the perpetrator's clothing and hair—most of which seem pretty badly scripted—and Darius promises to bring him swift Bama justice!

Then a very pretty, very made-up woman in sleek black athletic gear and a bulletproof vest sits on Thad's lap. Her outfit is no-nonsense but her hair is teased up to an unnatural volume and she's wearing long lavender acrylic nails. Her chyron reads "Vera" and I watch in morbid fascination as she runs her purple-tipped fingers up and down Thad's chest. As she does so, I spot a huge diamond engagement ring on her left hand. "Good luck, baby. Bring him into custody and I'll let you take me into custody tonight—"

In the lingerie store, Thad clears his throat and takes the phone back from me. "So, yeah. Verified bounty hunter. It *is* illegal in Illinois, but I technically practice out of Indiana, where it is legal, so."

I nod, pretending to still care about whether or not he has the right license, when I'm really still stuck on the woman in the video. Are they still engaged? Or married now? This video is date-stamped from a few years ago, and Thad no longer lives in Mobile or has a mohawk, so clearly some things have changed. But still…engagement usually leads to marriage. Was he kissing me in my apartment while he has a hot, high-maintenance bounty hunter wife at home?

All of this really shouldn't matter, considering the kind of trouble Dean is in. Still, I can't help glancing down at Thad's left hand. No ring. That could mean anything, though. Lots of people don't wear wedding rings, or they might still just be engaged…

Focus, Helen, I reprimand myself. I don't even like Thad as a person anymore, much less as a romantic prospect, and my attention should be on Dean and the best way to help him. "Why shouldn't I go to Shane instead of you? He's a private detective. That seems a little more legit than a bounty hunter who shouldn't even be bounty hunting in this state."

At the mention of Shane's name, Thad grimaces, like he's just bitten into something sour. "I don't know what kind of act Shane was putting on for you, but trust me when I say he's a complete douchebag. Finding Dean will be all about boosting his career and his ego, and if Dean gets fed to the sharks along the way, well, too bad, so sad, move on to the next job. *I* might be a lowly bounty hunter, but I only get paid if I catch my man alive."

He says this all matter-of-factly, and it's the first time it sinks in for me that Dean is actually, truly in danger. Not just his usual slap-on-the-wrist hijinks, but real and legitimate life-and-death danger.

It doesn't make any sense why I should trust Thad, but for some reason, I do. Sighing, I look down at my hands, where I realize I've been twisting the red lacy panties around. I drop them on the display, forcing myself to meet Thad's gaze and hoping he didn't follow the movement. "I'm going to see my parents on Sunday. They're coming into town and staying with my aunt Linda. Dean is supposed to call."

Thad's eyes light up, and he steps in closer to me, lowering his voice. "Bring me with you."

I suck in a breath, shaking my head. "My mom will freak out if she knows a bounty hunter is after Dean."

"So don't tell her I'm a bounty hunter. Tell her I'm your boyfriend."

My dumb heart speeds up a little. I feel myself reaching for the panties again—nervous habit, I guess?—and have to clench my hands at my sides to stop myself. "I don't know if they'll buy that. I haven't ever introduced someone to my parents, not since…" No need to be coy anymore. He knows it all. I square my shoulders. "…since ever. Even before I was a sister."

His eyes flicker down, then back up again. "The red panties suggest it's only a matter of time. I might as well be your first."

The words seem to register with him at the same time as they hit me, and he flushes. "First guy you bring home, I mean."

"Fine," I say quickly, hoping he doesn't notice my own rising blush. I hand him my phone. "Give me your number. I'll text you the information…"

And just like that, I'm bringing Thaddeus Hughes, bounty hunter, over for Sunday dinner.

Chapter 17
Helen

Beyond confirming the details of Sunday dinner with Thad, I don't have any contact with him for the rest of the week. Life goes on as normal at the library, except Shane seems to have disappeared completely. I guess he figured I was a dead end and moved on. Maybe he'll find Dean sometime in the next couple of days and I won't have to go through with bringing Thad to dinner with my family. Maybe then Thad will disappear, too, like none of this ever happened, and I can go back to my normal, boring life.

In the meantime, I use the Great and Powerful Google to find out as much information about Thad as I can. Now that I know about *Bama Bounty*, I find a whole treasure trove of details on the Internet. Apparently during the time of airing, Thad was something of a heartthrob to the show's small-but-rabid fan base, if the tribute videos on YouTube are any indication. (I may or may not have watched one video, devoted to zooming in on his muscles, more than once. For research purposes.)

The show went off the air about three years ago after some big scandal about Thad leaving the family business to start his own company in the Chicago area. At first I chalk this up to Thad wanting to spread his wings, or maybe getting a little too big for his britches as the *Bama* heartthrob.

Then I stumble across *the* thread that changes everything.

It all starts when I find the clip that Thad showed me at the lingerie store. Like some kind of masochist, I want to see the woman, Vera, again to try to piece together anything about his current relationship status. Not because I'm still interested in dating him myself, but because it feels a little weird bringing a guy who may or may not be married to dinner with my parents.

Could I just ask him myself? Sure. But if I have the option of stalking him late at night on the Internet to try and figure it out myself based on obscure clues and potentially meaningless details, that seems like a much better use of time, no?

I watch the clip a few more times, but aside from the uncomfortable feeling I get seeing Vera running her hand over Thad's chest, the scene itself doesn't yield too much more information.

The comments section, however, is on fire. All of the comments were made a few years ago now, but there's a surprising amount of engagement. People *really* do not like Vera, even though she seems fine, if a little handsy, in the clip itself. According to user MonkeyBrains49, this is the first taste we get of Vera's true colors, and her intentions are soooo obvious. ILoveDwayne-Johnson argues that it's not unusual for a woman to want to look made up for the camera, but Vera seems a little *too* fancy, even by *Bama Bounty* standards, and it's clear she's trying to catch someone's eye. LatherRinseRepeat24 writes simply that she is a slag. (I look that up and realize it is *not* a nice word.)

And so on and so forth. I realize there has to be more to the story with Vera and go to Reddit, hoping to unearth some more information about why everyone hates Vera so much. Finally, after searching a few years back, I find it. I stare in astonishment. I go back to Google to confirm what I found, and then I find the spread in *US Weekly* and the pictures to confirm *that.*

Vera was engaged to Thad during the run of the show, but then she ended up leaving him for his father, Darius, who was still married to one of his (six!) ex-wives at the time. Big scandal ensued. Thad left the show, and his family, to move to Chicago. *Bama Bounty* struggled on for a final season, but fans felt it didn't have the same flair without Thad, "the hot brother" (Internet consensus, not necessarily my personal ruling), and the ratings plummeted. Darius and Vera are now married, with two kids (who are Thad's half-siblings!), and continue to bounty hunt in Alabama with Amadeus and Orpheus, who seem to have sided with their father in the scandal.

Wow. If my past is embarrassingly squeaky clean, Thad's is wildly messy. No wonder he seems so reluctant to bring up his family and the show.

No wonder he's so cold and cynical, so determined to believe I'm pretending to be something I'm not. It must be incredibly hard to trust people, when the people you're meant to trust the most betray you. Not just Vera and his father, but his brothers, too, choosing not to take his side.

Of course, maybe I'm doing the same thing, bringing a bounty hunter into my family to track down my brother. I believed Thad before, when he said it would be the best thing for Dean, but how can I be sure?

The *Bama Bounty* stuff was a fun distraction, but the fact remains—I have no idea what I'm doing. And I might be about to make a terrible mistake.

On Sunday, Thad picks me up as scheduled in his 1969 Dodge Charger. This was Dean's dream car for a while, which is the only reason why I recognize it, and why I also happen to know it's an expensive vintage classic. I imagine most bounty hunters can't afford to drive something like this around, but maybe he's still getting royalties from *Bama Bounty*—which is syndicated on Hulu. (I've made it through season two, not that I'll be mentioning that to *him.*)

In fact, I don't know how much of anything I should tell Thad about the Internet sleuthing I did this week. It feels invasive to tell someone I've researched his entire history. Not invasive enough to not *do* it, but just invasive enough to not want to *tell* him I've done it. Then again, since he spent the first several weeks of knowing me pretending to just be a library patron so he could follow me around, I feel like we're kind of even.

The drive out to Buffalo Grove is a long one, though, so we'll need to come up with something to say. "Maybe we should go over some stuff about each other? Since we're supposed to be a couple."

Thad glances over at me, smirk-smiling. "I'd be surprised if you could tell me something I don't already know about you."

I raise an eyebrow at him. "You can't be *that* good, since you didn't even realize I used to be a sister until Dean told you."

There. Elephant in the room. I wasn't intending to address it, but maybe it's finally time to clear the air.

Thad's smirk fades, and now he looks vaguely irritated. "It came up in the background check, but when I saw the name, I thought it was some kind of religious school."

The Sisters of St. Elizabeth. I can see how he might have made that leap, especially since it didn't have anything to do with finding Dean, so he probably just skimmed over it.

"Besides," Thad continues, "you're not really what I think when I think *nun.*"

I furrow my brow at him, but he's staring at the road, and it feels like he's pointedly not looking at me. "What is that supposed to mean?"

He huffs, shaking his head. "Come on. You know what you look like."

I glance down at myself. I'm wearing a new dress that I bought at the mall after renewing my determination to move away from my shapeless sweaters. It's not a sexy dress, though—not skintight or low cut or in any way revealing. It's a pale green wrap dress, the kind of thing you wear home to Sunday dinner with your parents. I'm wearing a coat over it and tights underneath, so absolutely no skin is showing except for my face and hands, but I guess it is significantly more formfitting than what I usually wear. My hair is not in its normal bun, either, but combed and curled—again, for my parents' benefit, not for Thad's. Mom always likes us to dress in our Sunday best for Sunday dinner, even when it's virtual.

Can I help it that this shade of green makes my eyes look especially blue and my hair look especially blonde? Or that, as a natural hourglass, the wrap dress highlights all of my best features? No, I cannot. Nor should I have to. I am a confident woman in my thirties, allowed to feel vivacious and attractive if I so choose.

At one point, I might have fluttered and fretted over Thad's comment. But now, knowing that he has no romantic interest in me and I have no romantic interest in him, I feel free to be a little bold. "Were the huge sweaters too big of a temptation? I could see how the messy bun might be confusing for your hormones."

Now he does look at me, wryly amused. "Even a turtleneck doesn't hide" —he motions to the general vicinity of my body—"*that*. And combine that with the kind of stuff you were reading aloud at that sex club—"

"Writing group," I correct him, flushing.

"—it doesn't add up to nun. That's all I'm saying."

I'm still stuck on him gesturing at my body, his eyes flickering over me. I know I have larger-than-average breasts and a big booty—how could I not know, with a best friend like Matilda?—but I guess I naively believed the sweaters could hide my shape. I'm stuck between panicking about it and feeling curious, despite myself. Just what did he think about all of *this*, and has that all gone away now that he knows I used to be a sister?

I clear my throat. "My parents don't know about the romance novel, actually, so I'd appreciate it if you don't bring that up."

If Mom is having a hard time wrapping her head around me not wearing wool muumuus anymore, she really won't like knowing that I'm writing erotic love scenes that are thinly veiled copies of my own fantasies. I'm sure in her mind I don't have any kind of sexual urges, and any desire I've expressed to get married and have a family is purely out of a godly desire for children.

"Ah." Thad looks like he's about to glance over again but checks himself. "I can see why your folks might not be too keen. I thought it was pretty good, though. For a book."

I give him a skeptical look. "You really don't like to read? Not even those Agatha Christies you were checking out?"

I know it's possible for some people to genuinely not like reading, but…do I? As a librarian, I've always felt like it's my duty to help people find their thing. Not everyone is a reader like me who will gobble down practically any genre, but everyone has *that one thing* they would enjoy if they got hold of it. Dean, for example, used to always hate reading until he got into the Percy Jackson books, and then he read them over and over again on a loop. For all I know, he still does—wherever he is now, hiding from the mafia.

Thad shakes his head. "Don't really see the point. I'll read the news, or stuff about sports and whatnot. But stories? Happily ever afters? No offense, but I feel like that's little-kid stuff."

I roll my eyes. Right—the way that human beings have expressed themselves for centuries, told stories of war and love and imagination and social critique and hope. All kids' stuff. "You know, they say that reading fiction encourages people to have empathy for others. I can see why that might be a liability, in a line of work like yours."

Okay, yes, that might be unnecessarily snarky, but he just besmirched *books*. Books! Some lines should not be crossed.

Thad raises an eyebrow at me, making real eye contact for the first time on this trip. "So I don't have empathy?"

"Your whole job is putting people in jail."

"Criminals," Thad reminds me tersely. "Liars. People who agreed to abide by the terms of their bail. People who don't care that they're putting bondsmen and their own families on the line to come up with the money for breaking their bond, all because they're so selfish they can't see past their own noses. People who, I'd say, lack quite a bit of empathy."

There's no playfulness left in the back-and-forth banter, so I answer in kind, glaring back at him. "You mean people like Dean? My little brother?"

Our eyes hold for a moment before Thad slides his gaze away, shaking his head to himself as he looks out at the road. "You said it. Not me."

Chapter 18
Thad

I've always been pretty good with parents, even when I still had the mohawk. I think my glasses help. For better or worse, people trust people with glasses. That's why I wear them sometimes out and about, even though I really only need them for reading. Which, as Helen was so keen to point out, I only rarely do.

I also think being a ginger has something to do with it. It puts fathers at ease, for some reason. There aren't too many ginger heartthrobs out there, so maybe they think a guy with red hair and glasses won't be too sex-crazed with their daughter, or something.

I'm probably living proof that this assumption isn't true, though, if my recurring daydreams about Helen are any indication. She's being pretty huffy with me as we near her aunt's house, so I guess some of my sparkle has faded in her eyes and she's no longer interested. And that's fine, because I'm not interested, either. I have no use for criminals' sisters who happen to be former nuns and might potentially still be virgins. I have nothing against virgins, as a species, but I've never been the guy to think it was some kind of trophy to be someone's first. It seems like a lot of responsibility, frankly, and if she wants to wait to have sex until she's married, I'm definitely not the right guy for that. Again, live and let live and all, but I'm not a very patient guy.

We are all kinds of wrong for each other. I know that, and yet...

That wrap dress on her is something sinful. There's no reason it should make my mind go to such dirty places. But even though it's not low cut or short or slinky, my eyes keep catching on that little tie on the side, and I can't stop wondering if that's the only thing holding the whole dress together, and what would happen if I just give it a little tug. And if she'll be wearing those red lacy panties underneath.

Jesus. I will myself to think about anything else as Helen leads me up to the front door of her aunt's house. It's a quaint two-story on a picture-perfect little street, and today Helen looks like some kind of 1950s sweetheart with her blonde curls that bounce with every step she takes. I want to reach out and give one of them a tug, watch it spring and coil back into place.

What the hell is wrong with me?

Helen rings the doorbell and turns to face me. "Pam and Ken," she reminds me in a low voice. "And don't bring up Dean. Wait for my mom to do it." A little eye roll to herself. "It shouldn't take long."

Wait, what was that? There's some weirdness there between her and Dean. I myself am totally estranged from my brothers, but back when things were good, we didn't go months without talking to each other, even if it was just dumb little texts and GIFs and whatnot here and there. I make a mental note to figure out what the beef is between the two of them, ideally before the night is over.

Only because it might help me find Dean. Why else would I care? "Got it."

The door swings open and I hold up the flowers I purchased, pasting on my best nonthreatening, ginger-who-wears-glasses smile as I assess the group. The first person I see is Helen's aunt Linda—Linda Doherty (resident of Chicago for fourteen years, no prior arrests), a heavyset woman in her fifties whose blonde is running to gray. She looks me up and down with an unimpressed lip press, then moves aside so I can see—

Pam and Ken Flanagan, both late fifties. Just like with Helen, I've done some research on Dean's parents. I know they have good credit, regularly attend mass at their local church, are registered to vote, and have no criminal record, along with other miscellaneous tidbits. How these two managed to produce a kid like Dean Flanagan, I'll never understand.

Ken is balding but has darker hair and a darker complexion, suggesting where Dean may have gotten his coloring from. Pam looks more like Helen, only older, and with a much more sour face—or maybe that's only just for me. She and Linda exchange mutinous looks with each other, though Ken is all smiles. "Baby girl!" he croons, beaming at Helen like she hung the moon.

"Hi, Daddy. Mom. Aunt Linda." Helen hugs each in turn before reaching back for me. "This is Thad."

By the way she says it, I know she's prepped them for meeting me, and from the looks on their faces, I can see they're having a hard time wrapping their heads around it. Ken is the most friendly of the three, which is good—in my experience, dads are usually the hardest ones to crack. But I immediately start to second-guess myself on that front when I see the identical looks on Pam's and Linda's faces. Linda I'm less concerned about, since she's just the aunt; but if I thought Pam might be my inside track to finding Dean, I am now seriously reconsidering. The look she gives me is outright hostile—and she doesn't even know I'm after her son yet.

"It's so nice to meet you, Thad," Ken says, nudging his wife with his elbow.

Pam's face does not change much, though she does a weird sort of closed-mouth smile and speaks through her teeth. "Please, come in."

"Make yourself at home," Linda offers, but not before checking Pam's reaction first to make sure she's supposed to say it begrudgingly.

O-kay. I exchange a quick glance with Helen as we follow her aunt and parents over the threshold, and to my surprise, Helen takes my arm and gives it a reassuring squeeze. Because I'm supposed to be her boyfriend. Right.

"Don't take it personally," she murmurs. "It's not you. It's me."

Helen mentioned she's never brought home a guy before, but I guess I assumed her parents would react more like mine. My mom would be ecstatic about any step that might bring me closer to giving her grandchildren. And my dad—

Well, back when we were still speaking, he would have probably spent the whole night sweet-talking Helen and trying to touch her leg under the table. That seems like unlikely behavior coming from Pam, so all things considered, tonight probably won't go as bad as it could.

"We thought we'd bring a bit of Boston with us—I hope you like lobster rolls, Thad," Ken calls over his shoulder as he leads us to the dining room. I notice he is half holding Pam up, like she is in danger from losing her footing. Is she really that upset about Helen, her thirty-one-year-old daughter, bringing somebody to dinner?

Ken waits until we're fully in the room. "Why doesn't everyone have a seat? You too, Linda—we appreciate you hosting us, so you just relax. Pam, can you get everyone drinks?"

He and Pam have a wordless exchange for a long, uncomfortable moment before Pam reluctantly turns to face me. "Drink?"

"I'm easy," I tell her, smiling in what I hope is a friendly, ingratiating, don't-hate-me-for-dating-your-daughter way. "Whatever you got."

Pam gives me a none-too-impressed look. "So you're a drinker."

Holy shit. Helen steps in closer, protecting me from her mother. It would almost be funny, if her mother didn't scare the bejesus out of me. "He'll have a cider, and so will I. Thanks, Mom."

As Pam disappears into the kitchen, Helen pulls me over to the table, where we sit. Linda has taken Ken at his word and is watching *Masterpiece Theatre* in the living room at an incredibly loud volume, but I make sure both parents are safely in the kitchen before leaning in toward her. "What the hell is wrong with your mom? Why does she look like she's planning to poison my drink?"

"I told you, it's not you." Helen ducks her head in toward me conspiratorially. "I think my mom is still convinced that I'll eventually become a sister again. You would obviously get in the way of that, if you were really my boyfriend. Hence, the irrational hatred."

The thought has never crossed my mind, that Helen might take her vows again. I speak before I can catch myself. "That would be a waste." At her questioning look, I shift, realizing for the first time just how close we're sitting, the fullness of her lips and her big, too-blue eyes. I swallow, feeling compelled into honesty despite myself. "You becoming a nun again. Never getting a real, nice guy to bring home to your parents who isn't a bounty hunter with no empathy."

Her lips tug into a small smile. "Don't worry. I'm not going back. So there's still plenty of time to find that guy."

I feel a surge of irrational dislike for this nonexistent future boyfriend. He'll probably be some dickwad like Shane who looks impressive on paper but is actually the world's biggest douche canoe. I bet Pam Flanagan would like me if I were a private detective.

Feeling grumpy now at the thought, I'm in no mood for Pam's attitude when she returns with the drinks, holding out my cider like she'll get cooties if our hands so much as brush. It's not a good idea, I know, but I decide to play things up.

"Thanks so much, Mrs. Flanagan." I take the drink with one hand while I wrap my other arm around Helen and pull her close. "I'm so thrilled to be meeting you. Helen's told me all about you."

Pam zeroes in on where I'm touching Helen, then glares back at me. Oh well, at least it's all out in the open now. This is war. "That's strange. She's told us absolutely nothing about you, until a few days ago."

I laugh, like this is all in good fun, mostly because I know it will piss old

Pam off even more. "That makes sense, yeah. It was love at first sight for me, but it took some convincing to persuade Helen to give me a chance—didn't it, hon?"

Glancing over, I startle a bit as I realize just how close I've drawn Helen to me. Our faces are just centimeters apart, and up close her eyes are even more spectacularly blue, her face soft and sweet and guileless. I can't believe I ever thought this girl was a femme fatale.

Then again, that's how they get you, isn't it? With their beautiful, angelic faces and their big doe eyes?

Helen looks nothing but perplexed now, as if she can't quite figure out what game I'm playing—but, credit where credit's due, she rolls right along with it. "He showed up at the library almost every day. I thought he just liked to read!" She laughs, and it makes her skin do this kind of glowy thing that's... nice.

I realize I've been staring for just a little too long and clear my throat. "Yeah, so, confession. I'm not much of a reader." Looking at Ken, who's listening in on the conversation with interest as he brings some plates into the room, I take a gamble. "I'm more of a sports guy, myself."

Which is not a total lie. I'm an Alabama boy at heart, and college football is basically my religion. That being said, I wouldn't call myself the most faithful member of the congregation. I've been more like an Easter-Christmas worshiper since I moved to Chicago. I'm counting on being good enough at bullshitting my way through a conversation to get by.

Ken perks up, definitely interested. "Oh, really? Who's your team?"

"The Red Sox," Helen speaks up for me, smoothing a hand over my back. I don't know what's more distracting—her touching me, or just how quickly she jumps at the lie. "Thad loves baseball, don't you?"

I can tell by the way Ken's face brightens that he, too, loves baseball and the Red Sox. Thanks for that one, Helen. At least it's the sport with the easiest rules to follow—just hit the ball and run around the bases, right? "You're kidding," Ken crows. "We'll have to catch a game sometime, when you and Helen come to visit."

"I'd love that, Ken, I really would." I guess I'm getting a bit too into character because I drop my arm from Helen's shoulders so I can grip her knee under the table.

I hear her little intake of breath, but she recovers quickly. "Maybe we can all go. What do you think, Mom? The next time Dean's in town?"

This is the part I should be paying attention to, but I've gotten a little distracted by Helen's legs. I really wasn't thinking things through when I moved my hand, it just seemed like the kind of thing a boyfriend would do. The way she's sitting, her dress has ridden up a little—not anything too wild, but I guess because she's usually so covered up, I feel a shockwave go through me when I catch a glimpse of her thigh above her knee. The warmth of her skin seeps through her tights, and beneath the sheer material, I see a little freckle on the inner thigh of her left leg that I'm for some reason desperate to touch.

Swallowing, I force my gaze up again, only to find Pam glaring daggers at me. Her look seems to say, *That's my daughter, you dirty bastard, and I know what you're thinking.* And because I've apparently decided to lean into this archenemy thing, I give Pam a look straight back that I hope conveys, *You're damn right that's what I'm thinking, and there's nothing you can do about it.*

Pam fumes.

Helen clears her throat, sounding a little winded for some reason. "Mom? What do you think? When will Dean be back again?"

Pam blinks, then waves her hand irritably. "You know Dean. He'll be back when he's back." She rises abruptly to her feet. "Does anyone want some cheese? I made up a cheese plate."

She storms into the kitchen, slamming the separating door with such force that it swings back and forth for several seconds afterward. Ken seems to take this as par for the course and just goes back to setting out plates and utensils like nothing's happened.

Helen, however, does not seem quite so sanguine. She's giving me a look, like I've just kicked her favorite puppy. "Why are you antagonizing my mother?" she murmurs to me in a low voice. "I thought the whole point was to get on their good side."

Because your mother doesn't like me. Because she thinks I'm not good enough for her angel daughter. Because she wants to keep you wrapped up and hidden away. Because I really, really want to touch that little freckle on your thigh, just once.

I don't say any of those things, obviously, because I'm not cuckoo for Cocoa Puffs. "That got a little out of hand, didn't it? Maybe I should go talk to her."

"No." Helen holds me in place with a firm hand to my chest, standing up and making me lose my grip on her knee. Her dress falls back into place, covering up the little freckle, and an unexpected but profound feeling of loss surges through me. "I'll talk to her. You talk about sports with my dad."

"I don't know much about baseball," I confess to her quietly, daring a quick glance back at Ken.

She raises an eyebrow at me. "You're good at pretending to be things you're not, aren't you? Pretend you do."

Chapter 19
Helen

In the kitchen, I find my mother aggressively chopping up a block of cheese to lay out along with some crackers and meat for a charcuterie board. Oprah must have done something similar recently, because I can't imagine Mom hopping on the social media bandwagon and knowing about this trend otherwise.

"Mom?" I approach her cautiously, hands raised. "Let's put down the knife and talk."

Not that I think my mother would *intentionally* stab me. Our relationship is complicated, but not that complicated. Well, not unless Dean needed her to stab me for some reason. Maybe if he needed a kidney transplant and I wasn't cooperating or something. But she wouldn't stab me for bringing home a boyfriend, and so I'd call that a fairly healthy mother-daughter relationship.

Mom obediently puts down the knife, gripping the edge of the counter until she's white-knuckled. I notice the white wine bottle is almost empty, and the rest of us are drinking hard cider, which suggests she's been guzzling it back here in the kitchen. Lovely.

"I don't like that young man, Helen. He is not a nice boy."

I can't exactly contradict that, seeing as how he came here tonight to try to arrest her favorite child. Still, logically, I can't help but point out: "You can't know that yet, Mom. You've barely spoken to him."

"No, but I've watched him." She shakes her head, a little too vehemently.

"I've watched him watching you. That man only has one thing on his mind, and it's not taking you to mass on Sunday."

If only she knew how little interest Thad actually has in me. For a moment, I wish the whole situation were just a little less complicated so I could tell her everything—the ideas I built around him, that terribly awkward first kiss, the realization that he's only been using me to get to Dean. How much I wish I *were* on his mind, at all, as any kind of sexual prospect, even if I no longer hold out any hope that he will be the one to see beyond all the weirdness of my past and just love me, right now, as I am. I want someone to want me. I want someone to be unable to get me out of his head. I want someone to touch my leg like Thad just did, not because he's playing some kind of role, but because he can't keep his hands off me.

I glance through the kitchen partition, watching him fall into easy conversation with Dad, all the while sneakily glancing at his phone under the table to get his facts straight about the Bears. It's kind of endearingly Thad, but also kind of sad at the same time. I wonder if there's anyone else who sees *him* just as he is, or if he's just putting on an act with everybody to get something out of them. It sounds like a lonely way to live.

Sighing, I look back at my mother. "Be honest, Mom. It doesn't matter what he says or what he does or how he looks at me. You just hate the fact that I'm not going to be a sister anymore."

Mom stares at me, her gaze so blurry that I'm not entirely confident she's heard me. And then she bursts into tears.

"God had a plan for you, Helen. I had a plan for you. Why would you just throw that all away?"

I go to her, and hug her, and comfort her, because what else can I do? She's my mom. Some people get mothers who support them no matter what, and some people get mothers who smother them and question their every life decision. It doesn't mean she doesn't love me. It's just the best way she knows how to love. "I wasn't happy," I tell her. It isn't the first time I've said it, but I'm hoping that somehow, this time, she'll really hear me. "I was miserable. I felt like my life was over, like all my choices had been taken away from me and I was stuck playing a part for the rest of my life. And not just when I was a sister—everything leading up to that. Never going on dates, feeling guilty about having crushes, knowing I would never have kids or own my own house or—even ride a roller coaster!"

Mom sniffles. "I would have taken you to ride a roller coaster if you asked."

But despite her retort, I hope in her silence, in the way she grips me tighter, that she's processing the rest of it. Maybe really hearing it for the first time. Swallowing, I press on. "I know you had a plan, but it wasn't my plan. It wasn't what I wanted."

After a moment, Mom pulls back, wiping at her watery eyes. "And that's what you want? That *tattoo man* out there?"

She says it so disdainfully that I can't help but laugh. "Mom."

Mom, apparently, does not find humor in the situation. She levels a finger at me. "You might not be a sister anymore, but you're still a good Catholic girl, and you will still go to hell if you have relations before you get married. 'Let the marriage bed be undefiled, for God will judge the immoral.'"

Ah, yes, that old religious trauma that I've literally been going to therapy for. Thanks, Mom. I decide to turn the tables on her. "And you're gonna go to hell if you don't stop being so judgy."

She gasps at me, appalled. "Helen Margaret Flanagan!"

If she thinks she can out-Bible an ex-sister, she has another thing coming. "'Why beholdest thou the mote in thy brother's eye, but considerest not the beam that is in thine own eye?'" I level a finger right back at her. "You better be nice and not judge someone based on their looks. What would Jesus say to that?"

Mom actually looks a little cowed. "All right, I'll be nice." She picks up the charcuterie board, and I see her give a last, longing look at the remnants in the wine bottle, though she refrains from drinking it in front of me. "Will you grab the cards from the den? We can play a few hands while your father puts together the rolls. That boy does know how to play spades, doesn't he?"

"Mind your beam," I singsong back to her, though I obligingly head into the den. Passing by Linda in the living room, I see she's fallen fast asleep on her recliner. Good old Linda.

Even though I've spent many holidays and weekends here throughout my life, it takes a few minutes for me to find the cards. Every so often Aunt Linda gets bored and decides to reorganize the entire house—not for the sake of making it more functional, but for reasons unknown. Like with my mother, I suspect it probably has something to do with Oprah.

I finally find the cards, which for some reason have been stored—along with the other games—in a plastic wastebasket. It's clean and looks like it hasn't been used, but still, a trash can. Why?

Shaking my head, I start to leave, before my eye catches on something sitting out on the desk. It looks like a bank statement, but it's been highlighted several times and there are notes scribbled on it.

Curious, I move closer to get a better look. For the record, I don't typically look through other people's bank statements, but it *is* just lying out on the desk, and it looks like someone has gone to war with it, by how much it's marked up.

I see that a number of recent charges have been highlighted, with the total of all the various charges tallied at the bottom of the page. Did someone steal Aunt Linda's credit card and now she's having to file for fraudulent charges?

The truth hits me all at once, and I actually gasp out loud. Someone *did* use Aunt Linda's credit card, but I'm willing to bet he didn't steal it. Knowing Dean, he would have been smart enough to anticipate that an intrepid detective might look at my parents' credit card statements—but who would go so far as to dig through an aunt's payment history? That would explain why the charges have been tallied at the bottom—so my mom can know how much money she owes Linda.

I should be shocked, that my aunt and mother would be capable of aiding and abetting a fugitive who broke his bond, but…I'm really, really not. From before Dean was even born, Mom has been pitting us against each other. Never mind that I was on the honor roll; Dean placed in state on the swim team. I had perfect attendance? Well, Dean made Mom a paperweight in art class. I was a nun? Well, Dean cooked Mom a spaghetti dinner *by himself.* In a world of mediocre males being praised for doing the bare minimum, Dean is the undisputed king of undeserved praise. It totally makes sense that Mom must have spun some kind of narrative about this somehow not being Dean's fault, and Aunt Linda seems to have come along for the delusional ride. Or better yet, maybe Mom has found some way to argue that his misdeeds have something to do with *me* breaking my vows.

Gritting my teeth in annoyance at the way she is yet again coddling her favorite golden child, I try to focus on the information in front of me.

Charge after charge has been made from various places in the United States over the last week, but one place in particular starts to pop out more than the rest.

New Orleans, Louisiana.

"Helen?" I hear my mother calling from the other room.

Pulling out my phone from my pocket, I take a few quick snapshots of the bill pages and hurriedly put everything back into place just as my mother enters the room.

"What took you so long?" she chides me. "Don't leave me out there with those men."

"It took me forever to find the cards," I say, and technically it isn't a lie.

Nun Too Soon

Technically I'm not the one who broke the law, or helped my son break his bond, or aided my nephew in fleeing the law.

So then why do *I* feel so guilty?

Chapter 20
Thad

Dean never calls.

I don't know if he somehow got wind of me being here, or if plans just changed, but Pam's cell phone remains silent for the rest of the night. As for the dinner itself, it's pleasant enough, after Helen and Pam duke it out in the kitchen. Afterward I can tell Pam is making a marked effort to be cordial, though it's obvious she still thinks I'm not good enough to be mud stuck to the bottom of her daughter's shoe.

Well, won't she be pleased when she finds out she'll never have to see me again? The thought is irritating enough that I almost want to press Ken on his offer to go see the Red Sox sometime, just to really rub Pam's face in my sparkling personality.

We all part ways with vague promises to do it again sometime, and Helen and I get in the car to make the drive back into the city. I'm feeling kind of discombobulated, most likely because of Dean never calling, and Pam disliking me so very much.

And knowing that, after today, I won't have any reason to see Helen again.

She tried. I have to give her that much. She took me to her aunt's home for a family dinner and lied straight to her parents' faces about who I am and let me paw at her, all for the sake of trying to help Dean. And she was sort of alarmingly good at all that deception, frankly. If I hadn't already had ideas about her being some incognito femme fatale, I might be second-guessing myself. But that's stupid. She was a nun, for Christ's sake. Nice women who used to be nuns are not liars and schemers—right?

"Pull the car over," Helen says after we've driven about ten minutes.

I'm too surprised to argue much. Once the car's off the road, I see Helen studying my face intently, and for one stupid, irrational moment, I think she's about to kiss me.

Instead, she blurts out something that takes me completely by surprise: "I know where Dean is."

I gape at her for a moment, flabbergasted, before getting my wits back. "How d'you know that? Did your mom tell you—is that what you were talking about so long in the kitchen?"

Helen shakes her head. "No, I...I found my aunt's credit card bill. Dean's been using it to make charges."

"That's...brilliant." No kind of criminal investigative training and this woman somehow knows to go through credit card charges. She might really be more of a natural at this than I thought. "So where's he at?"

Helen bites her lip, and it's then that the other shoe falls.

Ah. Yes. I see. She's not going to tell me. She's going to double-cross me.

Lana Frickin' Turner, this one.

She's usually the one with a face like an open book, but something of what I'm thinking must be playing out across *my* face because Helen holds up a peremptory hand, as if to stop any negative thoughts. "I'm willing to tell you, I am. I'm not going back on our deal. But I want to amend it." She squares her shoulders, taking in a deep breath. "I want to come with you."

"Come with me?" I echo, frowning at her. "You mean to whatever hotel he's been holing up in? Where is it—downtown?"

She shakes her head. "It's far from here—a few states away." She holds up her phone to me. "I have all the info we need in here. But I want to come with you, to make sure Dean is okay."

I'm already shaking my head before she's even finished. "I don't bring along groupies. And especially not women."

"Because of what Vera did to you?"

What was merely irritating behavior before has now become outright infu-riating. I glare at her. "Someone's been doing a little digging into the past, I see."

"I'm good at researching things." Helen looks, and sounds, a little pleased with herself. "I might even be able to help you, if you'd let me."

"This isn't some fun road trip with a bus full of nuns and tambourines—I told you, there are dangerous people after Dean. I need to get to him before they do, and I can't have anyone slowing me down."

Helen sets her jaw defiantly. "Explain to me, exactly, how I'd be slowing you down when I'm the only one who knows where Dean is? Seems to me like you need my help."

She looks so smug that I don't think—I just act. One minute she's smirking at me, and the next I've snatched her phone right out of her hands. "Seems to me like I don't, since you already told me all the proof's on here."

Helen's jaw drops. She looks so genuinely shocked that I might laugh, if she weren't such a nuisance. "You can't just take my phone!"

"Can." I shrug. "Did."

"Well, you won't be able to log in without my passcode."

Now I do laugh. "Aww, aren't you cute, thinking I don't know how to break into a cell phone."

Helen stares at me for a beat. And then, faster than I would have given her credit for, she unbuckles her seat belt and lunges over at me.

I swear, it's only the fact that she's taken me by total surprise that gives her the upper hand. If I'd known she was coming, I could've been quicker, faster, gotten out of my own seat belt. As it is, I'm still pinned in place and she's climbing on top of me, with surprising strength as she wrestles to take her phone back.

"Jesus!" I shout at her when I'm able to catch my breath. "Who taught you to fight so dirty?"

Nevertheless, I manage to just keep the phone out of her grip, moving it from hand to hand as she struggles to get it back from me.

"I have a little brother," Helen reminds me, a little out of breath. "You think this is the first time I've had to wrestle someone to get back something that was mine?"

I don't doubt that's true, but I do doubt very much that this is what it was like when Helen wrestled with her brother. At least, I hope it wasn't. For starters, she is full-on straddling me now, the material of her dress rucked up to her thighs, her chest heaving inches from my face. I'm struck, once again, with the desire to tug on that itty-bitty little string holding her dress together.

With the phone still in my grip, I shove my hands under my backside, deep enough that she can't reach. And even a firecracker ex-nun won't reach under a grown man's ass, it seems. We're at an impasse. She's still on top of me, flushed and breathing heavy, but she can't get to her phone. I have the phone, but I can't move her or me without giving up my position.

Our gazes lock. We battle silently with each other, and all the while, I'm thinking she just might be the most beautiful woman I've ever seen. I don't know how or why she has this power over me, but it feels like I lose control of myself whenever I'm with her, like everything is weighted and meaningful in a way I don't totally understand.

"Don't be such a butthead," she says at last, breaking the silence.

I blink at her in surprise. So much for *meaningful.* "A butthead?" I echo.

"Yes, you're being a butthead." Helen sounds genuinely frustrated, like she doesn't understand why I could possibly think it's a bad idea to bring a nun turned librarian on a road trip to find a fugitive on the run from the mafia. "You told me to trust you to treat Dean fairly, and I'm doing that. I'm not going to get in your way. I'm not going to try to stop you. I just want to make sure my brother is okay. So why can't it be both ways? How can you ask me to trust you if you aren't willing to do the same with me?"

I stare at her, taken aback. I did ask her to trust me—and she has. And all she's done since then is help me as best she can.

"Trust me," Helen pleads with me again, eyes wide and earnest.

"O-okay," I hear myself stammering before I've fully made the decision to say so.

I regret it the instant I say it—not because of her, per se, but because I swore to myself I wouldn't do this again, wouldn't get tricked by a pretty face or a nice pair of tits. I have to be on guard, always on the lookout for people who're just looking to stab me in the back.

But then she grins at me, and it almost, almost, feels worth it.

Chapter 21
Helen

I can't believe it. I seriously cannot believe that I just wrestled with the Red Unicorn and demanded that he take me along with him on a recovery mission to New Orleans to find my brother.

I'm kind of awesome.

Of course, I didn't *tell* Thad that we're going to Louisiana, not yet. I'm not that much of an idiot. Despite the agreement we reached tonight, I have no doubt he'd leave me behind at the drop of a hat if he knew where we're going. I now have my phone, and the pictures of Dean's credit card charges, safely back in my possession. All Thad knows is that we'll be taking a lengthy road trip. We've agreed to meet up tomorrow at nine a.m. That gives me a little time to organize everything with my work and make sure my shifts are covered. I'm meant to have tomorrow off anyway, and I'm overdue some personal days, but since I don't know how long we'll be gone, I also want to cover my bases and reach out to some coworkers who I've covered for in the past, hoping they will do the same for me if necessary.

Not Erica, of course. I've taken many of her shifts at the last minute, but whenever I've reached out (almost always well in advance!) she's pretended not to get my texts. Funny how she's always able to receive them when she needs something from me…

In the midst of sorting through all the work stuff and packing, I send off a group text to Matilda and Nina, too. I'm going to New Orleans! With the Red Unicorn. 😬 Long story, but it has to do with my brother.

I don't expect to hear from Nina tonight, since her uncle usually insists on everyone in the house being in bed and having all lights and electronics out by nine p.m. (Apparently it's "ungodly" to be up too long after the sun sets...?) But it doesn't take long for Matilda to take the bait. Instead of texting back, she calls. "Are you insane?" she barks at me.

I put her on speaker so I can keep packing. "Not the last time I checked?"

"You barely know this man. He could be a serial killer. He could be a human trafficker. He could be someone who insists on playing marching band music the entire trip. You have no business going anywhere with him alone."

If I'm being honest, a similar worry has crossed my mind—well, not the marching band thing. That seems weirdly specific. But the truth is, I really don't know much about Thad, beyond the fact that he used to be on a TV show and that his fiancée left him for his father. That he's a licensed bounty hunter in the state of Indiana. That he doesn't like to read. That he gets abnormally territorial with middle-aged women like my mother.

Come to think of it, I guess I know a few things about him. Relaxing at the realization, I shrug off Matilda's concerns. "It's going to be fine. We've gotten to know each other better over the last week. I haven't asked him yet if he's a serial killer or human trafficker, but I'm sure it'll come up naturally in conversation sooner or later."

Matilda is clearly in no mood for my attempt at humor. "If you're going to insist on going on this fool's errand, I want you to take protection."

That was a bad time to be taking a sip of water, because I choke in surprise. "Condoms?" I ask, aghast at the suggestion.

"Pepper spray. Brass knuckles. A rape whistle." Matilda lists off all these items easily, like they're everyday things she carries around in her purse—and come to think of it, knowing Matilda, that's probably very well the case. "Although I find it very suspicious that your mind would go immediately to condoms. You're not thinking of sleeping with this man, are you?"

I consider the question. I am not going on this trip to try to sleep with Thad, nor do I think that's a possibility anymore, frankly. We are way too different. I get that. I've accepted it. The mystique of the Red Unicorn has been well and truly dissolved. So I'm not *actively* thinking about sleeping with him...

But in a nonactive, unintentional way...sure. Yes. Of course. I've *thought* about having sex with Thad, not because I plan on doing it, but because he's still objectively handsome. And smells good. Just stating the facts. Sure, when he touches me I feel like I lose control of my motor functions. When his hand was on my thigh earlier in the evening, I fantasized about what would happen if he just kept moving it up, up, up… When I was straddling him in the car, our bodies pressed together, his hot breath on my skin, I was so aroused that it was physically uncomfortable.

But I'm not going to have sex with him. I got the memo. It's not in the cards.

"This is not that kind of trip," I say primly. "We are traveling together to find Dean, and that's all. I'm not Thad's type, and frankly, he's not mine anymore, either. It's all going to be strictly professional."

Silence. Then Matilda groans. "Oh, God. You're totally going to sleep with him. Well, at least you'll get it out of your system, I suppose. I'll drop some condoms off with you in the morning…"

She hangs up before I can deter her from this line of action. "We are not going to have sex," I say aloud anyway, just to be clear to the universe or the CIA or whoever else might be listening that I know the score.

It would probably be a good idea to go to bed early, but I'm still waiting to hear back from some of my coworkers and want to try to get as much sorted tonight as possible. Plus I still need to pack more clothes after my load of washing finishes.

I guess I could always… No.

As soon as the thought enters my mind, I shut it down. Dr. Sandra and I have talked about this before—the irrational, knee-jerk flight response whenever I consider the possibility of…pleasuring myself. *Masturbation.* I even have a hard time allowing myself to think of the word, much less to contemplate the action. My body breaks out in a reflexive cold sweat, and I begin pacing the room just to get out some nervous energy.

The way I see it, the problem is this: I grew up my whole life knowing that my mother made a deal with God and I was supposed to be a nun when I got older. So all the normal shame I might be expected to feel about sex just from growing up in a strict religious household was amplified. If I were to let a boy kiss me, experiment with the bathtub faucet, or do anything even approaching acknowledgment of myself as a sexual being, I wasn't just taking something from myself, I was taking something from *God.* That's a lot of pressure for a teenage girl who was just experiencing totally natural urges.

And the issue is even worse now with pleasur—with *masturbation,* because the rhetoric I heard growing up about sex itself has some loopholes: sex outside of marriage is taboo, but sex within marriage is fine and healthy and normal, so sex in and of itself isn't inherently *bad*.

Nowhere, anywhere, in all of my time in church was masturbation (there! I did it!) talked about as anything other than evil incarnate. Masturbation, according to everything I heard in Sunday school, was evil and self-indulgent and *wrong*. So even though I no longer believe I'll go to hell for wanting to have sex, the taboo around touching myself has been harder to shake.

As I undress and get ready for bed, I try to talk it through with myself, like Dr. Sandra suggested in the past, even offering me a helpful metaphor: "Watching movies with your friends is a lot of fun, but your friends aren't always available to watch a movie every time you feel like it. So what're you supposed to do, just never watch a movie unless your friends can watch with you?"

Even though some time has passed since my earlier encounter with Thad, I still feel ramped up, energized, and—okay, I'll use my big-girl words: horny. I'm horny.

Of course, being a thirty-one-year-old virgin, I've gotten pretty good at deflecting these feelings. If the possibility of sex is never on the table, you develop some tactics for channeling that energy elsewhere. In the past, I might've exercised, or done some baking or knitting. More recently I've been putting all my untapped horniness into my romance novel.

But I realize all at once, I don't want to deflect. I don't want to suppress these feelings. I want to feel sexy and desirable. I want to feel *satisfied*.

I catch a glimpse of myself in the full-length mirror and do a double take. I'm halfway through getting out of my dinner clothes and into my pajamas, so I'm standing in the loose-fitting white tank that I like to sleep in and my under-wear. My hair is still curled, my makeup still done.

With all my efforts to hide away my body, I haven't allowed myself to really look at myself wearing so little clothing in a long time, and I'm surprised at how good I feel. Maybe it's leftover endorphins from being so close to Thad in the car, after pretending to be his girlfriend and hearing my mom tell me she can see *he's only after one thing*—but looking at myself now, I feel…dare I say it…?

Sexy.

I know something that would make it even better. Moving to my bureau, I open the top drawer and find the item I had wrapped up and tucked away in the back: the red lace panties. Yes, I waited until I was sure Thad left the mall and went back to buy them. Yes, part of why I wanted them was knowing that he'd seen them and imagining that maybe he liked to imagine *me* wearing them. Yes, I am a repressed weirdo. Let's move on.

I put on the red panties and apply some red lipstick that I've never been brave enough to wear out of the house, then check myself out in the mirror. Dr. Sandra has always encouraged me to try positive affirmations, so I give myself some now. Hot. Sexy. Desirable. Goddess.

And you know what? It works.

I am digging myself in a way that I haven't done…ever. Why have I been hiding this sex goddess away under baggy clothes and no makeup? I feel the sudden reckless urge to share this hotness with the entire world.

…I'm not really going to, of course. I'm into myself, but I'm not an exhibitionist. Still, a fantasy is taking over, helping me lower some of my inhibitions, so I just kind of go with it. Pulling out my phone, I snap some pictures of myself, trying to look as enticing as possible. Some in the mirror, some on the bed. I pose, I pout, I make myself laugh at my own ridiculousness, but I also make myself feel good.

So here's the fantasy: This version of me is much more sexy and confident, and Thad is someone I'm actually dating, not just someone who's forced to keep me around. (And sure, I could substitute in someone else, but it's easier to imagine Thad since I just saw him. There's no other significance to him starring in my fantasy. Really.) I introduced him tonight to my parents as my actual boyfriend, and in the car we were making out, not wrestling over a phone with details about my brother's credit card purchases.

Much sexier scenario so far, no? Thad and I haven't had sex yet, and he's trying to take it slow with me, so he makes himself go home, even though I tell him I'm ready, I want him, I need him. He's left me all hot and bothered, so I decide to show him what he's missing by sending him these pictures.

Of course that sends Thad running over, and when he shows up at my apartment, I convince him that we don't need to wait anymore.

In reality, I'm lying on my bed now, eyes closed, thinking about Thad's hand on my leg under the table, then our bodies pressed together in the car, his big, broad body flush against mine, with the same desperation and want… I'm running my hands over my body—my throat, my collarbone, then down over my tank top, cupping my breasts. My breath hitches as my hand—*his hand*—finds my nipple and teases it through the thin material. His other hand traces down my side, over my thighs, as I explore the sensation of each place, learning what I like best. Then he touches that urgent, aching place at my center, testing it—gliding, pinching, stroking. *"You like that, don't you, bad girl?"* he rasps into my ear, breath hot, voice ragged with need, and—

Oh. *Oh…*

Chapter 22
Thad

I am out of sorts the rest of the night, full of pent-up energy that has me pacing and moving stuff that doesn't need to be moved and basically climbing the walls of my apartment.

It's Helen. That damn freckle on her thigh and the feeling of her in my lap, her breasts heaving just inches from my face. Close enough to just lean forward and open my mouth and—

No. I'm not going there. Have I thought of the hot librarian when I took myself to O-Town? Sure. But that was before I knew she was a nun, when I thought she was playing some kind of game with me. Which I'm pretty sure she's not doing now. Not positive, but pretty sure. I think she honestly doesn't know what she's doing when she looks at me with those big blue eyes and bites that big full lip...and it would be wrong to think of her that way. Wouldn't it? Especially since we're going to be stuck in the car together for what sounds like a long time—I'm only guessing since she won't tell me where we're going, but I've packed a week's worth of underwear, just in case.

I wonder what underwear she's packing...?

Nope. I hastily change into my running clothes, knowing I need to get out some energy and fast. Get my blood pumping somewhere other than where it's all heading now.

Just as I'm about to head out the door, my phone buzzes. Like some love-struck idiot, my heart speeds up as I wonder if it's Helen. Just telling me something about the trip or something. There'd be no other reason for her to text me.

But it's not Helen, I know right away, my stomach roiling as I see the unknown number and the attached pictures. I've blocked her in the past but she just keeps finding new ways to reach me.

Vera.

I should just delete the texts, sight unseen. I genuinely don't want to see or hear from her again. My heart is pounding, and not out of excitement, but dread. I feel cold and clammy all over, like I'm about to open a text message with a picture of a severed head.

But curiosity and all that. And I guess a masochistic part of me wants the reminder that this is what I've been protecting myself from. This is *why* I have to keep up my guard.

I read the messages first. Some must have come through earlier while I was driving, because there are quite a few stacked up and waiting.

Hello Handsome

Did you block my other number? That wasn't very nice. Just want to know how you are

I miss you

We hoped you'd come back for Christmas this year. You won't believe how big the kids have gotten now.

I think the baby weight's finally off. What do you think?

Then come the pictures. Dear old step-mommy, posing in lingerie. I delete the whole text chain and block the number, hoping this will be the last time, but knowing it won't be.

The whole thing is such a head fuck, honestly. The way she swings back and forth between acting like she's trying to pull the family together again but at the same time letting me know she's open for business. I wonder if Dad knows, then decide that's not my problem.

Dad's always had a weakness for women. Women like him, and he likes them—all shapes and sizes and ages and colors of the rainbow. It's why almost all of his kids have a different mom. It's why it shouldn't have come as a surprise to me that he'd been screwing my fiancée behind my back. So far as I know, he's already moved on to someone else, which is why Vera is crawling back to me.

Or maybe she just likes thinking she holds this power over me.

Well, I'm never falling for that again. Not from her, not from anyone else.

Now I need the run for a very different reason. As I move through the streets of downtown, I focus my brain. Right now all I care about is finding Dean. Everything else is a distraction.

Everyone else is a distraction.

And I can't afford to lose focus.

Chapter 23
Helen

Have you ever noticed how beautiful the city is first thing in the morning? In the dim, early morning light, the window still half-frosted over, it feels like I'm looking into a snow globe. I sit and sip my coffee, waiting for Thad to arrive. As I catch a glimpse of my own reflection in the window, I grin at myself stupidly, the two of us caught in a guilty, complicit secret.

Last night was…amazing. I don't know why I waited so long to try this allegedly sinful thing. Whatever that was, that was *not* sinful. It was…incredible. Life-changing. Transcendent. I feel loose and happy this morning, relaxed in my body in a way that I haven't felt since…maybe ever. Forget yoga or meditation. This is the self-care practice that everyone should be raving about.

A knock at the door startles me out of my reverie. I jump, my calm of seconds ago shattered by swirling nerves in the pit of my stomach. Did Thad get here early? "Hello?" I call out tentatively, rising to my feet.

"It's me! Open up."

Matilda. Sagging with relief, I let in my friend, who is bundled up and holding a Jewel-Osco bag. "I can't stay," she says in her usual brisk tone, with no greeting or preamble. "Just dropping this off."

I take the bag from her, peer inside, and immediately feel myself blush. "Matilda!"

A box of condoms, two different kinds of lube, massage oil, personal grooming scissors, and Tic Tacs.

"Tic Tacs?" I ask in surprise, since even for a perma-virgin like me, the rest seems pretty self-explanatory.

"In case things get hot and heavy before you get a chance to brush your teeth. Whatever you do, don't let him chew cinnamon gum if he's going to…" She motions down to my pelvic region, then shudders. "Trust me."

This bag of unwanted gifts is both invasive and weirdly thoughtful—a pretty accurate summation of my friend. Even though I have no plan to use these things since Thad and I will *not* be having sex, I smile and pull her into a hug. "Thanks, Matilda."

She's always a bit of a stiff hugger, but today she's even more ramrod than usual. I realize why after she pulls away, frowning as she examines my face. "You look…radiant."

It sounds more suspicious than complimentary, the way she says it. "Thank you?"

Her eyes widen. "Did you orgasm?" Her eyebrows shoot even higher. "Was it the first time?"

I force a laugh, shooing her toward the door. "Okay, you better get to work, and I have to finish packing, so…"

To my surprise, Matilda is the one who lurches in for a hug this time, holding me in a vise grip with her strong, slender arms. "I'm proud of you."

Oh, Lordie. I pat her back. "Thanks." Because really, what else can you say to that?

She's grinning as she pulls away, really looking like a proud parent. "I try to orgasm at least once a day. It makes me much more relaxed."

This is the more relaxed version of Matilda? "Great," I say, still trying to not-so-subtly sweep her out the door. I do not want to be having this conversation when Thad shows up.

She stops abruptly, her face settling into its more typical frown. Good. Honestly, the smile was starting to freak me out a little bit. "You weren't thinking of *him,* were you?"

I hem and haw, not able to make eye contact. "I'm not sure that's any of your business."

Actually, I *am* sure it's none of her business, but that's never stopped Matilda. "*You* were the one who said nothing was going to happen between you," she points out pragmatically as I continue to all but shove her out the door. "Which is obviously bullshit, but if *you* don't want anything to happen, you probably shouldn't picture him while you're climaxing."

"Okay, thanks for the advice and the sex stuff. Bye!" And with that, I finally manage to slam the door behind her.

I've silenced Matilda. But unfortunately, I can't silence the thoughts she put into my mind as easily. Have I…made a terrible mistake?

By the time Thad arrives to pick me up, it's no longer a question in my mind.

Last night was monumental. And monumentally stupid.

Did I have my first-ever orgasm? Yes, yes I did. And was it amazing? Yes, yes it was.

But did I fully think through how strange it would be to get into a car and travel for days with the man who inspired said orgasm and has no idea of the role he's played in my fantasies?

No. No, I did not.

Maybe that's why things were so stilted between Thad and me this morning when he came to pick me up. We barely spoke a full sentence to each other, beyond him asking me if I had any more bags.

Now, an hour or so into the trip and making our way steadily through Indiana, conversation hasn't really picked up much. *These are the consequences of being a creep,* I remind myself in a voice that sounds eerily close to my mother's. This is really the kind of scenario they should warn you about in Sunday school. Thou shalt not fantasize about a man thou wilt be driving with for fourteen hours across several states.

I'm so preoccupied with feeling self-conscious about how weird *I'm* acting that it takes me a while to register how weird Thad is acting, too. It's not like we've ever been the best of friends, but yesterday, I felt like we'd come to some kind of understanding.

Today, he's barely looked at me. His only conversation has had to do with the mechanics of the trip. It's like he suddenly has this fortress that he's built up around himself and he's determined to keep me out of it. I understand why I'm being weird and quiet around him, but why is he being weird and quiet around me?

A sudden, sinking realization hits me: Thad knows I'm attracted to him. He can't know about what I got up to last night, but maybe he senses that I'm behaving strangely and he's guessed, in an abstract, roundabout way, the reason why. And he wants to make clear in no uncertain terms that he does not see me that way and nothing is ever going to happen.

I should have seen this coming. I climbed in the man's lap, for goodness' sake! He probably thinks I'm some lovesick fantasist. And, okay, sure, I thought about him last night, but not because I think anything is actually going to happen. He's attractive and he's convenient, in that we've interacted recently and there was a spark between us. I think? Or maybe that's all in my head, too. I don't know what I'm doing with all of this. I feel hopelessly, helplessly emotionally stunted in this area of life, especially knowing how easy it seems to be for everyone else.

"You gonna tell me where we're going, or am I gonna have to guess?"

Thad's sudden terse words pull me out of my spiral. I blink at him in surprise, motioning to the phone in my hand. "I have the map pulled up. Don't worry, I know the way."

He shakes his head, looking irritated. "Will you at least tell me how long we're gonna be driving? Which direction?"

I'm genuinely perplexed why he's so annoyed with me. This was the way we'd agreed to do things—and frankly, he has no right to give me attitude. I'm helping *him*, not the other way around. "I know where we're going. I'll get us there. And I'll make sure you don't have any reason to leave me in a roadside gas station in the middle of Kentucky."

He can't even argue that one—we both know it's something he might do. "Kentucky," he says after a moment. "So we're headed south?"

I feel a brief surge of panic that he might actually piece it all together and leave me behind. "Maybe. Maybe not..." Hoping to distract him, I fish around in my purse and pull out a Tupperware. "Brownie? They're homemade."

Yesterday was Sunday, after all, which is baking day. I think briefly about Tom at the library and how disappointed he'll be not to see me, but that's probably wishful thinking. If I'm not there to feed him, he'll just hit up a vending machine.

I'd hoped the offering of chocolate would diffuse some of the tension, but if anything, Thad looks even more horrified. "You can't eat in Kitty."

I stare at him blankly. "I'm sorry, I can't eat in *what?*"

"Kitty. My car." Thad says all of this through gritted teeth, like he knows it's a little ridiculous but he's mad and not willing to admit it.

"Is Kitty allergic to chocolate?" I ask in a hushed tone, patting the dashboard affectionately. "Does Kitty prefer poppyseed muffins, because I have those too."

My forced cheerfulness, and my baked goods, make no progress with his awful, terrible, no-good mood. "No crumbs in my car," he growls, scowling at the road.

We don't talk again until after we've stopped for gas about an hour later. I keep my phone in my pocket, just so he isn't tempted to take a peek at the directions while I'm in the bathroom, but I decide to try to play nice after that. If we're going to be stuck in the car together for another twelve hours, we can at least be civil to each other.

"I got snacks!" I announce as I approach the car, holding up my haul. "And I can take over driving for a bit, if you need a break."

Thad, who is finishing up pumping the gas, just glares at me. "No one drives Kitty but me. And I thought we already established that I don't want crumbs in my car."

Wow, he's being a delight today. I do my best to keep smiling. "No crumbs. See, I got licorice, beef jerky, and trail mix. All crumb-free."

He looks at me dubiously. "Trail mix leaves a mess."

"Not if you eat it carefully." I hold up the bag to him, giving it a little shake to make it look enticing. "Salted nuts. Raisins. Chocolate chips."

"I don't like raisins."

I laugh, like he's making a joke, even though I know he's being a grouchy complainer-pants. It's a skill I've developed as a public librarian—refusing to take offense when offense is clearly intended. Sometimes just pretending that you don't understand someone is being rude can diffuse a lot of situations, because you have to be a real monster to double down on someone who is being relentlessly pleasant to you. (It still happens, but I've gotten out of more than one sticky situation this way.)

"No one likes the raisins," I reassure him. "Just eat around them."

He grunts, but at least doesn't complain anymore or tell me I can't bring my snacks into the car, so I'll take that as a win.

I understand what he's doing. He wants it to be clear that he is not interested in me romantically. Fortunately, with the way he's acting, that is not as much of a blow as it might have otherwise been. I only feel a little ridiculous, for having even briefly thought there might be something between us.

After we're on the road again, both of us staring silently out at the countryside as it passes by, Thad clears his throat. "So. I did some more digging on you last night. Only seems fair play, since you were looking into my past."

I look over at him in surprise. "Oh?" Is that the reason he's being such a grouch today? I mentally run through what he might have found out that could make him so irritated with me. But there's nothing. Not even a speeding ticket. I'm—

"Squeaky clean," Thad says, shaking his head. "Almost *too* squeaky clean. You must have gotten into trouble at some point in your life?"

He says this almost spitefully. I try not to flinch. "It's hard to get into trouble when you've been on the fast track to becoming a nun since you were a toddler."

For some reason, this seems to annoy him. He shakes his head, like he's trying to figure something out, but the pieces just aren't fitting together. "Teenagers get up to things, though, don't they? You never snuck out? Shoplifted? Had a boyfriend you weren't supposed to have?"

I shrug again, finding it harder now to smile. "I guess I was just a rule follower. My mom…she had a hard time conceiving my brother. A really hard time." My mother's story is so much a part of *my* story, or at least what I was told my story was supposed to be, that it's easy and familiar to recite it now. "She asked God to give her Dean, and when He did, she decided that I should give my life to God to make up for it. And I never thought to question it."

"Until after you were a nun for five years?" Wow, Thad really did do his homework. "What happened—did something change?" His hands tighten a little on the steering wheel. "You got hot and heavy with a priest or something?"

Thinking of the seventy-six-year-old priest I worked with back at St. Elizabeth's, I laugh out loud. "Um, no. Nothing like that. It wasn't really anything crazy, I just…I woke up one day and realized I was living a life that I hadn't chosen for myself. And I didn't want to do it anymore." His face is no longer guarded, but genuinely curious, and I feel compelled to add, "It was like, my whole life I was propelled by this story about what I was supposed to be, and then one day I asked myself—is this even what you want? And I realized no one else had ever asked me that before."

For a moment, our gazes hold. An understanding passes between us.

Then Thad blinks, looking back at the road, and it's like the wall has come back up again. I feel it between us, something Thad is hiding behind. But why?

"I guess I just find it hard to believe that you've always been this perfect angel."

I flinch, frowning at the description. "No one ever said I was perfect—"

Thad scoffs. "Come on. Look at you. You're fucking perfect." He raises an eyebrow at me, almost challenging. "Can I swear in front of a former nun, or am I gonna go to hell?"

I'm the one to look away now, out at the road. He's not the first person I've encountered who's gotten hostile about my so-called saintliness. Some people seem to take my choice to become a sister as a personal indictment of them, somehow, like I must be judging them for not taking the same life path as me. If only they knew how little judgment there was. I always *envied* people who didn't make the same choices as me, who got to explore, make mistakes, live their own lives on their own terms. I never thought I was perfect, but the lifestyle I was living, that in some ways I'm still living, wasn't some carefree, happy existence. It was, and is, a lonely life, full of regret. "You can say whatever you want."

"But *you* won't say it."

I hear the challenge in his tone and find myself rising to it. I'm usually pretty easygoing, and I've been able to shrug off these kinds of confrontations before, but something about him and his presumptions gets under my skin. "I can say it. If I want to say it. But I don't. I think there are better ways to express yourself."

"Hmm," Thad says.

I clear my throat. "And anyway, I'm not *freaking* perfect." At the mean little laugh he does under his breath, I feel my temper rise. "I'm just a person. I might not have made some of the mistakes other people do, but I'm plenty messed up in my own way."

"Oh, yeah? Like what?" Now he sounds genuinely curious—but I don't know if this is just a ruse to goad me into saying something else he might make fun of.

I raise an eyebrow at him, warring between protecting *myself*, or proving him that he's wrong about me. "Well. I don't always recycle. Sometimes I'm too lazy to wash out a gross container and I just throw it away."

Thad doesn't just look unimpressed—he looks almost sorry for me. "That's the worst thing you've ever done in your whole life, Sister Helen?"

I glare at the unexpected nickname. "I broke my mom's angel figurine once and blamed it on Dean."

"Whoa. Easy, rebel." This said pityingly, like one might placate a small child who's tried their best but just can't quite play with the big kids.

"I'm still a virgin." The words are out of my mouth before I can stop them, but I need to prove Thad wrong about me. I've always had a bit of a competitive streak—hard to avoid, really, when you've been pitted against your brother your entire life. "I've been a layperson for four years and I still haven't done more than kiss a man."

That shuts him up. If Thad is doing the mental calculations, he's probably figuring out that when he kissed me that first night we met, that's the farthest I've ever gone with a man, sexually. What he hopefully isn't piecing together is that he's the *only* man I've ever kissed. That brief, embarrassing encounter with Thad was the total sum of my sexual experience.

He clears his throat. "That doesn't make you *bad*, though. If anything, that puts you even more in perfect, saint-like territory."

"I never said I was bad, I said I was messed up," I remind him. "And I am plenty messed up. I have spent my whole life trying to get my mother's approval, dedicating five years of my life to fulfill a bargain *she* made with God. And now I'm out, but it's like I'm stuck. I write about romance and sex but I don't have any idea what I'm talking about. It's all fantasy, only I've fantasized about it so long that now I'm terrified the reality can never live up to my expectations. Like, imagine you've never tried chocolate, and your whole life everyone is telling you how incredible chocolate is, and you want to have some but at the same time you know you've built it up to be this thing in your mind that it can never be. Right? Nothing will ever be as good as what you've dreamed chocolate could be."

A long pause. "I dunno," Thad says at last. "Chocolate is pretty damn amazing."

He says it so deadpan that I can't help but laugh—a sharp, gasping laugh that takes me by surprise and sets me off on the giggles. Thad laughs along with me, maybe more so because he's relieved that we've moved on than that he actually finds it funny. Either way, soon we're both laughing so hard that we're in tears.

"Noted," I say, wiping at my eyes. "I'll have to give chocolate a try. Someday."

I keep my eyes on the road in front of us, though I feel Thad studying me. "You should." He sighs. "Or maybe you shouldn't. Sometimes I feel like it can't be worth all the hassle. You know about Vera, but she was hardly the first."

He must register my surprised look, because he hastens to add, "The first woman to betray me—not 'hardly the first' woman to sleep with me."

I'd rather not dwell on who he has or hasn't slept with, frankly. "Who else betrayed you?" I ask quietly, looking over at him.

Still gripping the steering wheel with one hand, he extends his fingers on the other, folding each one in again as he lists a new person. "High school girlfriend dumped me right before she started college, even though she'd asked me to sign a lease on an apartment near the school to be closer to her. Another girlfriend, when I was in my early twenties, borrowed three thousand bucks from me to 'fix her car' but instead spent it on a trip to Malaysia with her friends, then ghosted me. Vera, of course. And honestly, even my own mom. She was in a pretty bad way when I was a kid, with drugs and whatnot. She basically gave my dad custody for an allowance so she could blow it all away.

She's clean now and we've patched things up, but that was…a rough couple of years."

Silence, as I take this all in. I feel like it explains a lot of my interactions with Thad, why he's always so prickly and ready for a fight. "I'm sorry that happened to you," I say stupidly, for lack of anything better to say. I can't commiserate and share my own love-gone-wrong stories, and he knows it.

He waves it off, and I can see the tough-guy walls coming back up, sliding into place. "Hardly the worst thing people've been through."

Afraid he might retreat back into his grouchy shell, I try to keep the conversation going. "Well, bless your heart."

He grins at me, a real grin, and it's like his whole face splits wide open, and those walls come crashing back down. "*Bless your heart*? Ouch."

I frown at him. "What? That's a nice thing to say, isn't it?"

"It's basically the Southern way of saying screw you." He shakes his head, laughing. "Where'd you hear that, anyway? I'm guessing that's not a Boston thing."

Blushing, I look back to the road. "I've, um, been watching some of the old episodes of *Bama Bounty*." What a loser. I'm totally bluffing. I watched all four seasons in about a week. They're short episodes and the seasons aren't that long, but…still. "Just to do a little background check, make sure I know who I'm working with."

His smile is a little more guarded now, but not faded completely. "And? What'd you think?"

"Well, you're the breakout star of the show, of course." I say it playfully, like I'm being a little facetious, but it's true. Orpheus and Amadeus are more comic relief, beefy and brawny and always fighting with each other. Darius is the slightly ridiculous, but somehow still compelling, seasoned veteran. Vera is…well, the bombshell. And Thad is clearly the broody, inscrutable heartthrob of the show, red mohawk and all. He has a quiet intensity to him that captures your attention whenever he's onscreen. It totally makes sense to me why there are so many fan pages devoted to him, plus homemade T-shirts, and even a tattoo I saw on one of the chat boards.

His squints at me, wary. "You're making fun of me."

"No, I'm not—I swear. I love the way you talk everyone through going back into prison and how you do those prayer circles together," I tell him. "It's…oddly moving." I should probably stop there, but for some reason I'm compelled to continue, "And for the record, Vera was never good enough for you. I guess I've had the ending spoiled for me, but…what a diva! That episode where she made everyone wait half an hour while she got her mani-cure fixed? Not the time, Vera!"

Actually, she reminds me a little of Erica, now that I say it aloud. Huh. I never put that together until just this moment.

I check his face. His expression has turned a little rueful now, but the smile is still in place. "Some of that was scripted," he admits, "but not entirely divorced from reality, I'll give you that."

A moment passes where he seems lost in some memory, and not a pleasant one. He clears his throat, and his smile fades again. "And somehow you still want all that, huh? Don't you think you were better off in the convent?"

I can't help but feel it as a rejection, even though I know this was never about me. I shrug, looking out the passenger-side window. "I want to be in love. At least once in my life."

"Even if it goes horribly wrong?"

"Even if," I agree.

He snorts. "You think that, until it does." He's silent for a while, and I imagine he's thinking about Vera again, until he asks abruptly, "Is that why you were out with Shane?"

The way he says Shane's name is so disdainful that I turn to look at his profile, gauging his expression. There's clearly more to their history than I realized. "Well, kind of. I wasn't looking for *love,* per se. More like experience."

More like, I'd just kissed the guy I really liked and found out he was only interested in me because he wanted to find my brother, and I thought Shane would be an easy ego boost. But I don't say that part out loud.

Another snort from Thad as he tightens his grip on the steering wheel. "That'd be an experience you'd have to get tested for afterward."

If I didn't know better, I'd almost say he sounds…jealous? But I don't let myself get carried away with that thought, because it's ridiculous. Thad could not have made it any clearer just how little he's interested in me. There are about a million other reasons why he might be testy around the subject of Shane.

So I let it drop, and we fall into silence again, both of us staring out at the scenery as it blurs by.

Chapter 24
Thad

We stop for the day just outside of Nashville. This is the part of the trip where it becomes obvious we're strangers. Some of those conversations we were having earlier, it started to feel like— maybe we knew each other? I know how stupid that sounds. I'm not saying we met in a previous life or something, but it didn't feel like we were two people who'd barely had any interactions together. She's easy to talk to, and she really listens, like it matters to her what I think. Maybe that's setting the bar low, but in my last relationship I was in a constant competition with social media (and then, unbeknownst to me, my father), so you can't blame a guy for enjoying the undivided attention for a change.

But now, trying to decide on a place to stay, it's clear just how much we really don't know each other yet. You know how with your family and friends, you can just be a grade-A asshole and make demands and shoot down ideas, but with an acquaintance you tend to be much more polite? All that "Oh, it doesn't matter to me…whatever *you* think" hedging and bullshit. It gives me a headache, honestly, and I just want the whole thing to be done.

Again, I'm used to dealing with personalities like Vera's, so I'm trying to suggest the kinds of things she would want. Not that we'll probably find five-star resort hotels on the side of the highway, but I'm aiming for the nicer end of what we're seeing. "What about that one?" I ask, indicating an advertisement for a hotel at the upcoming exit.

More hemming and hawing and squirming from Helen. Finally, I've had enough. "All right, say it. What's the problem?"

"Could we go somewhere a little less pricey?" she asks, wincing as she says it. "I'm sorry if that's not how you're used to traveling, but I'm a public librarian in an expensive city, so…gotta count my pennies."

I frown at her. "You aren't paying. This is my job, not yours—and you're taking time off work to do it." At the protest I already see forming, I cut her off. "Besides, I can write it off as a business expense."

And furthermore, I invested my *Bama Bounty* paychecks back in the day, so I'm not exactly hurting for income. But I don't mention that part. Seems crass.

I figure Helen will change her tune about staying at a nice hotel, now that she knows I'm paying, but instead she seems even more wary about choosing a high-end place. "It doesn't need to be anything fancy," she insists. "Just go with whatever you'd normally choose for a trip like this."

Normally I wouldn't be chasing anyone across state lines, so it's kind of a moot point. I don't mention that to Helen, though. It's hard to say what it is about the Dean Flanagan case. The money is obviously a nice incentive, but there's a feeling you get when you know you're on the trail of someone you're meant to catch. Dad used to say it was a sixth sense all natural-born bounty hunters have, a sort of obsession that feels almost like love. Plus it'd be nice to land something like this, prove that my business doesn't have to rely on my father's name.

I can't help but reflect, for maybe the thousandth time, just how different Vera and Helen are. I can't imagine Vera ever in a million years feeling uncomfortable about someone else spending their money on her. I don't think it's a bad thing, necessarily, to like the finer things in life—look at me, driving in my fancy car, fussing about getting crumbs on the upholstery—but I guess what stands out to me is the difference in how the offer's *received*.

Yet another reminder, I guess, that I don't really know Helen, or how she thinks, or what she wants. I don't ever know what to expect from her. She's not like anyone I've ever met before, and I don't just mean not like any other woman. I mean any other *person*. I've lived so long expecting the worst out of people, searching for the greedy or petty or mean reasons they do what they do. I've tried doing that with Helen, but I've been wrong basically every time. Which makes me almost wonder…if I should be expecting the best, giving her the benefit of the doubt, trusting that she actually might just be a good person.

We're taking so long to decide on a hotel that we've almost passed through Nashville completely, putting us in danger of hitting another empty patch of rural countryside and having to drive another hour before we can stop. My bladder very much does not like that idea.

I see another hotel advertised at the next exit. "All right," I say, making an executive decision for the both of us, "the Road View Inn it is…"

From the outside, the inn doesn't look too bad. It's obviously not a chain hotel, but the sign looks new and the paint is fresh. I see a bunch of bikes in the parking lot, but I'm not opposed to bikers on principle, unless they give me a reason to be.

As soon as we step inside, I realize I've made a mistake. The interior of the Road View Inn is a far cry from the freshly painted exterior. Fluorescent lights flicker overhead. The clerk sits behind bulletproof glass enshrining the entire front counter, with just a little intercom to talk through.

And the lobby is absolutely packed with bikers.

These are not retirees who bought a bike and formed a club with some buddies to fulfill a lifelong bucket list of traveling the country. This is a biker gang, full of the kinds of guys I usually only see in a database for breaking bail, or worse. Many are wearing matching jackets with white dragons stenciled on the back. This lot is big, mean, and rowdy…and their eyes all collectively turn to Helen as she enters the room.

Helen is oblivious to the attention, busy rifling around in her purse for something. "I can't find my wallet. I think I must have left it in the car…"

"We'll get it later," I tell her tersely, keeping my eyes on all the eyes that are watching her. Without really thinking about it, I put my hand on her elbow and pull her closer to me. "Come on, let's go check in."

"Won't I need my ID?"

I only half hear her, busy waging a silent stare-off with all the bikers who are watching us. *This one's mine*, I tell them with my glare, my posture, my hand on her. Yeah, yeah, I know it's archaic and sexist and blabbity blah. I'm only speaking their language, don't shoot the translator.

They suss me out a moment longer. This isn't my first tango with these sorts of men, and I know they'll clock my height, my frame, my tattoos, and the way I'm not pissing my pants staring them down. Hopefully all of that will translate to, *This guy isn't worth messing with.*

Nobody moves, and I swallow down a sigh of relief. They won't try anything, at least not with me around. "We'll be fine. I'm the one paying, remember?"

Helen grimaces at the reminder, but we've gone over it enough that she doesn't bring it up again. At least, not here, in this dump. I'm guessing she's already pieced together a room in this place can't cost *that* much, so she won't protest. But if I try to persuade her to go to a different hotel, the whole thing will probably start all over again, and frankly I've reached the point in the day of traveling where the thought of being in a car for even five more minutes sounds like excruciating torture.

Still, I won't feel safe staying in a place like this, not with Helen alone by herself in one of the thin-doored rooms, likely with a broken lock. Any one of these nasty assholes might pounce on her the moment I'm out of sight. They probably wouldn't even have to try that hard. Knowing her, all some guy would have to do is knock on the door with some bullshit excuse about needing to use the phone, and sweet little Sister Helen, with one of her sunny smiles, will throw the door wide open to the Big Bad Wolf.

I tighten my hand into a fist at the thought, gritting my teeth. The visceral reaction in my body surprises me—because nothing is actually, actively happening. It's all in my head. But tell that to my pounding heart, my clenching gut.

Thinking quickly, I come up with a solution. "There's a bathroom right here in the lobby. Your bladder must be pretty full by now, huh?"

Helen looks like she can't quite believe I'm bringing up her bladder in the middle of a hotel lobby. "My bladder is just fine," she says with no little amount of dignity, a very distracting flush creeping into her cheeks—two perfectly round little spots of pink that might have been adorable if we weren't surrounded by hungry predators all waiting to pounce on fresh meat. Her eyes dart over to the bathroom. "But, if you're going to check in anyway…"

"Go ahead," I encourage her. "I'll take care of everything." As she takes a few tentative steps toward the bathroom, I call after her, "Make sure you lock the door."

I watch her the whole time she walks, and so does the whole room, all of us holding our breaths. Dear, naive Sister Helen really has no idea what a loaded weapon she is outside of her bulky, shapeless clothes. She's wearing jeans and a sweater, nothing salacious, but even so. She has the kind of body that's made for sinful thoughts, all swaying hips and luscious curves, and I sigh with relief when the door shuts and I hear the lock click in place.

I move quickly to the glass-enshrined front counter, careful to keep the bathroom in my line of sight. The man behind the counter looks almost as tough as the bikers in the lobby, bald and tattooed, with a no-nonsense, gruff look about him. Damn. He might make things difficult for me.

"I need a room," I tell him, "two beds if you have it. And when my friend gets back, I need you to tell her there are no other rooms left, so we'll have to make due with sharing the one."

The clerk looks back at me, unimpressed. "Take whatever creepy shit you're trying to pull to another hotel. I'm not getting involved."

"No creepy shit, I swear." I put one hand on my heart and the other up in the air. "Hand to God, I'm not doing anything we couldn't tell her mom about tomorrow morning." Okay, so that's a bit of a lie, because I'm pretty sure Pam would have an aneurysm if she knew Helen and I were going to be in any type of bedroom scenario together, no matter how platonic. "I can't let her stay on her own with this group hanging around." I gesture behind me with a subtle jerk of my head. "Who are these people anyway?"

"The Iron Wraiths," the clerk tells me, and I can hear in his tone of voice that he's no fan, either.

I wince. "I grew up in Mobile. Never had any run-ins myself, but I know others who have, back from my bounty hunting days."

I let that dangle in the air a moment, see if he'll bite. It's a bit of a gamble, honestly. There are a lot of people who hate bounty hunters on principle, either because they've been picked up by one or a friend or family member has. This guy, by the looks of him, has had a few run-ins with the law, and chances are good he'll kick me out right now just for the affiliation.

Or, if my hunch is correct, he just might be the right demographic to have been a fan.

Sure enough, I see his eyes widen as a few things click into place. "Wait a minute—Mobile. You aren't...?" He examines my face, and his eyes widen even more. "You're one of those *Bama Bounty* guys, aren't you?"

Okay, not a big enough fan to know me by name, but I can still use this. People trust people they know from TV. God knows why, since being famous has nothing to do with being *good*, but I'll use it to my advantage if I can. "Yeah, I'm the oldest. Thad. I'm actually on a bounty hunting mission right now." I lower my voice, leaning in confidentially, like I'm sharing a secret. "Can't talk too much about it while I'm still on the hunt, but this guy's a big fish. *Big* fish, if you catch my drift."

I'll let him fill in whatever he believes that to mean in his own mind. "Wow. Is your dad here, too?"

Okay, this guy definitely isn't that big of a fan if he doesn't know that there's no way in hell I'd be traveling with my dad, but whatever. "No, just me." Before he can ask any follow-up questions, I motion over toward the bathroom. "The woman I'm traveling with is helping me, and believe it or not, she's a nun." A bit of an embellishment there, I know, but again, I'm using what's available to me. "Very innocent, a little gullible. So you can see why I'd be nervous about letting her stay on her own with this crowd around."

He looks at me skeptically, some of my credibility slipping again. "She's not wearing one of those robe thingies."

"They don't wear them while they're traveling." This is complete bullshit, of course, but I'm gambling on him knowing even less about nuns than I do.

I see the inner war waging on the guy's face. "I can't be responsible for you seducing a nun."

There's a sentence you don't hear every day. Even in his protest, though, I hear that he's softening. "I won't. Hand to God, nothing like that is gonna happen. I just want to make sure she's safe."

Before he can give me an answer, the bathroom door opens and Helen crosses the lobby to join me. She still hasn't noticed the ripple effect she causes just by existing in this room, surrounded by all these men, but the clerk sees it, and I hope it'll be enough to convince him that I'm right.

Helen smiles brightly as she joins me. "Are we all set?" Somehow she hasn't noticed the dark dankness of the lobby, or the dangerous men around her. I think she must have rainbow-tinted glasses, to see the world as such a good place. I feel my heart melt a little as I look at her, beaming at me with that newborn-kitten innocence and trust.

When I look back at the clerk, he isn't looking at Helen—he's looking at *me*. Whatever he sees there must convince him, because he nods to me, a short curt thing.

"Sort of," I tell her, trying to hide my grin and look appropriately put out. "There's only one room left—it has two beds, but we'll have to share the space."

"Oh." Helen falters a little at that, looking to the clerk. "Really? Only one room left?"

"Yep. All booked." He can't make eye contact with either of us as he says it, looking up at the ceiling instead.

I resist the urge to shake my head at him. Jesus. What a terrible liar. Instead, I turn my attention to her. "Two beds," I remind Helen. "We can hang up a sheet in the middle of the room, if it'll make you feel better."

"I'm sure it'll be fine." To the clerk, Helen says, "Thank you for your help."

He grumbles something back, suddenly intent on checking us into our room. I hand him my credit card, reassuring myself I was right to make this call. I don't have nefarious intentions toward Helen, but if I *did*, she would have been an easy mark. She barely even questioned the room situation, which means she probably would barely even question some biker trying to convince her to open her door late at night so he can force his way in…

The thought makes me shudder, and without thinking, I reach out to place a hand on Helen's upper back. It isn't so much a possessive gesture this time, meant to warn the bikers in the room that she's under my protection. I just want to reassure myself that she's safe, and not about to be snatched away from under my nose.

Helen looks at me in surprise at the unexpected contact. We really haven't touched each other much, I realize, as there hasn't been a reason to, but I'm surprised at how natural it feels.

"Room 203," the clerk tells us, dropping the key cards and my credit card through the slot in the glass. "Second floor. Elevators are down the hall, to the left."

He seems relieved to have us gone, but not as relieved as I am to finally get Helen out of that lobby, away from the peanut gallery watching our every move. "Do you want to get some food after we put our stuff in the room?" Helen asks once we're in the elevator.

"Whatever you want," I tell her tiredly. "As long as they deliver."

Once we're in that hotel room, I'm bolting the door and not taking her out again until we leave in the morning and put this place safely in our rearview mirror.

Chapter 25
Helen

There's something about traveling that's so exhausting, even though I've only been sitting in a car for most of the day. Thad never relented on letting me help him drive. Apparently my spotless driving record is still not good enough proof to show I can take care of his baby.

Whatever. I'm not jealous of a car. It's fine.

Thad must be even more exhausted than I am after all that driving because after he showers, he collapses onto his bed—the one closest to the door, at his insistence—and lets me take care of ordering the food. Considering that he's paying for all the gas and the room, and doing all the driving, I'm happy to take over finding dinner. That way I can put it all on my card and he won't be able to do anything about it, if he's even awake enough to notice.

"Pizza's on its way," I tell him, setting my phone on the bedside table. Actually, on second thought, I better take it into the bathroom with me while I shower. I have a passcode on it, but Thad seemed pretty confident that he'd be able to break into it without my help, and I don't want him figuring out where we're going and leaving without me.

"Hrrmm," Thad grunts from the bed.

If the thought of me getting naked in the next room is at all titillating, Thad does a really good job of not showing it. Rolling over onto his back, he reaches for the remote and switches on the television.

Whatever. It's not like during his shower, I was thinking about his naked body underneath all that hot water. That would be weird. And I definitely did not do that, not even once.

Thad may not care, but *I'm* self-conscious as I take off my clothes in the bathroom and step into the shower. I can hear him watching the TV through the wall. It's the most intimate I've ever been with a nonrelated man before, and even though absolutely nothing is going to happen, I choose to see this as a positive step forward instead of simply being sad. This man might not want to see me naked, but we are sharing a sleeping space tonight, and we will be in pajamas in the same room together, and that feels like progress.

If this were a romance, there would be some emergency that would make Thad need to come into the bathroom while I'm showering. My hair would get caught in the showerhead or there would be a giant spider on the wall or some-thing. Thad would be a gentleman and keep his eyes above my shoulders for most of it, but maybe he would sneak just one little peek and be overwhelmed with the sight of my puckered nipples and heaving breasts.

But this is not a romance, and nobody is interested in these boobies. I pat them consolingly. "Sorry, girls. Maybe someday."

I am a certified weirdo, but this has already been well established.

When I'm fully dressed again and absolutely no one has seen me naked, I find Thad in the same exact position, completely supine, like his body has been drained of all its energy.

"Are you alive?" I tease him, putting my toiletries back in my bag. I've decided to treat this whole sharing-a-room thing like a fun summer camp adventure with two buddies, since I need to stop thinking romance-novel thoughts so I won't act like a total creep with Thad.

He grunts at me. "Do you always sing in the shower like that?"

I honestly hadn't realized I was doing that, but it doesn't come as much of a surprise. A singing nun—what a cliche. "Sorry. Julie Andrews was a big hero to me growing up, go figure. Was it annoying?"

He grunts again but doesn't say one way or the other. He hasn't looked at me at all since coming out of the bathroom, I realize. I'm nothing more than a lamp in the room to him. An annoying lamp that sings.

A knock at the door saves us from this scintillating conversation. "That must be the pizza," I say, moving to answer it so he can keep resting.

Thad shoots up out of the bed faster than should be possible, considering he was practically catatonic moments ago, rushing to intercept me. "I'll get it."

Once he reaches the door, he peers through the peephole. "Who is it?" It's kind of cute, how paranoid he is. Like there's something rare and precious he has hidden away in here that he doesn't want anyone to take.

"Pizza."

Thad reluctantly opens the door, just enough to fit the pizza through. I approach from behind, cash in hand. "It's already been paid for, but here's the tip."

Thad snatches the money, then waves me back. "Go back to the bed." He waits until I've done so before thrusting the cash through the door, along with some more he pulls from his wallet. "Don't tell anyone what room we're in, if they ask." And with that he slams the door shut, bolting it for good measure.

"Such a people person," I tease him as he returns, pizza in hand. "And who's going to care what room we're in?"

"Don't worry about it." He drops the pizza on the bed. "Whatcha wanna watch while we eat?"

I glance dubiously at the TV screen, where an old black-and-white movie is playing. "What's this?"

"Oh." Thad runs a self-conscious hand over the back of his neck, and if I didn't know better, I'd say he was blushing. "It's an old film noir. *Double Indemnity.*"

I probably shouldn't comment, but I can't help myself—outside of being a bounty hunter, a minor reality television star, and an obsessive car owner, this is the first thing about *himself* that Thad's let slip. "I haven't seen much film noir," I say, treading carefully. "I like older movies, but I kinda stuck with the Judy Garland, Fred Astaire side of things. You know, the musicals, the romances."

Thad shrugs. "Yeah, I dunno. I've stayed at a lot of hotels over the years and they almost always have the classics channel. The noirs are decent."

I know enough about film noir to know the gist of what to expect—world-weary, warworn detectives and beautiful, dangerous women. No wonder he's into them. This must be a glimpse into his world, or as close as I'm going to get to it.

"Let's watch it," I tell him. "Can you catch me up with what's going on during the commercials?"

I pull out a slice of pizza, then hand the box across the gap between our beds to Thad. He settles back against the headboard, motioning to the screen. "Okay, so there's an insurance salesman, Fred MacMurray—that's the actor's name, not the character—and he goes to this rich guy's house to get him to renew his policy, only the guy's wife's there, Barbara Stanwyck, and she's this praying mantis. Gorgeous, but bad news…"

Thad fills me in up to the point where we are in the story, the final twenty minutes or so leading into the climax. I'm enjoying the movie a lot more than I thought I would, but what I'm enjoying even more is Thad's obvious enthusiasm for it. He's no longer a grunting, inert lump on the bed, but he's upright, animated, talking to the characters onscreen like they're old friends who can hear him.

"Don't go into the house," he warns Fred MacMurray's character. "She's waiting for you!"

When Barbara Stanwyck shoots him, Thad sits back with a sigh, like all of this could have been prevented if only people would listen to him. "Women," he says with a grin, shaking his head and biting wolfishly into his pizza.

I know he's joking, but something about it sits wrong with me. I wait, busying myself with cleaning napkins and other pizza detritus off my bed, until the final credits play. "Are all women like that in film noir?"

Thad finishes his last bite of pizza and reaches for another piece. "Like what?" He offers the box to me.

I hold up a hand, motioning that I'm full. "You know, either a Lola or a Phyllis. Either an angel or a she-devil?"

He considers it. "I guess so." He frowns at me. "Why, you didn't like it?"

Despite the frown, I sense a tenderness in the question. He's shared something with me that he genuinely loves, and I don't want to shoot it down. "I loved it," I tell him honestly. "The tension, the buildup, that denouement. It was all incredible."

He grins, looking visibly relieved. "I only know what half those words mean, but, yeah, it's great."

"And Barbara Stanwyck was incredible. Her shoes, her attitude." I couch my thoughts with compliments so he knows I'm not trying to tear the film apart. I decide to pose my criticism as a question. "I wonder why these films use the 'good versus bad women' trope? It's really entertaining to watch, but not all women are either good or bad, you know? There's a lot in between the Lolas and the Phyllises of the world."

Thad's grin fades into his usual frown, despite my best efforts. "Not really. At least in my line of work. There are bail jumpers, cheats, liars…and then the nun librarians." He gives me a tentative smile. "Don't worry, you're a Lola."

I know that's an olive branch extended, but it still bothers me. "But don't you feel like that's a lot of pressure on women? What about librarians who sometimes lie? Or bail jumpers who dream about being small-business owners?"

Okay, that was a stupid example, and I somewhat deserve the pitying look that Thad gives me. "That's cute you think so, Sister Helen. That's why you're a Lola."

I scramble for a better example. "Look at Phyllis. Even *she* couldn't go through with killing Walter in the end because she realized she loved him."

"And that makes up for everything she did before?"

I'm not explaining myself right. I shake my head, frustrated. "No, but... I'm just saying that it's not fair that women have to be all one thing or the other. Is Walter a bad guy because he fell for Phyllis's schemes, or does he get a pass because he had a conscience? Women should get to be complicated and complex, too, that's all I'm saying."

Thad raises an eyebrow at me. "And you don't think men get put into categories in your romance novels?" At my impending protest, he sits up a little straighter. "Either you're Prince Charming or you're the guy who deserves to get strung along because you're just the filler boyfriend until Mr. Right comes along."

I sit up, shaking my head at him. "That's not true. You obviously haven't read enough romance if you think that."

He motions to me. "What about your book—the one you were reading at the writing group? Rosamund has Wilfred lapping along after her, but he's all but scum beneath her boot once Axel turns up."

I glare at him. "Wilfred is not Rosamund's boyfriend. Him expressing an interest in her does not entitle him to dibs. And he isn't a bad person, he's just not the right person."

"Film noir splits it up into bad and good. Romance splits it up into Mr. Right and Mr. Wrong. That's all I'm saying."

I shake my head, determined to make my point. "But people aren't all bad or all good, that's the point—"

He laughs under his breath, shaking his own head. "Come on, Sister Helen. You can't really believe that. What about those assholes downstairs? You think there's good in any of those motorcycle creeps? Would you have invited them in for a Bible study if I'd let you have your own room?"

I'm about to retort, when my brain snags on something he said. "Let me have my own room?" I echo. "What does that mean?"

Thad, finally, has the good grace to look ashamed. "I...may have asked the clerk to lie to you about only having one room." Seeing my mouth drop, he sits up, protesting, "But it was for your own good. I was just trying to make sure you were safe."

The confession knocks the wind out of me. For a moment, I can only stare at him, and then I'm surprised by the sudden tears that blind my eyes. "You know, I've spent a long time with people making my decisions for me. Taking my choice away. I didn't think you'd be one of them."

I don't wait for a snarky reply, or a stammering apology, or a defensive explanation for why he's so right and I'm so stupid and naive that I can't take care of myself—because frankly, I'm pretty sure any one of those three responses would make me break down sobbing. Instead, I stand up, pulling my toiletries bag back out of my luggage. "I'm going to brush my teeth."

If he responds, I don't hear it, just the sound of a sweeping film score coming through the thin bathroom door.

Chapter 26
Thad

I'll be relieved once we put the Road View Inn in our rearview mirror, for more than one reason.

Reason the first: we'll get away from these Iron Wraiths, and I can breathe easy again knowing that Helen isn't about to be snatched up.

Reason the second: after last night, Helen and I are back to being polite strangers again.

"Hand it over," I say, gesturing to her bag. "I'll put it in the trunk."

"Thank you," Helen says, not quite meeting my gaze.

"No problem." And that's basically the total sum of our morning conversation.

Yesterday it didn't bother me so much. We are strangers, technically, so it makes sense there'd be a little weirdness between us. But last night felt…I dunno. Different. Just watching old movies in a hotel room, Helen with her damp hair and pajamas, giving me that big old smile. It felt—right? I know that's corny, but it was the closest I've felt to someone in a long time.

Then I had to go and ruin it with my big mouth. Honestly, I don't even know where most of that nonsense about good and bad women, Mr. Right and Mr. Wrong, was coming from. I guess it always kind of bothered me in those romance movies I'd watch with Vera how it was always so obvious who the Right Guy was supposed to be. Real life isn't like that. Even the Right Guy might be grouchy when he's hungry, or wear mismatching socks on laundry day, or be just a general pain in the ass at times. But I see what Helen was saying about the good women and the bad women in the film noirs. I get how that might be frustrating, especially after coming out of a vocation where there was probably a lot of pressure on her to be "good" and a lot of shame about doing anything that was "bad." I wish I would have told her that last night, instead of trying to pick a fight. Digging in my heels. Trying to prove I was right.

And then…I had to make an even bigger ass out of myself by telling her about the room. Although, I guess I'd already established myself as the world's biggest asshole when I decided to not even ask her about sharing. I know she's a former nun and everything, but she's also a woman in her thirties, living on her own in Chicago. It's not like I found her in a meadow where she'd been raised by fairies, or something. I'm sure she knows how to take care of herself. It was just, the thought of something bad happening to her because I'd dragged her into this whole mess… But that wasn't my choice to make.

So even though I'm eager to get as far away from the Road View Inn as I can, I stop Helen before she can get in Kitty's passenger-side door. "Hold up." I toss her the keys, then gesture to the driver's side, holding open the door for her. "I thought you could start us off, if you're up for it."

Helen blinks, then grins at me, her first real smile of the day. "Really?"

She hurries over as if afraid I'll change my mind. Honestly, I almost do as I watch her climb in and adjust the seat. Damn. I'd found just the perfect setting… But no, it's fine. I found it once, I'll find it again. "Just go easy on the gas pedal. She's a light touch. And if she starts shaking, you have to turn down the AC and let her have a little break."

Helen squints up at me, shielding her eyes from the light. "It's going to be all right, Thad. I almost never crash when I drive."

My heart misses a beat in the moment it takes me to realize she's joking, grinning at me like the cat who got the cream. "Think you're clever, huh?" I grouse, shutting her in before rounding the car to join her on the other side.

Despite her *hilarious* jokes, I can tell Helen is doing her best to be careful as she navigates onto the highway. That's the power of Kitty. She demands respect. Still, I can't help myself from gripping on to the passenger-side door as Helen approaches another car to pass. "She's wider than you think. Make sure to give her lots of space."

Helen rolls her eyes. "Is this you showing that you trust me? It's hard to tell."

We pass the other car without issue and I breathe easier again once we're in the slow lane. "I do trust you. You think I let just anyone drive Kitty?" I consider it. "Actually, you might be the first person I've let behind the wheel, come to think of it."

Helen looks over at me in astonishment—for a little longer than I like, but I resist the urge to tell her to put her eyes back on the road. "Seriously?"

"Seriously." I got Kitty after the breakup with Vera, and I haven't seen my brothers or my dad in all that time. My mom doesn't drive, and even if she did, I'd never trust her with my baby. I wasn't exaggerating before when I said I haven't felt close to anyone in a long time.

We drive in silence for a moment. I clear my throat. "What do you say, a show of trust for a show of trust. You wanna finally tell me where we're going?"

Helen gives me a sidelong, faux-suspicious glare. "You aren't going to leave me in a parking lot somewhere, are you?"

Maybe at one point I would have tried that, but that was before our run-in with those bikers at the hotel. I know she *could* take care of herself if she needed to, but I also know I don't especially want to see her try. She shouldn't even be on the same planet as guys like that. She should live in…Oz, or someplace like that. But without the wicked witches. Only the nice, bright, happy parts.

I must be taking too long to answer, because Helen frowns at me, no longer totally joking. "*Are* you?"

"No." I laugh, and hold up my hand. "Hand to God, I won't leave you anywhere."

She deliberates another moment longer before finally, sighing, she tells me: "New Orleans."

Mentally I run through the route in my mind. "Does that mean we'll be passing through Mobile?"

Helen shoots me a quick, worried look. "Shoot. I guess we probably will, if it's on the 65."

I grimace. "It is." Seeing the concern on her face, I do my best to wave it off. "It's fine. It's a big city." Somehow it feels like my dad and Vera will both know if I'm anywhere within a hundred-mile radius, but I know that's ridiculous. Trying to put Helen at ease, I change the subject. "So how'd you know to check your aunt's credit card bill to look for Dean?"

"I didn't do it on purpose. But I saw the bill out, with a bunch of charges circled and added up. I figured either someone stole Aunt Linda's card information, or, more likely…"

"Not bad," I tell her, begrudgingly impressed.

She shrugs, like it's no big deal, but I can tell she's pleased with herself for having figured it out. And she should be. She isn't the only one looking for Dean, not by a long shot. "I took photos of the bill, if you want to look at them. I figure there might be other charges on there besides the hotel—places that he's been going—that we can look into once we're there."

I pull out her phone and put in the passcode she gives me. "It should be the first thing that comes up in the camera roll," she tells me.

It is not the first thing in her camera roll.

The first image in Helen's picture roll is a selfie of her lying reclined in her bed, smiling up at the camera and biting her lower lip. Her hair is tousled, her expression playful and teasing. She's wearing a very thin white undershirt, through which I can see the full shape of her voluptuous breasts, and the red lacy panties I saw her looking at in the lingerie store.

My brain short-circuits. I stare at the image for longer than I mean to, longer than I *should*, unable to force myself to scroll away. The funny thing is, even a week ago I would've thought she intentionally tricked me into seeing this photo, a real *Gee, shucks, I forgot that sexy picture of me was there waiting for you* kind of thing. Now, after spending the last day on the road with her, I know that isn't what she intended. It isn't even a question in my mind. Which makes me a skeevy pervert for still looking at it when she didn't mean for me to see it, and I know this, but I also can't seem to tear my eyes away.

Finally I force my thumb to man up and do what my eyes can't. I scroll to the next picture, hoping to find the credit card bill. But no, of course it's another sexy picture. This time she's taking a shot over her shoulder in the reflection of the mirror behind her, so I can see her luscious ass straining against that thin red lace.

"What do you think?" Helen asks. "Did anything catch your eye?"

Again, if this were a week ago, I'd feel sure she was intentionally messing with me. Now, hearing the genuine innocence in her voice, I feel like even more of a scuzz for staring. "Um…" I try to swipe again, but am assaulted by yet another pose, another image that will be burned into my brain. "I'm having some trouble finding it."

Helen gives me a questioning frown. Then I see the exact moment she realizes what *else* was on her camera roll. Her eyes widen, and she jerks the steering wheel into the next lane before quickly correcting herself. Lucky no one was coming the other way or Kitty would need a new fender.

"Oh my gosh!" Helen reaches for the phone, throwing it into the back seat. She's tomato red now and I can see she's mortified. "I'm so sorry. I didn't mean to…I'm so sorry."

"No, no, it's…I didn't mean to, either, I was just…" I wave my hand inarticulately, looking out the window. Damn. Just when we'd started to break the ice. I realize if we go on like this, we're going to be two awkward strangers again, taking turns apologizing and pleasing and thanking after every other sentence. Sucking in a breath, I take a bit of a gamble. "So, you decided to go with the red lacy panties after all, huh?"

I glance sidelong at Helen, who stares at me, jaw dropped, before she starts to fight off a grin as she turns her eyes back to the road. "Well, obviously I did. Yes."

I laugh, and she laughs, too, shaking her head. "I can't believe I just made you look at pictures of me in my underwear."

"It was real torture," I assure her, and she takes a swat at me. Laughing, I catch her hand before she can make contact. As our fingers touch, our eyes meet, and a jolt of *something* passes through me.

Clearing my throat, I release her and look away again, not totally sure why my heart is pounding in my chest like I've just been sprinting after a bail jumper.

Then a sudden thought strikes me, souring the moment. I run a hand over the back of my neck. "Were those…for Shane?"

It's absolutely not a question I should ask, nor is it one that I have any right to know, but I'm still relieved at the perplexed look Helen gives me. "For *Shane*? Why would those be for Shane?"

Pure relief. There's no denying that's what I'm feeling. Most likely because Shane's a fuckboy of the first order, but also because I have to admit that the thought of him seeing *her* like that, of her smiling that way at the camera for *him*, makes me feel a bit sick to my stomach. "I dunno. I saw you two on that date. Wasn't sure how serious it was."

Helen shakes her head. "Not at all serious. The ten minutes that you saw us on that date were the only ten minutes we've spent together outside of the library."

I feel another surge of relief, until a new worrisome thought sours me again. "Some other guy, then?"

She shoots me a look. "How many men do you think I'm juggling at once?"

"Who'd you take the pictures for?" I counter. I say it like it's a frivolous question, just something to pass the time, but I'm holding my breath a little as I wait for the answer.

Helen takes a deep breath. "It's going to sound stupid, but…I took them for me."

A beat passes as I process her answer. "Like for a self-esteem boost when you post them for your followers?"

"My followers?" She connects the dots and shakes her head. "Oh, no. I'm not on social media."

Wow. Talk about a different species from Vera. "So how were they for you?"

Helen's entire face is pinkening adorably. "You know I'm still a *virgin*." She says that last word as a whisper, like it's a naughty word. It almost sounds that way, actually, coming out of her mouth. "Sometimes it's hard for me to think of myself as being sexy, so I thought I'd. You know. Practice."

Fuuuuuck me. I am *not* going to think about Helen practicing being sexy, or imagine the other things she might do to put herself in the mood. Nope. Definitely not going to think of that.

I clear my throat. "Well, for what it's worth, you nailed it. Those were definitely…very sexy."

Not sure why I said it. I'm not trying to be creepy, just trying to let her know her little post-nun homework is working. She deserves to know she's done a good job, that's all.

Helen looks over at me. Our eyes meet again. I feel that same charge to my chest, like someone's just put some defibrillators to me and gotten my heart going again. "Thank you," she murmurs, sliding her gaze back to the road.

We make pretty good time, the two of us taking turns driving, passing the hours with some deep questions, some bullshit. I learn that Helen is deathly afraid of snakes, that the place she'd most like to travel to is Greece, and that she didn't leave the convent to become a romance writer, though she laughs at the question. "I'm happy being a librarian. The writing stuff is just for me, kind of a way to work some things out."

I don't point out that, at least from what I heard, what she mainly seems to be working out is her libido, but I do tell her about my dream of road-tripping across the country in an RV, my childhood dog Mooch, and my manly fear of cockroaches.

She asks me some questions about my line of work, too: "So why don't you carry a gun? Wouldn't that make your job safer?"

I shrug. "Maybe, but it might also make it harder." She seems genuinely curious, so I explain, "Despite what the movies make it look like, most of my job is talking to people. Asking questions. And people close down real quick when they see a gun." I shrug. "Besides, I have other ways to take care of myself."

"Krav Maga," Helen says, seemingly without thinking, and then proceeds to turn bright pink.

I give her the side-eye, not saying anything. Krav Maga, huh? Seems like someone's been watching quite a bit more *Bama Bounty* than she's been letting on. I don't comment, though, because embarrassment is another way to shut down conversations fast. And I find, to my surprise, that I really want to keep Helen talking.

The time passes by surprisingly quickly. Close to the six-hour mark, Helen motions to one of the signs. "We're not too far from Mobile. Should we stop, stretch our legs, have a pee break?"

I've been bracing myself for this moment. As soon as I knew we'd be taking the I-65 from Nashville, I knew we'd be driving through my old stomping grounds. But Mobile is a big city, I remind myself. The likelihood of running into my dad, my brothers…Vera…is slim to none. Especially in a random gas station just off the highway.

Still, I catch myself tightening my hands into fists. "Sure," I say, forcing my tone to stay neutral. "Why not?"

I think I do a pretty good job pretending, until I glance over at Helen and see her frowning at me. "What's wrong? You sound weird."

Can Sister Helen read my thoughts? That's a disturbing idea. More disturbing for her than me, I'd guess, based on some of the things I've been thinking about. Things I definitely should *not* be thinking about, even if I can't get the image of her in that thin white shirt off my mind… I clear my throat. "I, uh, I haven't been back to Mobile since…"

Helen's read my Wikipedia page, so I don't need to fill in the blanks. Her eyes widen. "Seriously? Not even for Christmas?"

"Hard to be in the holiday mood when your dad was boning your fiancée for half a year before anyone had the balls to tell you."

Helen grimaces. "I'm sorry. I didn't realize. We can just keep going until we get to the next town."

I glance at her pointedly, eying the little dance she's doing in her seat. "Thanks, but I'd rather you *not* piss your pants on Kitty's original leather seats." Seeing the protest already forming on her lips, I reassure her, "It's fine. Honestly. We'll stay on the outskirts of town, just make a quick pit stop, then bye-bye, Mobile."

"I'll pee so fast," Helen vows, making a little cross-her-heart sign over her chest.

It's fine, I tell myself, fighting off the deep sense of dread I feel at being in the same state as my family.

Still, I'll be happier once we put Mobile in our taillights.

We pull into a gas station right off the highway, still on the outskirts of town. There's literally no way Vera would be caught dead in a place like this, so I relax, though I'm still determined to leave as fast as possible.

"I'll do the gas," I tell Helen. "You run inside so you can stop dancing around like a toddler. I'll meet you back out here."

"Aren't you going to go?" Helen asks me, doing that squirmy dance that little kids do when they're insisting they don't need to pee. It looks especially absurd seeing a woman in her thirties doing it, but for some reason, it's also adorable.

"I'm good," I tell her.

"But New Orleans is still hours away. Who knows when we'll stop again?"

"You worry about you and your bladder, I'll worry about me and mine." Still, I suppose she isn't wrong. I sigh. "Fine, just a quick piss, then let's meet back at the car. No snacks." I level my index finger at her warningly. "No snacks."

Helen looks at me with a guilty smile. "The sign says they have barbeque. Real Alabama barbeque."

"From a gas station." I consider my words. Actually, knowing Alabama, that's probably the place to get the best barbeque, but I'm sure as hell not gonna tell her that.

"The sign says they do crawfish boils, too. I don't know what that is, but it sounds Southern."

"You're certifiable if you think you're eating crawfish in my car," I growl at her through gritted teeth. The messiest food on the planet—she must have lost her damn mind. "I'm not joking, I'll leave you here if you come out with that!"

The smile she flashes back at me is not a good sign. The woman clearly has no fear of me anymore. I've lost all authority.

So then why the hell am I fighting a grin as I watch her half run, half waddle to the bathroom, like I'm some heartsick idiot?

Chapter 27
Helen

I'm about ten gloriously short steps away from the bathroom when the clerk calls after me: "Inside ladies' bathroom is broken, hon. You'll have to use the one out back."

Son of a preacher. I hope I can make it that far. "Okay, thanks!"

I hobble outside, attempting to keep my legs pressed together and not making very good progress as a result. Thad's busy filling up the tank, so I don't know if he can see me, but I make a waving motion and point behind the building to let him know where I'm going.

The bathroom is one of those creepy concrete things that is about a hundred yards back from the main building, which increases both its spooky factor (why is it so far away, is this the bathroom for plague victims?) and its inconvenience (again, why so far away?). At least we aren't in Chicago, so I won't literally freeze my tushy off, but it's still an outdoor bathroom with no heat in February.

But it's open and has a working toilet, and beggars can't be choosers, so I relieve my poor, overtaxed bladder. Ah, sweet relief.

When I step out of the stall to wash my hands, I stop short.

There is a middle-aged man standing in the entrance to the bathroom, leaning against the doorframe. He's on the shorter side but bulky, with scars on his face and neck, suggesting he's not an accountant or bank teller. He smiles when he sees me, but it is not a nice expression, and one of his teeth glints gold in the fluorescent lights.

"You're not supposed to be in here," I blurt out stupidly.

He straightens. "Here's what's gonna happen. My car's right outside. You're gonna come with me and get inside and not do anything stupid. And no one will get hurt." He lifts his coat to show me the gun he has holstered against his hip. "Understand?"

My brain freezes at the sight. I've never seen a gun before. Not in real life. Based on TV shows and movies, it feels like they should be everywhere, almost commonplace, but I realize in this moment just how bizarre it is to see one up close and know it might be used against me.

"I understand." I hear myself responding woodenly.

Another mean grin. "Good girl. Dean always said you were smart."

"Dean sent you?" For a moment, I'm calmed by the thought. This isn't some random man trying to kidnap me out of a bathroom. It's a man who knows Dean, and who for some reason has followed me here. The distinction isn't *great*, but it's something.

"In a way," says the man, with that not-nice smile, like he's laughing at some joke that's entirely at my expense.

I remember what Thad said about bad people coming after Dean, and any hope I feel about this being a gentler sort of kidnapping vanishes. He's not here to take me to Dean. He's here to use me as bait.

"You set off on this little road trip out of the blue, so I figured you and your boyfriend must know where Dean is. Think you can lead me to him, sweetheart?"

I don't know which is worse: To tell him the truth, that yes, I think I might know where Dean is, and throw my brother to the wolves. Or to lie, and give this guy absolutely no reason to keep me around. Maybe if he believes I don't know where Dean is, he'll just leave me here.

But there's also another alternative that does not end so well for me if he decides I'm worthless.

I make myself nod. "I can do that."

"Good girl." He reaches for me and I shudder, but obediently move toward him. "You are a good girl, aren't you? You wanna help your brother get out of this?"

I nod again, more out of fear than agreement. I don't want to do anything, especially in this enclosed space, that will anger this man.

"Good girl," he says again, making my skin crawl. "I'm sure you'll be able to help us convince Dean to give us back our Molly."

The first coherent thought that snags my mind is the word Molly. I may have lived a relatively coddled life, but I know that Molly is another name for a drug—I think maybe ecstasy? Dean stole this guy's ecstasy? I know from what Thad's told me that Dean has been getting into worse and worse crimes, but somehow it's still jarring to hear he's gotten mixed up in the world of drugs. And now, apparently, I'm mixed up in it, too. Because somehow I'm meant to persuade Dean to give it back, and something tells me I'm not going to have a lot of say in just *how* I'm used to persuade him.

Grinning with his gold-flecked teeth, the mobster grips my arm and leads me outside.

My mind is racing frantically, trying to figure out what to do next. My hope was I would see someone outside and be able to call for help, but there's no one back here—except for another man, sitting in the driver's seat of the car waiting for me. His expression, like the man holding on to my arm, is one of unambiguous menace. I don't know for certain what they plan to do to me, but I know it isn't going to be good.

I can't let them get me inside that car. I know that much. I may have spent five years as a sister, but I was a sister in *Boston*, and we were trained to be wary of our surroundings. Never let someone get you into a car and take you to a second location. When in doubt, cause a scene.

So, I do.

I have no idea if anyone's even close enough to hear me, but as soon as we're out of the bathroom, I scream like my hair is on fire. Like I've opened my car to find it's full of cobras. Like I'm swimming in the ocean and see a fin cutting through the water toward me.

I've heard you shouldn't scream "Help me!" because people will ignore it, maybe thinking that you're playing some kind of game, or maybe just not caring because you're a stranger. According to our safety training, you should yell "Fire!" which is something more likely to bring people running. That might be good advice, but instead I find myself shouting the only word that I'm confident will bring someone racing to my rescue.

"Thad!"

I shout his name again and again, praying that he didn't change his mind and go inside, or that he isn't sitting in the car with the radio turned on, drowning out my cries.

And while I'm screaming, I make myself the biggest possible menace to hold on to. I kick. I hit. I scratch. I wave my arms like a windmill. I make my body go limp. I drag my feet. Anything I can think of to keep this man from getting me into the car.

I have at the very least succeeded in pissing my captor off. "Hey, cut it out! Larry!"

The guy in the driver's seat starts to get out. Knowing I have to move quickly, I do the only thing I can think of and bite the arm of the guy who's holding me.

"Ow! You bitch!"

He releases me and backhands me, hard. It takes me by such surprise that I lose my balance and hit the asphalt.

"Hey!"

I open my eyes to see Thad rushing onto the scene, his face like nothing I've ever seen before. He is a storm cloud, a vengeful god. He is shouting a string of swear words like a war cry. He is Achilles, demigod and powerful warrior, exacting his revenge on Hector.

The way he moves is incredible. I know, this is kind of a bizarre thing to notice as I'm lying on the ground after almost being kidnapped by two mobsters who are after my brother. Maybe I'm in shock? All I know is I've never seen anything like this before, outside of those WWE matches Dean used to watch when we were teens. Thad half rolls, half propels himself across the hood of the car so he can get to the guy who threw me down. He seamlessly transitions this into springing onto the guy and tackling him to the ground.

The mafia guy is pressed down flat on his stomach with Thad on top of him, but still I warn him, "He has a gun in his coat."

Thad fishes it out and aims it toward the other guy, Larry, who's been edging back into the car. "Stay right there."

With the driver-side door still open, Larry starts the engine.

"Shit." Thad scrambles to his feet, pulling the other mobster along with him, aiming the gun at his temple. "Helen, get behind me, now!"

I do as he says, and realize why as soon as I'm on my feet. There's a very real possibility that the guy in the car will drive it forward and try to run us over. Thad's gambling that he won't want to kill the mobster Thad's holding hostage, but it's a bluff. There's no way to know which way this will go.

For one tense, breath-holding moment, Larry stares us down. Then abruptly, he backs the car up, swinging it around so he can drive off. Before he rounds the corner, he reaches out and pulls the driver-side door shut.

"Shit," Thad says again, but there's relief in his voice. It would have been better, sure, if he could have apprehended the other guy, too, but at least we're all still standing. "Helen, I need you to reach in my pocket and get out my phone. Passcode is 11-22-33."

The mob guy snorts. "Original."

Thad ignores him. "Call the police and tell them where we are."

I move to do as he instructs. As I reach into his pocket, our gazes meet. Thad's eyes roam over my face, searching, before catching my gaze again. He swallows. "You okay?"

My first instinct is to say something reassuring, to ease that almost furious worry on his face. But the mobster can hear everything we're saying, and I was seconds away from being kidnapped. As the weight of this catches up to me, I realize if I try to say anything, I'll burst into tears, and I really don't want the mobster to see that. It seems important for some reason that he never knows just how much he scared me.

Thad must see all of this on my face, because he nods to me like he understands, and tightens his grip on the mobster as I take a few steps away to call the police. "Hello? I need to report an attempted kidnapping…"

Chapter 28
Thad

The police arrive pretty quickly, but it takes forever to sort through everything, give our testimonies, show them my documents. The whole time Helen's in my line of sight, but she's not right here next to me, and I need her right here next to me. I need to touch her, to reassure myself she's okay and whole and not too damaged. I need to ask her if she's all right without anyone around listening, and look into her eyes when I tell her I'm not going to let anything happen to her, she's safe with me.

By the time they give us the all clear, it's obvious we aren't going to get back on the road today. Helen looks exhausted; I can see the adrenaline is starting to wear off and she's about ready to slump over. I need to get her to a hotel—a *real* hotel this time, with a security officer I can give clear instructions to and a door with a deadlock—and let her rest and recover. She might even want to fly home after what happened today. The thought makes my throat feel tight, but I'll respect whatever she wants to do. Whatever makes her feel safe.

I know Helen must still be a little shell-shocked because she doesn't say anything when we pull up to the Battle House Renaissance Hotel and I hand off my keys to the valet. A few steps up from the Road View Inn, no?

I go to ask for one room again, knowing there's no way I'll sleep tonight if she's in a different room, but I stop myself. I don't want to take any choices away from her, not again. Clearing my throat, I turn to her. "Do you want your own room or—"

"No." Her voice is quiet, and she curls her fingers into my jacket, holding me close. "I'd rather not be alone. If you don't mind."

"I don't mind," I say quickly, relieved. But it's more than just relief—I feel like a weight's been lifted off my shoulders. I feel like I would have been pacing like an animal all night, listening through the walls, checking the peephole every two seconds. Her muted tone and the way she's clinging on to me… I'll fucking kill anyone who tries anything, *anything*, again.

We make it upstairs to our room, and I realize my adrenaline is starting to come crashing down, too. I feel just about ready to collapse on the bed, but first I want to make sure Helen has everything she needs. "Are you hungry? Do you want me to order some food?"

Helen puzzles over this a moment, like she genuinely doesn't know. "Not yet, I don't think. I'm going to take a bath, if that's all right."

She sounds so dazed, I feel a lump forming in my throat. My God, she was almost kidnapped today. Who knows what those two psychopaths would have done to her? I honestly can't let myself think about it too much. I'm more than half tempted to call off the whole search, just turn Kitty around and head straight back to Chicago. Except, Helen might not be safe there, either. It sounds like those mob guys have been following her for a while, and I know Shane and I were doing the same. Who knows who else might be hanging around?

Maybe we should hop on a plane, go somewhere new? I'm not sure at what point this became less about finding Dean than taking care of Helen, but that's where we are now. We should fly somewhere unexpected. I wonder what it would take to convince her. Maybe I'll entice her with someplace warm like a tropical beach, where we can swim and sleep all day, and be somewhere no one's ever heard the name Dean Flanagan.

I realize this is crazy, of course. And I also realize I've been staring at Helen this whole time without saying anything. I try to smile, doing my best to let her know that everything's okay now, we're back to normal—or as normal as it gets after what happened today. "Yeah, sure. Whatever you need. Take your time."

She hesitates. "I think…I think they took my bag. Can I borrow one of your shirts?"

In the chaos of the afternoon, I hadn't even noticed she didn't have her luggage with her. They must have taken it when I went into the bathroom, probably hoping there'd be some clue inside as to where we were going. I always lock the doors, but I doubt that would be much of a roadblock to two mobster thugs. A sudden thought strikes me. "Did they get your phone?"

Helen shakes her head. "I threw it in the back seat, remember? After…"

After I accidentally saw those pictures of her in her underwear. I will not let myself think of that right now. The poor woman's been through trauma. I will not be the gross guy who is picturing her in red lacy panties after she almost got kidnapped. "Right. Shirt. You need a shirt." That's a nice distraction, at least, and I need something active to do to help her. I dig through my own bag and pull out a clean T-shirt. "Lucky that I overpack, eh?"

She gives me a wan smile, but at least it's a smile. It's the first trace of real emotion I've seen on her face since the police arrived. "Thanks."

"No problem. Let me know if you need anything else, okay?"

Without intending to, I reach up, gently touching the edges of the bruise blooming on her cheek. I never knew I could have such warring emotions inside of me. Rage at that bastard for hurting her, but also this…tenderness. I see the tears pricking her eyes and I instinctively cup the side of her face, careful not to touch the sore spot. "I've got you," I tell her earnestly. I wish I were more eloquent, that I could say it in a better, prettier way, but I need her to hear the words, even if they aren't polished. "I'm not gonna let anything happen to you."

Helen blinks rapidly, trying to smile, trying not to cry, as she nods into my palm. She reaches up, gripping my wrist for a moment.

Then she lets me go, and closes herself in the bathroom. A moment later, I hear the tub running. My mind instantly goes to Helen in that tub, warm water and bubbles enveloping her naked body…

Yep, that's what happens in a bathtub. I try to nip that line of thought in the bud right then and there, but my dumb brain keeps getting stuck. It would be creepy enough under normal circumstances, to be so immature about a woman taking a bath that I can't stop imagining her naked. But when you pair it with her almost getting kidnapped this afternoon, I feel like a complete dick. Seeing that guy grabbing her and throwing her to the ground awakened something almost primitive in me. I wanted to break every bone in his hand, throw *him* down onto the ground just to see how he liked it, let him and everyone else know that no one touches Helen like that and gets away with it. These aren't bad emotions, in and of themselves. I want to make sure she's safe, and that guy was trying to hurt her.

The problem is, the primitive man inside of me seems to have gotten loose with all that violence unleashed. I don't want to just stop at keeping Helen safe. I want to claim her as my woman. I want to take her mind off everything that happened today. I want to be in that bathroom with her, rubbing her neck and massaging her soapy breasts and reaching up between her legs…

Jesus. What the hell is wrong with me? I run over the list of reasons why Helen and I will never work out, yet again. Because she's an innocent and I'm an old jaded bastard. She's a nun, or she *was* a nun, and she's a good woman and a good person. She wants love, romance, babies. After what Vera pulled, I'm honestly not sure that's something I can offer to anyone ever again. But Helen deserves that. She doesn't deserve *me* out here fantasizing about her beautiful naked body or just how good I could make her feel…

I need something to do. Something active, to help her feel better. In her heart and mind and soul, not…anywhere else. I pace the room a moment, thinking through my options, before I realize the perfect thing.

Crossing the room to the phone, I dial down to the lobby. There's no way I'm going to leave Helen in here on her own, but this place is fancy enough and I'm paying enough money for the room that maybe I won't need to. "Hi, can I speak to the concierge, please? I need a favor…"

Chapter 29
Helen

I submerge myself up to my neck in the tub's hot water, piecing through the events of the day. There's a surreal quality to everything that happened, like it came from a movie I watched or a book I read. Like it didn't happen to me.

My sore body tells me otherwise. My cuts and bruises are superficial, but my side aches from when I was thrown onto the pavement. The human body isn't meant to be treated that way, and mine never has been. I've always been handled with kid gloves, I realize now, very rarely *touched*, much less manhandled.

A knock on the door startles me out of my thoughts. I stare, my muscles automatically tensing. "Who is it?"

A part of me knows that of course it must be Thad. He's been hovering around me ever since what happened at the gas station, and I believed him when he promised he wouldn't let anything else happen to me. When he looked deep into my eyes, his warm skin against mine, his voice low and ominous and gravelly.

For a brief moment, I think he might be knocking on the door to ask to come in here. Not just in the bathroom, but the tub. To massage my sore muscles and whisper words of comfort while he soaps my breasts, strokes my…

I inhale sharply against the thought. That's the sort of thing that would happen in one of my novels, not in real life.

This is not a romance, I remind myself.

I think I'm coping pretty well, all things considered, with nearly being kidnapped this afternoon by a member of the mob, but there has been one pretty weird side effect.

I cannot stop thinking about sex.

Every thought takes me in the same direction. Every road leads to the same destination. Everything in this freaking room is designed to turn me on, or so it feels. Like, I'm sorry, a bathtub big enough to fit two people? I wonder what *that* could be for. A transparent glass-doored shower? Yeah, like I'm supposed to look at that and *not* get completely hot and bothered by the idea of Thad standing in there, all naked and sexy and wet.

I wonder what Dr. Sandra would have to say about all of that? Probably, *"Go for it!"* So, I imagine what would happen if I did. If for some reason, in this unrealistic fantasy scenario, I'm unaware that Thad is showering and I wander in. I see his naked, lithe body, the crisscross of tattoos and smattering of scars. The crescent moon of his muscular buttocks in profile. I'm too startled to move, and he turns to face me. I don't mean to look, but my eyes dart down, down—

"It's Thad."

Right. I blink myself back into the actual, present moment in the bathroom, not the fantasy one where I'm ogling this man's naked body, and chastise myself to pay attention to what he's telling me.

"…I don't mean to interrupt you but I have something for you, for the bath. I can just leave it here if you'd rather wait for another time…"

If I didn't know better, I'd say he sounded almost nervous. Afraid he might actually leave, I sit up, calling out quickly, "I'm coming! Wait just a moment…"

I think about opening the door in just a towel, but despite my fantasy about him joining me in the bath, I'm not actually that brave. Instead I put on one of the soft robes hanging on the back of the door, making sure all of my bits are covered up, before I open it.

Thad stands on the other side, shifting from foot to foot and not quite meeting my gaze as he thrusts something toward me. "Here. I thought you might like some things for the bath. It's okay if you don't want them. So… here."

He thrusts a small bag toward me. Perplexed, I take it from him, peering inside to find a few items: bubble bath, gourmet chocolate, and a book. Pulling the book from the bag, I find it's a standard bodice-ripper romance. It's not one I've read before, though I've heard the title.

Looking up again, I study his face. He's still not making eye contact, and he's rubbing the back of his neck. If I were to hazard a guess, he didn't choose this book himself, but asked someone to pick out a romance, hoping I would like it.

The thought warms me from the inside out, and I feel my own blush rising. "Thank you, Thad." Clutching the book to my chest, I impulsively lean forward, kissing him on the cheek.

When I pull back, he finally meets my gaze. We hold there for a long moment, lost inside of something.

Then Thad clears his throat, swallowing—hard—as he steps away. "Okay, well. Enjoy. Give a shout if you need anything."

His tone is so curt and matter-of-fact that I might have almost convinced myself I was imagining that *moment* between us—if I didn't see him reach up to touch his cheek where I'd kissed him, just before I shut the bathroom door.

I can't stop thinking about that moment, replaying it again and again in my mind after I slip back into the bath. I try to read the book Thad gave me, but my mind won't stay on the words in front of me. I eat a bit of the chocolate but don't actually taste any of it.

Everything feels awake and alert and *wanting*. And not just my body. My thoughts circle around him, always drawn back toward him. Only him.

Thad.

When I'm finished bathing, I put on Thad's T-shirt, inhaling and recognizing the smell of his detergent. The thought makes me grin at myself in the mirror. What a creep. I imagine burrowing up against him, smelling his scent, getting twisted up in him…

I know I should stop, nip this line of thinking in the bud. When I go back out there, we will likely have reset back to normal. He'll be grouchy and distant, I'll be overcompensating-ly cheerful and obnoxious. To imagine any other scenario is probably setting myself up for disappointment.

But…what if that didn't happen? What if, instead of letting both of us fall back into our comfortable patterns, I decided to shake things up?

Some rational part of me warns that this is probably just a weird side effect of what happened to me this afternoon. Shock or PTSD or something else that's messing with my usual common sense.

But another, hornier part of me remembers the thought I just can't seem to shake since what happened this afternoon.

I don't want to die before having sex.

I mean, I don't want to die *period*. Maybe I'm being hyperbolic for suggesting that I was close to dying this afternoon. Regardless, the same thought stands. I don't want to die before having sex. I don't. I know there are other great things to experience, and not everyone gets to or wants to have sex in their lifetime. I get it. I'm on board. But I don't want to be one of those people.

I want to have sex before I die.

Preferably, with Thad.

The recognition of this honestly startles me. For so long sex has been this scary, foreign, unknowable thing that I feared almost as much as I craved. Maybe there's still some fear mixed in there, but it's like something happens to my body when I'm around him. I've never experienced this kind of feeling before, and it is heady. I want to walk out there in just a T-shirt and underwear, and I want him to want me to do that. I want to see him taking me in, unable to tear his eyes away.

I want him to *want* me.

With that thought in mind, I tousle my freshly blow-dried hair. All of my makeup was stolen with my bag, but I use the good old-fashioned method of pinching my cheeks to give them a bit of color. Finishing, I take a step back to honestly evaluate myself in the mirror and make sure I'm not making a ridiculous spectacle of myself.

Voluminous hair, extra big from just being dried. Fresh, rosy face, whether from the cheek-pinching trick or my own embarrassment at what I'm about to attempt, it's unclear. Thad's T-shirt, a little big on me, but still close-fitting enough that it's fairly obvious I'm not wearing a bra underneath. My breasts, which I have kept hidden for most of my life, seem eager to make their debut, my nipples hard and poking through the thin fabric of the shirt. The hemline covers most of my underwear, but a tiny little flash of purple cotton peeks through.

I look…sexy.

I *feel* sexy.

And it's absolutely terrifying.

Chapter 30
Helen

T had has the TV on when I come out of the bathroom, and he's found the classic movie channel again. It's playing a film I don't recognize, though from the dark coloring and intense expressions on the characters' faces, I'm guessing it's another noir.

He glances over at me, then immediately does a double take, eyes wide as he does a slow swallow that sends a little thrill of anticipation through me.

This is exactly the response I was hoping for, but I realize all at once that I have no idea where to go from here, and it makes me nervous. And when I'm nervous, I apologize. "Sorry! I didn't want to sleep in my jeans, so…is this okay?"

Thad looks me over one more time before forcing his eyes back to the TV screen. And yes, I know I'm a bit biased, but I don't think *forcing* is putting it too strongly. I can feel his energy still honed in on me, even though he isn't looking at me, even though he's trying his best to keep his eyes glued to the television. "Fine," he says, doing another heavy swallow.

I'm thrilled at his reaction. Short of him rushing across the room to throw me onto the bed, this feels like a best-case scenario. I know I don't have much experience with this—okay, *any* experience with this—but it feels like this response is good. He's attracted to me. He might not be overwhelmed with burning lust, but he's definitely aware of me in a nonplatonic way.

I think? I hope? Self-doubt quickly starts to set in, even as I do my best to stay confident and committed to my plan. It might only be that I've made him uncomfortable by dressing this way. I don't actually know what it feels like to have a man want to sleep with me. It's entirely possible that all of this is only in my own head, and he's wondering why the weirdo nun is walking around in her underwear while he's trying to watch a movie in peace.

I almost convince myself to retreat back into the bathroom and put on my pants again, but I stop myself. I know what I saw on his face, in his eyes. He's holding back, but maybe it's just because I haven't made clear what I want.

How one goes about doing that, I'm not entirely sure. In my romance novel, Rosamund knows from the beginning that Axel is driven to distraction by his desire for her. It's never a question of *if*, only *when*.

Worrying my lip, I glance at the TV screen that Thad hasn't removed his eyes from since I came out of the bathroom. A strikingly beautiful woman is pouting at the detective, eyes gleaming with mischief. She is wicked, confident, irresistible. Thinking back on what I saw from Vera in old episodes of *Bama Bounty*, she had a similar quality to her. This must be the kind of woman Thad wants.

I can be confident, I resolve with myself. *I can!*

Clearing my throat, I move over to the dresser, trying my best to walk sexily, not entirely certain what that looks like but determined to capture it. My body feels unnaturally aware of itself as I try to sway my hips and draw attention to my backside. Bottoms are sexy, right?

With my back to Thad, I pick up my phone, clearing my throat again. "Oh no." I look back at him over my shoulder with a little pout, trying to mimic the expression of the woman on the screen. "My phone's almost dead. Can I borrow your charger?"

Thad steels himself before looking at me. His eyes hone in on my face, seeming to hesitate before traveling down my body again. "Sure. My phone's been plugged in a while, so you can unplug it."

This might be the least sexy conversation two people have ever had together. Nonetheless, I press on, determined to get him hot and bothered. "Where is it?"

He motions to an outlet next to the sofa he's sitting in, opposite from where I'm standing, so it's blocked from my view. "I can toss it to you—"

"No, it's fine." A sudden idea strikes me and I saunter across the room again, hips swaying violently. There's plenty of space for me to just walk around the chair to access the charger, but instead I stop right in front of him and lean across him to reach for it. Our bodies are close enough that I can feel the heat coming off him, and I'm hyper-aware of my purple-underwear bottom sticking out. I'm pretty sure this would get him super excited, if he were a baboon. "There we go. Let me just stick it right in there…"

"Helen." Thad's voice sounds like I've never heard it before, sort of tight and curt, almost angry. "What are you doing?"

I straighten back up, trying to blink innocently, though I'm sure I'm red as a fire engine by now. "What do you mean?"

Again, his eyes stay honed in on my face, making some seriously intense eye contact. "You're all…wiggly, and talking in a weird voice. If I didn't know better…"

Wiggly? Weird? I am clearly not very good at this whole seduction thing, especially since he seems appalled to even put a name to what I'm trying to do. For some reason, unexpectedly, this brings out a surge of defiance in me. I fold my arms. "If you didn't know better, what?" Let him say it out loud, coward. I'm calling him on his bluff.

Thad seems to be struggling, and I realize why as his eyes finally dart away from my face, down to my chest. Frowning, I look down and see that the action of folding my arms has pulled the material even tighter over my breasts, not leaving much to the imagination.

When he looks into my eyes again, I feel a flutter of excitement run through me. Down there. In my panty region. It sends another surge of defiance through me. "If you didn't know better, what?" I demand again.

Thad is glaring at me—and okay, sure, *anger* wasn't at the top of my list of things I wanted him to feel, but for some reason that look makes me feel even more hot and bothered. "You're playing with fire, Helen. If you want something from me, you can't trick me into doing it. *You* have to be the one to say it."

He's right, darn him. If I'm going to be brave, I have to actually be brave, not just dangle myself in front of him and hope he'll take the bait. "Okay."

I'll take him up on his dare. I'll tell him, outright, that I want to have sex with him.

Only, as my mouth runs dry at the thought, I realize it's not quite that simple. Being that forthright, saying the actual words, is genuinely terrifying.

I wet my lips with my tongue, mostly for something to do, and feel another flutter of something as I see Thad's eyes follow the motion. "I want you to touch me," I say, breathlessly.

I must sound a little too winded, because Thad raises a skeptical eyebrow. "I don't think it counts if you can't say it without hyperventilating."

The challenge in his tone ignites something in me. "Then let me tell you *where* I want you to touch me."

His gaze intensifies, something scorching flashing through his eyes. He swallows. "Where do you want me to touch you?"

My arms fall down to my sides. I tentatively reach up one hand to touch my lips. "Here." I let my fingertips drift down the side of my face to touch my neck, the rest of my body already shivering. "Here."

I know where I'd want him to go next, but I hesitate, suddenly shy. No, not shy, *afraid*. I realize all at once that he's right—this is playing with fire. What will I actually do if he touches me where I ask him to?

Thad's gaze softens a little, and he looks away, running a hand over the back of his neck. "It's okay, Sister Helen. It's not too late to stop the game now."

He starts to stand up, and I know he'll find some excuse to lock himself in the bathroom, go get another room, or do something else that will end this moment forever.

"No!" Without thinking I move forward and stop him from getting up, pushing him back into the chair. He sits back warily, looking up at me.

"Everywhere," I tell him. "I want you to touch me everywhere."

A long moment passes. Something shifts on his face and he reaches for me, slowly, like he's waiting to see if I'll pull away. When I don't, he rests his hands on my hips, the thumb on his right hand playing with the hemline of the shirt.

It's such a little gesture, but it sets my whole body on fire, and I'm no longer shy, no longer afraid. Well, no, that's not exactly true, but those feelings become muted. The need throbbing between my legs drowns out any other feeling. "Please. Please, Thad."

He sighs raggedly, not advancing, but not releasing me either. "I want to, Helen. That's not the issue. But I don't want to take advantage of you when you're vulnerable. Your first experience, it should mean something—"

"I don't care if it means anything," I blurt out, and it isn't just the lust speaking. Maybe I'll regret this in the morning, but right now, I've never meant anything more in my life. "I'm thirty-one years old and I've never been touched by anyone. I'm not asking you to make any promises. I know this isn't some romantic fantasy. I just want to feel something. Please. *Please—*"

I guess it's the second please that does it. All at once, Thad pulls me forward, onto his lap. It's clumsy and I'm not expecting it, so I have to readjust myself so I'm straddling him. He twines his fingers into my hair and pulls me into a kiss, not gentle or exploratory like the first time we tried this. This kiss engulfs me, drowns out the rest of the room, the rest of the hotel, so nothing exists except for him and me.

Even if I wanted to laugh this time, I couldn't, because as our mouths are fusing, I feel his hands moving away from my hips. Roaming over my backside first, then up my back, around to my stomach, before finally finding my breasts.

I gasp into his mouth and Thad pulls away. *"Fuck."*

I already feel bereft of his mouth and am about to chase his lips when I catch his expression. He is watching my breasts as he fondles them, seeming mesmerized. His thumbs chase my nipples, still peeking through the thin fabric of the T-shirt, and he circles them again and again.

At my gasp, Thad looks into my eyes. What he's doing to my body feels incredible, but it's honestly almost eclipsed by seeing his response to me. Being desired by him is a heady high, and I want him to keep going, to do whatever he wants to do to me, so long as it keeps that look on his face.

"Thad," I breathe.

He captures my mouth again, hands releasing my breasts. I almost protest until I feel his fingertips sliding underneath the hem of my shirt and moving, ghost-light, over my skin, until he reaches my breasts again. His skin on my bare skin is electric. His mouth moves to the shell of my ear, down my neck, as he kneads my breasts. Almost unbelievably, his hot breath and warm mouth on my neck feels even more amazing than his hands on my breasts, but the dual sensation has my core throbbing. I am straddling one of his legs and start shamelessly thrusting against it, trying to relieve some of the pressure I feel building there.

"Fuck," he says again, breathing it into my neck this time. "You need this, don't you?"

With one hand, he reaches down to cup me over my panties. I cry out, begging, gasping, bucking against him wildly. "You're so sexy," he tells me as he rubs his thumb over my nub, again and again and again. "You're so goddam sexy."

I come apart, shaking and gasping and clinging on to him. After my shudders have subsided, Thad kisses me, long and slow, then nudges my nose with his. "Do you want to stop there?"

A murmur of protest escapes my throat. I grip on to his shirt, holding him in place, not wanting to lose his warmth for even a moment. "Don't you dare."

He laughs, quietly, under his breath. Then, standing, holding me, he puts me onto the bed.

I watch, breathless, as he takes off his shirt, his pants, leaving only his underwear on. He is…wow. I didn't know people could look like that in real life. He's broader than I would have imagined under his clothing, his shoulders wide and sturdy, his chest a map of muscle and ink and hair and scars. His erection tents through the thin material of his boxer briefs, and I stare at it, mesmerized and a little afraid.

"Can I?" he asks, reaching for the hem of my shirt.

I nod, helping him pull it up over my head. His eyes travel over my body, snagging onto my breasts again, before they find mine. He moves over me so our torsos are pressed together, my breasts against his chest, only the thin fabric of my underwear and his boxers between us.

His body feels so right against my body. The press of his warm skin, his hard muscles, his soft hair against my skin, my nipples, sends an unexpected jolt of want back down to my core, making my breath catch in my throat. I thought I was done. I didn't know there was…more. He kisses me—not gently now, but urgently, and I can feel the shift in his touch as it becomes less about guiding me and more about him losing his control. His hands move to palm my breasts like he needs them, he needs to be touching them. I reach up to stroke his back, to tangle my hands in his hair, encouraging him, and he breaks the kiss to look into my eyes. There is something almost wild in his gaze, and I see him fighting to hold on to control.

I don't want him controlled. I don't want him worrying about taking things too far or hurting me. I want to make him feel what I'm feeling—helpless with want, a prisoner to my need. I slide my hands back down his back, over his ass, and encourage him into the cradle of my parted legs.

He groans as his erection pressed up against my core, his eyes losing focus for a moment before honing back in on my face, and the intensity there is maybe the most erotic thing that's happened between us. He thrusts against me, again and again, moving now with wild abandon. He was right before, that I needed this, but I understand he needs it, too, maybe just as much.

The sensation isn't enough to make me come again, but it feels so good, his hardness pressed against my softness, the soft material of my panties rubbing against my core. His rhythm builds to a frantic pace, and then he shudders and groans.

He's holding himself up on his elbows, but I reach up, stroking his back and encouraging him to rest down on top of me. The weight of his body on mine, our skin touching, his hand wandering up to gently stroke my breasts again…it's incredible. Overwhelming, but incredible.

After a while, he rolls over to lie beside me, holding my hand, his warm body pressed close to mine. As we drift off toward sleep, I assess what just happened. It wasn't quite sex, but it was much, much closer than anything else I've ever experienced. I feel like in the last hour, I've gone from never having had sugar to eating an entire birthday cake by myself. It feels almost surreal, like it couldn't have actually happened to me. It's something I've imagined for Rosamund, or one of my other characters. Not Sister Helen.

I wait for the guilt or shame to catch up with me. I've been told for most of my life that everything I just did was a sin. But it didn't feel like a sin as it was happening and it still doesn't now. It felt...incredible. Not just the physical sensations, but the closeness, the intimacy. I understand why it's such a rite of passage and people might call it life-changing...but at the same time, that depiction doesn't feel quite right. I've heard it described almost as a fantastical experience, but that makes it feel far removed from reality. And yet it's the *realest*, rawest experience I've ever had. It's unlike anything else that's ever happened to me, and yet it all felt natural, instinctive. It wasn't magical, it was...holy.

For me, anyway. I remind myself that Thad has never made any promises. He's never told me that he loves me or wants to be with me. This isn't *his* first encounter, and we didn't even have real sex. To him this was likely nothing special—and I don't mean that in a self-deprecating way, but a practical one.

It doesn't matter though. For me, it was something sacred, not shameful or sinful. Relieved, I let myself relax and fall into an easy sleep with him beside me.

Chapter 31
Helen

I'm the first one to wake up in the morning. Thad is still flat on his stomach, eyes closed, breathing slow and steady. His face looks soft and open in sleep, and I spend longer than I want to admit just studying his features.

Then, I do what any thirty-one-year-old virgin would do the first time she's been brought to orgasm by her longtime crush and wakes up still in bed with him.

I sneak into the bathroom so I can text my friends.

It's still early, but I know Matilda will be awake since she has to be at her job first thing, and I think Nina wakes up around now to make her family breakfast.

Knowing my audience, I decide to get straight to the point: We hooked up.

I chew on my thumb as I wait for a response, half listening for any sign of Thad. My phone buzzes a few seconds later.

Matilda: Penetration?

I boggle at the screen. Wow. I thought *I* was being blunt. Blushing, I clarify: No. Boobies were touched though, and some contact in the bathing-suit areas. I realize that even for me, a former nun, this might sound a little prudish, but Nina is in the group chat and I don't want her to spontaneously combust because I've been too graphic.

Matilda: Oral?

Jeez Louise, Matilda. I quickly type back: No.

Matilda: Then you didn't hook up. You fooled around.

I roll my eyes. This is such a Matilda move. Here I thought I was going to have my *Sex in the City* moment, celebrating a new sexual milestone with my friends, and instead I'm getting a lesson on hookup terminology.

Before I can retort back something snarky, a GIF comes through from Nina. Nina is, unexpectedly, a big GIF-fer. I'm not sure she entirely understands the concept, since her GIFs often don't seem to have anything to do with what's going on in the conversation. Case in point, in this conversation about whether I've hooked up or fooled around, Nina sends through a GIF of a sleepy cat falling off a couch... At least she's participating, which means her phone wasn't confiscated by her uncle again.

I sigh, typing. Okay, I *fooled around.* With the Red Unicorn. Orgasms were had. I'm only ⅓ a virgin now. Woohoo!

Nina sends the GIF from *The Office* where Michael excitedly sprays Erin with a bottle of champagne in celebration. This GIF at least makes sense, though I doubt Nina realizes her inadvertent double entendre. Or maybe she does…? Hard to say with that one.

Matilda: So are you together now?

The question shouldn't have been unexpected, but it still knocks the air out of me a bit. Last night, I'd resolved myself to it being an ambiguous, one-off experience that didn't need to have any particular meaning. This morning, I'm not so sure. I don't know how to act when he wakes up. I've been so focused on overcoming the hurdle of being a virgin to these physical experiences that I hadn't really thought through what it means to be a virgin to these *emotional* experiences. Matilda has told me about hookup culture and I've read online articles about dating, but it doesn't prepare you for the reality of knowing that last night someone was looking into your eyes as you climaxed and this morning you might be almost strangers again.

Do I just ask him about it, up front? That seems like the mature thing to do, and probably what Dr. Sandra would recommend if she were here. But I'm so afraid to show my lack of experience. What if it was obvious last night that this was a one-time thing, to anyone who has an understanding of these dynamics? Thad might have thought he'd made himself perfectly clear, but I'm too naive to get it, and I'll be putting us both in a hopelessly uncomfortable position by bringing it up this morning.

I don't think so, I type back. I think it was just a moment.

Matilda, unexpectedly, is the one to send through a GIF this time—of a woman rolling her eyes and shaking her head.

My heart sinks in my chest. It was obvious, wasn't it? There was some kind of code I was supposed to understand about what happened between Thad and me last night, but I didn't because I'm a loser who doesn't know anything about sex or relationships. Every time I take two steps forward, I take one step back.

Matilda: I knew this would happen. Just don't be surprised if things get weird. DON'T get clingy.

Nina, also uncharacteristically, replies with words this time: I don't think he would have done something if it didn't mean anything.

Matilda: He's a man. Of course he would.

Antonina: Men have feelings too.

Another GIF from Matilda, this time of a woman hysterically laughing.

Antonina: Just talk to him. Tell him what you want and ask him what he wants.

Matilda: Let HIM do the talking. Do not show any weakness. They can smell it like blood in the water.

I turn off my phone. Holy cannoli. I think I've made a huge mistake.

Chapter 32
Thad

Last night changed everything.

The memories come back to me even before I'm fully conscious again—Helen's beautiful, supple body moving under me, her warmth, her trust, her readiness. I could replay it a hundred times in my mind and still find some new detail to snag my attention, something I missed before that suddenly comes into sharp relief. It wasn't my first encounter, not by a long shot. I'm my father's son, as my mother likes to point out, and I've never lacked for attention. In the past, my partners have been more like Vera—dangerous, sleek, confident girls who came after me. There was never any mystery about *if* it was going to happen, only when. And don't get me wrong, I've always enjoyed myself, a lot, but it felt more like a team sport we were playing together, two athletes who knew the rules of the game and had played with many others before, showing off our best moves.

Nothing with Helen has been like that. She is not dangerous by any stretch of the imagination. Whenever I've tried to treat this like a game and assumed she'd understand the rules, she thwarts me at every turn. She is sunny when I expect her to be sexy. Wholesome where I'm used to dangerous.

But as easy as it would be to peg her as the good girl, I also can't fully explain to myself why last night was so hot. It was obvious she wasn't as experienced, didn't know the game, so to speak…but it also didn't feel like a game. We weren't competing. I wasn't trying to impress her and prove to her I wasn't like any guy she'd had before because—hey, there's never been any guy before.

I was supposed to be the one who knew what I was doing, but I was in uncharted territory, too. Because if it wasn't about showing off, winning some challenge, then what were we doing? I was kissing her because I *wanted* to kiss her, not prove to her I was the best kisser she'd ever been with. I wasn't trying to surprise her with any new moves, I was just trying to make her feel good, because I felt like she deserved it. And *I* wanted to be the one to make her feel that way.

What the hell is happening to me?

I even came inside my underwear like a teenager feeling up my first girl-friend, and I'm glad I have time to quickly clean myself up and change before I see her again. Any moment, Helen is going to come out of the bathroom, and I have no idea what to say to her. What I *should* say to her or even what I want to say to her. The right thing to do in this scenario would probably be to not feel up an ex-nun without having a clear idea the outcome I want. But since we've already crossed that bridge, I think the decent thing to do is to solidify that we're together now. You don't one-night-stand a nun.

So…we're together now. Okay. I try to wrap my head around that, what it will mean. Helen is my girlfriend. My girlfriend whose brother I'm about to send back to prison—for his own good, but still. Moving past that, we put Dean in jail, drive back to Chicago, and…stay in each other's lives. Go to church together, probably, which I can deal with. Bonus points since it'll drive my megachurch-going Dad crazy that I'm switching over to the Catholics. And all the other stuff couples do, too—movies, food, markets, learning what we each like.

Spending some nights at her place and some at mine. Trading off who gets to pick movies. Old classic film noirs when I get to choose, of course, and probably rom-coms when it's her turn. I can deal with that.

I'll impress her with my gumbo. I can cook other things all right, but that's the one recipe I'm confident will knock her socks off. I know she likes to bake, so I'll have to spend more time at the gym to keep myself in fighting shape. I wonder if she'd like to come with me. I imagine those curves in spandex, heads turning as she walks across the gym floor. Knowing Helen, she'll be totally oblivious and think the dude at the weights who's trying to get in her pants is just a nice, helpful guy.

But with Helen, I know I'll never really have to worry on that front. There's something in her that's genuinely kind, guileless. I know instinctively that she would never hurt me, and in turn that makes me determined to never hurt her, or let anyone else get the chance.

I imagine lazy Sundays, sleeping in, then *not sleeping* but still staying in bed. This is all new to her, so I won't rush things, but I think I'll honestly enjoy that. Taking our time to get to know each other, figuring out what she likes, what she needs. Getting to see those red lacy panties in person, getting to be the one to take them off. Knowing when I find sexy pictures on her phone that she's taking them for me.

Holy shit. My heart is hammering in my chest with how much I want it all. I don't know how it blindsided me like this, how I didn't see it crawling up on me.

Helen's my woman. My sweet, awkward, sexy woman.

As if on cue, the bathroom door opens and Helen peers into the room, starting at the sight of me awake. Her head disappears from view, then reappears a moment later, and somehow I know she was in there coaching herself to come out and talk to me. "Um. Hi. Good morning."

I grin back at her, unable to hide my good mood. "Good morning."

Helen does a little double take, like she's taken aback by my cheerfulness. I guess I must've been a pretty sour bastard this whole trip if the sight of me smiling is *confusing* to her. I'll have to make it up to her.

"Hi," she says again, which lets me know she's nervous. It's kind of cute, how nervous she is. "Can you close your eyes?"

I frown in confusion, and my face must be so much more used to frowning than smiling because I feel my muscles relaxing instinctively. "Why?"

Helen's floating head blushes pink. "I need to run back to the bed and I'm not wearing any pants."

I can't help but laugh. "Are you serious?" A few hours ago we were basically naked together, but now she can't let me see her without pants on.

"Yes."

"Nah," I return, propping up my pillows so I can settle back against the headboard. "Think I'd rather enjoy the show."

"Thaddeus!"

She's never used my full name before. I think it's probably meant to sound intimidating, but she's about as intimidating as a baby chicken. I just grin at her, waggling my eyebrows. "Come on. Don't be shy. If it'll make you feel better, I'll take off my pants, too."

The sound she makes is kind of a weird half gasp, half strangled growl. The bathroom door shuts again. A moment later, it reopens and she edges into the room, eying me warily. She holds one of the white bathroom towels tightly around her waist, obscuring her bottom half.

If she'd just walked out wearing that in the first place, I don't think I would have made any kind of fuss. But the theatrics of it all—that look she's giving me and the way she's gripping the towel and edging along the wall like she's waiting for me to grab her and tear that towel off… Well, it makes me want to grab her and tear that towel off.

"Sister Helen," I tease her, "you know you can't play hide-and-seek with a bounty hunter. It triggers my feral instincts—like if you run from a dog, it has to chase you. If you hide from a bounty hunter, he has to come find you."

I give her my best smolder—the one my fans used to make into wallpapers for their computer screens. I guess I still got it, since she blushes, and I see her nipples start to pebble underneath her shirt.

No, strike that. *My* shirt. I was just playing around up until now, but the recognition of that makes my dick instinctively harden. My shirt on *my* woman. I'm going to get that towel off her if it's the last thing I do.

Helen must see the shift in my eyes because she puts even more distance between us, and a sofa. "Wait just a minute, Thad. Let me put on some pants and then we can talk…"

"We can talk after," I promise her, already off the bed and calculating the swiftest route across the room to get to her.

She still looks a little wary, but I can tell she's intrigued, too, by the way she bites her lower lip. "After what?"

"After I give you at least one more orgasm. Maybe two."

I give her just long enough to process that before I jump into action, hurdling over the sofa, grabbing her, and dragging her back down onto the cushions with me. I'm quick, but I don't think it's my imagination that she didn't try all that hard to get away from me. Her eyes are a vivid, electric blue as I hold her gaze, reaching down to tug the towel away.

"Thad," she moans, but makes no move to push me away.

What I really want to do is use this towel to tie her wrists over her head and make good on my promise. But I'm guessing that'll probably be too much, too fast, so I temper down the urge and kiss her, slowly, easing her into the moment as I feel her body shift and open up beneath me. I slide my thigh between her parted legs, pressing it against her core, and she gasps into my mouth.

My head is already spinning and we haven't even really done anything yet. My mind is racing through all the different ways to make her feel good, to try something she's never experienced before. It's like when you show a movie you love to someone who's never seen it, and you have to keep yourself from looking at them during all the best parts, just to see their reaction.

I already know in this scenario, I won't be able to keep myself from looking at her during the best parts, just to see her reaction.

Last night I paid a lot of attention to her breasts, and I'm more than half tempted to do the same this morning. They're spectacular breasts. I could spend all day touching them, holding them, rubbing them, sucking them. But she was going through such trouble to cover up her panties with that damn towel—maybe because last night we barely scratched the surface with just how good I can make her feel down there.

I think we better rectify that situation pretty quick.

Taking my time, I trail my hand down the length of her body, teasing up the soft skin of her thighs around her panty line, dipping a finger into the waistband, listening to her soft, urgent gasps, feeling the way she's already pressing into me. "Is this off-limits? Is that why you were hiding it from me?"

"N-no," she stammers, swallowing heavily. "I just didn't know if…if that was a one-time thing or…I didn't want to be presumptuous."

That draws me up short, and I still my hand. Is that what I'm being right now? Presumptuous? "Did you want it to be a one-time thing?"

Her eyes, which were at half-mast just moments before, fly wide open, searching mine. "Do you?"

"I assumed it wouldn't be," I tell her, not really thinking through the words, just speaking honestly. "I mean, with someone else, maybe, but not you."

I expect her to take that as a compliment, because that's how it's intended, but she frowns at me, her gaze intent. "What do you mean?"

I feel like I've accidentally stumbled into some dangerous territory, but I don't know how. I figure the best course is to just stay honest, as honest as I can. "Well, I know you aren't very experienced, because of the whole nun thing."

Her frown only deepens. "So you only want to keep fooling around with me because I'm not very experienced. You feel…sorry for me?"

"No! God no." I wince, remembering her earlier reactions to taking the Lord's name in vain. "*Gosh* no." Now that just sounds stupid coming out of a grown man's mouth, but I barrel on: "You're a good person. A good girl. A guy doesn't mess around with a good girl if he doesn't mean it."

She looks at me like I'm speaking gibberish—which, for the record, I'm not. I think it's totally fine if men, women, aliens, cows, want to have no-strings-attached fun, but if you sleep with a virgin ex-nun, then you go into it knowing that it's not a casual encounter. There are partners with whom you both know the score, and it's just messing around, and then there are partners you fall in love with.

Helen is in the falling-in-love-with category.

It's a compliment, but she really doesn't seem to take it that way. She puts a hand to my chest, forcing me back, and sits up, drawing in her legs. "Do you actually want to pursue something with me, or do you just think you should because I'm a 'good' girl?" She actually puts air quotes around the word "good," and I might find it adorable, if I weren't so totally confused about what's happening.

I honestly have no idea how to answer this. It feels like a trick question. Yes, I want to be with her, and yes, I think she's a good person. It's part of why I want to be with her. I'm not sure how one of these things is an insult, but it clearly is, and I'm walking through some kind of land mine that I don't totally understand.

Which is why I maybe give the worst answer of all time to a woman who asks if you want to be with her: "Yeah," I say, and shrug.

Take notes, Shakespeare. It was practically a whole goddam sonnet in one word.

The look she gives me is like a tiny kitten whose tail I've just stepped on. Before I can stop her, she's off the couch, retreating from me. "Wait—" I try, but she holds up her hands, stopping me.

"It's okay. Really. It's totally fine. You don't have to…I mean, you don't owe me anything. I knew this wasn't going to be a thing. Not long-term, anyway."

I'm the one to draw up short this time, blinking at her. "You did?" The whole time that I was thinking about us as a possibility, I for some reason took it as a given that she would want to be in a relationship with me, too. Not that I think I'm some great prize, or anything—Vera made the opposite clear to me when she left me for my *father*, thank you very much—but more so because of Helen's lack of experience. Her innate goodness. I assumed she'd want to be in a relationship, and if for some reason she wanted it to be with me, then who was I to argue?

But the more I think about it, the more I realize how shortsighted I was. She doesn't have any experience, or at least she didn't before last night. Maybe I'm the kind of guy you just play around and have fun with, not the kind you want to have lazy Sunday mornings with. Again, there is the glaring example of my fiancée leaving me for my father but still sending me thirst traps.

Helen is the one to shrug this time, not quite looking at me. "We're so different." Her gaze finally meets mine, and she looks at me expectantly, like she's waiting to see if I'll take the bait.

I get it. She wants to make sure I understand we're not compatible. She's a good woman, the kind of woman you marry. And I'm…a bounty hunter.

I nod curtly to show I understand. "Got it."

For a second, we both linger, neither of us seeming sure what to do. I clear my throat. "We should probably get on the road, try to make up for lost time…"

We still have about two and a half hours before we make it to New Orleans, after all. Nearly three hours, stuck together, in the car. That had been difficult enough when I was just attracted to her, but now I have real feelings for her. Now I know what she looks like when she's sleeping and the sounds she makes when she's turned on and the way her breasts feel in my hands.

Great. It's gonna be one hell of a day.

Chapter 33
Helen

What's worse than the third day in a row of hours upon hours of driving, you ask?

Hours upon hours of driving in a car, sitting next to a guy who gave you a pity orgasm and then felt like he was obligated to keep dating you because you're such a loser.

I'm starting to understand now why Dr. Sandra always insisted that sex wasn't going to answer all of my problems. I still haven't had sex yet, but even getting close to it has opened up a whole new can of worms. All the easy banter from the past couple of days is gone, and Thad and I have retreated into our opposite corners of our personalities. The more uncomfortable I get, the more I try to talk, hoping through sheer force of cheerfulness I can overcome the awkwardness in the car. And it seems the more uncomfortable Thad gets, the quieter he gets, becoming practically monosyllabic.

Exhibit A: This short snippet of our conversation—

Me, seeing a sign advertising boiled peanuts at a gas station: "Oh, yeah, I forgot that boiled peanuts were a Southern thing. But why boiled? Who decided, here's this peanut, I think I oughta boil this sucker and see how it tastes. How does it taste, anyway? Have you ever had them before?"

Thad: "Yep."

Me: "Do they boil them with any kind of flavoring? Does boiling them make them softer?"

Thad: "Can't remember."

Me: "So it's not something Southerners eat regularly, then? I guess not, since they sell them at the gas station. I can't really think of any gas station foods that I eat regularly. Nacho cheese, hot dogs, Slurpees. Maybe it falls into the same category of so-bad-it's-kind-of-good? Or is it the rare gas station treat that really transcends its surroundings?"

Thad: "Couldn't say."

So, yeah, take that and multiply it by about an hour and a half, and that's the trip in a nutshell.

By the time we make it to Gulfport, I think both of us are desperate to get out of the car and have a moment to ourselves. Even so, Thad surprises me by stopping me before I can go inside to use the restroom. "When you come back outside, come straight to the car. Don't go anywhere else without me."

In all the emotional turmoil and awkwardness of the morning, it somehow keeps slipping my mind that I was almost kidnapped yesterday. I know that must sound kind of idiotic, but it feels like something that happened in a movie I saw or a book I read. It does not feel like something that could happen to me in real life. I'm just boring Helen, recreational puzzler and eater of boxed macaroni and cheese. I am not the ideal candidate for a kidnapping.

"I won't," I promise, offering him what I hope is a reassuring smile before I disappear inside.

At least there's still that, I muse. Sure, it sucks that Thad doesn't see me as an actual romantic prospect, just someone he wanted to help get some experience; but I think on some level he does care about me. At least enough that he doesn't want me to get kidnapped. It's a small victory, but it's still a victory, isn't it?

We can be friends. Maybe someday, a long time from now after the dust has settled, we'll look back at that one time we messed around in a hotel room in Mobile and laugh about how foolish we were. The pang in my heart at the idea tells me this isn't something that's likely to happen *soon*, but…maybe someday.

When I make it back outside, I'm surprised to see Thad standing over Kitty, the hood popped open. His sleeves are pushed up as far as they can go, his hands and forearms covered with grease, and he's swearing softly under his breath.

If I didn't remember that we're just friends and that nothing romantic is going to happen between us again, I might feel another pang at how sexy he looks all greased up and glistening, forearms straining, oiled muscles rippling as he moves—

Instead I force myself to focus on the obvious problem at hand. "What's going on? Is Kitty okay?"

Thad straightens at the sound of my voice but continues frowning down at the interior of the car. "The check engine light was flashing earlier when we were driving, but Kitty does that sometimes when she's getting overheated. I thought after we got gas and took a break, she would be fine again, but now the car's not starting."

Getting stranded in Mississippi tonight might actually be worse than being stuck back in the car together. I imagine the awkwardness when we get separate rooms, the mortification at knowing he's probably relieved to have his own space.

But that is not a particularly helpful train of thought at the moment, and I'm nothing if not helpful. It's ingrained in my very being—Girl Scout turned sister turned librarian. I live to be of service. "Is there someone we can call? AAA, or does your insurance policy have a tow service?"

Thad runs a hand over the back of his neck, letting out a frustrated sigh. "Probably, but that's gonna put us back at least another day." He seems just as thrilled by that prospect as I am.

And of course. For him, this was always about finding Dean. I was stupid to ever lose sight of that.

"Hey, y'all okay?"

I turn, surprised to see two pretty, twentysomething girls approaching us. They both have bleached-blonde hair, lots of makeup, and they're wearing similar versions of halter tops, short shorts, and platform sandals.

They look great, and it makes me feel conspicuously underdressed in my day-old sweater, underwear, and pants. In my defense, my luggage *was* stolen by the mafia.

I hold up a hand against the sun so I can see them better, trying to smile. "We're having a little car trouble." And yes, maybe it's a sneaky thing to do, to phrase it as *we* to make clear that *we're* traveling together, even if it's in a totally platonic capacity. They don't have to know that, now do they? "Do you know of any mechanics nearby?"

"Oh, no!" The Southern twang is strong with these two, much more pronounced than Thad's own muted accent. "We're not actually from here."

"We're visiting from Ole Miss," the first girl confirms. "On our way to New Orleans for spring break with some other Delta Gammas."

Sorority girls. That makes sense, and maybe explains why they both look sort of vaguely similar, like they're in uniform, even though they're not.

Thad straightens, turning back to face us for the first time. He's frowning, absent-mindedly wiping off his greased-up hands on a rag. "How far is New Orleans from here? Are there any buses that run through?"

He must be pretty desperate to get to Dean, if he's even considering leaving Kitty behind.

Before the first girl can respond, the second gasps, clutching her friend's arm—and staring at Thad's face like it's the 1960s and she's just run into a Beatle. "Oh my God, Cassie." To Thad, she half points, half shouts, "It's you! *Bama Bounty*!"

Cassie's jaw drops, too. "It's you, isn't it? Thad!"

Thad shifts uncomfortably, his eyes darting to mine. He tries to smile. "Uh, yeah. That's me. How do you even know what that show is? It's been off the air since you were in grade school."

That's an exaggeration, but not by much. The two girls giggle, clutching at each other like they can't believe their luck. "We watch it every Friday night as a sorority. It's *our* show."

Girl Two nods her confirmation, still giggling. "We take a drink every time you take off your shirt."

I didn't think it was possible, but Thad is actually blushing. "Oh," he says, seemingly for lack of anything better to say. His gaze snags mine, and I don't miss the sheer discomfort in his expression.

I step in closer to Thad, feeling weirdly protective. Or maybe that's not the right word. Maybe it's more like *possessive*. I know we're just friends, but I do not like the idea of a bunch of sorority girls ogling Thad's body and acting like he belongs to them because it's *their* show.

"The girls are gonna lose their shit when they hear about this!" Cassie half whispers to the other one, then turns back to us. "Are you heading to New Orleans?" She gives me a quick, appraising look. "Is this your girlfriend?"

My mouth runs dry, but before I can say anything, Thad slips his hand into the back pocket of my jeans and pulls me up against his side. "Yep. This is my girlfriend, Helen."

I know he's only saying that to keep the sorority girls from fighting over him like he's the last big-screen TV on Black Friday. I know it doesn't mean anything. But feeling our bodies pressed together (and his hand on my butt!)… hearing him say that I'm his girlfriend…it makes me feel something. Something I know I shouldn't be feeling, but there you go.

Cassie appraises me for a moment longer before nodding. "She's so much better than Vera. I can't believe what she did to you. What a bitch."

Weirdly, it makes me warm to the girl. I mean, not that she called Vera a b-i-t-c-h—I don't like that language, and we're all children of God, after all—but knowing they really are in Thad's corner, even if they might still try to rip off his shirt if they get a chance. I smile back at them as a new idea starts to form in my mind. "She really is, isn't she? And to answer your earlier question, we *are* going to New Orleans. It's pretty urgent, actually." I lower my voice to a conspiratorial whisper. "Thad's on a case."

Thad shifts against me. "Helen," he starts warningly.

I ignore him, still grinning at the girls, who look absolutely thrilled that they've been let in on this secret. "I really hate to ask this, but…you don't happen to have any extra room in your car, do you?"

It's a long shot, but you never know. It doesn't hurt to ask, and sometimes the good Lord does provide.

Cassie and her friend exchange a glance. "Well, we do, but…it's not really a car."

She motions back to a vehicle parked at the far end of the parking lot—a party bus, absolutely teeming with sorority girls.

…which is how I wind up in a party bus full of singing and dancing sorority girls, on my way to New Orleans, sitting on Thad's lap.

Sitting on Thad's lap. Just in case you missed that part.

Turns out there are very few actual seats on a party bus. Most of the space is taken up by the minibar, the stripper pole (dear Lord), and a space for a large-screen TV. In Thad's honor, the girls put on episodes of *Bama Bounty* streaming in the background.

The girls are all pretty sweet, if a little overexcited to get to be near Thad. Most of them are already doubled up in the seats, which doesn't seem all that safe to me, but I'm trying very hard not to give off mom vibes and so I've refrained from commenting on it. A few offered to double up with Thad, too, but between his image on the jumbo TV screen and a few girls suggesting more than once that he can totally use the stripper pole if he wants, Thad has become the equivalent of a human turtle, withdrawing into his shell as much as possible.

"I'll sit with Helen," he speaks up quickly after the third seat-buddy offer gets made. "My girlfriend, Helen."

I know he's only using me as a shield because he's scared of the boisterous twentysomethings, but I still feel stupidly giddy every time he refers to me as *his*. And yes, I know this man only sees me as a friend, a sad little ex-nun who needed a little boost of sexual confidence. My mind knows this, but my heart does not care. It is programmed to be entirely too responsive to Thad, and I don't know how to access the factory reset.

Thad's quite a bit larger than the itty-bitty sorority girls who are doubling up on each seat, and my bottom is also no size 0, so we aren't doubling up so much as I am in this man's lap. I sit sideways with my legs across him, my left arm pressed to his chest, and I can feel the faint rhythm of his heart beating against me, his warm breath stirring my hair. I am aware of every single part of us that is touching—one of his hands on my leg, my thighs pressed against his. The side of my bottom is pressed up against his groin, my breasts roughly at his eye level, coming dangerously close to smashing into his face every time the bus jolts or moves too quickly, and I'm doing my best not to think about last night, that intense look in his eyes as he ground his hard erection against my panties...the groan he made when his hands closed over my naked breasts...

No, Helen. No. Pure thoughts. I start mentally reciting the lineage of Abraham, which is the least sexy thing I can think of and will hopefully take my mind off Thad's body and just where it's touching mine.

Abraham, Isaac, Jacob and Esau, Reuben, Simeon, Gad, Asher...

"So how did y'all meet?"

It takes me a moment to realize the question is being addressed to me. Twenty pairs of young eyes watch me expectantly, waiting for my answer.

"Oh, well..." I'm not a great liar. If there's a clear purpose in sight, like sweet-talking my way onto a party bus, I can sometimes manage it, but lying just for the sake of lying has never been my strong suit. Even before I was a sister, if I did something that I knew would upset my parents, I would just give myself up before they even had the chance to question me, knowing it was a fruitless endeavor. I can't fathom lying to these girls and actually managing to be convincing about it, but the thought of admitting that I was untruthful feels absolutely mortifying.

Plus, then they'll all know that Thad and I aren't actually a couple, and I really don't want to see the knowing looks on their faces when they figure out the whole thing was just a sham. They're probably too Southern and polite to say it outright, but I'm sure the looks on their faces will clearly say, *Bless her soul, but she didn't* really *think we bought them as a couple, did she?*

"We actually—" I start, but Thad cuts me off.

"Helen's a librarian, up in Chicago. I went into her library to get some information about a case, but once I saw her, I just kept going back. At one point I was pretending to read about a book a day before I finally got the nerve to ask her out. Just so I could have the chance to see her."

The hand he still has resting on my leg squeezes just above my knee, and I relax a little. I should have known that being a good bounty hunter translated into being a good liar, too. A lot of what he's said is true, but he's spinning it so it sounds much more romantic than it actually was.

The girls aww approvingly at Thad's story. "I pretend to read all the time for my American Lit class, too," one girl chimes in, a little too enthusiastically, earning her a few laughs.

Cassie, the only girl whose name I know, leans forward in her seat. "What was it about her that drew you to her?"

I tense, feeling myself prematurely growing embarrassed at the thought of him having to scramble to come up with an answer. Beyond the obvious *Her proximity to her brother,* that is. "I don't—"

But once again, Thad beats me to the punch. "Her smile," he says without missing a beat. "Her warmth. Her kindness. The way any room gets brighter when she's in it."

Another chorus of awws follows his answer, but I'm so surprised I hardly notice it. For the first time since sitting on his lap, I turn so I can look directly into Thad's face, searching his expression with a quizzical smile. "You didn't really think that," I say quietly, just to him.

He doesn't say anything, but his eyes burn into mine, so intense I have to look away, flustered. He is very good at pretending, I'll give him that much.

"And what drew you to him?" one of the girls asks. "I mean, besides the obvious."

A round of laughter follows this, and I play along with it, trying not to let on how much the question flusters me. "He is very handsome, isn't he?" I wet my lips as I think of the best way to answer, before deciding to go with Thad's method—the truth, or at least a version of it. "I never thought he'd be interested in me in a million years. We're from different worlds."

The girls are fully invested now in the love story, many of them literally hanging off the edge of their seats. Of course, that might also be because of the tequila shots I saw them taking a few minutes ago. "Opposites attract though," Cassie speaks up sagely, in the manner of a girl who is wise beyond her years, or at least trying to sound that way. "Sweet and sour. Naughty and nice."

"That might be it," I agree, conscious of Thad's eyes watching me closely as I answer. "But I don't think so. I think we're actually not so different. Not where it counts. The more I've gotten to know him, the more I think we're both people who've been hurt before, and who are a little scared of letting other people see us for who we really are. We might just have different ways of showing it."

I don't know when this turned into a counseling session, or why I'm being so honest with these Delta Gamma girls. Maybe it's because I know I'll likely never see them again. Maybe because it's easier to say these things when I don't have to look at Thad.

"So is it true love?" another girl pipes up.

The question catches me so off guard, I'm startled into looking at Thad. We stare at each other for a long, silent moment, and I don't know how to read the intensity of his gaze. I'm both completely aware of our audience, and sucked into this vacuum of a moment, where it's only Thad and me, our faces mere inches apart, our eyes holding in an unspoken exchange. He gives a slow swallow, looking down at my lips, causing them to part as I take in a sharp, expectant breath.

"NOLA!"

The shouted exclamation from the group of girls pulls me right out of the moment. I look back, surprised to see that we appear to have reached the city. Many of the girls are suddenly standing on their seats, crowding together to try to stick their heads through the sunroof.

With all the happy, frenetic optimism of youth, they've forgotten about us in an instant. But my heart is still hammering in my chest, and I feel Thad's thudding in response behind me.

Chapter 34
Helen

After the party bus drops us off at the Four Seasons (of course Dean wouldn't use Aunt Linda's credit card to book a Motel 6), I let Thad work his bounty hunter magic with the clerk at the front desk to see what information he can find out about Dean's comings and goings. As I wait for him, I scroll through the photos on my phone of Aunt Linda's credit card bill, trying to put together a little map of all the places that Dean's been making significant charges. He seems to be staying within a pretty small radius, with most of the charges going toward take-out food, although there are a few places that stand out to me as being unfamiliar. When I do some digging, I find out most of those unfamiliar locations are casinos.

I shake my head. Typical Dean. He breaks his bail, which my parents will likely have to take out a second mortgage to pay, then goes on the lam, using Aunt Linda's credit card to rack up charges at fancy hotels and casinos like it's *his* money to blow through. Of all the inconsiderate people in the world, I think Dean might very well be at the top of the list.

There's one final charge from a place that I don't recognize. When I pull up its information online, my eyes widen.

This is it.

Thad rejoins me, looking flustered. He's doing that thing where he keeps running his hand over the back of his neck, and it makes my heart warm. I feel like I'm looking at the little-kid version of him instead of the tattooed bounty hunter man.

"The front desk clerk was no help. Refused to divulge any information about customers, blah, blah, blah."

I refrain from reminding him that it's part of that poor woman's job not to give out information about customers, since he looks so put out by the rejection. "Aww," I tease him, unable to help being amused by his predicament. "I bet you're used to batting those blue-gray eyes and getting whatever you want."

Those blue-gray eyes narrow in on me, at first looking a little annoyed with my teasing. But then his expression shifts as something seems to occur to him. "Blue gray? Is that what color my eyes are?"

Too late, I realize that this is the exact color I used to describe Axel's eyes, when I read my chapter out loud to the writing group. Axel, who is not-so-loosely based on Thad himself. It didn't occur to me until right this moment that Thad wouldn't already know his eyes were blue gray, but I guess you don't really think of your own eyes in those terms, since you don't spend a long period of time staring into them, getting lost in them…

"Um," I hedge, averting my own eyes. "They're in the blue category, for sure."

When I dare a glance back at Thad, he is studying me with a ghost of a smile on his face. "Believe me, blue-gray eyes or not, I don't get everything I want. Not on the first try, anyway."

What does *that* mean? I'm not entirely sure, but even so, I feel like someone has just sent an electric jolt straight to my core.

Flushing, I avert my gaze to the screen of my phone, trying to steady myself. This is why we're here. To find Dean, not to do—whatever we're doing.

"I found something," I tell him briskly, trying to keep my tone businesslike. I start to hold out the phone for him to look at it, but instead he comes over, right behind me, his chest pressing up against my back, his closeness making every nerve in my body stand on high alert. Shaking, but trying not to show it, I angle the screen up so he can see it. "Dean's made multiple charges to something called the Carolina Belle. When I looked it up, this is what I found."

"A floating casino," Thad murmurs, and he's so close to me I can feel the words vibrating through my skin.

"A floating casino that's docked a few blocks away. Dean seems to be spending an awful lot of time there." More so than any of the other casinos on the bill. There's no guarantee he'll go back to the Carolina Belle, of course, but if we're going to start anywhere…

"I need to be on that boat tonight," Thad says, drawing the same conclusion—well, partly.

I whirl around to face him, eyes wide at his audacity. "*We* need to be on that boat."

"Helen," he warns me through gritted teeth.

It's amazing to me how not two seconds ago my entire body was trembling because of his proximity, and now I'm so irritated that he could be standing in front of me totally naked, and the only thing that would matter would be making sure he admits that I'm right. "Don't *Helen* me. I found this information. I'm the one who knew how to find Dean at all. Without me you'd still be back in Chicago, checking out books that you're pretending to read and hoping he might randomly turn up."

Thad narrows his eyebrows at me. "Let me count the reasons why it would be a bad idea for you to come along. One, you're a civilian. I'm a trained, licensed bounty hunter. Two, Dean will recognize you the moment he sees you and might get spooked back into hiding. He doesn't know who I am or what I look like. And three, yesterday you were almost kidnapped. If I'm on a crowded boat looking for Dean, how am I supposed to keep my eye on you, too?"

The ire I feel rising after each of his first two points unexpectedly deflates at his last question. I know that maybe I should be belligerent, insisting I can take care of myself, that he won't need to look after me, but I'm sensible enough to know this probably isn't true. I don't have any training. And I would stick out like a sore thumb, in more ways than one. Aside from the obvious fact that Dean (and anyone looking for him) would likely recognize me, all of my clothes were stolen, and I'm stuck in the same jeans and sweater I've been wearing for two days. Plus it's not really the attire I think they're going for on a fancy floating casino, where the low-stakes bid is more than one month of my rent.

"Then what am I supposed to do?" I ask, feeling frustrated and helpless. "Just go on a ghost tour and eat beignets like my brother's life isn't in danger?"

Thad rubs the back of his neck again—that telltale sign I now realize is buildup to him telling me something I'll likely not want to hear. "You need to stay at the hotel." At my jaw drop, he holds up his hands and hastens to add, "At least for tonight. Once Dean is back in custody, I can take you wherever you want in the city, I promise. But until then…"

"I'm still kidnappable," I finish for him, realizing the sense in what he's saying, but not happily. After everything we've been through to get here, it feels like an anticlimactic ending, just sitting in the hotel watching TV while I wait for Thad to find Dean and hope that everything turns out okay.

But at the end of the day, I'm a former nun turned librarian. I don't have any experience with apprehending bail jumpers. I'm not dressed to gamble on a luxury steamboat. And I don't want to get kidnapped by the mafia.

"Fine," I sigh, deflated, following him to the elevator. "I hope this place has the Hallmark channel…"

Thad lingers with me in the room for a few minutes, probably because he's afraid I'm trying to trick him; but finally, after I settle in to watch a movie with that actor I like from that show I used to watch, he grumbles about getting ready and disappears into the bathroom.

About half an hour later, the door to the bathroom opens again. I'm absorbed in my movie now and trying not to sulk, so I do my best to smile as I glance back toward him. "What time are—" I start, but the words cut off abruptly as I absorb what I'm seeing.

Thad's skin, fresh out of the shower, is glistening, his hair still a little damp but starting to dry in its usual soft waves. Along with his reading glasses, he's wearing a pair of pressed slacks and a dress shirt that's been unbuttoned down to his sternum, showing off a modest glimpse of chest that nonetheless gets my virginal heart racing. The sleeves of the shirt have been rolled up to his elbows, revealing his strong forearms, marked with dark tattoos that contrast his otherwise preppy look with a hint of something dangerous.

I'm staring. I know I'm staring. I try to stop, to get a grip on myself, but he cuts such a dashing, handsome figure that I feel a little shy. And a little pervy, too, because those exposed forearms are doing something to me. I feel sort of…tingly, in my lady parts. My entire body is alert and aware, like something is about to happen.

Which of course, it isn't, because he's about to go to the steamboat to find Dean, and I'm…staying here. All night.

"I look stupid, don't I?" Thad asks flatly.

I bark out a sharp laugh, because wow, has he misinterpreted my staring. "No. Not stupid. Different, but definitely not stupid."

My voice must actually sound as winded to him as it does to my own ears, because Thad's expression shifts. For a moment he frowns at me in that way I used to think was disapproving, but I now realize is just him concentrating— and then, unexpectedly, he grins at me.

I realize in that instant how infrequently Thad has smiled at me in all the time I've known him, because that smile, directed right at me, hits me like a freight train. If I thought the outfit was doing something to me, that smile knocks the rest of it out of the water. I would do anything he asked me to do when he smiles at me like that—and that recognition both thrills and terrifies me.

"So you like it?" he asks me, breaking what I realize is an unnaturally long silence as I've been staring at him.

"Y-yeah?" I'm trying to play it cool, not let on just *how much* I like it, but I don't have much practice and am not very good at playing these kinds of games. "I wouldn't have guessed you owned anything like this."

"Part of the job. Have to be able to blend in." He gestures to his shirt. "The collar's a little funny, though. Can you help me straighten it?"

"Oh." The surprised squeaking noise escapes my mouth without me giving it permission. I clear my throat. "Sure. Yeah. Fine."

I step toward him and am overcome with another wave of want as I get close enough to smell his cologne. Holy cannoli. I barely manage to catch myself from swaying into him, pulled toward his skin like a magnet. *Nice-smelling men are nice*, is the coherent, Pulitzer Prize–worthy thought that comes to mind.

Swallowing, I attempt to keep my focus on his collar. My hands are shaking as I flatten out the little crease in the back, and I hope he doesn't notice. "There. That's better."

I start to step back, but Thad stops me with a hand on my hip, holding me in place. The touch is light, not demanding or possessive, but it still elicits a gasp of surprise at the contact. I meet his blue-gray gaze, my heart thudding so loudly in my chest I'm sure he must hear it.

"You like me like this?" he asks.

There's teasing in his voice, but also a hint of something vulnerable. He's smiling, but his eyes move back and forth between mine as he waits for the answer. "I like you always," I tell him honestly. I'm too flustered to be anything but completely honest. "This is just…a new flavor."

The answer must satisfy him, because his expression relaxes. "When all of this is over, I'll take you out to dinner. In whatever flavor you like. If you want."

It's my turn to study him, doing my best to keep the worry off my face. This energy between us feels like fireworks, chemistry, all the things I've read about but never experienced, but I'm still afraid that because of my inexperience, I'll read into things, see things that aren't there. My knee-jerk response is to laugh, give him an easy out, but again this proximity between us seems to force honesty out of me. "Like a date?"

I wait for him to frown, step away from me, but he holds his ground, and my gaze. "If that's the flavor you want from me."

Now I'm the one to frown at him. Why does all of this—attraction, desire, feelings—have to be so complicated? Why don't people just say what they mean? "Is that the flavor you want from *me*?" I challenge back.

Thad's eyes drop down to my lips, then lower. He swallows heavily before meeting my gaze again. "I want to taste whatever you're willing to let me taste."

My jaw drops. Heat floods my cheeks, my body, as the words sink in. He grins at me again, squeezing the hip he's holding on to, before he abruptly steps back and lets me go. "Think about it. Get back to me."

And with that, he's gone.

Chapter 35
Helen

I do think about it. I can't stop thinking about it—especially since I've promised to not leave the room, so all I can do is pace in place like a caged animal, picking at the memory like a scab. *I want to taste whatever you're willing to let me taste.*

I might be a virgin, and a former sister, but I know what he's talking about. (At least I *think* I know what he's talking about… I'm pretty sure I know what he's talking about.) I've read lots of romance novels, after all, and I have a subscription to HBO. So. I'm pretty sure I'm caught up on most of the sex stuff, even if I haven't personally experienced it. Hypothetically speaking, if he meant what I thought he meant, then I would potentially be very excited to let him…taste me. Hypothetically.

After almost an hour of fretting over it, I realize I'm driving myself crazy. I need to find something to distract myself, to help pass the time, and ideally stop thinking about tasting altogether.

A nice hot bath sounds like just the ticket. I can do a little face mask, shave my legs and any other body parts that need to be groomed. Not for any specific purpose, of course. And not as a response to Thad commenting about wanting to taste me. Definitely not.

Except, I realize as I move to grab my nonexistent bag, I don't have a razor or anything that will make a bath feel truly luxurious: bubbles, face mask, the like. The hotel shampoo might do in a pinch, but if I'm going to be stuck in the room all night, I want to have a truly spa-like experience, not make do with whatever is available.

I remember spotting a little hotel shop off the lobby when we checked in earlier today. They should have at least a few of the things I'm looking for. And even though I'm technically leaving the room, I won't be leaving the hotel, so I won't be breaking my promise to Thad.

As I make my way through the lobby to the shop, I keep a careful eye on the people milling through the hotel as well as the people I can see passing by on the street outside. I know from the many mafia-themed romance novels I've read that my leaving the room creates the perfect opportunity for someone to kidnap me, forcing the hero into a dramatic showdown to reclaim his love. As fun as that is to read about, having almost been kidnapped, I can now safely say that I have no desire to repeat that experience. And as tempting as it might be to wonder how Thad would react if I were to actually be held for ransom, I'm not confident that I'm the kind of woman who would inspire a dramatic showdown.

Although…during my attempted kidnapping, Thad did rush onto the scene, throw himself across a car, and tackle a mobster who was holding a gun.

But that was because he still needed me to find Dean. Wasn't it?

I'm shopping and keeping half an eye out on the world around me, when I look out the window to the street and do a double take. Before I can check myself, I run outside, waving my arms. "Hey, Deltas!"

The group of sorority girls has transformed pretty significantly into sleek, dark, sexy outfits now that night is falling. I'm not sure I would have recognized them if they weren't in a huge cluster—and I'm really not confident that I could pick out any one of them individually. Still, I feel weirdly happy to see them. Or maybe I've just been bored in the hour or so since Thad left me on my own in the hotel.

Luckily the Deltas seem just as enthused to see me. "Helen!" they chorus, while a few crane not so subtly around me to search for my missing companion. "Where's Thad?"

I…did not really think this through, I realize as I try to come up with an explanation for why Thad has ditched me here at the hotel. Thinking quickly, I improvise. "We had tickets for the Carolina Belle—you know, the floating casino? Since my bag got stolen, I didn't have anything to wear, but I didn't want Thad to miss out on the experience, so…" I shrug, hoping that gesture will fill in the blanks of my story.

"No way!" Cassie exclaims, as ever the self-appointed spokesperson of the group, looking at the others in disbelief. "We're going there tonight, too! Why don't you come with us and surprise him?"

This…was not an alternative I'd been planning for. And honestly, it's a very good reminder why people shouldn't lie—me, in particular. Not only is it morally wrong, but I'm really bad at it. "What a weird coincidence," I stall as I try to come up with another reason. "Thad has our tickets, though, and I think you have to buy ahead. I won't be able to get on."

"We got you covered, girl! Caitlyn pregamed a little too hard and passed out at the hotel. You can use her ticket."

"Oh." That's convenient…and a little concerning. Hopefully Caitlyn is okay…but that's the least of my worries as I realize I'm running out of excuses. I motion down at myself again. "I can't wear this on the boat."

"Definitely not," another girl chimes in, eying my rumpled sweater and jeans with horror.

Cassie waves it off like it's of no consequence. "Our hotel is two blocks away, and I'm sure between the ten of us we can find something else for you to wear."

The girls all agree enthusiastically—except for the one who was so put off with my (very normal!) outfit, who adds, "We'll need to do hair and makeup, too."

Before I can really process that, or even fully agree to any of what's happening, I find myself being whisked off down the street by a gaggle of sorority girls, not quite sure how to stop what's been set in motion.

Chapter 36
Helen

That had is going to be furious with me.

In my defense, I'm not really good at thinking under pressure. I'm the reason we had to discontinue competing in our ex-nun group at trivia night—well, really, *Matilda* is the reason we discontinued because she shouted at me for so long about forgetting the name of the Winnie the Pooh author that we got kicked out of the pub. For the sake of our friendship, we decided not to do anything competitive together, ever again, largely in part to my inability to make quick decisions.

So, yes, I allowed the group of sorority girls to lead me out of the hotel after I promised I would stay in the room all night. And yes, I let them dress me up and do my makeup and hair, and I took Caitlyn's ticket to board the very boat where Dean will likely be apprehended and taken back into police custody tonight. (For the record, I checked on Caitlyn and she is okay—conscious, and binge-watching some reality TV show on her phone.)

But me being aboard the floating casino is not actually the biggest problem right now. The biggest problem is what I'm *wearing* aboard the floating casino.

Or, to be more accurate, what I'm *not* wearing aboard the floating casino.

Let me just say, to anyone who ever finds themselves in this predicament, if a group of sorority girls offers to dress you up and tells you to trust them, do not trust them. If they say they have extra clothing that will totally fit you, it will totally not fit your thirtysomething body in the way that it fits their early-twentysomething bodies. If you worry that the outfit they've chosen might be a little too flashy and they tell you that this is the kind of thing people wear to boat parties, by *people* they are referring to other young twentysomethings, not women in their thirties who are neither Beyoncé nor a Kardashian.

I know this, because literally no other woman on the Carolina Belle is dressed how I'm dressed. We were some of the last people to board before the boat launched on its leisurely three-hour round trip up and down the Mississippi, and I stopped short as soon as I stepped onto the deck. The other women my age and older are in cute, bright dresses and rompers, ranging from whites to pastels to bold floral prints. Some are revealing a tasteful amount of skin, like a high slit showing off a thigh, or a low-cut V-neck, or a dress with cutouts at the shoulders and back.

And I? I am wearing a black fishnet dress with a black bikini underneath. When the girls showed me the picture of the model wearing the outfit online, it seemed a little daring but tasteful—but of course, I didn't take into account the difference in body types. On a size 0 model, the fishnet reveals a little skin underneath, but all the important bits are pretty well covered, and the overall effect is sexy but stylish.

On this non-size-0 body, with my "larger than average breasts" (according to Matilda) and generously sized backside (according to the imprint I leave on my couch), there is a lot more on display than a little skin. Even though the bikini thankfully isn't just a piece of dental floss, it's still too small to fully cover everything I would want to have covered. June is bustin' out all over, if by "June" you mean my boobs, and the fact that it's only a few little strings holding the entire suit together makes me worried that it's only a matter of time before there's a Janet Jackson–level catastrophe.

At least my hair is a little more subdued, slicked back into a sleek ponytail. But the bright, fire-engine red lipstick and matching nails the girls gave me seem designed to draw even more attention. As I feel eyes watching my path across the deck, I fight back the urge to cover myself up and explain to the strangers around me that this isn't really me. I'm just a librarian who loves old musicals. Not a—

Well, a femme fatale. Honestly, I think I make Ava Gardner look pretty tame by comparison when I'm in this outfit.

The girls invite me to come with them in search of the pool on the top deck, but I decide that since I'm here, I might as well look for Dean. That was the whole point of coming to New Orleans, after all, and maybe Thad will be less irritated with me breaking my promise if I manage to find Dean first.

That's assuming, of course, that Thad hasn't already found him, arrested him, and taken him into custody. I really wish I'd thought of that possibility *before* the boat took off, since this is going to be a very long three-hour round trip otherwise.

"Helen?"

I turn in surprise at the familiar voice, my eyes widening. "Shane?"

Goofy-library-patron Shane, who I have to remind myself is actually undercover-private-detective Shane, approaches me, his jaw literally hanging open as he looks me over. His eyes linger on my breasts, none-too-subtly staring, before he manages to wrench his gaze up to mine. "What are you doing here?"

I don't have to ask him the same question, knowing now what his real interest in me has always been. I raise an eyebrow at him. "The same thing you're doing here, I imagine. How'd you know about the boat?"

"I have my ways." Shane gives me a half-cocky, half-goofy grin, before his eyes snag down on my breasts again. "You look...very different from the library."

Resisting the urge to cover myself, I clear my throat, trying to subtly call Shane out about his obvious staring. He meets my gaze, giving me another goofy, self-conscious grin and shrugging his shoulders. "Sorry—you just. Wow. Seriously. Wow. I knew you were beautiful, Helen, but this is something else."

Look, I may have been a sister, but I'm no saint, and I like a compliment as much as the next person. Fighting a blush, I reluctantly smile back. "Thank you, Shane." Despite enjoying the flattery, I want to steer the conversation away from what I may or may not be wearing. "Have you seen Dean, or Thad?"

Shane's eye twitches, just a little. "Thad's here?" He recovers quickly, rolling his eyes at himself self-deprecatingly. "Of course he's here. I should have known."

"Dean?" I prompt again.

"No sign of Dean yet, but I just arrived." Shane's eyes roam over my body again. "We'll look together. Let me get you a drink."

I don't know that I entirely trust Shane to do right by Dean. I don't know that I entirely trust Shane, full stop. But I also feel a little self-conscious wandering around this boat by myself, in this outfit. Shane might be a little overeager, but I imagine there are guys on this boat who might be far more aggressive, and this outfit seems to invite that kind of attention, whether I want it to or not. Maybe keeping the devil I know by my side might keep away the devil I don't.

"Sure," I agree at last. "White wine, please."

As Shane hurries off to fulfill my request, I continue to scan the main deck for Dean. Something I haven't been able to really piece together is why he's even here. Looking at the other people aboard, this doesn't seem like Dean's usual crowd. Sure, there are some partiers like the Delta girls who are just here for a good time. But most of the people around me seem to be fairly well-to-do, upper-class, on board to see and be seen as they do some serious, high-stakes gambling. After spending the last few days familiarizing myself with Dean's arrest record, I know he's not the innocent, wrong-place, wrong-time bystander that my mother paints him out to be. He's definitely dipped his toe into some seriously bad stuff, especially if the mobster who tried to kidnap me was telling the truth about Dean stealing their Molly. Who steals drugs from the mafia, anyway? An idiot, that's who.

I can't for the life of me figure out why he would be on this boat, unless he's trying to count cards or rig a game. But surely even Dean should be smart enough to figure out that when people are betting this much money just to buy in, the security on the boat won't be messing around. I've already spotted four security staff just on the main deck—one watching from the cockpit, one posted by the stairs leading to the upper deck, and two in plain clothes, circulating and observing everyone carefully to make sure nothing gets out of hand.

What is Dean up to? And where is he? My bet would be in one of the cabins, buying in on one of the high-stakes poker games. I'm half tempted to leave Shane here and search by myself, when I feel someone step in closer to me than is necessary, putting my body on full alert.

"What are you doing here?" a quiet but intense voice murmurs into my left ear, sending shivers coursing through my body.

Chapter 37
Helen

I feel like I've been caught by the principal—or what I imagine it must feel like to be caught doing something wrong by an authority figure, since I don't have much experience with that. Okay, *any* experience with that. I'm pretty sure my high school principal never even knew who I was. My grades were good but not stellar, I never got detention or ditched school or smoked in the bathroom or whatever else teenagers do to get in trouble. I don't even have the imagination to guess what other kinds of things might get someone on the principal's radar.

But somehow I have no trouble imagining Thad as the stern principal catching me doing something naughty. Calling me into his office. Telling me in that gruff, stern voice that I need to learn my lesson—

Whoa. Where the heck did that come from?

Swallowing, I pivot to face him, hoping that absolutely none of that weird mental detour is showing on my face. Knowing my face, however, that hope is probably in vain. I do my best to smile, probably overcompensating with my cheerfulness, and wave at him for good measure. Okay, definitely overcompensating. "Hi, Thad! Funny meeting you here."

"Is it?" he retorts, not looking in the least bit amused. "Is it funny?"

My whole body is on alert, bracing myself for the moment when he takes in my outfit. Half-anxious, half-hopeful that his eyes will linger like Shane's did. But Thad doesn't move his eyes from mine. He looks seriously pissed. And not in a fun-but-stern, spank-me-over-the-desk kind of way.

"I thought we agreed you were going to stay in the hotel," he says to me through clenched teeth, the muscle in his jaw doing that flexy thing again.

I'm so not used to actually being in trouble that I feel myself dialing up my positivity, as if through sheer force of sunny willpower I can convince him not to be angry at me. "So actually, it *is* a funny story—the sorority girls sort of ambushed me and did a whole makeover thing. That's why I'm here, wearing barely any clothes."

I wait to see if he'll take the bait, finally check out my outfit, but his eyes remain locked on mine, and his face remains unsmiling. I give a nervous laugh. "I guess it's more situationally funny than humorously funny."

Thad's eyes flash at me. "You need to get off this boat. There are other people on board who really don't want me taking Dean into custody. I can't have you getting in the way, distracting me."

His tone wipes the uneasy smile from my face. I no longer feel the need to diffuse the tension, because now *I'm* pissed, too. "I'm not here to distract you —but if I am, I feel like that's *your* problem, not mine. Because I'm here to help my brother and make sure he stays safe."

Thad inhales sharply through his nose, stepping in closer to me. That muscle in his jaw jumps, like he's clenching his teeth, hard. "If you're not here to distract me, then why the fuck did you wear this dress?"

I still haven't seen him actually *look* at what I'm wearing. But that look in his eyes, the closeness of his body, makes me feel more undressed than any single piece of clothing ever could.

"Helen, here's your drink."

I startle, turning to see that Shane is back, with my white wine in hand. He offers Thad one of his winsome smiles—though something about it seems a little strained. Calculated. "Hey, buddy," he says to Thad, as if just noticing him. "Glad you could join us. Sorry I didn't bring you a drink, too."

Shane steps in unnecessarily close to me. Too disoriented to think better of it, I take the drink he's handing to me. As soon as Shane's hand is free, he touches my arm. "You okay? Things seemed a little...heavy when I walked up."

I open my mouth to respond, but Thad cuts me off, taking me by surprise by closing his hand over my arm that's closest to him. "Fuck off, Shane. We're in the middle of a conversation."

Shane responds by closing *his* hand over my other arm. "Language, Thaddeus. The fair Helen of Troy is present." Despite his light tone, Shane is glaring at Thad over my head, and his grip on me tightens.

What the Hootie and the Blowfish is happening...? I don't fully understand the exchange going on between these two men—I mean, I get they're having some kind of pissing contest, but I'm not sure how I got dragged into the middle of it. And I'm a little worried they're actually about to start playing tug-of-war with my body.

"Hey, do I get a say in this?" I let stern-inner-city-teacher Helen's voice come out. "Or is it inconvenient when the fire hydrant has an opinion?"

Shane frowns at me. "There's a fire hydrant on board?"

Thad, at least, loosens his hold on me, though his expression doesn't become any less intense. "Do you want me to leave you with Shane?"

My mouth runs dry. Honestly, I'm a little scared of Thad's ferocity. Goofball Shane is a much more familiar, digestible alternative to…whatever is going on right now between Thad and me.

Shane must sense this, because I can hear the smirk in his voice as he trails his hand down my arm. "Come on, Helen. I, for one, would love to have your help finding your brother. And whatever else the night might bring…"

My body makes the decision for me. Shane's innuendo, the feeling of his fingers trailing down my skin, making me shiver—and not in a good way. I instinctively step in closer to Thad to get away from him.

Thad responds by putting his hand on the small of my back. It's a protective, almost primitive gesture—like he's announcing to anyone who might be looking, and Shane most especially, *This is my woman. Back off.*

I shouldn't find this absolutely thrilling. But I do.

"Come on," Thad says curtly, steering me through the crowd, and putting as much distance between us and Shane as possible.

I expect him to comment about Shane as soon as we're out of earshot, but Thad is completely silent as he guides me off the main deck and into the interior of the ship. He seems to know where he's going, so maybe his silence is just due to his concentration, but I'm not very good with silences. Especially not tense, angry silences. It was one of my major failings as a sister, and not in a fun, "How do you solve a problem like Maria" kind of way. At least, I'm pretty sure nobody ever sang a song about how much I annoyed everyone around me during times of silent meditation with my complete and utter inability to shut up.

"This is a big ship," I hear myself saying, almost like a disembodied voice coming from someone else entirely. "How old do you think it is? It *looks* like the one from *Show Boat*, but like it's been updated? I wonder if there's a whole market for boat renovators. You know, like the people who flip old houses on HGTV, but boats instead. I'd totally watch that show!"

Thad leads me through a series of hallways that I could definitely not find my way through again on my own, until we wind up in an empty, darkened room. The room opens up onto a balcony that overlooks the water below; some of the lights from elsewhere on the boat make it so the room isn't pitch black, but it's dark enough that I have to carefully make my way around so I don't trip over anything. That proves to be a moot point, though, since there doesn't seem to be anything inside.

Thad shuts the door behind him and locks it with a heavy click.

Turning in surprise, I swallow. "What are you doing? Is Dean in here?"

I know it's a stupid question as soon as it leaves my mouth. It's an empty room, with no closets or cabinets or furniture, so unless Dean is under an invisibility cloak, there's no one else in here. Thad stands with his back pressed to the door, his eyes following me in the shadows. "Dean isn't on board. I've searched all the decks, every room, twice. He isn't here."

I blink in surprise, worrying my lip with my teeth. "Do you think something happened?"

"I hope not. But we can figure it out once we're off the boat. Not much we can do now."

I swallow again. "So what is this room, anyway?"

"I think it's usually used as a private playing room. But not tonight."

"Oh." So no one will be coming into this room for the next two and a half hours. It's just Thad and me, and the door is locked.

Abruptly, I turn, moving to the balcony. There's an overhang above us, so I can't see any of the higher decks, but I can hear faint music and laughter trickling down from the top deck, where the pool is. "Do you want to go swimming?" I ask hopefully.

"Don't have my suit."

"Oh," I say again, stupidly. My heart is racing, my mouth dry. I focus on the dark water down below. "That's the Mississippi River, right? Do you think there are alligators down there?"

Of course it's the Mississippi River, and of course there are alligators. It's Louisiana, and it's a big body of water. But I couldn't stop the verbal bullet train coming out of my mouth if I tried.

I hear Thad approaching, and I grip the handrail as I feel him press in behind me. Brushing into the softness of my backside, he starts to harden against me, growling a little under his breath. "I honestly haven't thought about it. At all," he murmurs, his breath warm against the back of my neck.

"Thad," I gasp, gripping the handrail more tightly.

"Do you want me to stop?" He reaches up to touch the ends of my ponytail with a surprising gentleness.

"No," I admit, then shake my head. "Maybe. I…I don't want you to do this because you feel sorry for me."

A pause. "Sorry for you?"

"The nun virgin, who's never done anything." I take in a shaky breath. "I don't want to be pitied."

Another pause, then Thad laughs, just a little. "Are you serious?"

That makes me frown—at the dark water, since I'm caged in by his body and can't turn to look at him. "*Yes*. I have some pride, you know—"

"I don't pity you," he cuts me off. "I can't stop thinking about you. I can't stop thinking about all the things I want to do to you. That only *I* would get to do to you. I want to be touching you all the time. I want to make you feel good." His lips brush over my shoulder, and I shiver. "Will you let me make you feel good?"

A moment passes, where all I can hear is the rushing water below, and the pounding of my heart in my ears. "O-okay," I say at last, so quietly I'm afraid that maybe he didn't hear it.

But he must have, because the next thing I know, his fingers are dipping into the holes at the shoulder of the fishnet dress, finding the ties holding the bikini top together. "This fucking ridiculous bathing suit." His breath is hot against me. "I wanted to tear it off the moment I saw you." He sounds completely sure, confident, but I feel his fingers shaking a little bit, and it makes my breath catch in my throat.

"Oh," I say, stupidly. All night, I haven't been able to shut up, and now I can't think of a single thing to say. All the energy in my body is channeled into the feeling of him pressed against me, his hot words against my ear, his fingers tugging at my clothing.

A moment later, I feel the bikini give. He tugs it some more, and it drops to the ground. Except for the flimsy fishnet dress, my breasts are completely bare in the night air. Thad takes one in each hand and groans into my neck as he massages them. The thumb of his left hand works into the fishnet material of the dress, finding my hardened nipple and circling it, circling it.

A jolt of want courses through me, straight down to my core. "Oh," I breathe, instinctively arching back into his touch. I want more of it, whatever is happening to me. I feel greedy for it, needy for it, in a way that my logical mind is telling me should be embarrassing, but the aching inside of me won't let me be self-conscious. He's opened something inside of me that I understand will forever be left wanting if it isn't seen through to the end.

Thad groans in response to me pressing back against him, and it's a jolting reminder yet again that his actions aren't prompted by pity. He wants this, needs this, as much as I do. "Your body," he mutters into my ear. "Your fucking body. It's a sin it's been hidden away for so long. Your body deserves to be worshiped."

I feel like Thad and I have changed places. A moment ago he was dead silent and I couldn't stop talking. Now he's saying the sweetest, naughtiest things to me and my mind is a total blank. Everything is being channeled toward that pressing want building up inside of me.

Thad's right hand releases my breast, and I make a little whining noise in protest, but he just laughs into the crook of my neck. "You like that, huh? I bet it feels good. But I know other ways to make you feel good, too."

He trails his knuckles down my side, spreading out his hand again to grip me at my hip. Those clever fingers wrangle their way inside the fishnet again, finding the ties for my bikini bottom. My breath catches, and he notices. "Too soon?"

"N-no," I stammer, waiting for him to continue.

But he holds back, a little laughter now in his quiet murmur against my skin: "You want me to touch your pussy?"

Even the naming of it sends a spike of hot want through me. I can tell he's waiting for an answer. "Yes," I manage finally in a whisper.

"Good. Because I can't wait to touch your pussy. I can't wait to feel how wet you are for me."

Lord, give me strength. My head is spinning. I grip the handrail even tighter.

"But first"—Thad guides me back from the railing—"I want to see you."

He turns me around to face him, and my breath catches in my throat as our gazes collide. Everything up until now has been intoxicating, incredible, but facing him now, the intensity is instantly heightened. Keeping my gaze, he tugs at the string holding up one side of the bikini bottoms, then at the other. After a moment the strings give, and I feel the fabric slide down my legs and onto the deck. His gaze finally lowers, and I watch his face as he takes in my body, the way his jaw clenches and he gives a long, slow swallow.

"Holy Jesus," he mutters.

But as his eyes meet mine again, I can see that he's at last run out of things to say. I turn my face up instinctively as he leans in to kiss me, his hands burning through the flimsy fishnet to my skin beneath, his body pressing me up against the railing.

The kiss is consuming, and in any other circumstance, I would have been totally lost in it. But just a moment ago, he promised to touch my pussy, and the now-aching need down there is drowning out every other sensation in my body. I whimper, shamelessly rubbing up against him, and he finally breaks away from the kiss, looking a little dazed and disoriented for a moment before laughing under his breath, pressing his forehead to mine. "You need me?" he asks simply.

The first brush of his fingers over my folds is an electric shock to my system. I buck and moan, and when he touches me again, I cry out, overcome with it, this want, this need. "Thad!"

I'm not even sure what I'm asking him for, but he seems to intuitively understand. He slides one finger up into me, and that feels so good I could cry out again; and then he slides up a second, and that feels so good I *do*, my eyes flying open to find him watching my face intently as he slowly pumps his fingers in and out, in and out.

Some new pressure starts to build up inside of me, somehow even more powerful than what was already happening. It feels so good I'm starting to lose focus, but I know I need something else.

As if answering my unspoken request, his thumb snakes up, finding that little powerful detonator that's been throbbing, throbbing this whole time, and sets it off.

I come apart so suddenly that it knocks the wind out of me. My whole body stiffens, tightens, and then releases.

Holy…holy *shit*.

Chapter 38
Helen

It takes me a minute or two to come back down. When I do, I find Thad bracing me up against the railing, still watching me intently. Feeling a little loopy, I smile at him, in that sort of middle-hazy place like when you've just woken up from a nap.

It takes another minute to re-process that I'm all but naked, out here on this ship's deck, with this man who's played a formative role in my sexual awakening, but who's made it clear he couldn't see anything serious with me. I may be naive, but even I understand that sex does not always equate to commitment or *feelings*. I move to cover myself.

Thad stops me—not forcefully, his grip more like a suggestion. I could easily break free if I wanted to, but that intense gaze, still fastened on me, stops me. "You're so beautiful," he tells me solemnly.

I know that's probably just something you say to your partner, postsex. Kind-of sex? I was penetrated this time! But I'm sure Matilda will give me some other definition for what we just did. Still, we were *outside*, in a semi-public space, so maybe that will begrudgingly win me some respect from my more experienced friend.

Keeping her pragmatic, no-nonsense tone in my mind, I steel myself against anything sweet Thad might say now, in the moment. I know it doesn't mean anything, not really. "Thank you," I murmur, not quite meeting his gaze. Wanting to take the attention off me, I motion to his erection, still visibly bulging against his trousers. "Do you want me to…? I can do something, if you show me how."

My cheeks are already blazing red before the offer even fully escapes my lips, and I'm not sure if it's because of the nature of the offer itself, or the admission that I won't really know what I'm doing, even if I am a willing participant. An *extremely* willing participant, eager and ready to learn.

"Later," he says, sounding distracted. Surprised, I search his face to find his eyes roaming over my body. I flush more deeply as my greedy body reacts, my nipples hardening, my legs falling open just a little.

I close them again, resolved. "Thad," I protest, placing a staying hand on his chest. "That was—nice, but…I don't know if it's a good idea to—"

"You didn't like it?"

"O-of course I did," I stammer. "But—"

"You don't want me to make you feel good again?"

I shiver. "It's not that. It's just—I don't think I can do no strings. That isn't a judgment, it just isn't for me—"

"We can do strings." He traces his thumb where he's holding me at my hip. It's a completely PG touch, nowhere near the bathing-suit zone, but even that brief touch makes me feel like I'm on fire. Or maybe it's the intensity in his words, his eyes, as he holds my gaze. "We can do whatever you want. I want to be whatever you want me to be."

I blink at him in surprise, then uncertainty—sure I'm not understanding him right. "What does that mean?" I ask him point-blank, too frazzled to be coy. "I don't understand what you're saying."

He takes in a deep, steeling breath, and for the first time I can see he's nervous, too, and out of his element. "I want to be with you, Helen. I'm not sure I remember how to do this—but I want to try, with you."

Matilda did *not* prepare me for this. In all our conversations about dating, she's prepped me for the inevitable letdown, warned me about hookup culture and how no one wants to commit to anything anymore. But I don't know what to do with the man of my fantasies, begging to give me more orgasms and promising to stick around after. And I still can't quite shake the feeling that I must be making some rookie mistake. "You want to be my boyfriend?" I clarify.

"Yes. Great."

Remembering other things Matilda has warned me about, I ask, "You want to have sex with me—with *only* me?"

That dark, intense look comes over his face again, sending another shiver coursing through me. "Yes," he grinds out, like it's taking great effort for him to stop himself there.

My eyes widen. My mind searches for the loophole, whatever obvious thing I might be missing. "Are you sure you aren't just saying that because I'm naked?" I blurt out.

"I can't say it's not a good motivation." His eyes sweep over me again, and he swallows. "But it's not the only factor."

I can see from that wolfish look in his eyes that he's getting ready to do something naughty to me again. And I can tell from the pressure already building in my core that I'm going to let him.

Again, nervously, I say the first thing that comes to mind. "It doesn't really seem fair that I'm the only naked one around here." *That I'm completely at your mercy, and I already know I'm going to do whatever you want me to do.*

Something glints in Thad's eye. To my surprise, and chagrin, he steps back from me. "Okay."

Shoot. Whatever stupid thing I said without thinking, he's changed his mind about whatever naughty thing he was going to do. It's kind of what I wanted, but also—I realize now that it's happening—definitely *not* what I wanted. Stupid, inexperienced virgin!

I make an inadvertent sound of protest, but Thad surprises me by grinning as he takes another step back.

Then he reaches for his shirt.

I watch, wide-eyed, as he undoes each button. Somewhere, in a distant, logical corner of my mind, I'm aware that he could easily just pull the shirt off in one go, but he's intentionally taking his time. Teasing me. Watching my reaction as he slowly reveals more and more skin.

At last he reaches the final button, lingering a moment before he pulls the shirt off altogether. I suck in a sharp, unintentional breath—trying, in vain, to keep my eyes on his face, though they're pulled like magnets to his newly exposed skin.

But he isn't done yet. I watch the muscles of his arms and torso move and contract as he takes off his shoes, his socks, then works to undo his belt, pulling it off. Finally, smirking at something in my expression, he reaches for his pants and boxer briefs and shucks them off in one go, tossing them down on the deck with my discarded bathing suit.

I stare at him, speechless. He is completely and totally naked, without even a skimpy fishnet covering his skin, however inadequately. The sight of him is a shock to my system, so overwhelming I don't know where to look. Everything about him is big and solid and—his penis. I can't stop myself from looking at it now that it's unleashed. I can't believe that thing is supposed to fit inside of me. Just like everything else about him, it looks big and masculine and a little dangerous, in a way that makes me feel weak-kneed and nervous and aroused all at once in an experience that is completely, wholly new.

Something of this must read on my face, because Thad's face softens, just a little. He still has that intensity in his expression, but it no longer feels challenging or defiant. "Relax," he tells me. "We're not going *there*, not right now. I don't have a condom with me. And even if I did—we don't have to do anything you don't want to do. Ever."

I feel too shy to tell him I *do* want to do all the things. But I'm also a little relieved to know it doesn't have to be right now, all at once. We can take our time. Savor things.

"I want to touch it," I blurt out, my eyes dropping down to his erection.

So much for being one of his cool, sexy femme fatales. My dumb brain is short-circuiting, being next to a naked man, and *this* naked man in particular. I'm frankly surprised that I'm still able to put together coherent sentences.

Thad's gaze darkens. "Helen," he growls at me, almost warningly.

I tilt my head to the side, genuinely curious. "You don't want me to touch you?"

His eyes fall shut a moment before he seems to force them back open through sheer willpower. "I do, but...I won't be able to focus on anything else once we start down that road. And I have plans for you." His eyes flicker down to my pussy, and if I didn't know better, I'd swear he was talking directly to it. The thought should be ridiculous, but instead it sends a jolt of want straight through me.

"Oh." I dither for a moment. I like that he has plans for my pussy. I'd very much like to find out what those are. But I also can't stop staring at his erection. It looks uncomfortable, maybe even painful. And it feels like I should help him relieve that burden, if I can.

It's the Christian thing to do.

Swallowing, I step forward, reaching for him slowly. I want to give him the chance to stop me, if that's what he really wants. His eyes hone in on my movement, his jaw clenching. "Helen," he says, but he doesn't tell me to stop.

I touch him almost clinically at first, exploring this thing I've heard about and read about but never actually experienced for myself. It's both harder and softer than I thought. He's solid as a rock, but the skin is smooth, almost silky. I run my fingertips up and down the base, testing it a moment, before experimentally wrapping my hand around it. "Like this?" I ask, tilting my head to the side to study it.

Thad swears as he closes his hand over mine, adjusting my wrist and then guiding it back and forth a few times before releasing me to do it on my own. *"Fuck."*

I watch him, fascinated, as I continue the motion he taught me, experimenting with pressure and speed. Whatever I'm doing must be okay because he is almost incoherent in his want. The Big Bad Wolf who was threatening *pussy plans* a few moments ago has been completely and totally tamed.

It's a good thing he's too preoccupied with his need to pay much attention to my face, because I'm sure it's cartoonishly dorky—wide eyes, gaping mouth. In all the studying and researching and reading I've done about sex, there was nothing that prepared me for this—the vulnerability and the power, the heady thrill of watching someone come apart because of *you*.

With an abrupt grunt, Thad reaches down, stopping my hand. For half a second, I worry that I've done something wrong, made some beginner's error, until he half moans, "I'm going to finish if you don't stop."

Oh! Well, if that's all. "I don't care," I insist, reaching for him again.

"I do," he says to me through gritted teeth. "I have *plans*."

Before I can laugh at the absurdity of *that* statement, Thad surprises me by lowering himself down onto the deck, lying down flat on his back and urging me down with him so that I'm straddling him. I'm aware of too many things all at once—my nudity, my weight, whether or not I'm crushing him, the position I'm in and if it's making anything bulge or hang weirdly.

His voice pulls me back from the brink of a mini panic. "I've been wanting to do this ever since that day you were wrestling me in my car for your phone."

My mind cuts back to that night—me pinning Thad down with my thighs, our breathing thick and labored. "Do what?"

I'm distracted by movement behind me, and I turn to see that Thad has taken hold of himself and is pumping energetically. As I stare at the sight, hypnotized, his other hand grips my hip, urging me forward until—

"Oh, God!" I half gasp, half shout.

Forgive me, Lord. I can't help the profanity, truly. Not when I'm sitting on his mouth and he's exploring me with lips and teeth and breath and tongue. Pleasure so intense it's almost painful courses through me, muting out anything but this sensation, his hand on my hip, urging me on, the frantic pumping behind me.

When I implode, I try to be mindful of where my body goes so I don't crush him and he can breathe, though honestly, it takes Herculean effort to stay even that cognizant. He follows me a few moments later, his body jerking up all at once underneath me, then going prone again.

We lie there, the two of us, bodies awkwardly tangled as we try to catch our respective breaths. "Oh my God," I sigh finally, when I'm able to breathe.

"Oh my God," he agrees, one hand coming up to languidly caress my thigh.

Chapter 39
Thad

As we walk back to the hotel, Helen is glowing. To me, she's always been beautiful, alluring, and more distracting than I'd like her to be; but tonight, she is turning heads everywhere we go. And it isn't just because of the outfit. (Fuck me, that outfit. I was almost relieved that Dean wasn't on the boat once I saw her, because there was no way I would have been able to focus on anything but her all night.)

For as long as I've known her, Helen has been a turtle, hiding inside of her shell. The oversized sweaters, the messy buns. And even though she might have been making some moves to occasionally come outside of that, it was obvious she was still hiding a part of herself, not quite wanting to be seen.

She isn't hiding anymore. Everything about her begs to be noticed, from the way she carries herself, to the warmth and happiness she exudes—and yes, to the incredible body on display in that barely there fishnet dress.

Her glow isn't just from us fooling around, either—I mean, I'm sure the multiple orgasms didn't hurt, and I'm sure I'm walking around wearing one of my rare, shit-eating grins, myself. I think she's proud of herself, for trying something new, and everything about her radiates with pleasure and confidence.

And I think, maybe, just maybe, it has a little bit to do with me, too. We can't stop smiling at each other. Touching each other. Her hand gripping the sleeve of my shirt, my hand touching the small of her back, her body angling into mine to let other people pass. If I were seeing anyone else behave the way we're behaving now, I'd probably sucker punch them on principle for being so obnoxious, but I can't make myself stop.

As we near the hotel, I clock yet another pair of guys craning their necks to look after Helen as she walks by. Some of my innate sourness returns, and my face falls back into its usual, easy scowl. If I had a suit jacket, I would have found a reason to wrap it around her shoulders, even though it's an unseasonably warm night—anything to keep *their* eyes off *my* woman.

My woman. The thought makes me smile again, despite myself. My librarian femme fatale, too sexy to be a good girl, and too sunny to be a vamp. Helen. The only woman in the world, so far as I care.

My expression must be contagious because she sees my face as we step into the lobby and grins back at me, almost shyly. "What?"

I wouldn't know where to start without turning into mush. This thing I'm feeling is both overwhelmingly strong and incredibly delicate, like if I say the wrong thing or blink the wrong way, it'll snuff out. "Just thinking about how much I love New Orleans," I hear myself saying, like a prize idiot.

Either she can read between the lines of what I'm saying, or she's a bit of an idiot, too, since her smile just broadens, her heart in her eyes as she looks at me. "Me, too. I don't want to leave."

"Let's stay," I blurt out without thinking.

Her smile doesn't fade, though it does turn a shade skeptical. "Like, for a few more days? I have to get back to my job once we find Dean."

His name threatens to sour the mood, the happy bubble we've trapped ourselves in. Finding and arresting Dean was always the plan, and I meant it when I told Helen it would be the safest thing for him, with the mafia on his trail; but there's no way around it—arresting the brother of the woman you're crazy about is a bit of a buzzkill.

I push past it, blindly and willfully. "Quit your job. I'll move my business down here, get my bounty hunting license in the state of Louisiana. You can work for me."

I'm only half joking. If she says yes, I'll do it in a heartbeat; the joking part comes from knowing she'll never go for it.

She folds her arms, raising a skeptical eyebrow. "Doing what? I didn't know bounty hunters had a big need for librarians."

"Oh, they do. Someone who knows how to do monotonous research? Check. Handle even the weirdest members of the public? Check. Can navigate public records? Check." I'm kind of convincing myself with this whole bit, though she still looks dubious. Leaning in toward her, I lower my voice to a whisper. "Distract said bounty hunter when trapped on a boat for hours? Check, check, check."

She blushes, lightly shoving me away. "Call me old-fashioned, but I don't think it's the best idea to work for your boyfriend." She tenses as soon as the words leave her mouth. "Not *boyfriend*, but…whatever you would call this. If this even needs a name. I'm not saying it does." A sharp, nervous intake of breath. "Does it?"

Boyfriend is such a stupid word. I'm not opposed to the idea in theory, but it does sound a little bit like we're back in high school. "You can call me your boyfriend, if you want," I say quickly, mostly to ease her obvious stress. "I think I'd prefer to call you Sister Helen, though, but only in the bedroom."

The tension eases out of her shoulders just like that, and she laughs a little, even as she rolls her eyes at me. *"Thad."*

"The rest of the time?" I scratch my chin, as if considering it. "Maybe… my old lady?" I hook my index finger into one of the fishnet loops near her waist, tugging her toward me. "My ball and chain?"

She fights her amusement, half glaring at me. "You really like those better than just plain old 'girlfriend,' huh?"

My heart does a little stutter at that word. Girlfriend is much better than boyfriend, I decide right away. It doesn't sound stupid or immature at all. A girlfriend is the woman who can make your heart skip a beat when you pick her up for date night, but who is also unbearably cute in sweatpants, ready to binge-watch TV. A girlfriend makes you lose your mind with how much you want to touch her, all the time, but also makes you laugh and gives the best hugs when you've had a bad day. "Actually," I manage at last, "girlfriend sounds about right."

Her smile back at me is so bright, it almost hurts to see it. I feel like I've been sucker punched in the gut, but also, strangely, like I kind of…enjoyed it?

"Ms. Flanagan?"

We're so locked into each other that we both start at the sound of someone approaching. I turn to see one of the front desk clerks. That intense, electric chemistry between Helen and me must not be all that subtle, since the clerk is staring down at the ground, hard, like he's afraid to look at us too directly. "Someone left a message for you at the front desk."

He passes Helen a folded-up piece of paper before beating a hasty retreat back to the desk. Helen exchanges a quick, surprised frown with me as she looks down at the note. "What's this…?"

I watch her as she unfolds it, tracing the furrow of her brow, the widening of her eyes. "Who's it from?"

"Dean," she tells me, eyes still wide with amazement.

———

The message is curt and to the point: Meet me in 508 bring no one - D

I'm immediately skeptical that it's from him, though Helen seems to think it tracks. "He's not much of a chitchat guy," she explains to me as we make our way to our room. "This seems exactly like the type of message he'd leave—because he's much too important to write full sentences or punctuate." She rolls her eyes.

The fact that she becomes a belligerent teenager whenever she talks about her brother is weirdly cute. But I'm not letting that distract me from my distrust of the message. "Or it could be someone trying not to give you too much information so they won't tip off that it's *not* actually Dean."

Helen pauses in front of the room door and turns to face me. "You think it might be a trap?" At my grim nod, she nods back, but more so to herself. "I'd better change, then."

I follow her into the room, frowning. "I tell you that we might be walking into danger, and your first thought is about your outfit?"

Helen gestures down to herself. "It's not the most practical outfit to get ambushed in. Imagine being tied up in all this fishnet, helpless."

Oh, I'm imagining it now, all right, but I don't think Helen and I are quite on the same page with the visions that concept brings to mind. *Someday*, I tell myself before I can get too far off track. She's still a virgin, for goodness' sake. And if there's any life motto I live by, it's that you don't spring bondage-play on unsuspecting virgins.

"Change," I manage through gritted teeth. "Quickly."

As she heads into the bathroom to put on the clothes the Deltas had delivered back to our hotel, I'm half tempted to leave her here, go scout out room 508 for myself. Maybe it's a shady mobster, waiting to pounce on Helen and use her as bait. Or maybe it really is Dean, and this case will almost be over.

Hard to say which is the more comforting option.

Helen and I seem to be on the same page about continuing things…for now. But I'm not delusional enough to think that there won't be a hard transition back into normal life. It's one thing to have two such polar opposites, who are attracted to each other and in close proximity, act on their hormones. But when Helen goes back to working at the library, I wonder if my life of late nights and weekends and weird hours will start to seem less *exciting* and more *inconvenient*.

I manage to shake the thought as Helen reappears. I'm a little sad, and a little relieved, to see her in clothing more substantial than the too-small bikini and fishnet dress. I'm pretty sure that the memory of what she looked like on the deck of that boat will be the last thing I remember before I die, but this outfit looks much more like her usual style. Plus, it will make it way easier to concentrate, if we are about to be ambushed by mobsters.

Helen grins at the sight of me. "A part of me thought you'd go without me, for sure."

Feigning innocence, I point back to my chest with my thumbs. "Who, me?"

"If anything," Helen muses as we make our way to the door, "it should be me going without you, since the note said to come alone." At the look on my face, she laughs. "Don't worry—even I'm not naive enough to fall for that one. I'm just saying, as a matter of principle, if anyone's going on their own—"

I silence her by pushing her up against the wall—not hard, but with purpose—holding her in place with my body as I catch her gaze with mine. "How about from now on, we both agree that we're in this together?"

I mean that for much more than just finding Dean. I hope she knows that. I hope she can hear it in my tone, see it in my eyes.

Helen blinks at me in surprise, then tilts her head, studying me. For a long moment, we just gaze at one another, holding an entire conversation without saying anything at all.

"Okay," she says at last. "I can agree to that."

Chapter 40
Helen

I'm weirdly nervous to finally find Dean. And not because I think it might be a trap, like Thad clearly seems to. He's being even grimmer than usual, all no-nonsense and power shoulders as he walks, his eyes missing no detail in the hallway or elevator. He can't seem to decide if it's safer for him to walk behind or in front of me and keeps alternating positions, sometimes angling in front of me with his shoulder, other times staying close behind me, always restless.

I'm weirdly *not* nervous to have Thad this close to me. I'm not questioning what we mean to each other. I'm not worried that we won't see each other again after we've found Dean. I'm not worried about how I should be acting or if I should be playing it cool or if I should be giving him encouragement or any of the other things I expected to be feeling. It's like something has shifted into place, and we simply fit together now. We're a package deal.

At last we reach room 508. Thad is on even higher alert now, his gaze moving up to the ceiling, down the corridor to one side, then to the other, all while somehow still managing to keep an eye on me and the door. "You'd better knock," he says at last. "So if it is Dean, he can see you in the peephole."

I can tell it's killing him to make this concession, so I do my best to smile at him and avoid the urge to give him a somewhat condescending pat on the cheek. "It's going to be fine," I tell him quietly, reaching up to rap sharply on the door.

"You don't know that," he grumbles. Aww, there's my little raincloud. He's been so cheerful this last hour that it almost felt like I was with a different person.

"I feel it," I tell him back sweetly, and I can tell he's shaking his head behind me without even having to see it.

"She *feels* it. Huh."

Whatever diatribe he might have been building up gets interrupted as the door cracks open. "Helen?"

I recognize my brother's voice instantly. We may not have spoken regularly in quite some time, but you don't forget the voice of the boy who's called you Princess Bubble Butt for most of your life. "Dean!"

The door opens a little wider, and I see my brother's eyes, glaring at me through the shadows. "I told you to come alone."

I resist the urge to roll my eyes. Okay, yes, he's on the run from the mafia, but if he thinks he can boss me around, he has another thing coming. "Stop being melodramatic and let us in."

He does, hurrying us inside and slamming the door behind him, locking it before turning to face us. He looks exactly like the Dean I've always known, while simultaneously looking like a stranger. His hair is longer, and he has facial hair now, which is new. So are the tattoos on his arms. It's a weird look for a kid who used to be an altar boy and whose voice didn't change from its beautiful falsetto until he was thirteen. If I didn't know him, I might be afraid of him.

But I do know him, and I'm not. "Are you okay?" Ignoring his tough-guy glare, I pull him into a hug. "Mom is really worried about you. I can't believe you're on the run from the mafia. I can't believe you're hiding out in New Orleans. What are you doing here?"

"What are *you* doing here?" he counters in his deep voice that I suspect he pitches even lower than it needs to be, after years of being confused with me on the phone. That stopped a long time ago, of course, but it seems to have left a mark. "And why the hell did I get this tonight?"

He shows me a picture on his phone, and I'm surprised to see it's of *me*, from earlier tonight on the Carolina Belle, wearing my black fishnet dress. Whoever took the picture of me took it when I wasn't paying attention, looking off somewhere else. I feel uneasy knowing that someone was paying that close of attention to me without me noticing—but also, if I'm being honest, I can't help but notice how sexy I look in that outfit. Dang, Sister Helen! No wonder Thad couldn't keep his hands off me.

Thad steps forward, taking Dean's phone without permission. He studies the picture for a moment, looking equally grim as he meets my gaze. "Someone on the boat recognized you. Which means we probably don't have long." He looks at Dean. "We need to get you back into custody."

Dean scoffs. "Not gonna happen."

I put my hands on my hips, glaring at him. "Yes, gonna happen. The mafia is on your trail, Dean. I nearly got kidnapped in an Alabama gas station because of you. They know you're here."

"Wait, what?" Dean doesn't seem to know what to process first, but settles on, "You were almost kidnapped? Are you okay?"

I'm touched by his concern, and a little surprised, honestly. I thought Dean only ever cared about…Dean. Although, to be fair, I guess I haven't really interacted with him much as an adult, and I'm mostly basing all of my judgments off him from when we were teenagers—a time when most people are known to be thoughtful, caring, and considerate. (Ha.) "I'm fine," I return, a little flustered by the attention. "It really wasn't—"

Dean whirls to face Thad. "How could you let this happen?"

"He didn't let it happen," I interrupt before Thad can speak up for himself —presuming that he would. I'm not sure he fully believes it wasn't his fault. "He stopped it from happening—and he's why I'm here now, talking to you."

Dean paces the room, running an anxious hand through his hair. "How did you know I was here, anyway? I've covered my tracks so carefully."

"Aunt Linda's credit card," I tell him, and can't help but add, "Seriously, Dean? Letting Aunt Linda fund your getaway?"

"Mom's paying her back," Dean grumbles under his breath, though at least he has the good grace to look chagrined.

"And who's paying Mom back? You realize that's her retirement fund you're taking?"

Thad clears his throat, stepping in between us with his hands raised. "These are all good conversations to have *after* we've remanded Dean to the authorities. For all we know, whoever took that picture on the boat followed us here."

Dean's eyes widen. "Shit." He grabs a duffel bag on the sofa and begins hastily shoving things into it. "We have to go."

I watch him incredulously. "Go where?"

"Somewhere that's not here. I ditched them once—I can do it again."

"With what money?" I demand. "Mom's not an endless bank vault, you know. Especially after she has to pay your bond for skipping out on your bail."

Dean casts me an irritated look. "I know. That's why I came here—to win enough money to pay her back and get us to Mexico."

"That's why you bought the tickets for the Carolina Belle. To win enough money to pay off your bond." I can hardly process how shortsighted and ill-conceived and *Dean* the whole thing is. "Do you realize how stupid that is, Dean? Gamble what little money you have to try to get more money, when you're way more likely to lose it all and dig yourself into an even bigger hole—"

I could keep going with this all day. It's like all of my many years of pent-up irritation at Dean's carelessness has finally found an outlet. But Thad holds up a hand, his brow furrowed as he studies Dean. "*Us?*" he repeats.

It takes me a moment to follow what's happening. Dean said he was trying to win enough money to get *us* to Mexico. And unless he's started to refer to himself in the third-person plural...

The door to the bathroom opens, and a tentative head sticks out. "Dean?" asks a young, frightened voice.

Dean's face immediately softens. "It's okay, Molly. You can come out."

Chapter 41
Helen

Molly is young, but not quite as young as her voice sounds. It would put her in her early twenties, but she also might just have one of those faces that will always look a little childish, with her big brown eyes and round cheeks.

Molly is also very, very pregnant. Like, ready-to-pop-at-any-moment pregnant.

I stare at her, then at Dean, my eyes widening. I don't know whether I should be aghast or thrilled at this development. Aghast because Dean can barely take care of himself, much less a partner and child. Thrilled because…a baby! A little niece or nephew to cuddle and buy cute baby clothes, and honestly, Dean might have been a pain in my butt when we were children but even I have to admit he was the *cutest* little thing…

Molly must read at least some of what's on my face because she shakes her head. "It isn't his."

"It *is* mine," Dean protests, putting a protective hand on her belly. "I don't care whose DNA is in that baby. I'm gonna take care of both of you."

"Whose baby is it?" I ask, a growing sense of dread filling me at Dean's bravado and the haunted look on Molly's face.

Dean locks eyes with Thad, as if it's easier to explain things to him. "You know Eddie Cadorna?"

Thad swears, running a hand over his face. He looks to Molly, putting two and two together. "That's his—?"

"Yeah," Dean confirms grimly.

"And you?"

"Yeah."

I glare at both of them. "Care to include the rest of us in this conversation?" I guess by the rest of us, I really mean me, since Molly clearly knows what's going on, but still. Rude of them to use that shorthand.

Thad turns to me, taking my shoulders like he's about to brace me for something bad. "Eddie Cadorna is one of the big bosses of the Chicago mafia. And Molly is his daughter."

I really thought he was going to say child bride, so at first I'm relieved, until it sinks in. His daughter. I think of the lengths my mother would go to keep Dean safe, and she doesn't even have mafia connections. Something tells me that a mafia boss, accustomed to getting everything he wants, is not going to just calmly accept someone running off with his pregnant daughter.

And speaking of pregnant... I look down at Molly's bulging belly. "Whose...?"

"Nicky Gallo," Thad tells me grimly, like I should know the name. Because, yes, we librarians spend a lot of time keeping up on the who's who of Chicago mobsters. At my shrug, he elaborates, "Cadorna's right-hand man."

"We got married ten months ago." Molly's voice is so quiet that I almost don't hear her. "He wanted to get me pregnant right away, so I couldn't keep begging my dad to get it annulled. I was sneaking birth control, but he found it and made me flush it down the toilet. When I got the positive pregnancy test, it felt like a life sentence. But at least after that he left me alone."

I watch her uneasily, not wanting to prod, but reading between the lines well enough. I'm not sure what all Molly's marriage entailed, but I can tell by the rigid set of her jaw and her small-framed shoulders that it was deeply unhappy.

Frowning, I look at Dean. "How did you get involved in all of this?"

Dean won't quite meet my gaze. "I was Nicky's driver, and I ran some other errands for him. That's how I met Molly."

Again, reading between the lines, I can guess that Dean didn't just get the job off Craigslist. If he was working for a higher-up in the Chicago mafia, chances were very good that he was trying to become a member himself, get in the boss's good graces. My first instinct is to scold him for being so stupid and reckless, but I realize I'm not really sure I have the right. He's a grown man, and one I barely have a relationship with. And anyway, I doubt he'll get very far with his mafia aspirations now, seeing as how he "kidnapped" the wife and daughter of two of their most prominent members.

"We fell in love," Dean continues, taking Molly's hand and stroking it. "I couldn't see her suffer anymore, I just couldn't. I know that Mom's sacrificed a lot for me, but what choice did I have?"

I, for one, feel like there are quite a few choices between being a law-abiding citizen and breaking bond to flee to Mexico with a mafia boss's pregnant daughter, but apparently I'm naive.

And…I'm also not insensible to Molly's plight. Dean might have his faults, but I believe him when he says he couldn't just stand by and watch her suffer. Dean was the kid who would steal a teacher's car and fill it with rotten eggs, but who also would rescue injured animals and nurse them back to health.

The thing was, though, despite his good intentions…the wounded animals usually died. And even though I believe he really wants to keep Molly and her baby safe—he's *Dean*.

I exchange a glance with Thad, seeing in his gaze that we're roughly on the same page. We must not be too subtle about it, though, because Dean bristles defensively. "We'll be safe once we're in Mexico."

"You think they can't send people to follow you there?" Thad counters. "This is about honor to them. If they let you get away with it, then they can't hold absolute power. They'll kill you if they get the chance. They might not kill Molly since she's Cadorna's daughter, but you better believe she's gonna live the rest of her life under lock and key once they find her."

"They won't find us," Dean insists. "I disappeared once, and I can do it again."

Dean the ghost. I think he must have had his usual luck on his side, to go undetected for so long, but now the people who are following him will know his tricks. They'll know to keep an eye on Mom, and Aunt Linda, and most likely me. He won't be able to drop off the radar again through sheer dumb luck.

"I found you," I remind him gently. "And I'm just a librarian. These people are relentless, Dean, and they have resources. You need to let Thad help you."

"Thaddeus Hughes, the *Bama Bounty* guy?" Dean scoffs. At Thad's surprised face, he continues, "Yeah, I recognize you. Took me a minute without the mohawk, but I've seen the show." After a beat, he adds, "Do you think I could get your dad's autograph?"

This time I do roll my eyes. Leave it to Dean to focus on the least important detail when his life is literally in danger.

But if Thad is thrown by this, he doesn't let it show on his face. "I'll do you one better—I'll let you talk to him on the phone, if you like. Maybe you don't believe me, but he's seen this kind of shit before, man. He can tell you why going into custody is your best option."

That's a big concession from Thad, since I know he hasn't spoken to his dad in years. That's how high the stakes are, and how important it is to him to convince Dean.

I can see the war on Dean's face—getting to talk to Darius Hughes! But also maybe going back to jail. He glances at Molly. "What will happen to Molly?"

The thought comes to me before I fully intend to vocalize it. "I know some guys. Really important guys, who are connected, and can help Molly start life under a new identity."

Dean looks at me skeptically. "Monks?"

"Quinn Sullivan and Dan O'Malley, the heads of Cipher Security. Ever heard of them?"

Dean's face looks blank, but Thad does a double take. "How do you know Quinn Sullivan and Dan O'Malley?"

It's a little too complicated to explain all in one go, so I summarize it as succinctly as I can: "They're friends from church."

"Huh." Thad looks a little stunned, like I've just told him I know Brad Pitt or George Clooney, or something. Actually, to someone in the security busi-ness, saying I know Dan and Quinn is probably a bit like saying I know the security versions of Brad and George. "Those guys are seriously the best at what they do. They have this hacker who works for them, Alex Greene—"

The memory of a tall, quiet, dark-haired man I met in passing pops into my mind. "Alex—dark hair and glasses, right?"

Thad stares at me. "You know Alex Greene?"

"Not very well," I tell him. "We bumped into each other at IKEA one time. I know his wife."

Thad blinks at me, hard. "You mean this whole time we could have just shot Alex Greene a text and asked him to locate your brother?"

I shrug. "I guess so?"

With a sigh, Thad turns back to Dean. "Alex Greene is basically the best hacker in the entire world. If he agreed to do so, he could get Molly a new ID, new social security, a whole new identity, in a few minutes. I don't care who her father hires, he'd never be able to track her down."

Molly and Dean exchange a hopeful look. "Do you think he'd do that?" Dean asks me.

I really have no idea. But then, if he works for Dan and Quinn, and Dan's and Quinn's mothers have anything to say about it, then… "Yes. Definitely."

Molly and Dean retreat to the corner of the room to exchange fervid whispers. I look at Thad, who gives me a grim smile, an appreciative nod. "You did good. Who knew you were so connected?"

Grinning, I shrug back at him. "I'm full of surprises, baby."

I meant it to sound a little over-the-top cheesy, like a schmoozy Hollywood agent, but Thad's face softens as he looks at me, in a way that makes my heart skip a beat. "You sure are."

At the sound of a loud, mechanical clicking at the door, we all stop talking, turning to stare.

It takes my brain too long to process that it's someone opening the hotel door with a key card. By the time the thought has entered my mind, Thad is already stepping in front of me, shielding me with his body as he motions for the others to move back.

From where we're standing in the room, the view of the door is obscured by a wall, so for a few moments we wait—until a man steps into view.

Shane.

Holding a gun.

"Dean Flanagan," he says, with a steely focus that is as foreign to his features as it is unsettling. "You have no idea how long I've been waiting to meet you."

Chapter 42
Thad

For a long moment, Shane maintains his focused stare at Dean, gun aimed at his chest—and then abruptly, he doubles over laughing. "How badass did I just sound?" He lowers his voice to a gravelly, Clint Eastwood timbre. "Any last words, punk?"

At his continuing laughter, I exchange an uneasy look first with Helen, then Dean, before looking back to Shane again. I do my best to smile along, like I'm in on the joke, hoping that this is just Shane being Shane, despite my instincts keeping my body on high alert. "Good one, buddy." I reach out a hand toward him, slowly. "You can put the gun away, though. Dean's already agreed to go back into custody—haven't you, Dean?" I don't give him the chance to answer, just in case he gets it into his head to backpedal. To Shane, I say, "I'll let you remand him into custody—fair's fair."

That'll mean letting Shane collect the bounty, but I find I genuinely don't care. Because if Shane agrees, and puts away the gun, my gut is wrong and he isn't about to do something colossally stupid. We aren't all in danger. *Helen* isn't in danger, and we'll all walk out of this just fine.

I wait, biting the inside of my mouth.

Shane laughs again, but this time it's not a happy, playful sound. His hand tightens on the gun. "Wow, very generous of you, Thad. Too bad I've already gotten a better offer."

It's as I feared—and the worst part is, I should have figured it out a long time ago. Would have figured it out, probably, if I hadn't been blinded by

Helen. My first clue should have been when Shane popped up on the case, even though my mom never gave me the heads-up someone else was after the bounty. Or when Shane appeared on the boat, and Dean got that picture of Helen texted to him not long after. Shane wasn't hired by a bail bondsman—he was hired by the mafia to track Dean down. He won't be turning Dean into police custody, or letting Molly disappear under a new identity.

And he almost certainly won't let Helen and me walk out of here alive.

It's not the first time I've been held at gunpoint, but it's the first time it's happened to me with Helen by my side, and that changes everything. My instincts tell me to go into my usual calm, collected, problem-solving mode, but my nerves have other ideas. I'm finding it difficult to breathe, or think. My hands are shaking. I know I need to snap out of it, but I feel like I've been plunged underwater and I've forgotten how to swim.

"That's right," Shane crows, gloating at having pulled one over on me. "I'm working for—"

"Cadorna," I finish for him without fully meaning to.

It's a mistake, I see immediately, in Shane's sour expression. He's been looking forward to lording over me how badly he's outsmarted me. I shift tactics quickly. "But how? How did you know where we were?"

I don't care in the slightest, really, but I know Shane won't be able to help himself from boasting, and that might buy me enough time to think, to plan, to find some way to save us…

"Dude." The grin is back on Shane's face. "Those guys who were following you from Chicago? I sent those guys. I figured you'd recognize me tailing you, but it took you a long time to even notice *they* were there." His eyes drift beyond me, to Helen standing at my back. "Guess you must have been distracted."

I tense at his attention being drawn to Helen, and feel my stomach tighten as she responds back: "Were you the one who sent the picture of me from the boat?"

Her voice sounds totally calm, easy, and I would almost chalk it up to her naivety, Helen not realizing she's in danger once again, except for how tightly her hand is gripping the back of my shirt.

Shane perks up at the attention. "While I was getting us 'drinks,'" he confirms, using his free hand to make air quotes over the last word. "Lucky for me, I get to keep a copy as a memento. It's too bad you changed before leading me here to Dean's room, if you don't mind me saying so, Helen of Troy. I miss that outfit already."

I hate this. I hate that he's talking to her. I hate that he's *flirting* with her, while he's pointing a gun at us and insinuating he's going to kill us. I hate that he got to see her in that dress and that he has a pervy picture of her on his phone. I hate that Helen isn't back in the library in one of her big turtlenecks, absent-mindedly tucking a loose strand of hair behind her ear as she pretends to be working but is really writing one of her naughty books.

Think, Thaddeus. Think.

When she speaks again, Helen still doesn't sound remotely fazed. Maybe she's seen her share of public disturbances at the library, or maybe that's just her nature—warm and good and steady as a rock. "How'd you get a key to the room?"

"Stole it from the housekeeper's cart," Shane returns proudly. "Did it the first thing after I checked in. Figured it might come in handy." He motions toward me with the gun. "Bet you're regretting joining up with *him* now, huh? He might be the famous bounty hunter, but I've always had the real skills."

I don't know if it's his cockiness, or how idiotic he sounds, bragging about stealing a key off a hotel cart like it's proof that he's James fucking Bond, but at last I find my voice. "So what's the plan, Shane? You're gonna shoot all of us?"

Shane looks distinctly irritated to be talking to me now instead of Helen— or maybe it's because I'm calling him out, pointing to the fact that he really doesn't have much of a game plan. "Maybe. If I have to."

I run my eyes over the room, openly skeptical. "I don't know about that, Shane. The construction here is pretty good, but hardly soundproof. I'm pretty sure the neighbors will hear gunshots and call the police. What's your exit strategy?"

Shane stalls, clearly thrown. "There's a car downstairs, with a driver on standby. I can make a quick getaway."

Noted. I continue to look unimpressed. "It'll still be hard to get to it, once security locks down the elevator and stairwells."

"Then I won't shoot anyone, if I don't have to." Shane actually sounds disappointed about this. "As long as you all cooperate."

I assess him silently, running through the scenarios in my mind. If Shane gets us all tied up, what's to stop him from killing us some other way? If he's gagged us, we won't be able to make much noise, not enough to be heard through these thick, insulated walls. The real question is, is he capable of it?

A few days ago I would have said absolutely not—he's just a gung-ho, frat-boy idiot. But that was before I saw him visibly pouting at the idea of not being able to shoot us. I mistook his idiocy for incompetence, but idiocy paired with cruelty is a dangerous combination.

Taking a gun out of the equation changes the stakes, though. That requires you to get up close, fight against someone who's fighting back, look into someone's eyes as you take their life. I don't *think* Shane has it in him…but I can't be sure. Especially if he's determined to prove he's a tough guy.

No. No. I still don't think he's capable. He's a little boy playing gangster, but his priority will be getting Molly out and making a clean escape. He has no reason to kill the rest of us if he thinks he's getting what he wants.

"We'll cooperate," I assure him. "In fact, I'll help you."

"What?" Dean snaps, loudly enough that I glance his way without quite looking at him. Instead, I look at Molly, who stares back at me with those big, watchful eyes. Our gaze holds, just a moment, but hopefully long enough to convey one thing: *Trust me.*

When I look back at Shane, he looks dubious. I raise my hands to him. "Look, it seems to me you weren't really after Dean at all. You were using him to find Molly so you could take her home—and you found her. I'm sure her dad and her husband will be very grateful. And they'll be even more grateful when they know I've remanded Dean to the authorities. Add breaking bail, crossing state lines, and kidnapping to his record and I'm guessing we're looking at a nice, long sentence."

"Thad," Helen says from behind me, but I ignore her, stepping out of her grasp.

Shane raises the gun at me as I move, but I keep my hands up, my gaze locked on his. "Look, you can't hold the gun *and* tie us up at the same time. Let me help you, and you help me. After you leave with Molly, I'll take in Dean. We both win."

For a long moment, Shane studies me. Then he grins. It's not a nice grin. I know instantly I've miscalculated, played something wrong.

"I like your plan," Shane says, "except I want Helen to help me tie up everyone. Then she's coming with me."

Chapter 43
Helen

All hell breaks loose.

Dean is shouting that he won't let Shane take Molly. Thad is trying to be heard over him, demanding that Shane reconsider, that I won't be of any use to him.

Then Shane redirects the gun, directly at Thad's forehead. My heart stutters at the sight. Up until now, the gun's felt more like a threat to keep us in line, but something about the way Shane is looking at Thad now makes it feel more like a promise.

I'm not sure if the room actually falls silent, or if it's just the blood rushing in my ears. If Dean and Thad don't stop protesting, Shane is going to shoot Thad. Shane is going to *kill* Thad. He'll never tease me again, or call me *Sister Helen* just to get me riled up, or rub the back of his neck when I get *him* riled up. Those blue-gray eyes that hold so much in them will be lifeless, dimmed, forever.

And I can't let that happen.

Thad tries to grasp my arm, hold me in place, but I step around him and out of reach. "I'll do it. Just don't shoot anyone—please, Shane."

Thad tries to move between us again. "Helen—"

"Don't," Shane says sharply, and now the gun is aimed toward me, right at my sternum.

Thad hesitates, then steps back. We wait.

Shane visibly relaxes. "Good. I'm in charge here, Thad, not you. Don't try to pull anything on me—I'm not as stupid as you think." He blinks furiously, swallowing. "What should I use for rope?"

It takes me a moment to realize he's talking to me—and genuinely asking me. I cast my eyes around the room. I don't particularly want to help him come up with ways to tie everyone up, but there is the matter of the gun. Plus, I have a feeling that he weirdly trusts me. Maybe all that time chatting over books affected him more than he realized. We librarians are sneaky that way.

"Um…I can tie their shoelaces together?"

Shane barks a laugh at that. "Yeah. Let's do that. You two sit at the table." He motions Dean and Thad with the gun. "Tie them together, and around one of the table legs. Make it nice and tight, no tricks."

Dean and Thad both reluctantly, obediently sit at the table. I can't quite meet either of their gazes as I kneel to do what Shane's instructed, but I can feel both of them watching me. "I'm so sorry, Hel," Dean babbles. "This is all my fault. I'm so stupid."

I can hear he's close to tears, but I can't think about that too much. I focus on the task at hand, debating if I should chance leaving the laces loose. But if Shane checks, he'll lose trust in me, and somehow I know instinctively I have to try and keep him on my side.

As I finish, I glance up at Thad. I want to convey to him that I'm okay, that I have a plan, sort of, and that I knew all along what he was trying to do with Shane, that I didn't really think he'd betray us. *Me.*

It's a lot to try to say with one look, probably impossible; but it's a moot point, anyway, since Thad's not looking at me. He's looking over my shoulder at Shane, and his face is tight, furious. "Cut it out."

Shane laughs that irritating, frat-boy giggle I've only heard him use around Thad. "Just admiring the view."

It takes me a moment to realize he's talking about me. Kneeling down like this, my behind is straight up in the air, and based on Thad's expression, Shane's been putting on a show of ogling.

I know it's a show, too. Shane has no real interest in me. He's doing all this to get under Thad's skin, rile him up. I don't know their whole history, though it seems like there's some serious competitive energy between them. But Shane's never paid me any attention when Thad isn't there to witness it, and now is no exception.

"Come here, Helen," Shane orders me.

Wary, humiliated, I obediently stand up and move over to Shane. I force myself to meet his gaze, but he isn't looking at me—rather, at Thad. "Take off my belt."

"Shane," Thad says warningly.

"I'm in charge here," Shane reminds him. He's still grinning, but there's something dangerous in his expression.

Dropping my eyes, I undo the belt and pull it through the loops of his khakis, careful not to touch any part of him as I do so.

Despite this, Shane lets out an exaggerated moan. "Helen, you're so good at this."

"Fuck off," Thad snaps. Almost on top of him, Dean shouts, "Fuck you, asshole!"

Shane just chortles. "Belt their hands together under the table, around the table leg."

All of this testosterone in the room is making me nervous. I know Shane was only ever using me to find Dean and Molly, but even so, his energy when it was just the two of us at the library was radically different. Being near Thad seems to supercharge him, bring out his mean, spiteful side.

Maybe it's naive of me, but I think if I could remind him of our friendship, get his focus off one-upping Thad, I might be able to de-escalate things. It's not that I think Shane is good, per se, but maybe I could appeal to something good in him, some better instinct. "What a good idea," I praise him. "Did you read about that in that sailing book you checked out? I remember you told me about how you went down that TikTok rabbit hole, watching all those videos about knots."

It's a bit of a gamble, bringing this up, since I don't actually know if he read any of those books or watched any of those videos, or if it was all just a part of his act to ingratiate himself with me.

Shane blinks at me, as if genuinely having forgotten our history together at the library, and then his face clears. "Oh, yeah. I was tying knots with everything I could get my hands on for weeks."

I let out a sigh of relief, trying to cover it with a bright smile. "I think you showed me a few of them—wasn't there one called the Hercules knot?"

Honestly, I don't know what I'm doing, but I feel comforted by his relaxed posture, the grin that spreads over his face at the memory. "Oh yeah. That one took me like three days to get. I kept making a thief knot by mistake."

I laugh along with him, like I have any idea what he's talking about. "I should have paid more attention when you were explaining it to me. Would've come in handy now."

Glancing up, I'm taken aback by the earnestness on Shane's face as he meets my gaze. Unnerved, I feel the smile slipping from my face. "Shane—?"

"*I* should have paid better attention, to you. Maybe then we wouldn't be here now." He gestures down to the gun in his hands. "It's just…I had no idea how hot you were, you know? You always dressed so frumpy."

So if Shane had known I was "hot," he wouldn't have taken the job from the mafia, tried to have me kidnapped in Mobile, or shown up here with a gun to take us all hostage? I'm not really sure how that tracks, but Shane looks so *sincere*, it's clear that he, at least, believes it. "Oh," I say, for lack of anything better.

"And I'm sorry it has to be this way, for real. I think you're a nice girl. It isn't anything personal."

Oh, God. He's going to kill me. Maybe not right this moment, here in this hotel room, but after he's taken care of Dean and Thad. He'll find some way to kill them quietly so people won't overhear, but he can't leave behind any witnesses. That's what he's trying to tell me in his own clunky, self-serving way. And he isn't opening the door for me to change his mind—he's trying to get me to tell him that it's okay, no hard feelings, *I understand that you have to kill us all.*

My mouth runs dry. I try to think of something to say, some way to appeal to him, to change his mind, but instead I can't help but look over at Thad. I can see on his face that he's reached the same conclusion. We can do nothing but stare at each other, both of us lost, not knowing what to do. Not quite believing that we didn't get more time.

My attention is drawn back to the room by a quick movement out of the corner of my eye. My first instinct is that it's Shane, lunging for me, and I tense. But it isn't Shane moving.

It's Molly.

Petite, round-bellied Molly moves faster than it would seem possible for anyone in her current shape and size. One moment, she's a meek, quiet, big-eyed presence, lurking ghost-like in the corner of the room, and the next she's leaping onto Shane's back, knocking him to the ground with the force of her body.

"Molly!" Dean calls out anxiously over Shane's startled, then belligerent, shouts.

Again, my stupid instincts have me moving first toward Molly, until Thad barks at me sharply. "The gun, Helen!"

I look over, seeing that it's skidded out of Shane's hands. Molly's weight is pinning him to the ground, but even nine months pregnant, she isn't heavy enough to hold him for long. Pushing past the panic of having to (a) hold a gun and (b) potentially use it, I hop over Shane's prone body, careful to avoid his flailing limbs.

Once the gun is in hand, I point it, trembling, toward Shane. "Stop!" I order him with as much authority as I can muster into my voice. I channel the stern spine of Mother Lois, the rigid rule enforcer in my order, who would have found issue with anyone, even the Pope, for not being quite stalwart enough; the moxie of Erica, making up fake appointments and calling people the wrong name just to get her way; and the mettle of Julie Andrews, climbing over mountains to escape the Nazis. "Stop moving, or I will shoot."

Something in my voice must ring true, because Shane obediently goes limp. Still, I keep half an eye on him as I skirt around the room, giving him a wide berth, so I can reach the table where Dean and Thad are tied.

"Sis, that was so badass!" Dean crows, even as his eyes track back anxiously to Molly. "Baby, you okay?"

"I'm fine," Molly returns in that quiet, nervous voice of hers, muffled into Shane's shoulder.

"You did good, Helen," Thad tells me solemnly. He holds out his free hand for the gun. "Let me hold it while you call the police. Then you can untie us, okay?"

I'm relieved to relinquish my hold on the gun, relieved to call in the authorities. Relieved to have Shane incapacitated on the ground, and mostly relieved that, by some miracle, we're all going to be walking out of here tonight. "Okay," I agree, handing over the gun.

Chapter 44
Thad

It's a relief once the police show up, even though I've done this all enough times to know that their arrival signals a long night ahead of us. It's not like the movies, where the flashing red and blue lights mean we can slink off again—"There's your perp, officer. Good night!"—and this will all be over for us. There are witness statements to give, more than once. Paperwork to fill out. We have to wait until the ambulance arrives to take Molly to the hospital, and console Dean that she's fine, they just want to check on the baby with equipment the EMTs don't have on hand before they give her the all clear—and explain to Dean that no, he won't be going with her. He probably won't be seeing her again for a very long time, maybe never.

A month ago, I don't know that I would have been all that sympathetic to Dean. *People come and go in our lives*, I would have told him, if I'd deigned to give him any words of comfort at all. *Best not to get too attached.*

Now I can't help but think about how I'd be feeling if it were Helen they were driving away, Helen who I would never see again. That was almost what happened earlier tonight, what Shane was all but telling us he would do. Maybe he would have killed Dean and me first, or maybe I would have had to watch him take Helen from the room, knowing she was never coming back.

The thought is agonizing. Unbearable. It makes me feel like a caged beast. I know police procedure, I know how this all works, but I'm still restless, pacing, irritated that I'm stuck answering the same questions over and over again, unable to be near her. To check that she's all right. To comfort her. To comfort myself in the knowledge that Shane didn't succeed: she's okay, she's okay.

When they take us all down to the station, I make sure I keep my eyes on Helen as much as possible. I know when she's taken into one of the offices to give her statement, and I know how long she's there, and I check the look on her face when she comes out. She looks tired, but otherwise unharmed. If she's anything like me, she'll want to sleep for a thousand years once we finally get back to the hotel.

At one point, I see her speaking to an officer, who brings her over to talk to me. My heart catches in my throat at her sudden nearness. I want to pull her into my arms. I want to hold her. I want…to do things that would not be appropriate to do in a crowded police station. Instead all I do is stand as she draws near, swallowing hard as our gazes meet and hold.

She must be feeling similarly overwhelmed, because for a moment all we do is stare at each other. Then she clears her throat. "They're going to let me go down to the hospital to check on Molly. I can make some calls from there."

It's amazing that after such a short time of knowing each other, we can already communicate so much with just our eyes, a brief shorthand, but I know exactly what she's telling me. The police know that Molly was one of the people being held hostage in the hotel room, and I'm sure Shane will eventually crack and admit who she is and why he was following her. But these New Orleans police officers have no idea the significance of Molly's last name, Gallo, and no reason to hold her. Hopefully by the time they've figured it out, Helen will have made her calls—to Quinn Sullivan and Dan O'Malley and Alex Greene—and secured Molly safe passage to wherever her new life will be.

I'll need to stay here, to continue the process of remanding Dean into custody, more complicated than usual since we've crossed state lines and whatnot. It will be a long night. But it isn't the late hour or my tiredness that grates me now—it's not being with *her*, at her side, making sure she's safe while she makes sure Molly is safe. Shane and his accomplice are in custody, but there's no way to know if there are others lurking around.

I want to keep Helen locked in place, right next to me. But I know it's important to her, to keep the promise she made to Dean and Molly. And I also know, after seeing her with Shane tonight, that she's more than capable of taking care of herself.

"Be careful," I tell her. They're two stupid, insignificant words that don't nearly scratch the surface of what I'm feeling, but they'll have to do.

She nods, searching my face. "I will."

I wish I could take her hand, just for a moment. Touch her hair. Hold her in my arms. I guess I could actually do any of those things, but it isn't just embarrassment at being in a crowded police station holding me back. It's the depth of the feeling, how much is at stake. It's too raw and precious a thing to express, even in part, in front of all of these people.

I was terrified of losing you.

I don't know what I'd do if anything happened to you.

I...love you.

As much as the sentiment startles me, I don't resist it, because I know instantly that it's true. It doesn't make sense. We haven't known each other for very long, and most of that time I was pretending to be someone else. We're such different people, when it all comes down to it. So different that these past few days on the road shouldn't have had the power they've had, and yet...I admire her. I care what she thinks. I want to make her laugh. I want her to trust me, to respect me. I want to make the world be as good as she believes it is. *I want to be as good as she believes I am.*

I don't say any of this to her, though. Not now. I just hold her gaze, and nod. "I'll see you back at the hotel."

The words are nowhere near adequate. But I hope they're enough.

By the time I get back to the hotel, it's technically morning, though it's still dark as pitch outside. I'm half tempted to get another room so I won't wake her, but selfishly, I need to know she's all right, safe in bed where she's supposed to be. I need to be near her.

The room is dark when I let myself in, but I can tell instantly that Helen is awake. In the light from the hallway, I faintly make out her silhouette as she sits up. "It's me," I tell her quietly, just in case she's having as hard a time making out my features as I am hers. After the night we've had, I don't want to startle her or make her even in the slightest bit afraid, not even for a moment.

I shut the door behind me, plunging us back into darkness as I fumble for the deadbolt and the latch. No more surprises tonight. No one entering with a key card he shouldn't have.

Behind me, Helen switches on the bedside light. "You don't have to," I start to say. "I'm sure you're—"

Tired is what I mean to say, but I lose my voice as I turn and see her properly. She was asleep, I can see, tiredness still clinging to the corners of her eyes, her hair lightly mussed. She's put on my T-shirt again to sleep in, but her legs are bare, twisted up in the sheets.

It isn't just that she looks so incredibly sexy like that, though she does. She looks so *vulnerable*. I can't help but think about what would have happened if it had been someone else coming in here with that key card. She's so good, so trusting, coming along on this trip with me, putting her safety in my hands, but anything could have happened tonight. Anything almost *did* happen and I was there and I couldn't have done anything to stop it. I don't even carry a gun, because I'm an egotistical moron who, before tonight, didn't really believe anything bad could happen to *me*.

"Thad." Helen reaches for me, holding out her hand almost plaintively, like she can sense me spiraling.

I meant to ask her about Molly and how everything turned out. I wanted to tell her about how brave Dean was when it finally came down to it, how relieved he was that Molly was safe and that his mother wouldn't have to pay off his bond.

All I can do is go to her.

I want to touch her, feel her limbs and legs and fingers, hold her face in my hands and look into her eyes as I ask her if she's okay, really and truly. I want to kiss her, wrap my arms around her and hold her as she sleeps.

That's what I'm intending to do.

But as I grip her face in my hands and look into her eyes, I feel the full weight of what was almost lost. It hits me like a wave, threatens to pull me underneath its current. I want to apologize to her, tell her to get as far away from me as she can. Beg her not to leave me. Tell her I think I love her. Tell her she'd be better off going.

"Helen," is all I manage to say.

Somehow what I'm feeling must be conveyed in that single word, because Helen draws me in. Scooting back against the headboard, she pulls me so I'm half on top of her, my head cradled against her chest so I can hear her heart beating.

For several long moments, we stay that way, until at last, I lift my head so I can capture her mouth in mine. We kiss slowly at first, then more urgently. Our bodies are pressed together, her softness pinned beneath me. There are so many things I've wanted to do with her, so much that I've wanted to explore, but the urgent need to be inside her is outweighing almost every other impulse.

I push it down, reminding myself she's a virgin, that this would be her first time, and I'm not sure that's something she wants. Even if it is, the first time demands some kind of ceremony. It isn't a frantic, thrusting, needful thing done in the dark. There should be candles and rose petals. It should not follow a day of being held at gunpoint and very nearly killed.

I try to lose myself in the kiss, content to just be near her—until Helen pulls away with a frustrated little growl. "Why won't you touch me?"

Her hair is mussed, her lips a little swollen, and she's glaring at me like I've besmirched her honor, when that's the very thing I've been trying to avoid doing. I might even laugh at her irritation, if I weren't also feeling the same frustrating, pressing need. "I don't want to take things too far. Once I start, I don't know if I'll be able to stop."

"Then don't stop," she insists, spreading her legs wider.

Heat jolts down through me, straight into my cock. "Helen," I growl in warning.

"Please, Thad. I need you. I need you inside me."

I capture her lips in mine before she can say anything else, because I honestly don't know if I'm capable of self-control when she's begging me to be inside her. This time I do touch her, though, running my hand up her thigh, and hoping that if I help her find her release, she'll allow me to stay chivalrous and not deflower her before we've had a proper conversation about it.

She whimpers and gasps and twists around at my touch. After a few moments of teasing her, I dip my fingers into her panties to find her already soaking. Jesus.

To my surprise, she twists away from my touch. "I don't need that. I need you inside me. I want to feel you inside me."

I stare at her dumbly, heart pounding, sending all the blood in my body down to my dick. Struggling to remain coherent, I start running through the reasons why we shouldn't have sex, out loud this time. "It's your first time. We shouldn't rush it."

"I'm thirty-one years old. I'd hardly call that rushing it."

I grit my teeth. "We're both feeling the adrenaline from today. We should wait until we're thinking more clearly."

Helen grips my chin, forcing me to look at her. "If you don't want to, that's fine. But please don't try to come up with excuses for *me*. I'm a grown woman. I know what I want. I want you."

For a long moment, I stare at her, trying to remember again why I've been fighting so hard against this. Everything in me is urging me to sink into her warmth, feel her wrapped around me, and she is quite literally urging me to do the same.

Rolling off her, I push myself off the bed, shucking off my clothes. Naked, I move to the dresser for my wallet. I'm pretty sure I have a condom stuck in there. After checking the packaging for the expiration date, I tear it open, extracting the condom and rolling it on. It's been a while, but turns out it's just like riding a bike.

When I turn back, I see that Helen has also removed her clothes and is lying there, naked, waiting for me. For a moment, it feels like all the air has been pushed out of my chest. She is so *Helen* in that moment—brave and curious and determined and vulnerable all rolled into one—that it hurts to look at her.

"You're so beautiful," I tell her, gently easing her legs open. "Is this still what you want?"

"Yes."

I step in between her parted legs, encouraging her to wrap them around me, before I ease myself in slowly at her entrance, little by little. She is concentrating hard, her brow furrowed as she stares down at the place where our bodies meet. "Breathe," I remind her, then push in a little deeper as she does so. "This okay?"

"Yes."

"Does it hurt?"

"A little. But don't stop."

I won't, but I do pause for a moment, reaching up to take her breasts. Her perfect, voluptuous breasts. I become entranced, watching the way they move, seeing the rest of her posture relax into the sensation. I turn my face up so I can lick and suck and bite at her neck, her shoulder, her collarbone, her ear.

This time there's less resistance as I sink in a little bit further. She gives a little involuntary gasp, her eyes pressing shut, but I'm in deep enough now that I know the best thing is to keep going forward. "Move with me," I encourage her. "It'll help it pass more quickly."

I have only vague recollections from my younger years of this being true, but it seems right as I say it, and Helen obediently begins moving her body with mine. I've been so focused on her pleasure that it isn't until I've sunk all the way in that I allow myself to really feel mine. For a moment, I'm blinded by it—her warmth, her scent, her sex clenching around me as her body moves to draw me in even deeper.

I rouse myself out of the sensation, trying to focus on her, make sure she's all right, that this experience is memorable and meaningful and *enjoyable*. By now she's moving at an almost frantic pace, encouraging me to keep up, and I think any pain or discomfort must be gone, or long eclipsed by something else. "Thad," she breathes, urges, reprimands. There is so much need in that word.

Then all coherent thought disappears, and I'm simply moving, moving, bucking toward the sensation that's building inside of me and that seems to have possessed her, too. The last conscious action that I take is feeling for that sensitive nub in between us. She gasps, and moans, and pulls me in tighter, tighter, and I finally let go.

Chapter 45
Helen

I know something's wrong the moment I wake up.

Thad sits at the edge of the bed, his back turned toward me. He's fully dressed, just staring straight ahead, his shoulders tense. When I glance over, I see his bag is resting next to the door. He doesn't have to say anything. I may not have much experience, but I know what this means.

The hurt, the shock, the pain of it is almost unbearable. I don't move for several seconds, fighting back tears, my heart aching. If this had happened a few days ago, it would have hurt, but I could have understood it. We hadn't made any promises to each other then. We hadn't known what it would be like to almost lose each other.

But to have this happen, now? After what we've been through together? It isn't just about the fact that we had sex for the first time last night. It's the way he smiled at me when we were walking back from the Carolina Belle, like looking at me made his whole face soften. It's the way he stepped in front of me when Shane was pointing a gun at us, caring less about his life than mine. It's the way he held me when he got back to the hotel room, like he was terrified to let me go.

Matilda warned me that sex changes everything, that men don't always mean what they say. But what about everything he *did*? Does all of that mean nothing, too?

Sitting up to alert him that I'm awake, I wait for him to make eye contact with me. He does, swallowing, and his face is filled with pain.

I can see that he has something he's trying to work up the courage to say to me, but I don't want to hear it. Shaking my head at him, I cut him off before he can even start. "You don't have to do this. It doesn't have to be like this."

He swallows again, and the motion looks painful. *"Helen."*

Probably, if Matilda were here, she'd tell me to ice him out, pretend that this doesn't hurt me, but I can't. My heart has always been on my sleeve, advertising everything that I'm feeling for everyone to see. "Whatever scenario that's playing out where you think you have to be the lone wolf, or whatever—just don't. Change your mind. Please."

His voice sounds strained when he speaks, and if I didn't know better, I would have almost sworn that he's been crying. "It isn't that simple."

"It *is* that simple. What we did last night was *good*. You didn't take anything from me that I didn't want to give. It wasn't sinful or wrong. It was…" I gesticulate frustratedly, searching for the right words. "*Holy.* At least it was to me."

Thad starts to reach for me, then stops himself. "It isn't about that. I don't regret what we did together." Another long, painful swallow. "But I can't stop thinking about what happened before…what almost happened."

I frown at him. "With Shane?"

He flinches at the name. "If you hadn't distracted him…if Molly hadn't tackled him…"

This time I reach for him, curling my fingers around his. "But we did. And everyone's okay. I know it was scary, but—"

Thad withdraws his hand from mine, almost angrily. "It wasn't just scary, Helen. It was…" He shakes his head, as if there's no word to describe what he's feeling. "Shane was going to take you. He was probably going to kill you, and it would have been all my fault. You shouldn't have even been there."

I honestly don't know what to say to that. It takes me a moment to find my words again. "So—you're angry with me?"

He rises abruptly to his feet, pacing the small length of the room. "I'm not angry with you, I'm…furious that it happened. I'm terrified that it might happen again."

"Why would it happen again?"

"Because it keeps happening." Thad turns to face me on a rush, like all the words are pouring out of him faster than he can stop them. "Because you were almost kidnapped in Mobile, and you were almost killed here. And that's never happened to you before, not even close, so the common denominator here is me." He thumps his chest, hard, for emphasis. "And if I stay with you, if I pull you down to my level, it'll happen again."

I can tell that he means what he says, even though it doesn't make any sense to me, even though it sounds completely illogical. If you love something, someone, you protect them, you hold them close. You don't push them away.

Keeping my voice as calm as possible, I try to reason with him. "It happened because of my connection to *Dean*, not to you. And Dean is back in custody now. There's no reason to come after me anymore."

"But what happens when some guy I put in prison gets out and decides he wants to even the score? Or someone's family member wants to get revenge? It's only a matter of time, Helen. You're so…you're so *good*, so trusting. You're an easy target. And I can't let it happen because of me."

That word *good* hurled at me, is probably meant to be a weird sort of compliment, but I flinch away from it, blinking back tears. Rising to my feet, I clench my hands, waiting until I trust my voice enough to speak. "So because of a hypothetical possibility of something bad that *might* happen, you won't even try. I guess you could be right—but what if you aren't? Maybe I am trusting, and naive, and *good*, but I'd rather hope for the best than live for the worst."

That's all I can manage without bursting into tears. I make a hasty exit into the bathroom. And maybe I am naive, because a part of me still hopes he'll come after me, tell me he's changed his mind.

He doesn't.

Chapter 46
Helen

T*hree Months Later*

"Kimberly! Kimberly!"

I look up blankly from my computer screen, blinking as I realize that Erica has been trying to get my attention for the past minute. "Sorry—what?"

Erica points from her desk to the front counter, where I can see that a partially obscured patron is waiting to be checked out. "Someone needs your help."

Biting back my irritation, I refrain from reminding Erica that *she* could just as easily get up to help. But it's not like I'm doing anything, anyway.

When I reach the counter, I can see the patron more clearly, and smile when I recognize Kathleen from my writing group. "Hi, Kathleen! Long time no see."

"It's been ages! We've missed you at writing group."

I do my best to keep smiling. "I know, I've just been so busy." So busy *not* writing my romance novel. Normally I wouldn't have minded attending anyway to offer my feedback to the group, but I've had a hard time with anything romance adjacent lately. The only things I can really stomach these days are nonfiction and cooking shows.

"I've been pretty worried about Wilfred," Kathleen confides in me, referencing my character—the one who *doesn't* get the girl. "I hope you give him a happily ever after in the epilogue."

"Maybe," I say vaguely, keen to change the subject. "What are you reading?"

Kathleen hands me her stack of books. "I read about a new series I thought I'd try. It's supposed to make *Fifty Shades of Grey* look tame in comparison. I hear the second book has an alien orgy in it."

"Oh," I say, because really, what else can you say to that?

As soon as she leaves, I feel something light hit the side of my head. "Psst. Kimberly."

Frowning, I look down to see a stray paper clip on the floor. Slowly, I turn to face Erica. "Did you just throw a paper clip at my head?"

Erica ignores my question. "It says on the schedule that you're off at noon, but there's this fire sale I really want to go to. Can you stay on and cover my shift?"

I shake my head firmly. "I have an appointment."

"What kind of appointment?" Erica challenges, rolling her eyes, like I'm the one asking *her* to change her shift. Without waiting for my answer, she begins whining. "Can't you reschedule?"

It's my appointment with Dr. Sandra. Truth be told, I've been finding ways to avoid it for as long as I can, and I really wouldn't mind having another legitimate reason to postpone. But it's the principle of the matter. "Sorry, but no. Maybe you can still catch the sale after work."

Erica looks at me like I've suggested using her bare hand instead of toilet paper. "All the good stuff will be gone by then."

I really, truly couldn't care less. Still, I try to be as empathetic as I can. "You never know."

"Selfish bitch."

She mutters it under her breath, but still loud enough that I was obviously intended to hear it. And you know what?

Not today, Satan!

I rise to my feet, waiting until she finally deigns to lift her gaze. "You know what, Erica? Fuck off."

I'm not sure if it's the swear word, or the intensity in my eyes, or just the simple fact that I'm standing up for myself, but Erica's mouth drops open. For a moment, she is speechless. Then she rallies. "What did you just say to me?"

"You heard me, Kimberly."

She blinks incredulously. "That isn't my name."

"Well, it isn't mine either. So you can just fuck the goddam hell off."

And we work in silence together for the remainder of my shift.

Look, I know that telling off your coworker and swearing like a sailor aren't necessarily things to be proud of, but I gotta admit, it felt pretty good. That telling-off has been about two years coming, and I hope it will get Erica off my back. And even if it doesn't, I now know how good it feels to put her in her place, so I won't be avoiding doing so in the future if she steps out of line. In fact, I may even be looking forward to it.

Leaving the library, I have a little extra spring to my step as I make my way to my appointment with Dr. Sandra.

Which is a lucky thing, actually, since I've been dreading this meeting with my sort-of therapist. That's why I've been avoiding it for the past three months, ever since I got back from New Orleans. I'm sure she's been able to see through my fibs about why I needed to postpone, although I have gotten a bit better at lying. My first two excuses were fairly normal—needing to recover from the trip, feeling under the weather. But last month I may have panicked and told her my water heater exploded. I'm not really sure why. It seemed like a plausible excuse at the time.

Sure enough, as I spot her on our usual park bench, she brightens visibly and waves me over. "Hey, girl! I thought you might be getting ready to cancel on me again. I've been pretty worried about your household appliances all day."

Smiling sheepishly, I open my Tupperware offering and hold it out for her inspection. "Yeah. These are my sorry-I've-been-avoiding-you mini quiches." I'm pulling out the big guns today.

Dr. Sandra grins and happily takes one. After taking a bite, she chews thoughtfully. "Is that...pancetta and goat cheese?"

I nod in confirmation.

Her eyebrows rise a notch, impressed. "You must have something pretty big to tell me. So spill it. I've been appropriately subdued with eggy goodness."

I take in a deep breath, my stomach rolling as I brace myself to say the words. "I...had sex."

Dr. Sandra laughs, taking this as a joke—which I understand, since this is exactly the kind of joke that I might have made in one of our previous visits. But as she sees my lack of amusement, she quickly sobers, straightening a bit and shifting subtly into therapist mode. "Okay. That's a big development. How do you feel about that?"

Bless her, I know she's dying for the details, but I appreciate her checking in with how I'm doing first. "I'm fine. A little disappointed, I guess."

She grimaces sympathetically. "If it's any consolation, most people's first time isn't great. There's such a big buildup around it, and it's such a new experience—it can be hard for it to live up to the fantasy. But with time and practice—"

I shake my head to let her know that isn't the issue. "No, it was good." Unwittingly, memories from that night come back to me—the urgency and intensity, Thad's body moving against mine, inside mine—and I shake my head, drawing in a breath. "I...enjoyed it."

Dr. Sandra furrows her brow. "Okay, so what was disappointing about it?"

This is the part I've been dreading. A knot forms in my chest, making it difficult to breathe, to speak. "Well, I guess for starters, Thad and I aren't together anymore—"

"Thad?!" Dr. Sandra catches herself, clearing her throat before adding in a more subdued, professional tone, "The bounty hunter posing as a library patron to try to capture your brother. He was your first time?"

Dr. Sandra must have known I was traveling with Thad and helping him find my brother, since her husband helped Molly create her new identity and go into hiding, but there were obviously a lot of missing gaps in the story that she had not been privy to.

I nod, wondering where to possibly begin. "It's complicated but...we got to know each other a little better during that New Orleans trip. I think we fell in love with each other? At least, I fell in love with him."

Dr. Sandra is doing her best not to prod me on, to just let me tell the story, but I can tell she's confused and dying for some answers. "So...what happened?"

"I think he was afraid of something happening to me, because of his job. At least that's what he said."

"Do you believe him?"

I consider the question. "Yes. I mean, I think it was a stupid reason, but I believe that *he* believed it was true."

"But now you're disappointed that you're not together." Dr. Sandra's voice is kind, sympathetic. A truer testament, though, to the fact that she's really listening, is that she hasn't yet taken another mini quiche.

Again, I consider her words, then shake my head slowly. "No, that's not it. I mean, yes, I am disappointed about that. I'm heartbroken about that, if I'm being honest. But I guess it's a bigger sense of disappointment, more generally."

"What do you mean?"

I suck in a breath, trying to find the right words. "All this time, I felt so behind everyone else because I hadn't experienced the things that most people have experienced by my age. Love. Sex. Relationships. I guess I thought if I checked those boxes, then—I don't know. I would be caught up. Everything would make more sense. But I fell in love. I had sex. I had *good* sex—"

I must say this part a little too emphatically, because a passing jogger gives me a double take. Grimacing, I sink down a little lower on the bench, waiting until they've passed to continue. "I did all the things I've been waiting to do, and nothing's really changed. I'm still me."

Dr. Sandra nods, taking this all in. "Sex doesn't fix everything. They should really write that on the condom packaging, shouldn't they?"

"Yep." I take one of my own mini quiches, biting into it balefully.

For a moment, we sit in silence, eating delicious, savory, pastry goodness and staring out at the water. Then Dr. Sandra breaks the silence. "I can see why that outcome would be disappointing. But here's another way to look at it—if it ain't broke, don't fix it."

I'm not really sure where she's going with this, so I just take another bite of quiche and wait for her to elaborate.

"You started enjoying the pleasure of my company because you had some hang-ups about some life experiences you'd missed out on. There was nothing wrong with you—there was never anything wrong with you. In fact, in strictly medical, professional terms, you were what we like to call 'awesome sauce.' And now? You've had the sex, and the romance, and the heartbreak—all those big life experiences you were afraid you'd missed out on. And even after all that? You're still awesome sauce. You're feeling disappointed because it didn't change anything in your life, but *you* never needed changing. All of those things, they're just experiences, like going to the Eiffel Tower or running a marathon. They can enrich your life, or cause you a lot of unnecessary effort and pain, but they won't change who you are essentially. You're Helen, with or without sex, with or without a bounty hunter or any other romantic partner in your life."

The words, the kindness behind them, brings unexpected tears to my eyes. I haven't let myself cry over Thad since I left New Orleans. I haven't let myself cry for *me*, for all the jumbled emotions of everything that happened. But now, with these words of encouragement and support, I finally let myself break down, the emotions flooding loose.

"Oh, hon." Dr. Sandra pulls me into a hug, rubbing my back with practiced, maternal affection. "You know I literally could have him killed, right? Or at least audited by the IRS."

I'm not entirely sure that she's joking, but I laugh through my tears, grateful for the support, however unprofessional. "I'll keep that in my back pocket. Just in case."

Chapter 47
Helen

D r. Sandra and my writing group aren't the only people I need to make amends with, after disappearing for the past few months. I've been back in Chicago, but I haven't actually been *back*, not fully, and I've been avoiding Nina and Matilda. Nina, because her dark eyes would be full of too much sympathy as I told my story, and Matilda…because I don't want to hear *I told you so*.

That hasn't stopped them from texting me. A few days after I returned to the city, Matilda was the first to reach out:

Are you back? Did you have sex or what? Did you use the lube? When that got no response, she added, Pizookies on Tuesday?

When there was no response, even Matilda had enough tact to give me a few days, likely sensing that something had gone down on the road trip. I could almost imagine the separate text chain between Nina and Matilda, the back-and-forth while Matilda insisted on ambushing me at my apartment and Nina encouraged her to be patient, to give me some space.

But finally, Nina was the next one to reach out: Are you back? Do you want to meet up at Lou's at our usual time? 💟 After a few more hours, she texted again: If you need some space, we understand. Please just let us know you're all right.

When even that went unanswered, Matilda seemed to have gone off-book and fired off some uncensored messages. I texted Carlos and I know you've been coming to your shifts at the library, so you are therefore ALIVE and just not answering our texts, which I think you know is RUDE.

Are you there? Did you lose your phone??

Did that bounty hunter hurt you? Just give us the word and he'll disappear, no questions asked. I'm a paralegal - I know people.

So are you ghosting us now???

And after that, silence, except for Nina's gentle weekly reminders that they'll be getting Pizookies on Tuesdays, if I ever want to join them.

I don't know why it's so hard to face them. I think it's maybe because they've been with me through the whole journey, from meeting the Red Unicorn and dreaming about who he could be, to knowing and falling in love with Thad. Their hopes were built up along with mine—yes, even Matilda's, despite her odd way of showing it. My heart was broken in this process. I didn't want to break theirs, too.

But those were probably just the excuses of a coward. I was hiding from my life because I was hurt, I was embarrassed. I need my friends now more than I probably ever have, and I shouldn't have cut them out.

Luckily tonight is Tuesday. I think I have a pretty good idea of where they'll be.

My heart is racing as I look for our usual table at Lou Malnati's Pizzeria. Part of me is worried that Nina and Matilda might have changed their plans, chosen somewhere else to spend their Tuesdays. Part of me would honestly be relieved if that were true, because I'm a chicken and I'm terrified of what they'll say when they see me.

Nina is the first to spot me as I approach the table. The Pizookie must not have arrived yet, because they're just sitting and talking, but Nina stops midword at the sight of me, her eyes widening and her mouth opening in almost perfect, cartoonish symmetry at her surprise.

I might laugh, if I didn't feel like I was going to throw up.

Matilda frowns, following Nina's gaze, then her eyes land on me. She stares at me for a long time. Then she rises to her feet, folding her arms. Nina looks back and forth between us, her brow furrowed with worry.

"So you just show up, now, after all this time?" Matilda demands. "We thought you were dead. Then we thought you'd ditched us for your new boyfriend. We thought you weren't coming back." Her voice breaks a little on that last sentence, belying the coolness of her dark blue eyes.

I was expecting this from Matilda, and honestly, it's a little comforting. She is still Matilda, no matter what else may have changed in my life over the past few months. Her strong personality isn't for everyone. Her unflagging honesty can be brutal. But she is my constant, ever since I became a laywoman. Other people might come and go, might change, might bend, might waver, but Matilda will always be there, firm and unyielding as a rock as the waves crash around her.

"I have no excuses," I tell her, and Nina, but mostly Matilda, earnestly. I know I've hurt Nina, too, but she made clear her door was always open. I need Matilda to understand how much I need to know that hers isn't closed. "I was embarrassed. I was hurt. I was being selfish and wallowing in self-pity. I'm sorry. I missed you. I need you. Both of you. Please forgive me."

Matilda's face remains unreadable, but Nina is already shaking her head. "There's nothing to forgive—"

I cut her off before she can finish, needing them to understand me. "Yes, there is." Again, I look at Matilda, holding her gaze. "I abandoned you. I was hurting, but I could have still texted. I could have asked for time. Instead, I shut you out. And that isn't how you treat the people you love." I know that kind of hurt, after all. That's exactly what Thad did to me, and it's taken me months to even be able to say it. "I'm sorry."

Nina's eyes are filled with sympathetic tears. Matilda stares at me for a long moment before abruptly lurching at me and pulling me into a too-tight hug. It's a little hard to breathe, actually, but I'm so relieved she's accepting my apology that I don't protest.

After a moment, she pulls back, blinking furiously. "You'll have to tell us everything, of course. Then we can decide what we'll need to do to take our revenge on that no-good bounty hunter."

Nina wipes at her eyes, laughing a little. "We don't even know that there's any reason to take revenge."

Matilda levels her eyes at me again. *We will take our revenge*, she mouths at me, nodding once, a solemn promise.

Despite the old hurt rising again, knowing that I'll have to regurgitate all the details, the emotions, I can't believe how good it feels to be with my ex-nun tribe again. Nina's kindness and empathy, Matilda's ferociousness and loyalty. I smile at each of them in turn as we take our seats. "I'll tell you everything," I promise.

So I do—I tell them about how I've been writing Dean once a week, trying to keep up his spirits while he waits for sentencing after pleading guilty. I tell them about the mysterious, unaddressed, generic postcard I received that simply read *All good x2*, which I choose to believe is from Molly, letting me know that she and the baby are all right, wherever they are.

And I tell them about Thad. I tell them how rocky the start of the trip was, but how we slowly grew to understand each other better over time. I tell them all the strange details of our journey—almost being kidnapped, being saved by sorority girls, being held hostage by Shane. Falling in love with Thad. Having my heart broken.

When I'm finished, Matilda is predictively, protectively furious. "That bastard. I hope his dick rots off."

Nina, as always, is a little more circumspect with her judgments, watching me carefully as she speaks. "Have you heard from him at all since then?"

My heart lodges in my throat. Not once. Not a text. Not an email. Nothing. "Nope," I say when I'm able, hardly recognizing my voice.

"Who cares about him anyway?" Matilda interrupts. "He's dead to us. What we need to do is find someone new, someone *better…*"

I shake my head at that, firmly, even though I know she's only trying to help. "I think I might keep romance on the page for now." At the impending protest I see on Matilda's face, I cut her off. "Not forever. Just for now."

After all, Rosamund has been waiting for me patiently, wanting to get her happily ever after. I think I'm ready to give it.

More time passes. I bake. I read. I knit, badly, but finish my first hat, which will go to my father, since it is very poorly constructed, and he is likely to be the only person who would wear it. I go out with my friends, and I meet up for my monthly visits with Dr. Sandra. I make Matilda go through my clothes with me because I know she will give me her honest opinion on what looks terrible; and then I ask Nina to go shopping with me for new items, because I know she will give me her honest opinion on what looks good. I send care packages to Dean and start up a more regular correspondence by writing him letters, because I want to know my brother as the adult he is, not as the kid I remember him being. And I start writing again, after deciding to take my story in a new direction.

My life is full. I would even say it's happy. I know, and have always known, that I don't need a man or sex or romance to feel fulfilled. I've spent most of my life living without any of those things, and I slip back easily into life without it once again. It's better that way, honestly, to just push it all behind me. To not think about him, as much as that's possible. But when thoughts of him do slip through, more often than I would like, I wonder what he's doing, where he is, if he's happy. Mostly I wonder if he ever thinks about me. Probably not. He was this huge, monumental milestone in my life, but I was likely just some brief blip in his romantic history. If he thinks of me at all, it's probably just on occasion.

The thought is meant to help me move on, but it brings me no comfort, only misery.

Which is why, one morning when I come out from the back room of the library, I'm stunned to see Thad standing at the service counter.

At first, I think it's just my imagination. Part of me wants to see Thad, and so I'm seeing his features in a stranger. If I look at him long enough, change my angle, close my eyes and open them again, I'll see that of course it's not really him. There's no reason for him to be standing there.

But I stare, and shake my head, and all but rub my eyes, and it's still Thad, watching me silently as I stare back at him.

My body stiffens instinctively at the sight of him, my stomach roiling with nerves. Beyond the shock of him actually being here, now, in my library, I'm honestly not sure what to feel. Confused, mainly, I think. Angry that he's here with no warning, no explanation, just as I was getting my life back on track. Hurt that it's taken him so long.

"It's you," I blurt out.

Of all the lines I practiced with myself for if I ever saw him again—all the ways I planned to play things so mysterious and sexy and cool—that response was never on my list. I regret it immediately, but it's too late to take it back. Instead, I straighten my spine a little, determined to recover. "What are you doing here?"

"I came to see you."

Thad's tone is direct, firm, like he's been practicing the words. I am unfortunately not as prepared or as practiced. My mind swirls around what he just said, trying to parse out its meaning. He came to see me? He's not just in the neighborhood, or in desperate need of a book recommendation—he came to see *me*. Why?

"Why?" I ask the question aloud, because again, I did not have the benefit of preparing ahead of time how this conversation would go.

Thad holds steady, not breaking my gaze. "Because I missed you."

The words hit me like a blow to the chest. It's what I always hoped would be true, but realize now that I didn't believe it was actually a possibility. He's missed me. He's *missed* me? "Why?" I ask again.

"Do you know Philo's—the coffee shop down the street?" At my uncertain nod, Thad continues, "Will you meet me there on your break?"

I check my watch, mostly for something to do, some way to stall. "It isn't for another hour."

"I'll wait." Thad's steady gaze holds mine captive. "Will you meet me?"

I honestly have no idea if this is something I even want to do, until I glance down at his hands, and notice the way he's gripping the edge of the counter in a way that belies the steadiness of his voice. He's just as nervous, uncertain, as I am. And for some reason, that compels me to nod. "Okay."

"Thank you." Thad's shoulders lower a little, and he holds my gaze a moment longer, nodding to himself, before leaving. "I'll see you then."

Chapter 48
Thad

I feel like I'm going to throw up.

And I probably deserve to, after everything I've put Helen through. My nerves, my racing heart, my indigestion, are mild prices to pay for abandoning her, for taking the choice out of her hands yet again. So, yeah. Penitent projectile vomit. It feels like the least I can do.

There are still a few minutes before Helen is supposed to come here to meet me, but I'm looking up and down the street, straining my head every time I see a flash of blonde hair go by. I check my phone, just in case she texted, then check it again a moment later to make sure I didn't accidentally put it on silent. I haven't. The ringer is all the way turned up, too, just for the record.

I honestly wouldn't blame her if she stood me up. I know I put her on the spot before, just showing up at the library, but I didn't know how else to do it. A text felt too casual. An email, too impersonal. I wrote a long letter, too, but I got too paranoid about it getting lost in the mail. So I decided to hand deliver it to her apartment, but then I worried that might be too creepy, like I'm trying to remind her that I know where she lives, or something. In the end, showing up at her workplace seemed like the best bet, because if she felt unsafe or just didn't want to see me, there would be plenty of other people around to back her up when she told me to get lost.

She's not coming, my pessimistic inner voice warns me. I need a distraction, so I pull out *The ABC Murders*. That's right—an Agatha Christie book. One I'm actually reading this time. I worry it might seem a little manipulative, like I'm trying to prove to her I've changed, or something, but the truth is, I can't stop reading them. Helen was right to recommend them to me, back when we first met, because they're great books—but that's not why I'm reading them. They could be the worst drivel of all time, and I'd still be hooked.

I knew, when I left Helen in that hotel room in New Orleans, that I'd miss her. I probably knew even then that I was making a mistake, but I think I got caught up in my head, like I was some kind of fucking film noir character who was proving his nobility by leaving the girl behind so she could live a good life. Only…I didn't leave her behind. She was with me everywhere I went. I saw her in strangers on the street. I heard a laugh that sounded like hers and it felt like someone was squeezing my heart. I remembered the way she smiled at me after the Carolina Belle and I genuinely, truly loathed myself for being the person to hurt her.

I needed her back in my life, even if it was in some small, insignificant way. So I went to the library—not hers, but another branch where I was sure she wouldn't be—and picked up my first Agatha Christie. And I actually started going through them as quick as I used to pretend to read them, back when I was following Helen. It felt like the closest I could get to actually being with her—reading the books I knew she'd read.

Glancing up from *The ABC Murders*, I see Helen standing on the other side of the window. It's hard to read the expression on her face, and even that feels like a small blow to the gut, because she used to be so open and sunny. So sure of being treated kindly and fairly because she didn't know any other way of dealing with people.

Until I came along.

My heart starts pounding as I rise to my feet. She's here. I can't believe it. She's really here. I try to smile as she comes in to join me, not sure what tone to strike. I'm genuinely relieved to see her again, but I don't want it to come across like what passed between us was no big deal, like it's been easy for me to be away from her.

"Sorry for the wait," she says as she joins me at the table. Her voice, too, is guarded, closed off, and even though she meets my gaze, her eyes quickly flinch away, like it hurts to see me.

"No problem." I hold up the book, like a peace offering, as we take our seats. "I've been catching up on…" I realize suddenly that I have no idea how to say the detective's name, since I've only ever read it on a page, never heard it out loud. "Porrot," I try, and know immediately that it's wrong.

That earns a ghost of a smile from her. "You're actually reading the books? Not just using them as a cover to stalk librarians?"

I can hear she's trying to keep her tone light, even though there's obviously barbed wire around those words. I do my best to match her, minus the cutting undertone. "They're really good. This is my fourth one." I swallow, hesitating before adding, "I can see why you recommended them to me before."

Her gaze flickers again to mine before sliding away. "That's the best compliment you can give to a librarian, you know. That she's helped you find the right book."

Silence stretches out between us. I honestly have no idea why I've been talking about these books for so long—well, no, that's not true. I'm delaying the actual conversation I came here to have, because I'm a coward.

I clear my throat. "What do you want to drink? I can grab it for you—I'm due for a refill anyway."

"No, thanks." Helen shifts, folding her hands on the table in front of her. "I actually don't have too much time, so maybe we can just, you know. Get to it. Whatever you wanted to talk about."

I'm the one trying not to flinch now. I told myself not to take up too much of her time, but I'm scared to get to the meat of things, because if she says no…that's it. We're out of each other's lives, forever. "Okay. Sure. I just…I wanted to see how you're doing, after everything that happened."

"I'm fine," Helen says tersely. "Great, actually. No complaints. You?"

This is it. No more waffling. I steel myself, clearing my throat again. "I've been doing okay. I've actually been seeing someone."

I realize as soon as the words are out of my mouth that I've phrased things incorrectly because of the way Helen reacts—like she's been slapped. I backpedal furiously, realizing what *seeing someone* usually means in the context of two people who've slept together and are meeting up after a breakup. "A therapist, I mean. We've been working through a lot of things together, and it's made me realize…I was really unfair to you. I made the decision for us to end things, without you, and I didn't listen to what you had to say. I thought I was trying to protect you, but that doesn't mean I should have shut you out, or not given you a say. I'm sorry, Helen. Really."

I've practiced the words so many times that I know them by heart, but I'm so nervous it comes out too hurried, some of the words half stumbling over each other. Holding my breath, I wait to see how she'll respond.

Helen stares at me for a long moment, her face blank. Then she shifts in her seat, casting her eyes around the room, like she can't bear to look at me.

And even though I deserve it, even though I've done much worse, my heart clenches painfully in my chest.

"Thank you," she says finally, but without much feeling. Like you might thank a stranger for holding open a door. "I appreciate that."

That's that, then. She couldn't make it more obvious that she wants nothing to do with me. And again, I deserve it, I half expected it…but it still hurts.

"Is that all you wanted to say to me?" she prompts, watching me carefully, her brow furrowed.

No. That isn't all I wanted to say to her. If I weren't such a coward, I would tell her I'm still in love with her. That I can't stop thinking about her. That even though we only knew each other for a little while, she burrowed herself so deep into my heart that I don't know how to go on with any chance at happiness without her.

It's more than just cowardice, though—and I think I'm being honest with myself when I say that. Helen spent so much of her life with people taking away her choices, and I ended up being one of those people. I'm afraid to bulldoze her again, to coerce her into something she doesn't want to do, because she's nice and doesn't want to hurt my feelings.

But I have to be honest, don't I? I can't only tell her part of the truth, because that's taking her choice away, *again*. That's what Dr. Zahn would say, anyway, if he were here.

I rub the back of my neck, building up my courage. "I want to be in your life. If you want that." I don't want to pressure her, though, or maybe it's just me being a chickenshit again, but I tack on, "As your friend."

No. Definitely chickenshit. I realize it as soon as the words are out of my mouth.

"You want to be my friend?" Helen echoes, sounding confused, maybe even a little frustrated. "Why?"

Okay, sure, maybe this is the coward's way out. Because I don't want to be her *friend*. I want to be the first person she calls when she needs something, the person she tells about her day, the guy who gets to see her face first thing every morning.

Then again, I haven't earned that privilege. I threw that away when I left her in New Orleans. Maybe *friend* is the most I deserve—and I will honestly take whatever she will give me, if I get to be a part of her life.

"Because…" Another scrub of my neck. "Look, I don't like that many people, okay? People as a general rule are shitty. They're liars and backstabbers and…just shitty. But you? You're a good person. And I want good in my life."

I must have said the wrong thing again, because Helen cringes, shaking her head. "I'm not that good."

"Trust me. You are." For the first time since we started talking, I catch her gaze and actually manage to hold it. I try to put everything into that look—my hope, my sincerity, my regret at hurting her and my resolve to never, ever do it again. "Look, I understand if you don't want anything to do with me. But I'll be a good friend to you, if you'll let me."

Helen holds my gaze, her eyes searching for something in mine. I wish I could read her, but I realize now I never really could. She's always been an enigma to me, acting in ways I can't predict, with motives I'll never be able to fully understand. But I want to. I want to know everything about her. All the goodness and warmth and humor and sassiness, yeah, but every freckle and scar on her soul, too.

I think some of this must show on my face, because I can see Helen's gaze softening, just a little. Still, she sounds bewildered as she asks, "What would we even do together? We have nothing in common."

Grinning through my racing heart, I hold up my book. "What are you talking about? We both love to read. I've read four—no, five whole books now."

She fights a smile, but loses, and my heart clenches again, in a good way this time. "You want to talk about books?" She tries to load her voice with sarcasm, but neither of us is buying it.

I feel my own smile broaden, so wide it hurts. "And go on walks. Get food. Go to the movies. Friend stuff." I only wince a little when I say that last part.

"I guess…we could try it." She levels a finger at me—and despite the silliness of the gesture, I can see in her eyes she is dead serious. "But no deciding you need to protect me, or ghosting me, or saying you're not good enough—none of that nonsense. If we're friends, I need to be able to trust you."

I swallow, trying to convey in my eyes, my tone, my smile, just how important, how *sacred*, all of this is to me. "I promise, Helen. I'm not going anywhere."

Chapter 49
Helen

I'm in week two of officially being Thad's friend. I never realized what a loaded word that was before. *Friend*. I always assumed it must have a positive connotation, but now—now, it's complicated. Because despite everything that's happened between us, I trust that he hasn't come back just to toy with me. If he says he'll be a friend to me, he will.

My worry is that all he wants from me is friendship, and that every time I'm near him, my heart will race, and I'll get clumsy and awkward and won't know what to say, and I'll wonder what he thinks about me, and I'll catch my breath every time we touch.

My worry is that I'll always be just a little bit in love with him.

But maybe…maybe with time that will dim. Maybe being friends might actually be a good thing, because it will take him off the pedestal in my mind. He'll stop being this unreachable being—my first love, first kiss, first time— and just be Thad. My friend.

My friend, who brought me donuts at work to surprise me. And who took me to the film noir festival last week. And who texts me cute GIFs of puppies falling asleep before bed every night.

Normal friend stuff. I think. Nothing I should read anything into, right? Because we are just…friends.

"This is a terrible idea," Matilda told me when I broke the news to her and Nina about Thad popping up in my life again.

Which, all things told, is a pretty standard Matilda reaction, and I'd braced myself for that. What I hadn't braced myself for was Nina's reaction—sort of the human equivalent of the grimacing face emoji.

And maybe they're right. Maybe I am being stupid. Maybe this all will go catastrophically wrong.

But even knowing all of that, what I also know is that I'm not ready to let him go, even if we'll only ever be friends.

I can get used to it. I will get used to it, and I'll move on. Eventually.

Tonight, my *friend* Thad is making me dinner—his meemaw's gumbo, which everyone knows is not a romantic food, so I'm in no danger of getting swept up in my feelings. And if it weren't for the constant worry that I'm only falling more deeply in love with him with every minute we spend together, I might just be enjoying myself.

I give myself a mental slap to the face. I don't want to be one of those creepy people who tries to force someone to be with me, especially when he's made his feelings so clear. I've agreed to friendship, and so I will be his friend. I will move on, and he will, too, and I won't let myself be weird about his new girlfriend, whenever she inevitably makes her grand appearance, and I won't let pining over him keep me from being happy with someone else.

This too shall pass, and all that.

"You did not guess the murderer," I chide Thad through my laughter, shaking my head as I dutifully chop up the peppers and celery and okra for dinner. Technically he's supposed to be making dinner for me, but I couldn't just sit around while he did all the cooking, especially in my own apartment, so I'm on vegetable-chopping duty.

"It was obvious. I figured it out by chapter three."

I roll my eyes. "Arguably Agatha Christie's best novel, and you guessed it by chapter three? Bullarky."

Thad glances over at me from where he's making the roux, looking deeply offended. "I'm a bounty hunter. I can read people. I know when someone's lying."

He's smiling as he says it, but the words send a jolt of panic through me. For the first time it strikes me that that's what I'm doing, in going along with this whole friendship thing. I'm lying. To him, to myself. I'm pretending that my heart isn't broken, that I'm not hoping something will change, that I'm not waiting for him to change his mind and tell me he loves me, he wants to be with me, he can't live without me.

Matilda was right. This is a terrible idea.

"Hey." Thad's low, gentle voice pulls me out of my panic. He's standing close to me, frowning with concern. "You okay? Where'd you go just now?"

He steps in closer, raising his hands to tuck my hair behind my ears. His fingers gently trace over my cheekbones, the shell of my ear.

The air in the room instantly changes from friendly to intensely charged, at least on my end. At his nearness, his light touch, a jolt of want shoots through me. I've been making my brain repeat the mantra that *we're just platonic friends now, that there's nothing romantic or sexual between us*, but my body has not gotten the memo. It remembers those same fingers tracing other parts of me, his skin on mine, and it responds so quickly and urgently I'm afraid he'll notice.

I step back, just a little, but it's enough. The spell is broken. Thad's hands fall back to his side. "I was just remembering something I have to do for work," I say, lying yet again, because the truth is too mortifying to say out loud. "I'm back now."

"Okay." Thad's hands flex at his sides. "You ready to make the roux?"

His smile and tone are both easy, like none of that affected him in the slightest. Of course it didn't. Just in case I needed another reminder, I tell myself again—*he's the one who left me.* He's the one who didn't want me. Even though he's popped back into my life again, he hasn't made any gestures that could be read as romantic. I have my answer.

It's only that, looking into his blue-gray eyes, I realize what I've probably known all along: no matter how long we're friends and what we go through together, a part of me will always yearn for him.

"I'm going on a date," I blurt out without meaning to.

Thad stills, blinking at me. "What?"

"I just thought I should be honest," I continue, because the only way out of this mess is through it, I guess. "His name is Barry something. He works with Matilda. She's setting us up."

I could tell him how much prodding and cajoling it took on Matilda's part, how I agreed to everything before Thad showed up again at the library that day…but if I'm being honest, what I really want to know is what *he* thinks of all this. It's sneaky and manipulative, I know, but I want to call his friendship bluff. Is this what he really wants? Us dating other people and filling each other in on the details? I think of him telling me about some new woman he's met and know that no matter how much time has passed and how long we've been *friends*, it will be pure agony. And if he doesn't feel the same…

Then I guess things really are over between us.

Thad's expression is impossible to read. He just stares at me for a long time, blinking. Is he trying to compose himself, or is it the raw onions I just chopped? After a moment, he grunts. "Does he have a criminal record?"

Despite the immense tension I'm feeling at this conversation, I have to roll my eyes. "I don't know, bounty hunter. I haven't checked."

"You should run a background check if you're meeting a stranger, *Sister* Helen."

"Well, he's a paralegal and he works with my friend, and we're meeting in a public place, so I think I'll be fine."

"I'll run a background check on him," Thad mutters under his breath, quiet enough that he probably thinks I didn't hear him. "What did you say his last name was?" Glancing over and seeing my expression, he shakes his head. "Never mind, I'll figure it out on my own."

"Please don't." I shouldn't have brought this up. With a sinking feeling in my stomach, I realize that I have my answer, and all I'm doing now is picking at old wounds. "It's not, like, a real date. It's not going to go anywhere. It's just…practice."

"Practice for what?"

"For…" I gesticulate around. "I don't know. The real thing. So when I meet someone I actually like again, he won't run away after having sex with me because I don't know what I'm doing."

Whoops. Another thing I definitely didn't mean to say tonight. That glass of wine I've been nursing as we've been cooking must have gone to my head. "Sorry, I shouldn't have said that."

"That's not what happened," Thad says quietly.

"I don't want to talk about it," I say quickly, because I don't. I don't want to rehash what happened. I don't want to hear some horse-manure excuse about not wanting to hurt me. I also don't want to scare him off. Despite knowing that being around him will only bring me misery now, it's still better than the alternative. "It's fine. Honestly. I'm not trying to make things weird."

Thad's voice shifts, and I can tell even without looking that he's turned to face me. "I need you to understand that isn't what happened, though. You don't need practice to be good at dating or sex"—he says the word quickly, like it pains him to even put that suggestion out there—"or anything else. We didn't work out because of me, not you."

My heart squeezes in my chest. "Thad, come on."

"Come on, what?"

A humorless laugh escapes my throat. "I'm naive but I'm not stupid. I know what the whole 'it's not you, it's me' speech really means. It's fine. I don't hold it against you. But men don't break things off with women they're actually interested in. We weren't a good match. I get it."

"Helen, look at me."

Reluctantly, I do. Thad looks at me solemnly, his eyes full of meaning. "I meant everything I said to you. There's nothing wrong with you. You're perfect."

It actually physically hurts me, to be coddled this way. "Thad, come on—"

"You're the first person I want to talk to every morning. I used to hate waking up and now all I do is think about what I'm going to text you that day or when I'm going to see you next." He takes in a deep breath, almost like it's freeing to get this off his chest. "I fucked up. I shouldn't have let you go. *I* was the problem. Not you."

I stare at him, trying to process his words. "So you were interested in me, but you thought…*you* weren't good enough?"

Thad nods.

"Even though I was a thirty-one-year-old virgin who'd never had a boyfriend or kissed anyone before, and I sing dorky old musicals in the shower, and I can't swear without flinching?"

"I like all of those things about you," Thad says.

I frown at him. "Like, as in present tense? As in, you're still interested in me? Romantically?"

"Like, as in present tense. As in I'm in love with you."

Thad says this simply, as if it's obvious, as if he hasn't just detonated an emotional nuclear bomb in my kitchen. He says it so matter-of-factly that I can't believe this is actually a romantic expression of love, so I rack my brain for some other explanation. "You love me like a good slice of pizza?"

"I love you, Helen," Thad says simply. "Not like a slice of pizza." He takes in a bracing breath, and for the first time I see something in his quiet, guarded expression that I realize isn't him holding me at bay. He's been holding *himself* back, only I was so caught up in my own head that I didn't notice it. "I know I hurt you, and I made all the choices for us before. I don't want to bulldoze you or try to force you into something you don't want to do. If you're set on dating Barry"—his voice tightens at the name—"or anyone else, I'll accept that. I meant what I said about being your friend, if that's all you want from me. But you should also know that I'm in love with you. And I always will be."

For a long moment, I can only stare at him. I bite my knuckle, tasting the various veggies I've been cutting, as I think over what he's just said. "You're in love with me. But because you're allegedly so terrible, you just want to be friends. You're never going to try to kiss me, or have sex with me, and you're going to sit by and watch me date other people?"

He swipes his hand over the back of his neck. "I guess so. If that's what *you* want—"

I hold up a hand, silencing him. "I understand."

And I finally do. I finally understand what happened between us, what's happening between us.

This idiot thinks we're in a film noir. I'm the good girl, the counterweight to the femme fatale, held up on a pedestal so as to not be corrupted by the anti-hero. The good girl may not get her happily ever after, but at least she's safe; and in leaving her alone and chaste, loving her always from afar, the antihero proves to himself he's a good man.

Little does he know, I'm about to show him this isn't a film noir.

It's a romance.

Chapter 50
Helen

After a strained couple of minutes of dancing around the awkward conversation we just had, I excuse myself to go back to my room. When I return, Thad is finishing adding all the ingredients for the gumbo into the pot, his back turned toward me. At my reentrance, he glances back over his shoulder. "Hey, we have a little time to kill while we wait for everything to set. Do you want to—"

He stops, doing a double take back at me, and I hold my breath as I wait for his response.

I've tousled my hair and put on lipstick, but that isn't why Thad is staring. I'm wearing the sheer red panties and the same white tank top from the sexy selfie I accidentally showed him on the road trip.

And nothing else.

Thad looks almost afraid as he takes all of this in. When he meets my gaze, his expression is grim. "What are you doing?"

"I'm seducing you," I tell him with more bravado than I feel. A few minutes ago I was absolutely certain this was the right call, but it's hard to hold on to certainty in sheer red panties.

Thad seems to be exercising Herculean effort to keep his eyes on my face, and that at least is a confidence booster. He swallows. "Why?"

"I need you to understand that I'm not who you think I am." I advance a step toward him, and he presses back against the counter, trapped. "You've been acting like I'm Lola, but I'm not."

I don't need to tell him that I'm referencing *Double Indemnity*, the movie we watched together on the road, and the character Lola. The good girl. He shakes his head at me, smiling an indulgent little smile, like it's cute that I'm trying to be so sexy. Except, when I take another step toward him, he convulsively grips the edge of the counter.

"So who are you, then?" he challenges, trying to recover. "Barbara Stanwyck?"

The femme fatale. I shake my head. "No. I'm not her, either. Not all the time." I'm trying to channel some of her confidence now, but no one can be that uncomplicatedly one-dimensional. "Sometimes I am."

"Helen." That pitying, mildly condescending tone is back. "You're not a femme fatale. You're just not. You're a good person. I like that about you. I respect you for it."

I flinch away from his words. "I don't want you to respect me from a distance. I don't want you to leave me for my own good. If you don't want to be with me, then don't be with me. But don't act like you're doing some noble thing by keeping me at arm's length. Don't pretend that's *my* choice." Taking in a deep breath for courage, I plough on, summoning the spirits of Lana Turner and Ava Gardner and Marilyn Monroe for strength and resolve: "I'm in love with you, too. I want to be with you. I want to kiss you. I want you to be insane with jealousy at the thought of me going on a date with Barry or anyone else. I want to feel you inside me again. I want you to rip these panties off me and fuck me on the counter."

Thad gapes at me. *"Helen!"* The word is a shocked exclamation, with no trace of that gentle pity from before. Good. I don't want that from him. I don't want his pity, his condescension. And I don't want his friendship if it's just some form of self-flagellation.

"Maybe I seem like a good girl to you. I guess I have the whole nun-virgin thing working against me. I try to be a good person, and I'm happy if that's how I seem to you. But I don't want to be punished for being too good, whatever that means. I don't want decisions made for me. If there's some other reason you don't want to be with me, that's fine. But if it's up to me, I want to be with you. Please respect me enough to let me make that choice."

I've advanced on him little by little during this speech, so that by the end of it, I'm mere centimeters away. My braless breasts are straining against my tank top, my bare legs close enough to brush up against him if I move any further. I see Thad take all of this in, see the war across his features.

After a moment's hesitation, he reaches up, gripping my hair near the base of my head, rougher than he's ever touched me before. I'm surprised how thrilling it is, this sudden gruffness. I meant what I said. I don't want to be treated like porcelain. I'm tougher than that.

"I don't want to hurt you," he tells me in a strained voice.

"So don't."

A moment passes in which I think he really isn't going to kiss me, that he's really going to let me go. I start to retreat, but he stops me, pulling me back, and fuses his mouth to mine. He releases me only long enough to flip our positions, so I'm the one now standing with my back to the counter, the edge of it digging into me. His big, muscular frame crowds me in, caging me in place. This time he doesn't hesitate before kissing me, even more forcefully than before, hard enough that my head knocks back against one of the cabinets.

It should hurt, but it doesn't—or, at least, the thrill of being manhandled by him outweighs any temporary smarting. For the first time, I feel like he's letting himself lose control with me, not holding back and playing nice with Sister Helen.

His hands release my face, moving down to grip my breasts through the thin material of the tank top. It doesn't seem to be enough for him, though, because he lets out a frustrated grunt, pulling down the neckline of my shirt so my breasts come popping out. "Goddam, you have the best tits. Do you have any idea how hard it's been to be near you and not be touching them all the time?"

I blink at him in dazed amazement. He honestly never gave me any indication that he was struggling at all. "You can touch them whenever you want."

He takes one in each hand, kneading them, looking deep into my eyes. "They're mine?"

The brutal possessiveness in his tone makes me feel weak in the knees, and other places, too. "They're yours," I confirm breathlessly.

He growls in appreciation, leaning in to take one nipple into his mouth. His tongue lavishes it, teeth lightly grazing over the sensitive tip. I grip his shoulders to stay standing. "Oh my God," I sigh.

As if in answer to my prayer, he raises one of his thighs between my legs, pressing up against my throbbing core. The feeling of the rough denim through the flimsy material of my panties creates a delicious friction that's almost painful against the softest part of me, but somehow feels incredible. "Thad," I half gasp, half whine.

He releases my breast from his mouth with a lewd popping sound and grins up at me, wolfish. Any sense of hesitance or holding back seems to have disappeared completely. "Is this what you want? For me to—what did you say?— fuck you on this counter."

I manage to nod. "Yes."

"If you'd gone on that date with Barry, you would have been thinking about this the whole time, wouldn't you?"

"Yes."

"But I'm not gonna let you go," he tells me gruffly, smile fading as something fierce and possessive flashes through his eyes. "Because this is mine, too, isn't it?"

He lowers his thigh so he can cup my pussy with his hand. I whimper, my head falling back against the cabinet again. "Yes. Yes."

"No one else gets to touch it."

"No," I vow.

He angles his hand so his thumb can stroke at my clit through the mesh material, and I mewl and howl like a wild creature, head banging from side to side as my pleasure builds and builds.

When I feel like I'm on the brink of losing my mind, the pressure releases from my sensitive place. With my eyes still closed, I moan in protest, clutching at his shoulders. *"Thad."*

"Mine," he reminds me, and I feel him yanking down my panties, hard enough that I hear the fabric tear. I gasp as he hoists me up so my ass is resting on the edge of the counter, and he pushes my legs open so my pussy is exposed, wet and throbbing with need.

I expect him to put his finger into me, but I'm surprised when there's a delay. Dazed, I open my eyes to find him rolling on a condom, his eyes locked on to my spread center almost hungrily. A moment later he thrusts into me, sliding in easily, and groans, swearing under his breath.

The same pressure that has been building and then ebbing awakens again, mounting to a new frenzy as he moves in and out of me at a frantic pace. This is not a gentle bedding. This is an I-won't-be-able-to-walk-tomorrow fucking and I love it. I can't believe I've spent my whole life without this, deprived myself of this holiest of communions.

I scream out his name as I break, and a moment later he follows, groaning as he finds his release inside of me.

For a moment we stay that way, sweaty and clinging together. Then he lifts his head, grinning at me with an almost woozy happiness before he playfully nips at the top of my breast. "I never realized you were such a bad, bad girl."

I laugh quietly, running my hand over his spine. "You love it."

"Yeah," he agrees, his eyes heavy with emotion as he strokes my face. "I do."

Chapter 51
Helen

For the first time ever, I'm late for my writing group. Bad luck that it happens to be on the night that I'm reading my pages.

Thad looks completely unrepentant as we walk down the corridor together, hand in hand. "I told you we wouldn't make it on time," I remind him under my breath as we approach the doors to the event room.

I try to sound a little stern, but honestly, it was as much my fault as his. I should have known not to wear the cutout dress with the sweetheart neckline that basically makes it impossible for him not to ogle my breasts. And I really should have worn underwear if I'd wanted to ensure we made it out the door when we were supposed to.

Thad just smirks, with all the smugness of a man who's managed to give his partner multiple orgasms in one quick, frantic session. "You're the one reading," he reminds me. "What are they gonna do—start without you?"

As we enter the room, Florence and Deb are both frowning down at their phones. "...have her number?" Florence asks, looking up at my entrance, then staring for a moment before her jaw drops open. "Helen?"

At first I assume the sight of me holding hands with a man must be what's throwing her off. Then I realize that, between my road trip with Thad and skipping several reading night sessions over the past few months, Florence probably isn't used to seeing me without my oversized turtleneck and messy bun. I haven't retired my sweaters completely, since they're ridiculously comfortable, but from now on I'll only be wearing them in wintertime. And I've decided I like putting a little more effort into my appearance—not for anyone else, but for my own sense of confidence. No more hiding.

"Hi, ladies. Sorry I'm late. Are we ready to go?"

Deb and Florence both exchange befuddled looks before Deb manages to nod. "Sure thing, sweetie."

I spot Matilda and Nina at the refreshment table. Between the night of the ruined gumbo and now, they've already been filled in via text that Thad and I are officially back on, though they've yet to see us together in person. Even from across the room, I can see that Matilda is skeptical and disapproving, though Nina gives me a quiet, supportive smile, and even a little thumbs-up when Matilda isn't looking.

I'm not worried about Matilda, though. She'll come around. She's not necessarily all bark and no bite, since I'm pretty sure she *would* bite if she felt the situation called for it, but she'll adjust once she realizes that the only person who rivals her protectiveness of me is Thad.

And maybe Dan O'Malley and Quinn Sullivan, but only when their mothers get involved.

As Florence tells everyone to settle down for the reading, I see Kathleen rush to grab a seat in the front row. Oh, no. With all the turmoil of the past few days, both good and bad, I'd forgotten that my writing group received very different pages than what I'm going to read tonight. That's kind of a big no-no with writing groups, since people will have already formed their critiques based on what I sent out, but oh, well. It's good to break a few rules every now and then.

"Good luck," Thad murmurs in my ear, giving my hand a squeeze as I make my way up to the podium.

Standing up in front of a sea of expectant faces, I clear my throat. "Hi, everyone. Sorry about the wait. The last time I read for you, Axel and Rosamund had finally given in to their feelings, but as you all know from some of the developments in the months in between, Rosamund was having second thoughts about giving her heart to such a sexy outcast."

I cast a quick, guilty glance at Thad, but he just grins at me, leaning back in his chair. Apparently that's just another ego booster, now that he knows how much Axel was based on him.

"And she began to realize how much someone like Wilfred could bring to her life," I continue, turning my focus back to my writing group, "with how much they have in common."

From the front row, Kathleen actually fist-pumps into the air, Judd Nelson–style. This is everything she's been waiting for.

"In the pages I sent you at the beginning of the week, Wilfred and Rosamund finally share their first kiss and express their feelings for each other." I take in a deep breath, bracing myself. "But what I'm going to read for you tonight goes a little differently. Sorry for the last-minute change, but the muse demanded it."

I proceed to read my now-revised story, in which Rosamund thinks about what a good man Wilfred is, but worries that she'll never fully get over Axel. Wilfred and Rosamund go on the walk that is supposed to end in them revealing their feelings for each other—but this time, they're interrupted by Axel, who crashes their planned picnic.

"'What are you doing here?' Rosamund demanded, her breath catching at the sight of Axel. She'd tried so hard to forget him, to get over him, but the second he walked back into her life, it was like he'd never left.

"'I can't live another day without telling you how I really feel,' Axel insisted, his blue-gray eyes sending currents of feeling running through her body. 'Maybe it's too late. Maybe you love someone else. But you have to know that I'm still yours, and I always will be. And I believe, I hope, you're still mine.'"

A cheer goes up in the group—from everyone, basically, except for Kathleen, who shrieks and covers her face.

Ignoring both types of outbursts, I finish out the happily ever after for Axel and Rosamund, and hint at the beautiful secretary who's been pining for Wilfred all along, in the hopes that maybe it will appease Kathleen enough that I don't get another sixteen-paragraph email from her on the subject.

When we finish up the official round of critiques, various members of the group come up to congratulate me and tell me how much they like the changes. "Thank God you switched the love interest back to Axel," Deb tells me conspiratorially. "Wilfred was such a drip. Don't tell Kathleen I said so."

"I won't," I promise, for both our sakes.

Deb leans in toward me. "I couldn't help but notice that Axel bears a striking resemblance to your gentleman friend. He's very handsome, though I gotta say, I never pictured you with such a bad boy."

I catch Thad's gaze across the room, where he's talking to Nina and a sulky Matilda. For a brief moment, we just smile at each other, and in that moment, I feel the weight of everything we've been through, the promise of everything to come, a pleasant premonition.

"He's not so bad," I tell her with a knowing smile. And I'm not so good, either.

I'd say we fit each other just about right.

Epilogue
Helen

After the reading, Matilda, Nina, and I go out for drinks, as is our tradition, only this time, I invite Thad to come along.

"Are you sure?" he asks me quietly. "I don't want to interfere with friend time."

I can see why he might be hesitant, considering that Matilda has literally not stopped glaring at him all night, but Nina is actually the one who insisted on it, and it's so rare for her to assert herself on anything that I feel like I have to capitulate. "It's fine," I reassure him. "Don't worry—I don't think Matilda will actually poison your drink, even if she might strongly consider it…"

Normally we go to the wine bar down the street from the library, so I'm surprised when Nina insists that we try out a pub a few blocks over instead. I assume that she must be trying to help Thad feel more comfortable, though it does little to ingratiate him any further with Matilda.

"An Irish pub?" she scoffs as we enter the place. "If I wanted a stranger to get blackout drunk and puke on my shoes, I'd ride the L after last call."

Seeming to sense the brewing mutiny, Thad offers to buy the first round and elbows his way through the crowd up to the bar while we ex-nuns find a table. The atmosphere in this place is definitely a bit more raucous than the wine bar, and I'm frankly surprised that Nina was brave enough to set foot in here, much less suggest it. "Where did you hear about this place?" I shout-ask her over the live band.

"A friend recommended it," Nina says vaguely, not quite meeting our eyes as she says it.

Glancing over, I see that Thad has made some headway at the bar, though there's still quite a line. He might be a while.

When I look back, Matilda has turned her glare to me. "Is he going to stick around this time?" she asks me flatly.

"Yes," I say without hesitation, and can't help but add, "But only because of how welcoming you've been."

I don't really blame her though, truly. Matilda is just looking out for me, in her own prickly, aggressive way. It's how she shows that she loves me. And I know that Thad will prove her wrong, whatever else she might think.

Before Matilda can get out the retort I can see she has planned, a tall, dark-haired, handsome man approaches the table, his gaze on Nina. "Excuse me." Even raising his voice to be heard over the band, it's clear he has a faint Irish accent.

Already primed to be grouchy, Matilda openly rolls her eyes at this familiar interruption. "Not interested, buddy. Move it along."

He frowns at her in surprise before looking back to Nina. "Sorry—Antonina, right? I thought we said nine."

As Matilda and I both turn to Nina with matching expressions of astonishment, she blushes but sticks out her hand to the man. "Yes, sorry. I'm Antonina. You must be Grady." Darting a quick side-eye at the two of us, she continues on boldly, "It's been a busy night and I haven't had a chance to tell my friends about you yet."

Matilda groans, burying her face in her hands. "Not you, too, Nina!"

Ignoring her theatrical outburst, I extend my hand to the man. Grady, apparently. I also have no idea what's going on, but if Nina wants to invite a date along to our group hangout, I don't want to be the reason he's scared off. "Hi! I'm Helen, and our rude friend is Matilda." I say it with no spite in my tone, hoping to convey to him that he shouldn't take her too seriously, since we don't.

"Grady Kelley," the man returns, shaking my outstretched hand with obvious relief. He's really a handsome man, I notice, with his strong jaw and dark eyes, though he looks a bit older than what I would have chosen for Nina, closer to his forties than her own twenty-four years. I guess age is only a number, though.

I turn to Nina, hoping she'll offer some explanation. "Did the two of you meet online?" I prompt her.

"No. Deandra gave him my number."

"Deandra?" I echo, taking a moment to piece together the not-so-common name. Unless I'm mistaken, she must be referring to Deandra Wilcox, the ex-nun who used to organize the meetings for former sisters where Nina, Matilda, and I first met. But why would Deandra give this man Nina's number…?

My confusion must read on my face, because Nina hurries to fill in the blanks. "Grady met Deandra at one of the meetings, but he had the same problem we all did—everyone else was so much older. So she recommended that he give me a call."

I feel like I'm being excessively stupid, but my brain is having a hard time putting all of this together. Matilda must be in the same boat, since she blurts out, "Why would you go to a meeting of former nuns?"

Grady shifts, looking a little nervous. "Because," he returns, "I used to be a priest."

About the Author

Lissa Sharpe is a mom, a wife, a teacher, a PhD, and an award-winning writer. She has written plays, screenplays, teleplays, short stories, songs, and now for the very first time, a romance novel. When she isn't having mental arguments with her characters, she is hanging out in the American South with her husband, son, and golden lab.

Find Lissa Sharpe online:
Facebook - https://www.facebook.com/profile.php?id=100095127281327
Twitter - https://twitter.com/AuthorLissaS
Instagram - https://www.instagram.com/lissasharpeauthor/
Pinterest - https://pin.it/1n38Ml7Vy
Website - lissasharpeauthor.wordpress.com
gmail- lissasharpeauthor@gmail.com
Newsletter: http://eepurl.com/iwYxdA

Find Smartypants Romance online:
Website: www.smartypantsromance.com
Facebook: www.facebook.com/smartypantsromance/
Goodreads: www.goodreads.com/smartypantsromance
Twitter: @smartypantsrom
Instagram: @smartypantsromance

Also by Lissa Sharpe

As Elizabeth Gilliland:

What Happened on Box Hill

The Portraits of Pemberley

Sly Jane Fairfax

Dear Prudent Elinor

As E. Gilliland

Come One, Come All

Round and Round We Go

Also by Smartypants Romance

<u>**Work For It Series**</u>

Street Smart by Aly Stiles (#1)

Heart Smart by Emma Lee Jayne (#2)

Book Smart by Amanda Pennington (#3)

Smart Mouth by Emma Lee Jayne (#4)

Play Smart by Aly Stiles (#5)

Look Smart by Aly Stiles (#6)

Smart Move by Amanda Pennington (#7)

Stage Smart by Aly Stiles (#8)

<u>**Lessons Learned Series**</u>

Under Pressure by Allie Winters (#1)

Not Fooling Anyone by Allie Winters (#2)

Can't Fight It by Allie Winters (#3)

The Vinyl Frontier by Lola West (#4)

<u>**Out of this World**</u>

<u>**London Ladies Embroidery Series**</u>

Neanderthal Seeks Duchess by Laney Hatcher (#1)

Well Acquainted by Laney Hatcher (#2)

Love Matched by Laney Hatcher (#3)

<u>**Wolf Brothers Series**</u>

Truth or Wolf by Anne Marsh (#1)

www.ingramcontent.com/pod-product-compliance
Lightning Source LLC
Chambersburg PA
CBHW022023310726
48972CB00006B/1787